Dust and Roses

by

Wes Brummer

Dust and Roses

Cover Art by *Debbie Taylor*

The Wild Rose Press, Inc.
PO Box 708
Adams Basin, NY 14410-0708
Visit us at www.thewildrosepress.com

Publishing History
First American Rose Edition, 2017
Print ISBN 978-1-5092-1789-2
Digital ISBN 978-1-5092-1790-8

Published in the United States of America

Dedication

To my wife, Debbie

Part I: Defiance

"The bold defiance of a woman is the certain sign of her shame. When she has once ceased to blush, it is because she has too much to blush for."

~*Charles Maurice de Talleyrand*

"A woman is like a teabag—you never know how strong it is until it's in hot water."

~*Eleanor Roosevelt*

A distant horn blew,

its blast rising in pitch. A farm truck bore down on them, the young driver motioning frantically for them to move aside. Sara and Bea leaped for the ditch as the huge truck roared past. Behind the vehicle swirled a fantail of fine powder, a faint imitation of what was to come.

Sara climbed onto the road on hands and knees, pushed to her feet, and helped Bea up. The air thundered. Darkness drew around them like an enveloping cloak.

Bea took a step and collapsed. Sara heaved her up, wrapping her arm around her waist. "Come on! I'll help you. The driveway is just ahead!" She yelled to be heard.

They set off with Bea leaning on Sara's shoulder, pacing in sequence like runners joined in a three-legged race. With time all but gone, they left the road, entering the curving driveway. The wind shrieked. The steps were just around the curve. But even as they neared the porch, the storm rushed upon them.

A black wave surged around the tenant house and obliterated it from existence. Before Sara could scream, a blast of cold air gave her goose bumps, and dirt pelted her like buckshot.

The darkness swallowed them.

Sara and Beatrice were trapped in the belly of the storm.

Kudos for Wes Brummer

Won second place in "first chapter" category
Kansas Writers Association Writing Contest

Chapter One

KSKN Radio Station
Prepares to Join Alliance Network
Since their announcement April 3 of joining the Alliance Broadcasting Systems, Wichita's KSKN radio station has been hard at work. Announcers are promoting network shows. New equipment is arriving daily. More positions are being added. There is an air of expectancy as KSKN prepares to join the fastest growing radio network in America.

"We are getting ready for the big changeover," says W. L. Tabor, owner and manager of KSKN. "Alliance Broadcasting offers a wide variety of programs, including dramas, comedies, news and sports. Soon, we will air live professional baseball games, directly from the ballpark." In addition to baseball, KSKN will air all of ABS's most popular shows including Saddle Tramp, Lew and Mabel, and Graveyard Tales.

Currently, Alliance Broadcasting has stations in Newark, Detroit, Cincinnati, Chicago, and Omaha. Each station adds their unique shows to ABS's line-up. Which KSKN show will ABS choose? "The secret is out," said Mr. Tabor. "Alliance has aired several KSKN programs. The audience favorite is Heaven and Earth, Pastor Samuel McGurk's half-hour Sunday morning commentary."

"Everything is in place to bring the resources of Alliance to Wichita listeners," says Jeremy Gorham, chief engineer at KSKN. *"All that is needed is the wire linking KSKN to its sister stations. Once connected, a concert in New York will sound as close as The Forum Exposition Hall downtown."*

KSKN's Alliance premiere will be Sunday, May 12. "More details are coming," says Gorham. *"Stay tuned."*

The Wichitan
6 April, 1935

"Are you sure?" Sara McGurk asked for the second time.

Dr. Daniel Payton fidgeted in his swivel chair, peering through bifocals at a flimsy sheet of paper. "Miss McGurk, the pregnancy test we use is ninety-eight percent accurate. You're going to have a baby around mid-November. I know this is a shock. The good news is you're young and healthy. I see no complications at this time."

"Oh, the complications are just beginning." She looked about the too-small doctor's office. Certificate hung on the wall above a cluttered wooden desk that seemed to take up most of the room. Nearby were family photographs and a calendar that hadn't been switched to April. Three months. If only she could undo her mistake as easily as turning the page of a calendar. But she couldn't.

Doctor Payton was doing a poor job of hiding a grandfatherly smile. With a start, Sara realized she voiced her first thought aloud. "We'll schedule you for another visit, this time with the father. He should be involved as well."

She sighed. "I'll have to tell him. That won't be easy."

The elderly physician jotted some notes on what could have been her medical chart. *He* was certainly taking it well. Probably wasn't the first time he had to tell an unmarried woman she bore a child. And now she had to share her news.

He scratched his rumpled gray hair. "Nevertheless, it's important he understands your condition as you get closer to delivery."

"After I tell him, I'll need to tell my parents. Daddy's old fashioned." She threw her hands to her face. "It feels like the world's coming apart."

Dr. Payton touched her wrist. "Tell the father what you know. Make a plan together. Then face your parents together. It may be troublesome now, but every parent secretly wishes to be a grandparent. Keeping up appearances is what gets in the way. I'll have you come back in a month. But before you go, I want to check your information." He drew a fountain pen from his white coat pocket and retrieved her chart. "What is your full name?"

"Sara Kay McGurk."

"Your birth date?"

"May 23, 1911."

"Street address?"

2234 Parker Street."

"And that's in Wichita?"

"That's right."

"Do you have a telephone?"

"Yes, MO-55545."

"Finally, I need the name of a relative in case of emergency."

"That would be my mother, Katherine McGurk. Same telephone number and address."

"Very good, Miss McGurk. See my nurse on the way out. She'll set up your next appointment."

"Thank you, doctor." Sara stood. Dr. Payton pushed himself to his feet as well, shaking her hand.

"See you in May, Miss McGurk."

Sara made her appointment, gathered her handbag, donned a lavender hat, and left the doctor's office. She had one more task before going to work—breaking the news to Larry.

Downtown Wichita bustled with activity this crisp April morning. Women in long tapered dresses peered in shop windows while men in homburgs and fedoras hustled to work, holding their hats against the occasional of wind. The pleasant smell of bacon turned her head as she strolled past Woolworths. She could stop for a cup of coffee to steady her nerves, but she had no time. Turning, she picked up the pace, making her way through the business district.

Would this be the end, or a new beginning for her and Larry Bigger?

They'd been seeing each other for five months. Larry was fun, always telling hilarious stories about his customers at the mercantile. Even when he did something boneheaded, he could still get her to smile. Come to think of it, she couldn't remember when they ever had a serious conversation.

She met Larry by way of his father, Gerald Bigger. Jeremy Gorham—that bookish engineer from the radio station—bet her she couldn't sell radio advertising to the owner of Bigger Mercantile. Yet, she pulled it off, earning her the friendship of Wichita's savviest businessmen. From that escapade, Gerald introduced her to his son, Lawrence Bigger.

Larry was like a real-life Lamont Cranston from *The Shadow* radio show, a carefree man about town. Nearly every week he took her on a different adventure, showing her places and experiences she never imagined.

One week they dined at the Kit Kat Restaurant in the newly completed Allis Hotel. Then they rode in an elevator seventeen stories to the rooftop and gazed at the lights of Wichita far below. Another time they flew in one of Boeing's newest planes at an air show. On Sundays, they sped along country roads in Larry's 1933 Chevy Roadster. He paid extra for the silver paint job.

She also learned to dance.

Dancing was the best, whether it was a New Year's ball in the Allis or a dance marathon at The Evergreen Club. She loved twirling with the flow of music. The closeness, the thrill, and the vitality, all made dancing an exuberant celebration. To share the bond together, to perform with other couples; this was the heart of it. To dance was to be alive.

Sara approached the corner of First and Market. The cement fortress of the Hotel Lattimore rose before her. The notorious lodging held a speakeasy beneath the ballroom. She accompanied Larry to a Valentine's dance here two months ago. That night changed her life.

It began as an adventure—going to a speakeasy in a notorious hotel. They entered the lobby wearing red and white. Larry sauntered to the bell desk handing the employee a gold card and a five-dollar bill. The bellman escorted them to a closed door with a sign:

DANGER!
EXPOSED WIRING

Inside, muffled drums thumped behind a partition. After the bellman rapped a hurried code, a hidden door slid opened.

The joint, as they say, was jumping.

Men and women shouted to each other in a large smoke-filled room with a jazz band playing on a small stage. Couples, dressed to the nines, were laughing and drinking from small glasses. A pretty cigarette girl worked the crowd. Long-legged waitresses, dressed as cabaret singers, served eager young men. A rotating mirror ball scattered beams of light across a brilliant dance floor.

The combo finished a breezy number with sax and trumpet amid muted drums. A hush fell as the room blacked out. Moments later, a spotlight kindled to life over a statuesque colored woman in a white evening gown. She sang "Blue Moon."

They danced the night away. After relentless teasing, Larry talked Sara into trying a martini. Actors drank them in movies. They came in such small glasses. How bad could they be? She gulped one down, as instructed. Then Larry ordered her another.

Things got fuzzy after that.

She couldn't remember leaving the speakeasy, but she did recall the drive out of town. "Larry, take me home. My head is spinning." She cupped her hands over her temples, trying to keep the world steady.

"In a bit. It's Valentine's Day, and there's a lover's moon." The dim light from the car's dashboard gave his face a predatory look. "Don't you want to see it?" He turned the car onto a country path.

A silent bolt of lightning penetrated the fog in her head. Sara gasped. With awful clarity, she realized what was about to happen.

What followed was an act, not of passion, but of regret and sorrow.

And now…shame.

She pushed the memory aside as she hurried past the dreadful hotel, crossing the next block. Catty-cornered was the Orpheum Theatre, its corner marquee shouting in bold letters:

NOW SHOWING
"THE GAY DIVORCEE"

Maybe Gladys from work could watch it with her. Gladys was a big fan of Fred Astaire.

She would have a serious talk with Larry. He'd snort and complain but would do the proper thing in the end. He had to. After they married, they could rent a small house. Mother would love the baby, as would Mr. and Mrs. Bigger. Daddy would be hard to win over, but in the end, all should work out.

At Emporia Street Sara turned north. Bigger Mercantile was one block away.

The brick and limestone building stood four stories tall with rows of tall windows on all sides and marked the dividing line between the business and warehouse districts. The mercantile traded in practical goods. Those looking for trendy fashions or delicate jewelry should go elsewhere.

Sara entered the store and climbed the stairs. As she rounded the third-floor landing, she spotted Gerald Bigger stepping down from the fourth floor, talking to another man. The stranger wore a brown woolen suit and flat-brimmed derby. Mr. Bigger looked impressive in his black three-piece suit and large watch-chain. His striking blue eyes and gray temples could turn even a young woman's head. He stopped in mid-sentence when he saw her. "Sara! This is a surprise!" Bigger turned to his companion, gesturing. "Eustis, this is Sara McGurk. She and my son have been seeing each other these past few months. Sara, this is Eustis Case. Mr. Case does business in Kansas City."

Sara curtsied. "How do you do, sir."

"Hello young lady." Case tipped his hat.

"Sara's father is a notable radio pastor in this town," said Bigger. His program *Heaven and Earth* is quite popular." He turned to Sara. "Did I read that your father's program will be on the Alliance network?"

"Yes sir. His premiere will be in six weeks."

"I imagine your workload will soar when your father gets a nationwide audience."

"We're already seeing more listener mail."

Bigger motioned to his colleague, "Mr. Case is helping me put together a mail-order catalog for out-of-town customers. It could double our sales."

Gerald Bigger exhibited the most commonsense of any businessman Sara met. His store was always clean, prices well marked, and every light bulb lit. Details like these would stand out if neglected. He had a simple, yet ingenious method of keeping customers; he wandered around, viewing the store the way a customer would. Sara often glimpsed him poking among the racks, straightening stock, checking signs, and talking to customers. Bigger carried a notebook, noting what needed attending. His help hated that notebook, Larry most of all.

Eustis chuckled. "Mail-order customers can order

anytime from anywhere. Work clothes and hard-to-find tools are appealing to rural customers. Bigger Mercantile could become a major mail-order business in the next two years."

"That sounds grand." Sara shifted her feet. "Is Larry still working the fourth floor?"

Gerald pointed upstairs. "In the men's department, re-arranging clothes unless he wandered off." He tapped his fingers on the rail. "Say, when you see him, tell him to head straight home after work. Mr. Case is having supper with us tonight." He shook his head. "I swear, managing a business in the middle of a Depression is easier than raising a son. Tell him it's important."

Sara nodded. Gerald's demeanor always seemed confident, but today she saw something else. Exhaustion.

"I'll tell him, Mr. Bigger. Good day, gentlemen."

The fourth floor was essentially one large room. Rows of tables and shelves sat in neat rows beneath lights hanging from long cords. Piles of goods occupied every flat surface. Easy-to-read signs listed items and prices:

Work Shoes $4.00
Fine Hats $3.00
Leather Jackets $17.00
SPECIAL SALE!
Winter Coats $5.00

Sara spotted Larry stacking bib overalls. Beside him sat a cart of unsorted work clothes and price tags. She picked her way to his table. "Hello, Dancer. Think we'd cause a ruckus dancing on this floor?"

Larry glanced up. "Hey Gold-digger."

Uh. She hated that nickname.

Larry Bigger wore a pale blue suit with matching vest, white shirt, and black tie on a lanky frame. A strong chin made him look like a matinee idol, but Larry had ears the size of dipper handles. He parted his long blonde hair down the middle, but no amount of combing could cover those incredible ears.

Larry frowned as he folded a pair of overalls, placing them on a stack. "We could kick off these clothes and dance on this table. By the end of the day, they'll all be jumbled anyway."

"Oh, don't be a crybaby," Sara teased as she adjusted his stacks. "You fold so well. I can see you washing and hanging laundry. A girl could make good use of you around the house."

"Thanks. This is my dad's idea. Next week I'll probably be sweeping the stairs, or changing the ceiling lights."

Sara laughed. "Things are tough all over. You've got to admit, though. Your father is a shrewd operator. Learning every job in the store will make you a better manager. Keep your eye on the brass ring. And when you change the lights, don't look down."

"Don't tell me you agree with this learn-every-job plan of his. I'm wasting my time. Lifting and moving merchandise is what employees are supposed to do. All I need to do is supervise."

"Lawrence—"

"Don't call me that!" His voice was sharp. "I hear enough of that home. You know I prefer Larry."

Sara sighed. "Your father is simply looking after his business. He wants to leave it in good hands. He's preparing you for the day you take over. You've told me all this yourself."

"Yeah, yeah, I know. It's just that…I feel like I'm doing time." He flashed a broad grin. "I just had an idea."

"Oh, yeah?" She gathered more clothes and straightened the folds.

"Maybe you can change the lights, and I can hold the ladder."

Sara stifled a smile. "That's kind of you, Dancer, but I have a job. Besides, I'd have to wear these overalls. Otherwise I'd be wondering if you were trying to peek up my dress."

"Just admiring the view, my dear." Larry made a ridiculous smirk.

Sara took a step back. "Too true." She set down the overalls. "I have something to tell you." She paused— there was no way to sugar-coat the news. "I'm going to have a baby."

At first, nothing happened. *Maybe he didn't hear me.*

Then Larry's face changed. Eyes widened. Brows arched. He retreated, staring at her as if she'd slapped him. "You're kidding me."

"It's true. I just came from the doctor's office."

Larry shook his head. "No, no—this is not supposed to happen."

Is he blaming me?

She stepped in close. "Listen." She had to see his eyes. "I'm just as shocked as you are. In seven months—next November—I'll have a child. *We* will have a child. So, *we* need to plan. Make arrangements."

"I get it. You don't need to pound it into me." His voice turned irritable. "This news came out of

11

nowhere!"

Sara glared at him. "I seem to recall a particular night in February. After the dance? You were there."

"For crying out loud, stop with the sarcasm. I need a chance to think."

"What about?" Sara bit her lip from saying more. *Is he going to deny his part in this?*

"I need time to decide...what to do." Larry jerked his arm up as if he was tossing a coin.

"It's obvious what we should do. We tell my folks. We tell your folks. Then we pick a wedding date."

"A wedding!"

His shout echoed off the walls. Nearby customers turned to watch the show.

Sara wanted to shake him. "It's the proper thing to do. The sooner, the better. We could go to a county judge and dance on our honeymoon." Sara flashed her best smile. "A wedding will turn this little problem into a celebration."

Larry's scowl deepened. "I'll work this out myself—without any help from you."

Sara resisted the urge to withdraw. "Take the whole day. In the meantime, leave a message at home when you're coming. I don't have a telephone at work. Daddy thinks we would be talking instead of answering fan letters."

He stared at the floor. "Call your house. Got it."

Sara touched his arm. "Thank you."

Larry turned away.

Sara sighed. "I'm late for work. See you tonight." She turned and headed for the stairs. As she took the first steps down, she remembered Gerald's message. She hurried back to Larry's work area. The cart still sat half full of unsorted clothes. Price signs lay scattered on the floor. Sara turned a complete circle, glancing around.

Larry was gone.

Chapter Two

The stenciled sign on the frosted glass door read:
Heaven and Earth Mailroom
Pastor Samuel McGurk, Director
Sara and her workers simply called it The Mailroom. The office took up a quarter of the space on the second floor of the Kramer Building, a narrow two-story warehouse converted to office space. Much of the building was empty, though a couple of lawyers, an accountant, and even a bookmaker—the gambling kind—leased downstairs. No other renters on the second floor. The Mailroom was the only office that kept regular hours.

Sara arrived at work around eleven a.m. that Saturday. The bus ride felt relaxing after the confrontation with Larry. By the time she climbed to the second floor, she was ready for work.

Sara breezed in, peeling off her hat and jacket. "Good morning, ladies."

"Mawnin', Miz Sara." Sylvia waved with a handful of letters. The tall, ebony-skinned woman sorted and bundled mail at the heavy oaken worktable in the center of the roomy office along with Gladys. Sylvia was two years Sara's senior, but looked much older. "Ridden hard and put away wet," Gladys told Sara at one point. "The rod wasn't spared on this child." Sylvia wore a patched dress made from dyed bedsheets. A tightly

14

bound checkered cloth hid her hair.

Marilyn Krieble, a grandmother of four, was already typing at her desk. "Morning, Miss McGurk." A short wave, a quick smile, and she went back to answering letters. Marilyn had bad knees. Sitting much of the time gave her a dowdy appearance, but Marilyn had the quickest typing fingers Sara had ever seen.

Sara stopped at the big worktable to examine the bundles of letters. Gladys Pickering snapped a rubber band around another stack. "Hi, boss. We were wondering if you decided to play hooky."

Sara smiled at her old high school friend. "And leave you in charge? No, I had a doctor's appointment. How's the mail today?"

Gladys brushed auburn bangs from her eyes. While Sara was tall with straight lines, Gladys was petite and curvaceous. "The word is out. People know your father's radio program is joining the Alliance. Many are asking why. We've gotten some three hundred pieces this morning. No telling what the two o'clock delivery will bring."

This was the listener mail in response to Daddy's Sunday program. The show seemed like an extended monologue, laced with a bit of scripture and quotes from dead people. Two thousand letters arrived in an average week. Many contained donations. The job of the Mailroom was to answer fan mail and keep track of donors who sent in money.

Sara retrieved a bundle, running her fingers through the stack. "This is just the beginning. By mid-May, we'll have letters coming in from all over the country. I'll need to hire more help by then. Maybe even expand the office."

Sylvia heaved a dramatic sigh. "We be needin' the help soon, Miz Sara. We're jumpin' like frogs now." Sylvia was always respectable, yet surprisingly candid. Sara's thoughts flashed back to when the gangly black woman approached her for a job. All she saw at the time was a colored woman who could do with a meal. The office needed a cleaning lady, so she hired Sylvia on the spot. Since then, Sylvia taught herself typing and now answered the mail like everyone else.

Sara nodded. "You're right. We need help now." She divided the bundles into four groups. "For now, we'll have to make do. Running behind is the best way to convince Daddy we need more typists. Then it will be a matter of hiring and training the right people. In the meantime, we keep plugging away. So, Gladys, you take the local mail. Marilyn gets the out-of-towners. And Sylvia, you work on the out-of-state pieces. You all know the drill. Keep track of donations and send any problem letters to me. Use the sample letters in your files whenever possible and keep your responses short. If a listener asks an opinion, make it general. Our job is to foster the belief that Pastor McGurk just answered their letter. One last thing, don't seal your envelopes. We're getting new leaflets this afternoon, about Daddy's Church of the South Wind. Those leaflets go in the envelopes as well."

"What do we do if someone asks about the show joining the Alliance network? We don't have a standard response covering that." Gladys handed a letter to Sara.

Sara read through the note. "I'll work on a sample response today and mimeograph copies for you to use on Monday. The show will remain on Sunday. Carey Salt is still the sponsor. Put those letters aside for now.

We'll tackle them next week."

Marilyn held up a hand. "Is there any chance that Alliance will drop the program?"

"Not unless something goes terribly wrong." Sara pursed her lips. "Come on, ladies. Going national is a good thing. It's steady work for us, and there'll be new jobs as well. Anything else?"

No one spoke. Sara listed several more instructions, grabbed a bundle of mail, and headed to her desk in the back corner.

Reading the mail was her favorite part of the job. The letters revealed who the listeners were. Their words told the stories of people: of good fortunes and bad, of survival in the city, and of holding onto the land. These were stories that deserved to be re-told. But that wasn't likely to happen.

Besides KSKN, four other Kansas stations carried *Heaven and Earth* via transcription discs: Topeka, Hays, Coffeyville, and Garden City. Some hobbyists would re-broadcast the program by shortwave. Once, they received a letter from Sydney, Australia. Daddy boasted about that one on the air.

Sara opened an envelope and took out the letter.

Dear Preacher McGurk,

I heard your radio program a couple of weeks ago. This Hitler fellow sounds like the kind of leader Germany needs right now. He is doing a marvelous job of whipping his country back into shape. Mr. Roosevelt could learn a lesson from him. I agree with you about Europe. Whatever their problems are, they shouldn't be our problems. We have our own troubles. Let the leaders of Europe work on theirs.

Yours truly,

Calvin Dieffenbacher
Greensburg, Kansas
~*~

Dear Pastor,

My husband and I listen to your show every Sunday. You are one of the few people who understands what is going on. My husband rents land owned by the bank to grow corn. Recently, the federal government passed a law paying farmers NOT to grow crops. They say it will help the farmer by raising prices. That may be true, but it's not helping us. That taxpayer money will go to the bank since they own the land. And the bank still charges us rent. Today, we're told not to grow anything. How can we make ends meet if we can't grow crops to sell? We can't even grow food to feed ourselves. It is just a matter of time before the bank kicks us off the land. I've never seen my husband cry 'til this week. I don't know where else to turn.

Your servant in Christ,
Elaine Daniels
Eskridge, Kansas
~*~

Dear Sir,

I don't like your show. It is full of vile rumors and name-calling. If you cannot say anything good about President Roosevelt, then don't say anything at all. He is doing the best he can. So what if some of his programs don't work as well as others? Doing anything is better than doing nothing like Herbert Hoover. There was only a single verse of scripture quoted in your program. I'm not so sure you're a real preacher.

Mrs. Quinton Messenger
Zenda, Ks.

****

As she read, Sara made notes and underlined passages for her response. The farmer-losing-his-land letter was a good one to show Daddy. He liked using examples of government failing to work for the average person. She set the letter aside and reached for another envelope.

A shadow fell across her desk. Sara glanced up to see three faces peering at her. "Ladies?"

"Sara…" Gladys included the others with a wave of her finger. "We have concerns about what's happening."

"What concerns?"

"We don't think the program should go national. Better to keep it the way it is."

"Daddy's been working on this show for years. Chances like this don't come twice. I know there will be more work. I promise to get extra help."

"That ain't it, Miz Sara," Sylvia jumped in. "Those folks writin'? Your daddy started with them. Most write ev'ry week. Just like clockwork. They're…familiar. They'll be swallowed up like Jonah when loads of new folk start writin'. It'll be hawd takin' on these new'uns and still take care of our friends."

"We can't have favorites." Sara scooted her chair back. Sylvia leaned in much too close. "The number of listeners determine ratings. Ratings determine the future of the show. It means not only keeping our jobs but hiring new people to answer the mail. You move up and supervise the new workers. Paychecks grow as well."

Gladys turned to Marilyn and Sylvia. "She's right. We all go up the ladder, and a bigger paycheck is a blessing." She turned back to Sara. "But there is a problem. Marilyn, Sylvia, and I work together day after day. We're a team. Being supervisors is fine, but it means we have to split up. And one more thing…"

"Wait!" Sara rose to her feet. "If we're going to discuss this, then let's sit out in the open. I'm getting a crick in my neck from looking up."

They brought their swivel chairs in a tight circle between the worktable and front desks. The short break relieved the room's tension. *At least I can talk eye to eye.*

Sara glanced at her crew. "Remember. All of us work for my father, and he is pleased that Alliance picked his program for their network. Airing your feelings is good. But understand this. Nothing will change."

Gladys shrugged. "We know that." She sat down, staring at the far wall. "At least listen to what we have to say."

Sara nodded, taking her seat.

Gladys pursed her lips, leaning forward, "Pretending to the fans that one person reads and answers every single letter is phony. It feels like we're deceiving the people."

Sara swept her arm. "It's our job to help the fans feel that Pastor has read and answered their letter." Sara paused. "We want them to feel special."

Marilyn met her gaze with a firm jaw. "I think what we do is important, even though Pastor gets the credit. We can't always say what we want to, but we provide a personal touch. You'd never know that from listening to his show. What's truly sad is we end up burning all these wonderful letters. All the words, all the feelings these pages hold—turns to ash. Years from now, people will only remember Pastor's voice."

Sylvia looked up with doleful eyes. "It's a world of hurt, Miz Sara. Hawd times. Folks feel like it's their doin'. They askin' for help. I got a letter where a grandmama loses her child and grandbabies. I tells you, Miz Sara. It hurt me readin' this letter." Sylvia sniffed. "The pain grabs at you."

Sara reached out, holding her wrist. Both Gladys and Marilyn gathered close, each extending a hand in support.

"I know we often get sad letters. Some are impossible to answer. Give the letter to me. I'll take care of it."

"It is hard," Gladys said. "People are suffering. They reach out to Pastor—to us. All we can offer are words."

Marilyn looked to Sara. "Can we send money to some of these unfortunates? Pastor could start a charity."

Sara shook her head. "We're not in the social work business. Radio people will tell you what Daddy does is entertainment."

Gladys's eyes narrowed, her voice edged with resentment. "You know that's not true. When people listen to your father, they hear a man of God. To them, he is a symbol of salvation. He can't be an entertainer and a man of faith at the same time. Isn't there something in the Bible about that?"

" 'A servant cain't serve two mas'sas. Either he be hatin' one and lovin' the other, or devotin' to one and despisin' the other,' " Sylvia recited. "It's from Luke."

Sara bit off a rueful grin. "Sounds like *Elmer Gantry*."

Marilyn pointed at Sara. "Folks worry about their homes and families while Pastor speaks of government spending or the country going in debt. Listeners care about the pastor, but Pastor cares little about his audience."

Sara frowned. "I never heard it put that way before."

Gladys sighed, "Well, Sara, you live with him. Was he like this when he had a church of his own?"

"I was six when Daddy became a pastor." Sara closed her eyes, thinking back. "Things seemed simpler back then. It wasn't until near the end that he became interested in radio. I knew Daddy took long drives and sermonized on some stations. It was a shock when he quit his own church. He had Mother tell them and this got some people angry. I felt humiliated. Daddy didn't care; he got what he wanted—a radio program. You'd think the pressure would be off with the Alliance adding his show, but now he seems more agitated than ever."

Sylvia tapped Sara's wrist. "Seem like we be pickin' on your Pa. That's not what we mean to do. It be you we worry about."

Gladys nodded. "We think you're under a lot of pressure. You holding up okay?"

Sara drew out a long breath. "Four hours ago, I would have said yes, but now...I'm not sure."

Gladys leaned forward. "What's wrong?"

"I might as well tell you. It seems the pastor's daughter has let her guard down in her wild romance with a certain young man. I'm expecting."

Marilyn clasped her hand to her breast. "Sara, this will change everything. Have you told anyone yet?"

"I went to Larry's work and told him right away. He didn't take the news well. I'll tell my parents tonight. Hopefully, Larry will be there for moral support."

Marilyn gripped her arm. "This will shock your parents. Their first instinct will be to hide you. Send you away. You'll have to quit your work here."

Sara drew in a breath. "I'm here to stay. All of you have convinced me of that."

Gladys waved her finger to include Marilyn and Sylvia. "We want you with us, Sara. Becoming a mother might be tough at home but it won't be a problem here. We'll make it work."

Marilyn drew a hand across her forehead. "It won't matter. Your parents will have the final say. If my oldest daughter became pregnant, I would send her to my sister in Missouri. Her protests wouldn't matter."

Sylvia clasped her hands. "The Lawd will show you the way."

"Thank you, Sylvia." Marilyn's disturbing comments seemed all too plausible. "I'm not looking forward to this evening, but I'm glad I told you." She stood. "Half the day is gone. We really should get back to work." Sara scooted her chair back to her desk. "Gladys, there's a musical at the Orpheum. Would you like to see it tomorrow?"

Gladys shook her head as she replaced her chair. "Eddie and I are going to Wellington for a quick getaway. No kids. But I'll be back Monday."

"Maybe later in the week?"

"It's a date. I love musicals."

Sara glanced at the electric wall clock. "It's almost dinnertime. Let's take a short break and restart at twelve-thirty. We can knock off at three o'clock and start fresh Monday morning."

By three, Sara completed her second handwritten draft explaining the benefits of moving to the Alliance network. It sounded terrible. She set it aside and peered at the newly arrived boxes of leaflets.

She opened a container and scanned the flyer. "Give a dollar to The Church of the South Wind, a place that will feel like home." Those were her words. The cover showed a country-style church blown up to gigantic proportions. The actual church was an empty lot on the north edge of town. It was a lure for more donations. And she was the shill.

Daddy would demand that she quit. As much as she wanted to shepherd the changes to the Mailroom, it wouldn't happen. Still, she could talk to him. Convince him to start a charity, or at least learn more about his listeners.

Sara rose and stretched. "Okay everybody. We won't be using the leaflets. Too many printing errors. So seal your letters, and we'll pick up again on Monday."

"I got washin' at home. The extra time'll come in handy." Sylvia dashed off one last address, picked up a letter, and carried it to Sara's IN tray. "This be the letter I told you about."

"Thank you, Sylvia." Sara grabbed an empty box to gather the mail. Marilyn sealed her remaining letters while Gladys helped Sara collect envelopes.

Sara set the outgoing mail by her desk. "All that's left to do is postage. I'll finish up here. Enjoy your Sunday, ladies. Have a good trip, Gladys."

Gladys tossed on her jacket—then searched for her

hat. Marilyn found it perched atop the Philco radio against the back wall. "See you Monday, Sara." Gladys waved as the door closed behind the three of them.

Sara blew a heavy breath, dropping into her seat and savoring the silence. Affixing postage and stuffing envelopes in a burlap bag was quick work. After mailing off the letters, she could catch a bus and be home in fifteen minutes. Going home meant telling her parents. *Please come, Larry. Do the right thing.* Sara cleared her desk, placing her handwritten draft in a tray. She would type it Monday.

Her fingers brushed Sylvia's letter. Sara retrieved it, glancing at the return address, R. R. 3, Elkhart, Kansas. Few letters came from the southwest corner of the state. As she opened the letter, some grit fell onto her desk along with four sheets of tightly scrawled penmanship.

Dear Pastor McGurk,

I'll be leaving here soon. Another duster is bound to come, but I won't stay for it. I hate this land, and I know it hates me. We live in a world of desolation. There is no rain. No green anywhere. Rabbits and grasshoppers have eaten nearly every surviving plant. It's as if the wrath of God has descended upon us. I can't take anymore. My husband is out. I'll be gone when he returns.

I keep thinking about joining Trisha, my daughter. She has escaped this place. Joining her and my grandbabies would be paradise.

Until four years ago, our farm had done well. My husband and son-in-law bought a tractor a few years back. With it, we pulled in record crops of wheat. Even when the price of wheat fell, we made enough to get by.

The rains held. Life was good. Daughter Trisha had beautiful twin babies, Thomas and Mary-Beth. I treasured them like my own. Sometimes life here is hard, but my babies made it pure joy.

In '31 the rains stopped. My husband dedicated just about every bit of our land to wheat. We still pulled in a decent crop, but wheat prices were hitting rock bottom. Between fuel, upkeep on the tractor, and the cost of seed, we could barely make do. The next year was even worse. That's when the dusters started to blow.

For the past four years, we've had little rain. Not a week goes by that we haven't had at least one duster. Some would last for days. The only thing keeping us going was faith and family. Then last year the grandbabies got sick. They started wheezing and coughing up mud, thick as paste. They couldn't breathe through their noses because they were full of dirt. Finally, the little ones couldn't keep their food down.

Trisha tried to keep the dust out of her house. I helped best I could. We taped windows, stuffed rags around doors, and tied wet towels around their little faces. Nothing worked. Trisha tried. I know she did. I forgive her. For everything.

We took the babies to the hospital in Elkhart. Doctors there said the babies had dust pneumonia. Lots of babies are getting it. Old folks, too. The hospital has a special room where babies can get free of the dust. But it was too late.

Little Thomas broke his ribs from coughing so much. But it was Little Mary-Beth who succumbed first. She choked to death from the mud in her throat. Little Thomas coughed constantly. It was almost a relief when he died. The twins were barely four years old.

Five days ago, Trisha must have found out she was expecting again. Or maybe she just guessed. She didn't tell anyone. Not even her husband. Our son-in-law ran to our place about midnight, shouting about Trisha. She was bleeding, having terrible cramps and screaming in pain. We ran in the dark the half-mile to their home. Trisha lay in a pool of blood. I suspected she miscarried.

It was far worse. While the men went for help, she told me what happened in between waves of pain. She didn't want to give up another baby to the dust, so she found a midwife, the kind that knew how to stop a baby. This woman put Lysol in Trisha's womb. Trisha cried, not just from the pain. She begged me to forgive her. Here she was, dying in my arms, and she worried about how I felt. I kissed her and wiped the sweat from her brow. She died in my arms.

I held her until the men returned with the doctor. I held her until my husband pulled me away.

Her funeral was yesterday, and we buried her in hallowed ground. No one knows about the abortion. My husband and son have pledged to stand by the farm. They think the worst is over. It's not. The gates of hell will open soon, and Satan's breath will spew black across the land.

I'm tired. I don't sleep much anymore. When I do, I sit in a chair. The coughing spells aren't as bad that way. Today, my husband is helping with another rabbit roundup. They're killing the critters with bats and shovels so they won't eat what little green is left. No shooting. People get hurt that way. My husband's gun is by the front door. All that's left to do is put this letter in the mailbox at the crossroad. And then I can see my babies.

I hear them calling now. I hear Trisha, too. They're in a land of gentle rivers and green grass, clear skies, and soft breezes. Pray for the people here, Pastor. Pray for my husband and son-in-law.

I'll be seeing Little Thomas and Mary-Beth soon. We got some catching up to do.

Mrs. Jennifer Stotermeyer
Elkhart, Kansas

Sara closed her eyes, imagining the life of this woman. The land she and her family depended upon was lashing back, destroying them. With shaking fingers, she slipped the letter in its envelope and placed it and the Eskridge letter in her handbag. *Daddy needs to see these messages. He needs to know people are calling to him.*

Silence hung like a shroud. She stood and shuffled to the Philco. It sat on a hall table next to a divan. Sara flipped the radio on and waited for the tubes to warm. She needed music. Once the sound came up, she dialed the tuner knob, finding an orchestra playing a German waltz. That would do. She turned the cathedral shaped cabinet toward her desk and inched up the volume.

Sara slumped back in her chair, covering her eyes. If each letter was a cry for help, then her father was forsaking the call. Gladys, Sylvia, and Marilyn wanted her to take up the banner, to rally for the listeners and push for a new course.

They couldn't have picked a worse time.

Larry's behavior was worrisome. What if he didn't come through? Daddy was harder to defend. An ugly truth festered in her mind. *My father is a fraud, and I'm his Judas goat.* He wasn't going to listen to her. It would interfere with his ambition. *I'm going to fail...with both fathers.* A Bible verse came to mind. Something about the sins of the fathers shall be visited upon the children. *How will I pay for my father's sins? What about my own sins? Can my baby escape? What must I do for my child to break free of this cycle?*

Losing her job was only the beginning. Her life was about to change. All the work she put in helping her father would come to nothing. She'd become a burden.

Her chin quivered. Tears brimmed in her eyes. A black storm seemed ready to engulf her. For a fleeting instant, she thought about keeping quiet. She had no business telling Daddy what his obligations were. Let someone else fight this battle.

There was no one else. The Judas goat was about to turn on her master.

Tears spilled down her cheeks. She bent over her desk, her face buried in her arms. She cried for her unborn child and for the neglected child within herself.

The music played to an audience of one.

Chapter Three

Sara pushed her way through the front door of her home holding a bag of groceries. "Hi Mom! I brought some things from the store!"

Light from electric wall lamps, as well as pale blue wallpaper, gave the living room a cozy look. In the right corner sat a floor model Emerson radio with three overstuffed chairs arranged in front. On the wall above hung a decorative plate with a drawing of a wedding cake in the center. Gold script circled the picture:

Sam and Katherine
July 19, 1910

"I'm in the kitchen!"

Sara hung her jacket and hat in the closet, grabbed the groceries and stepped through the sewing room into the kitchen. Daddy was nowhere in sight.

A wide cupboard trimmed in green and eggshell white stood by the kitchen door. In the center of the room was an oak kitchen table with four chairs. A telephone hung by the screened back door. From the kitchen, a hallway led to a bathroom, her father's office, and her parents' bedroom. A closet-sized pantry sat between the hall and back door.

Sara set the groceries on the kitchen table. "I got a few things from the Corner Market on the way home. There's a bakery opening. Maybe this Depression is about over."

Katherine McGurk peeked in the bag. "Stores come and go. It doesn't mean a thing." Dashes of gray streaked her mother's black curls. Deepening lines appeared around her hazel eyes. At forty-four, time was catching up with the only person in Sara's life who didn't seem to age. "Spinach, beets, pickles, and sauerkraut. Your father *might* eat the pickles. Do you want any of this with supper?"

"The spinach. I'm having a taste for it. Where is Daddy?" Telling Mom about cravings would be hard enough. Telling her with Daddy walking in would be disastrous.

Her mother pointed down the hall. "Your father's in his office working on his next talk."

"Is he coming out soon?"

Katherine shrugged. "I doubt it. You know your father. When he's writing, he could stay in there all evening if I let him."

"What about the boys?"

"They're running errands. Getting magazines and newspapers. Your father has become a newshound."

"How soon?"

Katherine glanced at Sara. "Half-hour, I suppose. Maybe longer. If Jason had gone alone, he'd be back by now. With Michael tagging along"—her mother smiled—"It could be a while." She pointed to the groceries. "Keep the spinach out and put the rest in the pantry. You can help me with supper." After storing the groceries, Sara tied on her apron. "What are we having?"

"Meatloaf and mashed potatoes. I'll mix the hamburger. You can peel the potatoes. We'll heat the green beans and spinach later."

Sara filled a bowl of potatoes and took a paring knife from a cupboard drawer. Her mother placed the meat in a large bowl and added crackers, eggs, and a tin of tomato sauce. "How did work go today?"

Sara dropped a quartered potato into a pot. "We were busy. More letters are coming in. People are inquiring about the show being picked up by the Alliance."

"That's not surprising. Are you keeping up?"

"For now. But before the show goes national, I'll have to ask Daddy for more help."

"Your father is a practical man. He'll agree to that."

Sara guided the small blade with her thumb, a strip of potato skin spiraling below her fingers. "That's the problem. The girls are worried the new letters will bury our regular fans. They are the listeners who've stayed with the show from the beginning."

Katherine pursed her lips. "It's the price of success. Something that's very rare these days. And so we make the most of it. You never know when it could end."

Her mother worked the mixture with sure hands. She never followed a recipe or measured ingredients. If she didn't have what was needed, she made do with something else. All her dishes were unique creations because she never made anything quite the same way twice. And it always turned out right.

She couldn't keep her secret much longer.

Katherine smiled without looking up. "You better finish those potatoes."

Sara let out a breath, peeling and slicing the russets into pieces. When she finished, she filled the pot with water and placed the container on the stove. Katherine packed the ground beef in a loaf pan and slid the mixture into the oven.

With the immediate kitchen chores completed, now was the time. Sara bit her lower lip. "Mom, there's one more thing I need to tell you."

Katherine flipped the oven door shut. "Oh? What's that?"

Sara's hands quivered. A lump formed in her throat. She could barely get the words out, "I don't think I can do my job anymore." Sara closed her eyes against stinging tears.

Comforting arms embraced her. "You're shaking. What happened today? Ever since you came home, you've been as skittish as a rabbit." Katherine wiped Sara's eyes with a towel. "Tell your mother."

Sara brushed hair from her eyes. "I got some news from Dr. Payton today. I'm going to have a baby."

Her mother gasped, then grabbed a chair, pointing to another. "Sit down." Her voice was heavy with dread.

As Sara sank into the chair, Katherine held her trembling hands. "Tell me what you know."

Unspoken pain crept into Sara's green eyes. "I'm due in November. Larry is the father. I told him after I found out. He didn't take it well. Did he call?"

Katherine shook her head. "It would be better if you could marry. In any case, you'll have to move away in a month or two. Have your child somewhere else. We'll say you were overworked and left Wichita to rest. After you give the baby to an orphanage, you can move back home and live as before."

Sara lifted her gaze with cold defiance. "I know that's the right thing to do, but I want to protect my baby. I can't do that by giving him to strangers."

Katherine's eyes darkened; her voice became low and urgent. "You don't have a choice." She glanced down the hallway. "It's a terrible price to pay, but it will be over in a few months. Keeping your child would mean accepting the scorn of others or living with elaborate lies for the rest of your life."

Sara tilted her head, "I don't understand."

"There is another way." Katherine met her daughter's eyes with surprising resolve. "You and Larry marry and move away. Change your life. Make new friends. Decide on a different wedding date for yourselves. Move it, say, six months earlier. Make a plaque or decorate a plate that proclaims the new date. The fictitious anniversary will soon become fact."

Sara stared at her mother open-mouthed. "How do you know so much about this?"

She spoke in a detached tone. "You're not the only one with secrets. Twenty-four years ago, I wore your same shoes."

Her words hit like a hammer. Sara buried her head and held on sobbing. "We're quite a pair. So much alike. I've prayed I'd never have to tell you, but you deserve the truth. Please forgive me."

Sara trembled in her arms.

"Sam and I married just before we moved to Wichita, well before you were born. I felt so ashamed at first when I learned I would have a child. But you are a special creation. My baby. And you grew to become the wonderful and unique person you are today. Now, look around. Nothing has changed."

Mother was wrong. The everyday familiar—that sense of order and balance—was dashed to pieces. A sense of uncertainty rocked her, like a boat yanked from its moorings and cast adrift on a windswept sea.

Sara stood up and turned away, unable to mask a cold, bitter emptiness looming inside. She had to be strong and find her way through this. "I can't sort this out. When did you and Daddy marry? I want the real date."

Katherine shuffled to the stove, stirring the potatoes. "Our true wedding date was December 2, 1910, five months before you were born."

Sara closed her fingers into a fist. "How did this idea...changing your anniversary, come about?"

Katherine turned around and smiled. "The idea came when I decided to keep you as my child." She grabbed a towel and wiped down the cupboard. "I first met your father when I was nineteen. My parents and I lived outside of Hutchinson. I spent that day in town with friends window shopping downtown. It was early May of 1910. Some boys followed us in a sickly green Tin Lizzie. The driver was this tough looking rooster in overalls." Her voice trailed off as she stared out the kitchen window. "He followed me home, driving that contraption into my parents' yard. The car kept backfiring, and our dogs ran around barking up a storm."

"Is this Daddy you're talking about?" *Impossible.*

A faraway look touched her mother's eyes. "Oh yes. He wore these goggles. Dust and wind plastered his hair down, and he was filthy except for his eyes. He honked his horn, waving at me. Daddy took a pitchfork after him. Me? I was already falling for him."

"Oh, my."

"My parents forbade me from seeing him. I did

35

anyway. I felt like the luckiest girl on earth. At least, until the day I learned I was with child."

Sara drew in a breath. A pang resonated within her, but she had to know the rest of the story. "What happened?"

"My parents were shocked, of course. Mother was disappointed in me. Daddy took his shotgun in search of Sam—I mean your father. He hid in an old dugout we found one day while driving. A friend took me there. I begged him to marry me. He was my last hope because I was about to be sent away. We married two weeks later. I wouldn't call it a shotgun wedding, but my uncles covered every door in the church."

Sara shook her head in amazement. It was impossible to imagine her mother as a prim, but reckless young woman, stepping beyond the bounds of acceptability. A stunning truth hit home.

This was her story as well.

"After we married, I insisted we move away. We arrived here in January. I was clearly a mother-to-be by then. We rented a house, joined a church, and made new friends. I even made a plate—it's in the front room—stating our wedding date as July 19, 1910."

"Six months difference, just like you said." Sara's voice was low as if reciting the facts to herself.

Katherine shrugged. "What's an anniversary but a date on a record nobody sees?"

Sara blew out a breath. "Larry isn't about to give up his job and move away. He wants to run his father's business."

Katherine set her jaw. "I'll write to my sister in Hutchinson. You can stay with her. It's only fifty miles away."

"I'm not going away just to wait out my time and let someone take my child."

Katherine gripped her daughter's hand. "You must. It's the price you pay for having sinned."

Sara flinched, stepping back. "*My* price? And you, Mother. What price did *you* pay?"

Katherine recoiled, glancing down the hall. "I made a decision. People don't always marry for love. Love may come later. Or not at all. My sins are my own. Spare your child—and yourself. Do you love this man?"

"I enjoy his company."

"That's not what I asked. Do you *love* him?"

Sara's rose, trudged to the sink, and turned on the tap, running water in cupped hands and splashed her face.

Katherine offered her a clean towel. "Don't add to your mistakes, Sara." She leaned over and peeked in the stove. "Let's go to Sunday worship tomorrow, the way we used to."

Sara bit her lower lip, shaking her head. "I can't. I don't want to see those hypocrites again. Not after all that's happened. I'm surprised you still go."

"Your father didn't commit a crime for leaving. He moved on because he found a new passion. The radio station needed programs to fill its schedule, and his idea of a Sunday morning commentary fitted their needs perfectly." Katherine gazed out the kitchen sink window "But I have to admit. Being the pastor's wife was exciting. I chaired committees, took part in social events and greeted parishioners as they came in the door. Those were crazy, busy years—raising three children and organizing church projects at the same time. I still miss it."

Sara's lips held a quiet smile. "I had some good times as well. Singing solos when I was ten and still being the youngest member of the choir at seventeen. I felt so grown up. Then Daddy quit."

"Some people were bitter toward your father. Those were not easy times."

Sara poured water from the potato pot and retrieved a masher from the cupboard. "I hated the whispers and side-long glances. I called them phonies and quit the church." She added salt, milk, and butter to the potatoes, stirred in the ingredients, and tasted the mixture. All done.

"The thought of leaving the church never crossed my mind."

Sara bowed her head. "I wish I was as strong as you."

"You are. You just don't know it, yet."

Sara heated the green beans and spinach and Katherine set the table. Brakes squeaked outside announcing the arrival of Sara's younger brothers, Jason and Michael.

Michael McGurk banged through the back door, carrying a stack of newspapers and magazines. "We must have gone to half the newsstands in town!" The wiry eighteen-year-old dropped the papers onto a kitchen chair and tossed his newsboy cap onto a wall peg. Small for his age, with curly brown hair and freckles that refused to disappear, Michael looked like one of the older tough kids in the *Our Gang* comedies.

Katherine stepped forward. "Take those papers to your father's office. And tell him supper's about ready. Where's Jason?"

"He's working on the clutch. Says it's too tight. You know how he likes to fiddle with that Model A."

"Well, he better not get attached to it. Your father's talking about trading it in for a Nash or a Mercedes."

"A Mercedes! That'd be neat!" Michael grabbed the papers, racing down the hall.

Sara scooped the cooked vegetables in bowls while Katherine removed the meatloaf from the pan and added flour to the drippings to make gravy. "Is Daddy serious about a Mercedes?"

"Your father wants a car that will make a statement."

Sara raised her brows. "He's going to buy a fancy car before his show is on the network?"

Katherine held up a palm. "When I tell you kids to learn from your father, it doesn't always mean to follow his example."

Sara set the bowls on the table. "I have to call Larry."

Katherine pursed her lips as she placed the gravy by the vegetables. "Supper first. Larry can wait."

Sara frowned but said nothing. She set the meatloaf by her father's plate.

Katherine surveyed the table. "Everything's ready. Let's get the men in here. Time to eat."

Chapter Four

Sara passed the last of the meatloaf to her father. "Would you like any more, Daddy?"

"I'll take that." Sam deposited the remainder on his plate. A large man with hooded eyes, massive hands and thick shoulders, Samuel McGurk looked more like a boxer than a preacher. "Now, where was I? This new car I want will be either a Nash or a Mercedes."

Jason McGurk frowned. "What's going to happen to the Model A?

Sam pointed an index finger at Jason. "I'll get to that. The Nash is a roomy, elegant car. We could all ride comfortably in it. But I've been eyeing a Mercedes at Ziegler's car lot. It's been sitting there for weeks. I'm betting the dealer will give me a discount just to get rid of it."

Jason bent forward. "I've put in a lot of time keeping the Model A in good shape." Three years younger than Sara, Jason had his mother's slight features, black hair, and blue eyes. "A second car could come in handy for running errands, especially if you're out of town."

Sam's fist fell to the table with a thump. "Forget the Model A. It's an average car, built for the masses." The big man wolfed down a mouthful of meatloaf. He seldom wore pastoral clothes these days, preferring flannel shirts and suspendered denim pants. "I'm selling the car. One vehicle is enough for this household."

Jason set his fork down. "So, does that mean I can drive this new car?"

Sam settled back in his chair. "No. This car will be special. Since my program is going national, I want a vehicle that commands attention. Not one of Mr. Ford's cookie cutters."

"You're going to sell the Ford and leave us with nothing?" Jason shook his head. "Fine with me. I've been saving my money. In four months there'll be enough to make a down payment for a used car."

Sam McGurk rose and bent forward, his thick arms pressing down on the table. "Watch your tongue, young man."

Katherine held Jason's arm. "Sam, owning a car will teach Jason responsibility. We could keep the old car until he buys his own."

"Maybe." He turned to Jason. "Or you could buy the Model A."

"No. Sell the thing and run your own errands."

Sara gasped. Why was Jason goading Daddy?

Sam shoved the table forward, as his voice simmered with controlled rage. "You've made your point. Now hear mine. As long as you live in this house, I will expect your full respect. Either you give it to me, or you can live under a different roof. Do I make myself clear?"

"I'm sure Jason didn't mean—"

"Stay out of it, Katherine. This is between Jason and me. What's it going to be, boy?"

Jason's eyes searched about the room as if avoiding his father's penetrating stare. "All I want is to own a car." All defiance was gone.

"The subject under discussion is respect. I'm not interested in you owning a car."

Jason's eyes focused on the table. "You have my respect, Father, for as long as I live under your roof. May I be excused now?"

Sam nodded. "We'll keep the Model A. For now." Samuel sat back down, extending a pointed finger. "But I warn you. Any more lip, and I'll take action."

Jason rushed from the kitchen.

Sam finished eating as if nothing had happened, then wiped his lips. "A fine meal as always Katherine."

"Sara helped as well."

He shrugged. "Daughters are expected to help their mothers."

Sara sighed, closing her eyes.

"Can I go now?" Michael asked. Katherine nodded, and Sara's youngest brother bolted from the kitchen.

Sara picked up plates. "I'll wash dishes tonight, Mother."

Katherine waved her hand. "You and your father should visit."

Her father turned his head. "Oh? Are you going to lecture me on how I handled your brother?"

Sara clasped her hands together. "My helpers are worried how joining the Alliance will affect the Mailroom."

Sam leaned back. "Well, let's get to it. Katherine, is there any of that strawberry cake left? Or did the boys eat it all?"

"There's still two slices. Sara, would you like some?"

"No, thank you." Sara retrieved the two letters she brought from work while Katherine plated a wedge of pink cake and brought it and a clean fork to the table.

Sam licked some icing from a fingertip. "Cake doesn't last long around here." He ate with deliberate slowness, savoring each bite. Sometimes he dabbed his mouth with a napkin between bites. Finally, he ate the last bit of frosting before pushing the saucer away. "Very tasty, Katherine. A lemon pie would be a nice treat next week. Could you do that?"

Katherine nodded. "Sara has some business to discuss with you."

Her father glanced at her as if noticing her for the first time. "Can this wait? I should be polishing my talk for tomorrow."

Sara shook her head. "No, Daddy." She pushed the "duster" note across the table. "This first letter is about a grandmother who loses her daughter and grandchildren. It's very sad."

Sam pulled out the pages with a bit of dust as well. "They don't keep a clean house, do they?"

"Just read it, Daddy."

Sam donned a par reading glasses and flipped the pages before reading through the letter. A frown etched across his face. After he finished, he settled back in his seat, scowling.

Sara couldn't contain herself. "What do you think?"

"Quite a story. Two unfortunate children die from an obscure disease. A mother aborts because she doesn't want another child. And we have an insane grandmother ready to commit suicide. You tell me what to do with this mess."

Sara stared at her father. "It's possible Jennifer may still be alive. We need to call the sheriff down there. Get her family some help. You do that from time to time. She turned to you, Daddy. She believes in you. We have to make an effort to help her."

Sam pushed the letter away. "Do you remember what I said when I gave you the job of answering fan mail? We're not saving the world. If you get a sob story, tell them to look to their church for help. Then move on. Don't let one piece of mail bog down the works."

"This one is special." Sara tapped the pages. "Don't you see? Dust storms are destroying their lives. You can tell their story. Prevent another tragedy like this from happening."

Sam gathered the pages. "Have you answered this letter?"

"I thought you should see it first."

"Good." Methodically, he ripped the paper into confetti. "Coming from a demented woman, this may not have happened at all."

Sara gasped—it was hard to breathe. "Don't!" She grabbed his arm to stop the mutilation, but he batted her away.

"The matter is settled." He brushed the pieces aside and then picked up the other letter. "So, what's this one about?"

Sara stared at the bits of paper, Jennifer's words flashing in her mind. *They think the worst is over. It's not. The gates of hell will open soon, and Satan's breath will spew black across the land.* Was this a cry for help from a saddened woman? Or was it a premonition? Should she let this moment pass? Or should she make her stand?

Sam slapped the pages of the second note. "Now

this is a good letter. A farmer is losing his land because of a New Deal program. He can't plant any crops to feed his family or make a living. Here's proof FDR's farm programs are failing. No fireside chat can smooth *this* over. I'll pay a couple of months rent to keep this story alive."

Hot anger shot up the back of Sara's neck. "The bank controls the situation. Not Roosevelt."

Sam flicked his fingers. "Let's not muddy the water. You take care of the letters. I'll take care of the show. Where are the donations?"

Sara drew a thick envelope from her handbag. "I could deposit in the bank. I go by it every day on the way to the bus."

"No bank is touching this money. Are we finished?"

Sara's eyes narrowed to steel slits. "Not quite."

"Oh?" Sam raised an eyebrow. "I know that look of yours. Out with it."

"These letters are calling for your help, Daddy. They're from listeners who look to your authority. They see you as a pastor. So they write about the things that matter to them—the lack of control in their lives. Many folks think this Depression is punishment for sins they've committed. And they're looking to you for hope."

Sam threw out his palms. "I do give them hope."

Sara spoke with urgency, knowing it was a futile effort. "You spew out anger and criticism. You talk about the economy, Congress, government programs—the average person sees these things as remote. You can use your role as Pastor to ease the anxiety, to build charities. You can be more than a mere entertainer."

Sam's eyes narrowed. "Don't lecture me on running my business. We are not a charity. The program is my concern. And I expect you to encourage fans to write back with at least a dollar donation."

"Daddy, if you want to call yourself a pastor, you need to act like one. Listen to yourself. The problems of these people mean nothing to you. Their only purpose is to donate. Remember what the Bible says about serving two masters?"

"Stop right there." Her father's voice wore a warning.

"You have to hear the rest. You take, but give nothing in return. Your show is one big advertisement. A half-hour commercial all about you."

Sam slammed a fist on the table. "Why you smug little whelp. Don't get pious with me. When was the last time you've been to church? Or cracked a Bible? You've gone dancing, living the carefree life, running around with that well-dressed pansy, yet you insult me in my house—"

"Sam!" Katherine stepped from the sink, grasping his arm. "Be mindful of your blood pressure."

He turned to Katherine, glowering. "The doctor said it was benign hypertension. Benign. There's nothing to worry about."

"That not completely true. Dr. Payton said your blood pressure was close to malignant, and you should avoid anger by counting backward." Katherine shot a look at Sara. "And you shouldn't irritate your father."

Sara breathed a sigh of relief. Thank goodness, Mother distracted Daddy with his recent doctor's visit. "I'm sorry for saying those things. The volume of mail is going up, and our in-state listeners will likely get

46

buried under the avalanche of new mail."

Sam grinned. "I would say now is the time to send out those new leaflets. Did they come in today?"

Sara nodded.

"With the flyers in place along with the increase in mail, donations should pour in. How many leaflets went out today?"

Sara's mouth went dry. She couldn't find a way to soften the truth. None. "I decided not to send out an advertisement for a church that doesn't exist."

"You couldn't..." He stared at the ceiling for a moment then leveled darkened eyes. "You're fired."

Sara closed her eyes. Losing her job was inevitable. But now, it meant Daddy would be overseeing the office and supervising her friends. She had to help them. "You'll need to hire more workers. Gladys, Marilyn, and Sylvia—they care about their jobs, but they'll fall behind due to the increasing volume of mail."

"They put you up to this. And you expect me to help them?"

"They care about the fans. That's all that matters."

"You're harboring their little mutiny." He smiled, showing uneven teeth. "Firing you may not be enough."

Sara sucked in a breath, "What're you saying?"

"I'm taking your suggestion. Get new help. But first, I'll clean house and start from scratch."

Sara jumped to her feet, "You can't! Those are my friends. They've worked hard for you, and they've created a bond with the fans. Would you destroy that? What would you put in its place? A sweatshop churning out identical letters asking for money?"

Sam chuckled. "Not a bad idea when you put it that

way."

Katherine rushed behind her husband, rubbing his shoulders. "Sam, you already have many responsibilities. Hiring and training new people on top of writing and managing your program—it's not wise. Give the job of running the office to someone else."

Sara pointed a finger at her father. "You'll always be looking for new help once they see what a fraud you are."

Only later did Sara piece together what happened next. Her father lurched to a fighting stance, thrusting out his massive hand. He swung his arm around in a sweeping arc. Sara froze, transfixed by the approaching blow. A force shoved her aside. In the next moment, a dull crack of flesh against bone, and Katherine fell to the kitchen floor. For a long moment, she lay unmoving.

"Mom!" Sara dropped to her knees, cradling her mother's head. Tears spilled down her cheeks. *How could this happen?* She moaned. Sara gasped with relief, pulled herself to her feet and rushed to the sink. She ran water over a dishtowel and hurried back to her mother's side. Daddy deposited her in a kitchen chair. Sara thrust the towel toward him, not daring to say a word.

He dabbed at his wife's swelling cheek. "How could you do such a stupid thing? You *knew* she had it coming, and you still stepped in the way? *Why?*"

Katherine groaned, taking the towel and pressing it against her jaw. "You can't hurt her, Sam." Her voice was barely understandable.

Her father scowled. "I wasn't going to *hurt* her, but someone has to teach her a lesson."

She focused on her husband. "You can't."
He crossed his arms. "And why not?"
Sara bowed her head. "I carry a child."

Chapter Five

"I can't believe this!" Samuel McGurk paced the kitchen, waving his arms while Sara held a cold towel to her mother's jaw. "I've given you a job, paid you a wage, and this is the thanks I get? You've brought shame to this family. You've brought shame to *me*. Critics watch every word I say. They're *waiting* for me to make a mistake. And you've given them a gift! A pastor with a disgraced daughter under his roof. I could lose everything. All because of your irresponsibility. You'll have to leave. Sooner the better."

"I'll write my sister in Hutchinson." Katherine spoke slowly, her voice muffled. "Once Sara has the baby, she can give the child up for adoption. She should be able to return home."

Sara shook her head. *Not my baby.* "Mother…"

Katherine shot her a glance. "Not now."

McGurk rubbed his chin. "I don't like it. Word can still get out. I want her in a sanitarium. Somewhere secure where the staff can be trusted to keep quiet. The Meisenheimer Clinic might work."

Katherine's eyes widened. "You can't be serious."

Sara balled her hands into tight fists. "I won't go. But there may be room in that sanitarium for you."

Her father whirled around, his eyes frosty. "That's it. You're leaving tonight. Now, I have work to do. I expect you to be gone when I come out." With that, he stalked out of the kitchen to his office, slamming the door.

Katherine stood in shock. Sara rushed to embrace her. "I'm sorry. I didn't mean to push him."

Her mother wiped silent tears. "We need to think. Is there a place you can stay tonight?"

"There's Gladys—but she's gone this weekend."

"Go upstairs and pack some clothes. I'll see about where you can stay."

"I can't leave you like this. You jaw is swollen."

"You have to. Now go." She released Sara.

A minute later, Sara was in her room throwing clothes in a carpetbag. Michael appeared at her bedroom door. "We heard yelling downstairs. Sounds like Dad's all fired up."

Sara sighed. "We had an argument. He would have boxed my ear if mother hadn't stepped in the way."

"Wait'll Jay hears about this!" Michael raced out of the room.

Moments later, both boys stood at her door. Sara related the events downstairs. "You might as well know. In seven months I'm having a baby. That's what set him off."

"You mean we'll be uncles?" Michael's eyes grew large.

Jason gave a low whistle, glancing at his sister. "That would do it."

Sara packed her box of stationery. "Anyway, he's kicked me out. Seems I'm a threat to his radio career."

Jason took the bulky container from her. "I'll carry it. Where do you need to go?"

"There's a flop house," said Sara, "near the tracks on Lincoln. They might have a place for women."

Jason gave a rueful grin, "Fat chance. Mom'll have a better idea." He carried the bag downstairs with Sara following.

Her mother was waiting. "I've got a sheet, a couple of blankets, and a pillow. Is that couch still in the back of the office?"

"It's still there."

"Good. I've got a spare key. Leave your keys on the table for your father to find." She touched her jaw. "Here's some money for train fare. I've called the depot. Two trains run daily to Hutchinson. One at 10:05 in the morning and the other at 4:45 p.m. Call here tomorrow and tell me your plans. I can send my sister a telegram before your arrival."

"Mom, you should take some aspirin."

"Already done that."

"I'm not sure I want to go to Hutchinson."

"They can help you. Now promise you'll call."

Jason lifted her bag. "I'll run this to the car." The screen door banged shut behind him as he left.

"I promise."

Their time was growing short. Katherine stepped forward, hugging Sara. "Please forgive your father. When he first started, he was grateful to preach before a small church. Now, he has this burning desire for fame. Nothing else matters and it scares me. I've had dreams of his career falling like a house of cards. And your father was the last to know he was ruined."

"Why is Daddy so afraid of me?"

Katherine closed her eyes. "He frets about everyone he meets: you, the boys, the radio station, even me. But most of all, I think he's afraid of himself. That he'll make a mistake."

Jason returned, gathering up the blankets and pillow.

"Sara will be out in a minute," Katherine told him.

As Jason left, Katherine and Sara embraced, tears flowing down both their cheeks. "Be careful. I love you Sara."

"I love you too."

As Sara stepped to the Model A, she turned to wave goodbye. In the gathering dusk, she saw her mother behind the screen door. She looked like a trapped creature. A minute later, Jason backed the car out of the drive, turned onto the street and drove away.

****

Sara sat staring out the window as Jason drove through the downtown streets. Bands of light and shadows chased through the interior as they passed beneath Wichita's newly installed electric streetlights. Jason half-turned to her, but kept his eyes on the road. "I wish I could have been there. I could have stopped the argument."

"Be glad you weren't." Sara gave him a sideways glance. "You'd be looking for a place to stay as well."

Jason stopped at a traffic light. "Pop's changed, hasn't he? This idea of being heard all across the country has really taken hold of him."

"Daddy's wrapped up in his dream. You and Michael take care of Mom. Help her with dishes, the housecleaning, and doing the laundry. Don't let her feel like she's alone."

"I know. It's easy to take Mom for granted." Jason turned onto Douglas Avenue. "But this should all blow over. Pop hates to admit mistakes. Tomorrow, he'll act like nothing ever happened. By Monday, he'll be grumbling why you're not answering his mail." Jason glanced at her. "Right?"

"Not this time. Things have gone too far."

"You could find work at one of the big stores downtown."

Sara sighed, her eyes downcast. "For another month, maybe. After that, it's going to become obvious I'm expecting."

Jason watched the streets ahead. "This is a strange question. But I'm curious. How does it feel?"

"How does what feel?"

Jason hesitated, working his lower lip. "I wouldn't ask if you weren't my sister. But how does it feel...to be a mother?"

Sara arched her brows, looking baffled. Then burst into laughter and scooted next to her brother, slapping his knee.

"I didn't mean to sound stupid."

"Oh Jay, it's not you. I've been jumping from one thing to the next all day and haven't had a chance to think about my feelings."

Jason turned onto Broadway. "Can I ask...who's the father?"

"His name's Larry. He works at Bigger's Mercantile downtown. His father owns the store."

"Did he eat supper with us last Christmas?"

Sara nodded. "He entertained Daddy all evening with jokes."

They were moving through the southern end of the business district now. Ahead were mostly darkened buildings.

"I never realized how creepy this part of town is at night," Jason said. "Will you be okay?"

"I promise to lock the doors." She swatted his arm. "Don't be a mother hen."

"I've got some change. You'll need to eat."

"Mom gave me some money. Thank you, though."

The electric lights gave way to occasional spots of illumination that dotted the area.

"You can always go through the mail and pull out donations. Nobody would know. That's how Pop is paying for his fancy car."

Sara's jaw dropped. "Be careful who you say that to. That money is for Daddy's Church of the South Wind—whenever that will be." She sighed. "I couldn't do that, anyway."

Jason shrugged. "You're right. I was thinking how a person could get back at him."

The Kramer Building loomed ahead. Office lights burned on the first floor. Sara pointed. "The bookie's working tonight."

"I wish you had a telephone." Jason pulled to the front door. The glass reflected the car's headlights.

"There's one in the diner across the street."

They entered the building. Sara carried her travel bag while Jason held the blankets and pillow. She unlocked the Mailroom, entered, and turned on the lights. She dropped her bag to the floor. Jason flung the bedding onto the couch. Sara turned to him. "Thanks, Jay."

Jason glanced around. "At least you got a radio."

"There's also a washroom down the hall."

Jason grunted. "All the comforts of home." He stepped forward and embraced her. "You take care of yourself. And call home tomorrow, or I'll come looking for you."

"Mom's given me the lecture." Sara smiled. "Now get, you big worrywart, or Daddy'll take away those car keys."

Jason left the office, averting his face. Two minutes a horn tooted, and the clatter of the Model A merged with the rest of the evening sounds outsides her open widows.

Sara locked the door, flipped off the lights and made her way to the couch. She clicked on the radio and busied herself with making her bed. Outside, a dog growled at an intruder, and a trashcan in the alley tipped over. Was someone outside? Sara listened, staying clear of the window. Soon, the barking faded. Somehow, the silence seemed more intimidating than the clatter. She turned up the radio, hoping to impede the encroaching night.

Could Mother's dream come true? Could Daddy's career fall like a house of cards? It seemed impossible. His fame was about to skyrocket with plump fees for speaking engagements, product endorsements, and book deals. Daddy's future seemed secure.

And what about her? Her work as a office supervisor was over. The world that seemed so ordinary that morning had turned into a tempest, propelling her into uncharted waters. What was she to do? Strike out on some new course? She couldn't. Not yet. She needed to see Larry one last time. Give him one last chance to do the right thing. If he wouldn't listen, that left staying with her aunt and uncle in Hutchinson. To lose her child would be terrible. But to learn too late that she could keep her baby—*that* would be unbearable.

Chapter Six

"In closing, friends, I wish to extend prayers to the beleaguered in hostile lands. To the Jew in Germany. To the Christian in Russia. To the tribal peasant in Iran. May they overcome their persecutors and find peace.

"But most of all, I want to extend my prayers to the people of the United States. To the struggling American farmer, fighting to save his land. To the laborer, who has lost his job. And to the mass of humanity roaming this country in search of work.

"All of these people are abandoned. They are abandoned because Washington is not letting the Depression take its natural course. We have an administration that thinks it can fix everything but the weather. The New Dealers want to control business as well as government, and it is the American people who must pay the price. Even our Congress is swooned by the promise of prosperity. A promise from a president who has failed to make a difference.

"Thomas Jefferson once said, 'In matters of style, swim with the current; in matters of principle, stand like a rock.'

"So, friends, I'm asking you; is this a government of style? Or is it a government of principle? Have you seen signs of happier days? Believe me when I say there are those who are getting fat from this Depression.

You've worked hard, yet there is never enough food on the table. Is FDR helping you? Or is he crooning in your ear while your tax money goes in someone else's pocket?

"Alexander Hamilton died in a duel, and yet his style of big government lives. Thomas Jefferson was president, yet his principles of small government are dead. Isn't it time we turned things around?"

~Excerpt from the *Heaven and Earth* radio broadcast
Sunday, 7 April 1935

Sara awoke early, washed in the lavatory down the hall, and headed across the street to the Farmland Café. She found a stool at the front counter and ordered breakfast from a waitress wearing a starched blue uniform. The waitress was her mom's age with short graying hair, much in the style of ten years ago. The name embroidered on her lapel read CARRIE. Ten minutes later, Carrie slid a plate before her. "Careful, Missy. Plate's hot."

As she ate, Sara pondered her visit with Larry. Would he see reason? Or fail her? His father wouldn't stand for such nonsense. Gerald Bigger was a man of integrity. But should she use him as a way of getting at Larry? Was forcing a man into marriage a good idea? How best to approach him?

With breakfast over, Sara fished a nickel from her handbag and made her way to the phone booth near the entrance. She picked up the receiver, deposited the coin, and rang through to the operator. "Could you connect me to City Cab?" A minute later, the dispatcher came on the line. "I'd like a taxi at the Farmland Café, 1610 South Broadway. Thank you."

Sara returned to her seat. The mirror behind the

back counter gave her a good view outside. As she drank her coffee, Carrie stopped to refill her cup.

"Can I pay for my meal now? My cab could show up anytime."

The waitress flipped open a ticket book. "That'll be forty cents with the coffee."

Sara placed two quarters on the counter. "Keep it."

"Thanks, Missy. Cabs run slow on Sundays. You might be waiting a while."

Sara nodded. Another customer left his newspaper on the counter beside her. Fearing the waitress was right, Sara spread the paper before her and settled in for a long wait.

The front-page story was about the new bus station near the Innes Department Store. After months of construction, it would open tomorrow morning. All city buses would meet in one central location. That would make getting home a lot easier. Except she couldn't go home anymore. Another article related news about an engineer working on a system for sending and receiving moving images over cable. He called the system "television."

A car honked outside. Sara glanced at the mirror. A cab sat in front of the restaurant. She grabbed her purse and bag, bustled out the front door, and entered the cab. "I'd like to go to 1217 River Boulevard."

The taxi drove northeast to Wichita's Riverside area, following the winding road that bordered the low waters of the Little Arkansas River. The street followed a wide bend, and stopped in front of a modest two-story Craftsmen-style house facing the water. Sara paid the driver and carried her bag up the steps to the front door. Gerald's La Salle was gone, but Larry's silver Roadster sat in the driveway. Biting her lip, she ascended the steps and knocked on the screen door.

A long moment passed before the inside door flew open. Larry leaned on the doorframe, rubbing his brow. Unshaven, red-eyed, and wearing nothing but a long nightshirt, he squinted through the screen door. "You could have told me I was supposed to come home after work yesterday." Larry rubbed bloodshot eyes.

Sara gritted her teeth. "You said you'd call me."

"So, does that make us even?"

"Not even close." She shook her head. "It doesn't matter anymore. I'll wait out here. Your parents should be returning home from church soon. I'm sorry to have bothered you."

Larry pushed the screen door open. "Don't be so bullheaded. Come inside. It's chilly out there, and my parents won't be home for hours. They're going to dinner after church."

"I'm not coming in with you undressed." She retreated a step, crossing her arms.

He shrugged. "Have it your way. I need some aspirin. Give me a chance to wash up, and then we can talk. Even better, I can pick you up at work tomorrow and take you to supper."

Sara stared at him through narrowed brows. "Daddy fired me. In fact, he turned me out of the house just last night."

Larry grunted and turned away, trudging up the steps. It *was* chilly out here. Sara slipped into the house, closing the door behind her. "Larry, I'm downstairs," she called.

No answer. Squeaky water taps turned upstairs. Larry must be taking a bath.

Sara sat on the living room sofa. Lois Bigger kept a fine house. The wallpaper was a pale green print of vines and flowers. In one corner sat an upright piano. Small table lamps bracketed the sofa, and several chairs set around a large radio. Against the stairway was a bookcase full of recent hardbound titles in colorful paper jackets.

Sara wandered to the shelves and examined the volumes. Most were fiction with "Book of the Month Edition" printed on the inside front jacket. *Good-Bye Mr. Chips* by James Hilton, *So Red the Rose* by Carolyn Miller, *Elmer Gantry* by Sinclair Lewis, *Grand Hotel* by Vicki Baum, and *The Good Earth* by Pearl Buck. Among the many books was a small wind-up clock: 10:50.

She had read *Elmer Gantry,* skimming through the book at the city library after her father blasted the book on the radio. How many readers would have not read the novel if he kept quiet? The story of a conniving preacher was captivating. Even more thrilling was the delicious dread of getting caught while reading the forbidden pages.

Heavy footsteps tromped down the stairs. Sara glanced up. Larry wore a gray pinstriped suit and Panama hat. His sunken eyes still betrayed a rough night before.

"You look terrible. Did you drink last night?"

"I had a few." He plodded the rest of the way down the steps, and stopped before her. "When I came home, the old fuss was waiting for me—harping like an old woman 'bout how I should have returned hours ago. And what was I doing out so late? I kept quiet, but I wanted to sock him good. If he wants me to take over, he should step out of my way."

"So, you haven't told your parents yet…about us?"

Larry pursed his lips. "I'll get around to it."

"You've had most of a day."

Larry shrugged. "Sorry."

"It's quite all right." She flashed a false smile. "I'll take care of it."

Larry blinked. "*You're* telling them?"

Sara countered, "You weren't listening at the door?"

Larry's eyes grew dark. "Don't get smart with me."

Sara retreated a step. Larry was altogether too surly this morning. Perhaps it was time to leave. "It's almost eleven. I should go. Later, this evening I'll come back when your folks are home. Can I use your telephone to call a cab—"

"What time?" He glanced at the clock and grabbed Sara's travel bag. "Get your purse. I have an idea. Let's go for a Sunday drive. Kill a little time and…talk. I think better behind the wheel. Whaddaya say?"

Sara gazed at him, tilting her head. "Sure, but why the rush?"

"No rush. Just need to clear my head." He yanked open the front door. "Daylight's burning."

Sara retrieved her purse. Larry hustled her out. What had gotten into him?

He slammed the front door, and tossed her bag in the backseat of the car before opening her door. "The road beckons."

Sara got in. Larry slammed her door shut and jumped in his seat. Gunning the engine, he backed out of the driveway, raced up the Boulevard, and turned east to Broadway. Larry flashed a grin at Sara. "Let's

take a drive north. Might see something interesting."
With one hand on the steering wheel and the other
draped over the front seat, he stepped on the gas as they
took the highway out of town.

In Newton, thirty miles from Wichita, Larry
stopped for gas. Sara walked next door for some dime
burgers and nickel pop. By one o'clock, they were
bouncing along on a rutted dirt road. Sara crossed her
arms. Her stomach was cramping. The greasy food and
rough roads didn't mix well. She gazed out the side
window, watching the countryside. Anything to take
her mind off the waves of nausea.

The landscape west of the Flint Hills was flat and
open, dotted with gray farmhouses and painted barns.
The geography was a hodge-podge of plowed fields,
tall grass pastures, and a few scraggly trees along dried
creek beds.

This was Mennonite country. Farms were small
and well kept. Some of the barns looked to be in better
shape than the houses. While phone lines stretched to
some of the houses, there were no electrical lines.
Power stopped at the edge of town.

This land wasn't much different now than when the
pioneers first came here. She imagined empty plains
under a forever sky. Wildlife would include deer, fox,
coyotes, and bobcats. Even cougar. Not many trees, but
there would be wildflowers. Did the young pioneer girls
gather flowers to decorate their homes?

She couldn't have endured the pioneer life. Even
today, it was hard to imagine living without electricity.
*Give me an afternoon at Innes Department Store or
even Bigger's Mercantile.*

"Larry, we haven't seen a decent-sized town since

Newton."

"I know. Isn't it great? An open road with nothing to get in the way. Hold on. You can't do *this* in Wichita." Larry stomped on the gas.

The Roadster leaped like a startled deer; engine racing like a heart beating fast. A rooster tail of dust flew behind.

"Slow down!" She grasped the flimsy dashboard. Close objects hurtled by in a blur. Larry hit a bump, and the speeding vehicle leaped from the ground, landing with a jarring thump. Sara pushed down the lock on her door. "This is dangerous!"

Larry eased his foot off the gas pedal, his eyes blazing. "Did you feel that? It's like a rush of energy racing through my head! The only thing slowing me down is this crappy road."

Sara forced herself to steady her breath. "I'm not interested in thrill rides. I'm about to have a baby. Take some responsibility."

He scowled. "You're ruining the fun."

"It's time you acted like an adult." Sara shot him an irritated look. "What's gotten into you?"

"Nothing. I'm fine." Larry frowned. "Don't get so testy."

Sara sighed. "You said at the house you'd rather talk in the car. I'm listening."

Larry sucked in his cheeks, thinking. "You don't *have* to have this baby, right? Couldn't you decide *not* to have it?"

Sara stared at him. If only she could jump out and run. Dash away and never lay eyes on this stranger again.

"Larry." Reasoning with an obstinate child would

be easier. "I could never do that. You have no inkling what a woman goes through when she faces the prospect of ending the life of an unborn child. The physical experience is dangerous enough. Women die from abortions. Even if all goes well, it's never over. There are always lingering questions: Did I make the right decision? What if the infant had lived? Imagine that child becoming an adult."

Larry grunted. "You're making too much of it."

Sara held up a palm. "Women have an emotional connection. It's not just deciding with our head. We choose with our heart. Men make a decision—and that's that, right or wrong. No turning back. There are no consequences. Just new problems. Your head and your heart are detached."

"Thank God for that. That's what makes us stronger."

Sara huffed. "Don't be so sure. You have thin-skinned areas where you don't like me to tread, Larry Bigger. It doesn't take much to set you off like a rocket."

"Impossible. Try me."

"Are you sure you want to play this game?"

"Sure. I got you beat already. Even if you hit a nerve, I can keep a straight face."

"We'll see." Sara hesitated. This could be a dangerous contest.

"What are you waiting for?" Larry darted a look at her. The Roadster increased speed again. Without warning, he whipped the steering wheel to the left. Sara glimpsed a tilted signpost, *"Carriage Road,"* as the silver car spun around a tight corner. Wheels shrieked.

Thump!

Sara's head slammed against the side of the car. Salty blood filled her mouth from a split lip. Larry fought the wheel as the car skittered across the road. A shallow ditch raced to within inches of the wheels as Larry shouted a curse.

We're going to crash! My baby will never live!

Larry leaned forward, grabbing the wheel with both hands. The car straightened course. He turned to Sara, a smirk on his lips. "Well? I'm waiting."

Her head reeled; a bolt of fear shot through her. "Stop this car. I've had enough."

"Oh no. You started this. Let's finish it. What do you got on me? Spill it."

He didn't stop.

"Okay." She eased a sigh. There was no going back. "It's about your work." Her stinging lip made talking difficult. She found a handkerchief in her purse and dabbed at her mouth. "You know your father wants to season you. He doesn't think you're ready to supervise yet. He fears you'll never be ready. You see the things you've done, but he sees the things you need to do. Try to put yourself in his shoes, and then maybe you'll succeed."

"Is that all you got?"

Sara nodded.

"Pretty weak. Now it's my turn."

"I don't want to play this game any more."

"Game's over." He chuckled. "Now, we're showing our cards." Larry punched the gas. He glanced at her, a lopsided grin on his face. "Rides well, doesn't it?"

Sara said nothing. Her upper lip felt puffy, but the bleeding had stopped.

Larry stared ahead, keeping the car to the center of the road. "I knew you wouldn't like the abortion idea. You could still get rid of the baby, and we could have gone back to having fun. But no. Instead, you wanted to trap me into marrying you. So you got yourself pregnant—"

She gasped. "That is not true!"

"It doesn't matter. I know what you want. I figured it out."

Sara gripped her hands together to keep them from shaking. She'd gone down the rabbit hole, and the Mad Hatter was behind the wheel.

"You want my job. I saw you and the Old Man talking on the stairs yesterday. Both of you are in it together, but it's not going to work." The engine screamed as he mashed down on the gas.

"None of that is true! Believe me."

"Save it!" He gave a mirthless chuckle. "I didn't tell you the rest of the story. When I came home last night, he stood in my way and pointed a finger at me. Said I failed to meet his expectations and called me— *me!*—a disappointment. And then he talked about *you.*"

Sara covered her mouth. Her body trembled. When was this madness going to end?

"See? You know you're guilty." He snorted in triumph. "The Old Man said it was too bad you weren't working for him. You would have easily taken care of all the tasks I failed to do. Well, that will never happen. I'm ending it now."

A spike of adrenaline coursed down her spine.

Larry chuckled. "I love that look of fear. But don't flatter yourself. I'm not going to hurt you. Just the opposite. I found a place for you to stay. It's out of the way. A bit rustic. But it'll do. Someday, you'll even thank me." He glanced up. "And lookee here. It's the end of the line."

Larry braked hard. The Roadster skidded over loose dirt and gravel, sliding to the roadside near a T-shaped intersection. Dust engulfed the car, obscuring the world.

Sara peered through the dirty windshield. As the haze dissipated, details of a strange building became clear.

The structure faced an adjacent road about thirty yards to the left of the car. The construction looked like a fortress, three stories tall, built of rough-hewn limestone. On the other hand, it resembled a Victorian cathedral, but with a stark, imposing air about it. Front steps ran up to a wide porch with six windows in from. The massive edifice extended back from the road by a good two-hundred feet with an arching roof covering a lofty attic. A steeple towered in front with a small attic window placed where the bell should have been. Sitting on the ledge of the attic window was a small feminine figure.

"Look!" Sara pointed at the person, her fears at bay for the moment. "In the steeple! It's a girl!"

"I'll be..." Larry's eyes flashed. "I think she's about to jump."

Her jaw dropped. "Oh, dear God."

The figure did not move.

Sara stared in fascination. "What kind of place is this?"

"I'll tell you later." Larry tore his eyes away from the person. "First, let's get a few things straight. You drove me to this. It's all your fault. If you hadn't gotten pregnant; if you had agreed to an abortion; if you didn't scheme to take my job; things could've turned out better for us. Even if you weren't after my job, the Old Man would've demanded we get married, and you would've taken over the business. I can't have that. It's mine."

She held her arms out to him. "I understand your feelings. I'd never do that. Larry, this is insane!" Exasperated, she lowered her arms. Her left palm landed on top of the shift lever. The metal knob fit snugly in her hand.

"Funny you should say that." His smirk turned into a scowl. "The bottom line is this: you're staying here. They'll have to take you in because you're with child. And if you don't like it here, go somewhere else. I don't care. But if you show up in Wichita, I'll hurt you. I'm a desperate man, Sara. I'm prepared to do anything to keep what belongs to me."

The gearshift knob felt loose. Probably from all the shaking the car took. Sara twisted the metal lump until it came free. It nestled in her palm like a stone. She grew up with two boys. She knew how to throw a punch.

With her left fist cupping the round handle, Sara straight-armed Larry in the face, missing his nose but slashing him across the cheek. The edge of the knob ripped skin from nose to ear. Blood spurted. Larry grunted, knocking her arm aside. The heavy chunk of metal shot across the interior of the car, cracking a window. Larry punched her twice in the side and then threw a fierce jab to the temple.

Sara yanked on the door handle, trying to get out. *Locked!* She fumbled for the latch as more blows hit her in the ribs. Larry raised a foot and kicked her as she threw open her door. She landed hard on the gravelly dirt road, eyes closed against the stabbing pain coursing through her body.

A car door creaked, and measured footsteps crunched on the gravel, circling the back of the vehicle, stopping behind her. Another door squeaked, and her carpetbag and purse landed inches from her head. More shuffling, then a shadow loomed over her.

Sara remained motionless. Finally, the passenger door closed, and the footsteps retreated to the driver's side. The door slammed, and the engine roared to life. The Roadster backed away, turned, and retreated, its engine diminishing to nothing.

An intense, visceral bubble throbbed inside her head.

Sara opened her eyes to see the strange house and the figure watching her. She struggled to her feet, but a thousand knives jabbed at her side. A moan escaped her lips as she collapsed to the ground. Lying on her back brought the stabbing knives down to a hundred.

How could she communicate with this girl? *Could you bring me a glass of water?* Sara tried to shout, but her words were a faint cry.

Gritting her teeth against the pain, Sara pulled the purse beneath her head. She'll try for the house later. *Rest now.*

The last thing she saw was the girl climbing back into the window.

Part II: Deliverance

"Affluence, unless stimulated by a keen sense of imagination, forms but the vaguest notion of the practical strain of poverty."
~Edith Wharton, The House of Mirth, 1905

"As we come marching, marching,
we battle too for men,
For they are women's children,
and we mother them again.
Our lives shall not be sweated
from birth until life closes;
Hearts starve as well as bodies;
give us bread, but give us roses!
~*~
As we come marching,
marching, unnumbered women dead
Go crying through our singing
their ancient cry for bread.
Small art and love and beauty
their drudging spirits knew.
Yes, it is bread we fight for—
but we fight for roses, too!
~*~

As we come marching, marching,
we bring the greater days.
The rising of the women
means the rising of the race.
No more the drudge and idler—
ten that toil where one reposes,
But a sharing of life's glories:
Bread and roses! Bread and roses!"
~Bread and Roses protest poem originated from
the Lawrence, Maryland, Textile Strike of 1912

Chapter Seven

Sunday, April 7, 1935

Beatrice Mullens sat outside the attic window of the tenant house, listening to the voice in her head. It was Sally. *Come on Bea. You can do this. Put your arms down by your side and push off. Then we can be together. You do want us to be together, right? Then, push off when I say.*

Sally said it would be daring. Bea had to agree. Climbing to the attic was exciting. No one knew she was here. The view was enormous. What a thrill it was to lift the heavy attic window, throw back the shutters, and climb onto the outside ledge. There was danger here. She could fall. That was the point. Eternity was seconds away.

Except now, she was cold. The thrill was gone, and she just wanted to finish it. Bea placed her hands on the wind-battered wood. Thin muscles tensed, ready to push off.

Wait! Not yet! You're spoiling it! I give the word. I decide. You do what I say. Or I will leave you. Just like that! Now look around. Pick the last thing you want to see.

Bea hung her head, waiting for the tirade to end. The chill of a stiff wind gave her goose bumps, tousled her short blonde hair, and fluttered her thin flour sack dress. Bare feet dangled in space over the porch roof below. Could she push hard enough to clear it?

In front of the porch was a semi-circle drive that led to Miller Road. Bea traced the two-lane eastward. A grove of willows covered one side of a small cemetery a quarter mile away. The town of Joshua lay eight miles farther. She lived there after leaving the orphanage, learning to be a proper adult. It was a short stay. Bea shuddered. No one knew the truth of her time there. Only her and the Bergkamps. And Sally.

White-faced cattle grazed on the east side of a gravel road going south, and still-dormant buffalo grass lay on the west. Both cattle and grass disappeared in the haze of the southern horizon.

Only, it wasn't haze. Dust billowed, racing up the road along with the growing whine of a car engine pushed wide open. Long and silver with a sloping canopy, the car screamed like a wounded animal, speeding forward. Brakes squealed, and the vehicle slid to a halt near Miller Road. The silver car sat quiet and unmoving as the dust settled.

Bea watched mesmerized. Then—a piercing scream!

There was an impression of movement on the passenger side; the door opened and someone fell to the road. The driver, a well-dressed man, jumped out, one hand to his cheek, and stalked around the car. He yanked open the back passenger door and tossed a bag to the road. For several seconds, he stared down with one fist raised—about to pummel the unseen person on the ground.

Beatrice held her breath, but the blows never came. The man lowered his fist and came back around to the driver's side. The tall figure in the white hat turned his attention to the building. She gasped. The man wasn't interested in the house. He was studying her. Waiting.

What was he waiting for? And why was he smiling?

Then the man did the oddest thing. He bowed, making a grand gesture of tipping his hat and sweeping his arm as if greeting her at a ball. Holding the bow for a long moment, he swept his arm back up, donning his hat. The curious figure waved a final salute, jumped in his car, whipped the vehicle around, and roared off.

Silence returned to the flat plain. Bea turned her attention to the woman by the road. She stirred, pushing herself up with one stiff arm and raising her head. For one brief moment, both women locked eyes before the battered form crumpled.

Sally, what do I do?

No answer.

Sally was gone.

Bea shifted her position on the ledge. With clumsy effort, she climbed back in the window. She pulled the attic shutters closed, but couldn't get them to latch. The hook would not reach the eyebolt. She did manage to shut the window. Now, she must leave the attic unobserved.

She peeked out of the hatch and surveyed the infirmary hallway. No one about. She lowered herself from the ceiling onto a massive linen closet, replaced the attic board, and clamored to the floor.

She opened the closet drawer and pulled out her apron, tying it on. She retrieved her slate and chalk, putting them in her apron pocket. Now, she was ready to find the matron. Miss Gloria would know what to do.

Bea crept down the long stairway that ended in a landing by the front door. Miss Gloria sat on a couch in the big common room with Patrick Arnesdorff, a pleasant boy two years younger than her. The matron was trying to teach him how to thread a needle, but it was clear Patrick wanted to be somewhere else.

The matron was a small woman, her hair always wrapped in a tight bun. Tiny spectacles magnified piercing eyes gave her the appearance of an alert barn owl. She once called Patrick feeble-minded to a well-dressed man from the county, but that wasn't true. Sure, he was slow and didn't see well, but Patrick knew how to avoid a chore if he didn't want to do it.

As she padded across the front living space, a pine board creaked underfoot. Patrick glanced her way as she pulled slate and chalk from her apron. She printed her message in careful block letters:

LADY ON OLD CARRIAGE ROAD—HURT

"Um...Miss Gloria? Bea has something."

The matron peered at Bea's message, then jumped to her feet. Sally found it amusing that the fifty-six year-old matron stood only to Bea's chin.

"Patrick, go to the road with the cattle," she said with urgency. "Look for a young lady—perhaps laying on the road. Then get back here and tell me what you saw." She turned to Beatrice. Her gaze bore into her; it was a look even Sally found disconcerting. "Go to the dinner bell. Ring three times. Stop. Take a breath. Then ring three more times. Keep ringing until Mr. Eisner comes. Show him what you wrote. I'm getting my medical bag."

Beatrice stood transfixed, staring wide-eyed at the older woman. Patrick didn't move either.

"Get moving!"

Bea dashed through the dining room, kitchen, and out the back door. The railed porch was strewn with rockers and stools. A stout iron bell set mounted on a metal frame by the steps. With both hands, she grasped the handle and rocked the bell.

Bong. Bong. Bong. The piercing ring hurt her ears.

With difficulty she held the bell in place after several swings then rocked the frame again.

She so wanted to meet this stranger. Why didn't Miss Gloria choose her to check on the lady's condition? After all, she saw the injured woman first. And what was keeping Mr. Eisner? What if he was in the barn and couldn't hear the bell? Not wishing to stop again, Beatrice pushed the handle harder, and the bell changed with each swing.

A broad-shoulder man in drooping slouch had, white shirt, and washed-out overalls emerged from the barn about forty yards away. He loped to the back porch, waving his arms and yelling. It was hard to tell what he said with the bell ringing. Miss Gloria said to show him the message—that was what she would do.

He came up the steps, reeking of straw and manure and grabbed the frame. "All right. You got my attention. Did the missus send you out here?" He looked to the house. She tapped the slate with the chalk. Anything to get him to read her note.

"A woman's hurt on Old Carriage Road. Who is she?"

Bea shrugged.

"Does Gloria know?"

The blonde resident shook her head.

"Can't you tell me anything?

She bowed her head, trembling.

"Forget it. I remember now. You can't talk. Well...the missus says I snore like a bear. So we all got something."

She tucked her slate in her apron and pointed inside. The matron was waiting.

He smiled. "Come on," he said. "Gloria has probably issued orders to half the residents. Let's see what we have to do."

Bea followed the overseer into the dining room. If she stayed out of the way, she could learn more of the stranger.

"What's this about an injured woman?" he called from the kitchen.

"I'm in the dining room."

Miss Eisner sat at a table peering inside a leather bag. She closed it with a snap. "A young woman is lying practically on our doorstep. You and I are bringing her in. We need the litter in the infirmary."

"I'll get it. Anything else?"

"No. I'm going out to find this girl. Once we load her onto the litter, we'll bring her back to the house."

Excitement jolted Bea—she wiped the slate with her sleeve and wrote:

CAN I GO??

The matron frowned. "It's up to you. Just stay

out of the way." With that, she grabbed her bag, and bustled out of the house. Bea followed behind.

A cold wind blew as she hurried to catch up with the matron. The huddled woman hadn't moved. Mrs. Eisner knelt down, cradling the lady's head in her arms. She looked to be in her early twenties with beautiful glowing skin, thick brown hair, and clothes fit for a princess. Those well-kept curls reminded Bea of the dusty movie star magazines in the front room. She knelt beside the matron and wrote on her slate:

HOW IS SHE?

"She's taken a beating, but her pulse is good." Mrs. Eisner pressed on the stricken woman's side. A loud groan escaped her cracked lips. "Bruised or broken ribs. We'll have to get Doctor Zwiefel out here to check her." The matron bent to whisper in the girl's ear. "We'll get you inside."

The girl blinked and her lips moved, but no words came.

Mrs. Eisner placed her ear to the woman's bloodied mouth. "Say it again, honey."

Bea leaned forward.

The hurt woman's single word was a sigh. "Baby."

Mr. Eisner arrived a minute later with the stretcher. They loaded the stranger and carried her to the house. Bea rushed ahead to open the front door.

"Put her in the empty room, second door right." The matron pointed down the long hallway that separated the main rooms from the resident bedrooms. They carried her in and transferred her to an iron bed.

Mr. Eisner locked the metal bedrail in place and rolled the bed closer to the window. He stepped back, looking at his wife. "I'd better fetch the doctor. Need anything while I'm in town?"

"No, but hurry. The woman's with child."

Patrick brought towels, and the matron sent him for hot water. Bea stood near the foot of the bed. This was exciting! Would Mrs. Eisner let her stay until the stranger awakened? Who was she and where did she come from? With her fine clothes, she must be from a big city. A place like Wichita or Kansas City or New York. And she must be rich with her own house servants and ladies in-waiting.

Mrs. Eisner closed the door and glanced at Bea. "Still here? Well, sit down and don't be a nuisance. You might come in handy." She dug in her first-aid bag, retrieved a pair of scissors, and then slashed the dress from hem to neckline. While it was disturbing to see such a fine dress ruined, it was fascinating to see the matron performing as nurse.

Someone knocked. The matron pulled a sheet over the still form and received a pan of steaming water from Patrick. "Now, bring me a dipper of water and some women's bedclothes. They're in the big bureau upstairs." As the door closed, her friend's footsteps thumped away. As she closed the door again, she stared at Beatrice. "You take the water when Patrick returns. I don't want to be disturbed for the next few minutes."

Bea nodded. She moved aside the manacles attached to the bed. One was laying in front of the sleeping girl's nose. She wouldn't need them. Such a beautiful princess shouldn't need restraints. Would she?

With towels, water, and some soap from a nightstand, the matron set about cleaning the stricken woman. "Dear, this is hot water. It's going to sting. Not waiting for a reply, she applied the steaming towel to a swollen lip.

"*Oww!* Stop!" The girl came to life with a start, batting away the hot towel. "That hurt!"

"Ahh, you're awake. That's good. How's your head?"

The woman felt her left temple. "I've got a splitting headache." She tried sitting up, but fell back, eyes squeezed shut. "My side is on fire," she said through gritted teeth. "I've never hurt this bad in my life."

"I've seen worse. It looks like you've been kicked by a mule. We'll fix you up. What is your name?"

"Sara."

"How old are you?"

"Twenty-three."

"Good." Miss Gloria nodded, satisfied. "Your memory's intact. How in the world did this happen?"

"My boyfriend. We had a fight."

Bea wanted to tell what she saw, but then Mrs. Eisner might guess about her trip to the attic. Best to remain quiet.

"I'll want to hear more about that later. What I'm more concerned with now is the baby. How far along are you?"

Sara widened her eyes for a moment, and then she nodded. "I remember now. I told you outside. The doctor said I was at least seven weeks along."

There was a knock at the door, and Bea jumped to her feet to answer. She retrieved the dipper and night clothing from Patrick. When she returned, Mrs. Eisner found aspirin, shook out three tablets, and gave them to the pretty stranger. Bea handed her the tin cup.

"Sara, I'd like you to meet Beatrice. She saw you on the road. Bea, this is Sara."

Bea wrote in her best script:

SARA IS A PRETTY NAME.

"Uh…thank you." Sara arched her brows to the matron.

"Bea can't talk, but she has a good ear and doesn't miss much."

Miss Gloria always said kind things about her. It was a good thing she didn't know about Sally. She wouldn't say those good things if she knew about her hidden friend.

"Since you're expecting, it would be wise to have you checked by a doctor." The matron wiped more dirt from Sara's face and neck. "A beating is not good for mother or child. We have a physician, Dr. Barry Zwiefel, who comes out once a month on the county's dime. He does checkups and the occasional emergency. I think we can call this an emergency."

"It hurts to move. I can't even take a full breath. Can I rest for a while before leaving?"

Bea sucked in a breath. It would be grand if she could stay.

"Dr. Zwiefel makes house calls. My husband left a few minutes ago to fetch him."

Sara nodded. "Thank you. Who are you? Are you a nurse?"

"I'm Gloria Eisner. People here call me Miss Gloria or Mrs. Eisner. I do a bit of nursing when the need arises."

"Is this some kind of hospital?"

Bea bit her lip. *Not the kind you're thinking of Miss Sara.*

"No hospital. I manage the house and supervise the residents. My husband oversees the work farm."

"Residents…" As Miss Gloria re-filled her kit, Sara surveyed the room, looking from the ceiling and walls to the iron bed. She gasped, staring at the manacles. The injured woman gripped the bedrails on either side of her, pulling herself up and hooking one leg over the bedrails. She gulped for air, her arms shaking. A low moan came from deep within her throat. Her shallow breathes increased and her cheeks flushed an alarming tint of red.

Something stirred in the sub-cellar of Bea's mind. No! Stay away! Not now! She jumped to her feet, tapping her scrawled letters with the chalk.

THE BED IS SCARING HER!

Miss Gloria dropped her bag and rushed to the incapacitated woman. "Get your hands back!" She slapped at Sara's wrist. Sara jerked back, still wheezing. Miss Gloria whacked the metalwork with her palm. The top half of the heavy iron rail fell with a loud clang, and the matron clamped a palm over Sara's mouth. "Breathe through your nose. You're taking in too much air. Relax. The cuffs and straps are not for you. You're not a prisoner. You can leave anytime. Take slow, deep breaths. Not so fast. You're not a prisoner. That's it. Relax. Breathe steady. You're free to go anytime. That's much better." Gloria took her hand away. Sara lay on her back, eyes closed. "How do you feel now?" She dabbed at the woman's forehead with the now cool towel.

"Exhausted," Sara said just above a whisper. "I'm so tired."

"We'll be leaving in a minute. I'll return later with

the doctor."

"Wait a minute!" Sara's hand darted out, grasping Miss Gloria's wrist. "There's something I have to know."

"What is it, dear?"

"What is this place?"

Miss Gloria raised an eyebrow. "You mean you don't... We can discuss this after you've rested."

"No. I have to know *now*. Nothing makes any sense."

"Very well. Keep an open mind. In spite of our name, we're rather proud of what we have here. We keep a clean house. No pests—well, few anyway. And we are a safe place."

"Where am I?"

"You're at the Joshua County Poor Farm."

She'll learn. Beatrice's chalk squeaked as she wrote, then turned her slate to Sara.

AND ASYLUM

Chapter Eight

Sara awoke in a darkened room. Through the window, the silhouette of cedar trees pointed to a sky of brightening stars as dusk gave way to nightfall. Where were the lights from neighboring houses? Why was it so quiet? Then she remembered; she was in the country, in a strange house. Realization brought understanding, but not relief.

Faint lights flickered as footsteps approached. The door creaked open, and two shadowy figures loomed over her, each holding hurricane lanterns. Sara shielded her face, stifling a growing terror. "Who's there?"

The smaller shadow set a lamp on the bedside stand, revealing the diminutive features of Mrs. Eisner. "Sara, I brought Dr. Zwiefel."

The doctor spoke in a sonorous voice, "Hello, young lady. I hear you got some pain." He wore small silver glasses that sparkled with reflected light from the lanterns. The mirror on his forehead sent a point of light dancing about the room whenever he moved his head.

Sara exhaled with relief, unbuttoned the front of her nightdress, and moved it aside. "It's a stinging pain. Along here." She traced the curve of her lower ribs.

The doctor probed the area, gauging her reaction. She gasped when his jabs struck a tender spot. A prickling sting high on her left side became a jagged-toothed blade sawing across her lower ribs the lower his

87

fingers probed. Sara gripped the side of the bed, yearning for the torment to end.

Finally, Doctor Zwiefel released her and drew from his black bag a spool of soft cloth. "I'm going to bind your ribs for now, loose enough for normal breathing, but tight enough to keep you from taking a full breath. Let's bring you up."

Mrs. Eisner cranked the long rod running beneath the metal frame. Sara's back rose to a sitting position as the top half of the mattress lifted. The doctor wound the strip around her mid-section several times and then clipped it in place.

"If it loosens, you can re-wrap it to your liking. Or leave it off. The cloth is to help with the pain. Your ribs will have to heal on their own."

"Thank you, doctor." Sara squinted against the harsh light.

He stepped back. "You have two bruised, possibly cracked ribs, but I don't think anything is broken. In two to four weeks you'll be good as new."

"Is the baby okay?" Sara asked.

The doctor took out his stethoscope, adjusted the earpieces and held the bell against her chest. "Your baby is at an early stage, so it's hard to say. There doesn't seem to be any harm at this point. Has anyone gone over your pregnancy with you?"

"No, I just found out yesterday." Her visit with Dr. Payton seemed like a long time ago.

Dr. Zwiefel grunted. "Let me ask a few questions then. How are you feeling? Nausea? Morning sickness? Mood swings?"

She sighed. "All of it. Especially the mood swings."

"Your doctor probably gave you a guess on the due date, but I'm going to ask you a direct question. Be honest. Do you know what causes a woman to have a baby?"

Sara gasped. "Of course, I do! I'm not a child!"

The physician chuckled. "You'd be surprised how many grown women don't know the answer to that question."

Sara shook her head, shocked by the candor of this country doctor. "I see what you're implying. I've been pregnant since February fourteenth. No other possible date."

"So you should deliver your baby around mid-November."

"That was my doctor's guess. What other signs can I expect in the coming days?"

"Let's see." Dr. Zwiefel tapped his temple. "You might get a heightened sense of smell. At times, you may feel overwhelmingly tired, and you may get cravings for unusual foods. Some foods you normally like may taste awful. This is happening because your body is preparing for the baby."

"Is there anything I should do?"

"Nothing special. Anything beneficial for the mother is beneficial for the child. The good news is you haven't miscarried."

Sara's eyes widened. "Is there a chance of that?"

"Unfortunately, yes." Dr. Zwiefel checked her pulse. "Especially during the first three months. However, with time, the risk will lessen. Think positive, young lady. You're about to have a healthy baby. Eat well, get lots of rest, and don't get into any more fights. If you're still here next month, I'll see you again."

Sara glanced at Mrs. Eisner. "I need to ask you about staying."

She smiled. "We're not going to kick you out, child. There are certain requirements for staying, but we can talk about that later."

The doctor put his instruments away. "When I return, your child may be around twelve weeks old with fingernails, a chin, and a nose."

"Mrs. Eisner?" Sara asked, "Can I have lantern? In case I need to get up?" She didn't want to be without a light.

Gloria nodded. "Keep this one." She produced some stick matches from her apron pocket and laid them on the stand. "It's about eight o'clock now. Lights out is nine-fifteen. I'll return then with some clothing for tomorrow. Right now, I need to check the other residents. Doctor, if you're ready, we'll find James and get you back home."

"Before I go," the doctor said. "I'd like to check on the infirmary. Especially the TB and cancer patients."

"Certainly. Sara, I'll be back to check on you later." She cranked the bed flat and left with the physician.

She was alone in a strange house, miles from home. The city held music, lights, and color. Here was silence and shadows. She'd visited the country as a child, spending weekends with her relatives. That was an adventure. To live without power would be an adjustment.

Still, it felt safe here. These people rescued her, given her a bed, a place to stay, and even brought medical help. For all this, Sara was grateful. She could rest and get her strength back. In a few days, she could go…where? She had no job, no home, and no future. All gone. What was she going to do? What *could* she do? She would have to come up with a plan. Sara squeezed her eyes shut, sighing. The task seemed impossible.

She extinguished the flame and relaxed. Laying on her hurt side made it easier to breathe. Closing her eyes, she drifted off to sleep.

Sara woke with a start. Someone was rapping on the door.

"Come in."

Mrs. Eisner entered, pushing a cart. The wooden trolley held a bright lantern, ceramic pitcher, metal basin, and a tightly wrapped bundle of clothes. She set the items on top of the nightstand. "I want to go over how we do things here. This will take but a few minutes. Would you like your bed raised?"

Sara nodded. "Are these house rules?"

"In part." She turned the long crank and brought Sara to a sitting position. "Tomorrow, I can give you a tour of the house."

"I'd like that. I'm sure this place isn't like the terrible stories I heard growing up."

The matron gave her a pensive look. "Pay no attention to what you hear on most matters. Telling a simple lie is far easier than explaining a complicated truth."

Sara swallowed. "I understand."

"Many people have an irrational fear of poorhouses, poor farms, almshouses—whatever you wish to call us. Maybe they see an unclean purgatory or a prison for paupers. That's not how it is here. I have three simple rules. Keep your room clean. Do your assigned chores. And get along with the other residents."

"Yes, ma'am."

She waved a hand. "Oh, please, don't call me ma'am. My official title is matron, but most of the residents call me Miss Gloria or Mrs. Eisner."

"Can I call you Gloria?"

A ghost of a smile crossed the matron's face. "You're a bold one." She shook her head. "To keep the harmony, I think Mrs. Eisner will do." She sat in the rocker. "Our purpose, if you will, is to provide shelter and work for the poor and the indigent. But it's also the aged, the feeble-minded, and the insane. We're a community of sorts, but not one normally seen by polite society."

Sara wrinkled her brow. "It's not just the poor?"

"Half the residents here are elderly and bed-ridden. Many of the others can't do farm labor for different reasons. Times have changed. Very few residents work outdoors anymore."

"Who takes care of the farm?"

"The county bought James a tractor two years ago. A couple of the residents help in the barn and garden."

"I see. How many people live here?"

"Eighteen. Four men, four women, and ten in the infirmary. You'll meet the active residents tomorrow."

"I'd like to stay, at least until I can get around better."

"Stay as long as you wish. We often get people who've had a bad turn. They stay for a few days and then move on. Most, though, have nowhere to go. Don't be surprised by the attention you'll receive tomorrow. New residents get a lot of scrutiny."

Sara shuddered, "I'm not sure I want that kind of attention."

Mrs. Eisner laughed. "I'm sure you'll do fine." She retrieved the bundle on the nightstand. "I've brought you some clothes for tomorrow."

Sara glanced at the grayish parcel. "Thank you, but I have my own clothes."

The matron's cordiality faded. "I'm afraid you misunderstand. There's no choice. If you wish to stay, you *will* wear these clothes. We'll put away your possessions for safe keeping while you're here. No one is to stand out by wearing store-bought clothes. Beatrice, the girl you met earlier, made these dresses. She's picked up some sewing skills along the way and is quite a good seamstress." She unrolled the parcel and held up a garment. It was a feed sack dress with a daisy print. *"Classen's Feed and Grain"* was stenciled on back.

Sara pursed her lips. "Rather plain, isn't it?"

"It's a rule of the house. One other thing, if you decide to stay, I'll need some information. If you have family or relatives nearby, you cannot live here. The county commissioners believe family must provide the first line of support. Kin look after kin. Most don't have any kindred at all.

"No family. That seems a little harsh." *How can I stay here if Mrs. Eisner learns of my parents?*

"Only the truly destitute can remain here."

"I understand." *No one must know about my family.*

She set the clothing aside. "Morning will come early. The wake-up bell is five a.m."

Sara groaned.

"You'll get used to it. We don't tolerate laziness.

93

Breakfast bell is at five-thirty. If you're not in the dining room by the time breakfast is served, you'll have to wait until dinner to eat. At night, everyone is expected to be in their room by nine p.m." Mrs. Eisner stood and carried the lantern to a corner of the room. There set a wooden chair with raised arms, and an oval hole cut in the seat. On the floor nearly was a tattered catalog. "This is your potty chair."

"You're joking!" She gulped. The house had no plumbing.

"It's the white owl here or the privy out back. I expect you to scrub it out every day. Cleaning time is after breakfast." She stepped to the nightstand, opened the small door, and retrieved a bottle of clear liquid. "Feel free to use as much bleach as you want. And yes, I do check."

Mrs. Eisner reclaimed her seat in the rocker. "I know what you're thinking. The rules are unforgiving, and the accommodations are minimal. There is no electricity or running water. A poor farm is not a hotel. The residents here have little. Only the truly needy would want to stay here. It's only for the deserving poor. So you have a decision to make. Ask yourself, 'Is my situation hopeless? Is there somewhere I can go?' If there is, then make your plans to go there. If you stay, you'll have to give up your possessions and a certain amount of freedom. So think about alternatives. You seem resourceful. Consider what is best for you."

"I will. And thank you for the clothes."

"Thank Beatrice. She'll love the praise."

"I'll be sure to thank her."

"Do that. After the morning chores, I can give you a tour of the house. Say around nine o'clock?"

"Nine o'clock. I'll be ready."

"It will be quick. Commissioner Krause will be here for his weekly visit around ten."

"What does he do?"

"He oversees all relief programs in the county, making sure they are carried out. Not just us, but medical services, food relief, and direct payments."

"It sounds like a lot of responsibility."

"It's not a popular position to hold either. The newest elected commissioner gets the job by default. Most of the time an official will bumble their way through the job, hoping to pass it on when they become a senior official. But I have to say, Commissioner Krause has done commendable work for such a young man."

"A person who takes his job seriously? I'd like to meet him."

Gloria's brows narrowed. "I don't think that would be proper. Residents do not communicate with Commissioners."

Sara bowed to hide her eyes. "Yes, Mrs. Eisner. Thank you for helping me."

The matron huffed. "Let's see how you feel in twenty-four hours."

Chapter Nine

Throughout Sunday, Jason McGurk had been nursing an idea. At first, it seemed preposterous, but it was clear that family would see the task through to the end. No distractions. No setbacks would stop him. And he would pursue the trail wherever it may go.

But he couldn't do it alone.

That night, He dashed in the bedroom he shared with his younger brother Michael. Music from *Country Hoedown* played on the radio downstairs.

Michael lay sprawled on his bed reading a copy of *Black Mask*, a pulp magazine full of gun-blazing gangsters and murder. Jason scrutinized the cover. A square-chinned man in fedora and trench coat held a drawn pistol peeking around a corner to a dark man shoving a blonde into a black sedan. What does he see in this trash?

Michael glanced up, flipping the monthly over to keep his place. "What's with the serious look?"

Jason turned the magazine around. *Three Complete Detective Novels in This Issue!* "How would you like to try your hand at being a real-life private-eye?"

Michael wrinkled his nose. "How's that?"

Jason pointed at the cover. "You and me. Tracking down a missing person."

"Who are we looking for?" Michael looked blank, and then his jaw dropped. "You're talking about Sara!"

"Bingo." He nodded, unsmiling. "She should have called home by now."

Michael's eyes dazzled. "Count me in!"

"Shh. Not so loud. Pop doesn't need to know." He hooked a thumb downstairs.

"Why don't we call the police? That's what they're paid to do." Michael flipped the magazine back around.

"They'll say she ran off."

"What makes you think something happened to her?"

Jason crossed his arms. "Because Sara told me she'd call home when I took her downtown last night. Something's wrong. I know it. And don't be trying to weasel out of this. You said you were in." Jason snatched the magazine. "Give—or you're not getting it back."

"Okay! You sold me! Don't lose my spot. I was just thinking out loud." He grabbed for the magazine, but Jason yanked it out of reach. "I said I'd help, now give it back."

Jason tossed the pulp to Michael, pages flying.

"Thanks for nothing," Michael mumbled as he looked for his place. "You've been thinking about this longer than I have. Where do we start?"

No kidding. Like all afternoon. Jason pulled up a chair. "I thought we could go to her office tomorrow and talk to the help. We can find out if she went anywhere else that day. There's a diner nearby with a phone. She may have met somebody there.

Michael found his page and bent the corner. "A friend maybe?"

"Can't say. It's all guesswork. We can start finding answers tomorrow."

"Can't wait." His brother rubbed his hands together. "The game is afoot."

Jason tilted his head. "What game?"

Michael smiled. "Never mind."

Chapter Ten

Monday, April 8, 1935

Sara awoke to the shrill din of a bell clanging outside her door. She covered her ears until it stopped. After a few moments, the bell rang again a short distance away. She eased out of bed, moving carefully to avoid the worst twinges of pain in her side. The room was dark, with starlight shining through the eastern window. No sign of dawn. Sara found the lantern and matches. After striking a light, she removed the thin, frosted chimney, lit the wick, set the glass in place, and adjusted the flame.

The travel bag and purse lay next to the bed. It was tempting to wear one of her own dresses. Best not. No reason to create a ruckus. She unfolded the sackcloth dress, examining it at arm's length. The material was coarse and stitched in odd places. She sucked in a breath between gritted teeth. Okay then. She shrugged off the nightclothes and slipped on the sack. The material hung to her knees. If only it was longer. She'd look presentable if she had a scarf to cinch at the waist.

The thought of meeting strangers meant she needed a new name. Sara…what?

She sat on the edge of the bed, rubbing her temple. The name had to be easy to remember, similar to her real one. Sara…McCain, McDonald, McPherson,

McGuire? *McGuire!* That's it!

Now, a new past for Sara McGuire.

The story should be adequate, but not too detailed.

The five-thirty bell rang.

Time for breakfast. Using a worn cake of soap, she washed her face and hands in the basin and dried with a coarse towel. Was she ready to meet the oddities who lived here? Sara gave a mental shrug, put out the lantern, and stepped into the narrow hall.

A kerosene wall lamp flickered outside the door. The wallpaper looked like autumn leaves in faded greens, browns, and reds. A pale ceiling arched overhead. It was like being alone in a rundown gothic manor haunted by murmuring ghosts.

She wasn't alone.

Ahead, voices chattered and chairs scraped on a wooden floor. The scent of greasy food and wood smoke hung in the air. This forest path led to a gathering. With her heart in her throat, Sara crept forward.

A doorway opened to the left, revealing a spacious dining room. Two wooden tables spanned the center of the room with white cupboards along the east wall, and a row of tall, narrow windows to the west. The south wall was a blazing fireplace that separated the dining room from the one beyond. Bright and whitewashed walls made the space brilliant and inviting. A few people milled about, but most were seated.

The blonde waif, Beatrice, sat at the end of one of the tables. A weather-beaten man with gray whiskers and slouch hat poured her coffee.

While Sara picked her way between chairs to join Beatrice, the hairs on the back of her neck tingled. To the left, a stern-looking wheelchair-bound woman scowled at her, a deep frown that made her face droop like a bulldog's.

Sara reached the end of the table. "Good morning, Beatrice." She waved to the thin girl. Bea's blonde hair fell straight, just past her ears, and she had serious dark blue eyes. "Care if I sit with you?"

Beatrice shrugged, pointing to an empty chair next to her.

"Coffee?" The battered-looking man held a dented metal pot. "Still hot."

"I'd love some." She slid into a rickety Bentwood chair. "What's for breakfast?"

"S.O.S. Same Old Stuff. Hobos call it stuff on a shingle. Or worse. I wouldn't want to offend, and the matron has ears like a bat. She was just here, asking about a person named Sara. Would that be you?"

"That would be me." She liked this man's easy manner.

"She wishes to welcome you to the charming rogues of our humble home. I'm Don Holland. Friends call me Dutch." He stuck out a hand.

"Nice to meet you." She flipped a wave, refusing to touch hands with strange people before eating.

Dutch tipped a metal cup to his lips. "So what do you think of the house?"

Sara scanned her surroundings. "It's rustic, but clean."

Dutch chuckled. "It's not the Muehlebach Hotel, but the matron runs a tight ship. The food is plain. That old bum, Wheatley's been serving S.O.S. since I came here three years ago."

Sara drank some coffee. It cooled fast in the metal

cup. "You've been here three years?"

Dutch leaned back in his chair. "Just the winters. I leave in the spring and tramp 'til November, working odd jobs and sending the money to my wife."

"What work do you do?" Dutch was intriguing. She had never met a tramp before. At Union Station in Wichita, she kept her distance from panhandlers. And here she was, talking to one.

"The kind that pays. Helping Mr. Eisner is fine, but it doesn't pay cash money. What few jobs there are in the spring and summer disappear when winter comes. Too cold to tramp then. So I come back here to winter. The matron doesn't approve of me staying. 'You're not deserving enough,' she says. But she hasn't turned me out yet."

Sara tilted her head. "Mrs. Eisner mentioned that to me—the deserving poor. But it seems odd. What makes one person deserving and not another? Seems to me, no one deserves to be poor."

"Well now…" Dutch took off his hat and scratched the top of his head. "You've touched a question that's vexed the minds of charity workers for the last hundred years." He leaned forward. "The deserving or undeserving part has nothing to do with being poor but has everything to do with judgment. Who deserves relief? Who doesn't? And how do you keep the undeserving from getting the goods? These are hard questions with elusive answers. Religious charities use faith as a yardstick. These days, social workers for the county think they have the answers as if wisdom comes with a job title."

"So why would Mrs. Eisner think you don't deserve to stay here?" Sara put down her empty cup.

Dutch fetched a new pot and re-filled their tins. "The missus and I get along well enough, but she sees tramps as ungrateful and uppity. There's some truth to that. If we don't like the pay or the boss, we walk. Traveling gives us independence. We fend for ourselves and don't act humble or needy. That's what makes us undeserving. When the matron talks about the deserving, she means the docile."

"But with the way you move about, aren't you taking advantage?"

Dutch lost his smile. "Tramping isn't romantic. A lot of us die on the road. We get sick, fall under trains, and get rolled for money we don't have. Sometimes we die because it's too much trouble to keep living." Dutch stared at his cup. "A tramp is no freeloader. I work for my keep."

"It sounds like a bleak life."

"Often, late at night, I think about my wife. I used to teach history and Latin at a high school in St. Louis. When the Depression hit, the powers that be cut back on courses. I got the ax. My wife and I soon lost the house, and she moved in with her parents while I searched for work. I've been tramping three years now. Some have taken to the life. But I'd gladly trade it for a paying job."

"Why don't you spend the winters with your wife?"

Dutch closed his eyes, sighing. "I ask myself that same question sometimes. I know it wasn't my doing, but losing my job still makes me feel ashamed. I failed as a provider. My wife might understand, but her parents don't. To redeem myself, I must find steady work."

A rattling cart popped out of the pantry entry, pushed by a stumpy youth with unkempt brown hair. His too-long pants bunched at the knees and ankles, dragging on the floor.

"Ahh, here comes Patrick. Now, some people will tell you he's slow. He might be sixteen going on eight, but he's a great kid. Just don't ask him to prove how strong he is. Mr. Arnesdorff can get a bit enthusiastic."

Patrick's wooden cart held a tray of tinware. He stopped at the end of their table. "Breakfast is coming!" He peered at Dutch while handing out forks and spoons. "Miss Gloria said it's your turn to wash dishes, Mr. Dutch. She wanted me to tell you."

Dutch grinned. "Tell the queen I shall comply. Miss Sara, this is our messenger from the kitchen, Patrick."

Patrick squinted at Sara for a long moment. Sara sucked in a breath. *The boy can hardly see.* "I know you. You were laying on the road yesterday. I found you."

"A shining knight. That's our Patrick."

The youth leaned over the table. "You're sitting in my chair."

"I'll move. That way you can have—"

Dutch jumped to his feet. "Nonsense. Patrick, Miss Sara wants you sitting across from her so you two can talk. I'll give you my seat if you do the dishes for ol' Dutch." The rumpled tramp winked.

"Oh boy!" Patrick flung the tray of utensils back and forth, twirling in a tight circle. Spoons and forks rocked shrilly from side to side, pieces threatening to fly out. He finally set the tray back on the cart. "Thank you, Mr. Dutch." He moved to the next table, passed out the tinware, then bustled back to the kitchen.

Sara gaped at Mr. Holland. "Why did you *say* that? You got him all stirred up, so you wouldn't have to work in the kitchen. I can't imagine the kinds of thoughts you may have planted in his head!"

Dutch moved to the next seat over. "Don't worry, Missy. Patrick bumbles, but means well. He's Don Quixote without the horse. You couldn't find a more loyal friend."

"Still, I don't like—"

A hand grabbed Sara by the wrist. It was Beatrice. She pointed to her slate:

WE ALL LOOK AFTER PATRICK

Dutch clapped his hands. "Bea knows. You tell her."

Beatrice rolled her eyes. This got Dutch chuckling even more.

Patrick returned, flopping in the seat across from Sara. "It's coming," Patrick stage-whispered. "Mr. Wheatley is bringing out the big pot."

A minute later, a large, full-bearded cook brought out a cart holding a steaming pot of gravy, a stack of pie tins, a large knife, and two loaves of homemade bread. As the cook shuffled back to the kitchen, Dutch cut the loaves and ladled the soupy mixture over the slices. Each person passed tins down to the end before getting their own.

Sara stared aghast at her meal. The gravy was a thin greasy mixture of flour and milk festooned with undercooked pieces of scrambled egg, peas, and bits of meat. The bread had a hard, thick crust with a pasty center. Back home, she would have pitched it.

Sara picked at the unappetizing mess. The smell of

grease and eggs turned her stomach. Across the table, Patrick wolfed down his meal, using bread to soak the fat. After the third mouthful, she had enough and reached across, nudging Patrick. "I'm not hungry. Would you like my breakfast?"

He shoved his plate to one side. "Oh boy! More food!"

"It's all yours." She pushed the plate to his side. Patrick grabbed the tin, shoveling in the food.

Beatrice tapped her shoulder.

YOU'LL GET USED TO IT

"I don't see how," she said.

Dutch pulled a dirty rag from his pocket and wiped his mouth. "You're talking about Wheatley. He's an old rummy from way back. I've traveled with him a time or two. Don't know what the matron sees in his cooking." He lifted the pot, frowning. "I'll get us some more coffee." With that he left for the kitchen.

Beatrice wrote

MAYBE YOU COULD COOK FOR US

"I helped at home." She touched sore ribs. "I'm not sure I'd be able to do the job right now."

Beatrice nodded.

WHERE ARE YOU FROM?

"I'm from…" Sara froze, remembering her story. "Denver. How about you?"

AN ORPHANAGE IN KANSAS CITY

"Oh." Sara tapped Bea's wrist. "I'm sorry for being nosy."

She shrugged.

"How did you get here?"

I TURNED 18. HAD TO LEAVE.

"You came directly here from the orphanage?"

NO. THEY BONDED ME TO A FAMILY IN JOSHUA.
Bea erased her slate, and wrote,
    BIG TROUBLE. HAD TO LEAVE.
Sara raised her brows. "What kind of trouble?"

Beatrice wrote a few letters but stashed the slate in her apron when soft footsteps approached.

Mrs. Eisner stepped to Sara's side of the table. "I'm glad you made it to breakfast." Her eyes narrowed when she spotted two plates in front of Patrick. "You know, you're not doing your baby any good by skipping meals."

Sara glanced up at the small woman. "I couldn't eat the food."

"You'll eat the meals provided, or your stay will be short. I will not allow an unborn child to starve because of a finicky mother."

Sara nodded. "I'll try harder."

The matron huffed. "See to it." She glanced at the faces around her. "I see you've met Patrick, Mr. Holland, and Beatrice. Let me introduce you to the others before they wander off."

Sara rose and followed the small woman, trying not to wince from the knives digging in her side. At the other end of the table sat two elderly men. One was a grizzled old coot with a hooked nose, no teeth, and huge ears. "This is Mr. Wunch. He'll bend your ear about building the capitol dome in Topeka if you let him." Mrs. Eisner turned to the other man, a thin fellow of medium height with wispy white hair, scratched eyeglasses, and overalls. "This is Mr. Emerson. Both these men help James in the barn sometimes. Gentlemen, this is Sara."

"Pleased to meet you," Mr. Emerson said.

Mr. Wunch gave her a toothless smile. "Well ain't you a pretty chick-a-dee!" The hawk-nosed codger flapped his elbows like a bird.

The matron's eyes flashed. "A word later, Mr. Wunch." She took Sara by the arm, and they stepped to the next table.

"This is Mrs. Robson and Miss Underwood. Both work in the infirmary." Mrs. Robson had well-kept red hair streaked with white and wore a full-length apron. Miss Underwood wore men's trousers cut off at the ankles and men's shoes as well. The handsome woman nodded. Mrs. Eisner then stirred Sara to the woman in the wheelchair.

"This is Mrs. Chapman. Mildred, this is Sara. We have a special rule for Mrs. Chapman. She may ask, but no one may push her in her wheelchair.

The stout woman glared at Mrs. Eisner. "The matron thinks I don't need my special chair." Her voice was deep, almost masculine. She thumped on the armrest. "But she's wrong. I have a rare disease that demands special treatments. And there are secret experiments happening upstairs. Doctors put me here because I know too much—"

"Enough!" Gloria clapped her hands once.

The woman stopped jabbering like a needle lifted from a phonograph.

"We're all accustomed to Mrs. Chapman," Mrs. Eisner said as she led Sara back to her seat. There are ten more residents in the infirmary upstairs. When you're able, I'll introduce you to them. One has consumption. No one, except those taking care of him, may enter his room."

"Shouldn't he be isolated?"

Mrs. Eisner smiled, but her eyes remained serious. "He is. The county hospital sent him to us. I don't win all my battles."

Sara nodded, catching a whiff of greasy food. Her stomach lurched, and then tightened into a small ball. She doubled over, her forehead breaking into a cold sweat, and a wave of nausea spread upward. She grabbed a pie pan, heaving.

A few of the remaining tenants stared at her. One edged away. Sara coughed. This was embarrassing.

The matron appeared before her, holding out a cup of water. "Wash out your mouth. It's been a while since I've seen this. You have a full-blown case of morning sickness. Welcome to motherhood."

Chapter Eleven

While waiting for breakfast, Jason watched his father sip coffee and read the paper with a stack of uneaten pancakes to the side. His neck-tie hung over the back of his chair. The search could not begin until Pop left for the radio station. Jason tapped his foot. Every minute meant time wasted.

Katherine set hot plates of pancakes before Jason and his brother. "Meetings today, dear?"

"Detail work. We're going over rules that KSKN must follow to comply with the other Alliance stations. The higher-ups call it 'standards and practices.' Since Alliance is broadcasting my program, I need to be there."

"Is there anything the boys can do to help?"

Pop shook his head. "Maybe later this week." After eating a few bites, he set down his fork. "I haven't got time to eat. The meeting doesn't start until nine, but I have some business downtown. Can you help me with this miserable thing?" He held the black-tie like it was a loathsome snake.

Katherine slid her skillet off the burner and hurried to stand behind her husband, working over his shoulders to loop the knot together. "Stand up," she said. "Let me adjust it."

Sam rose to his feet and turned around. Katherine straightened the knot, pulled it tight, and adjusted his collar.

He grabbed his hat, a battered trilby, and shrugged into his coat. "I'll be home by five." A few seconds later, he was out the door, and the Model A chittered to life.

Jason carried his plate to the sink, and his mother rinsed it, her face averted. "There's something you should know, Mom," Jason said. "Today, Michael and I are looking for Sis."

She turned off the burner, sank into Sam's chair, nibbling at his food. Her eyes were red and puffy. Was she crying? Jason sat beside her and reached for her arm. "We'll find her."

She stared at the half-eaten pancakes. Finally, she glanced at Jason. "I know she can't come home. Just make sure she's safe."

"We'll do that. Right Michael?"

Michael nodded. "Should be easy."

****

The city bus dropped the boys off a half-block from the Kramer Building. *What a wreck.* To Jason, the structure looked even more rundown during the day than it did last night. Giant empty planters full of dirt and cigarette butts sat on either side of the front steps, and tattered newspapers covered the inside glass of the front doors.

They entered the cramped lobby.

Michael tapped his shoulder. "Wouldn't it be funny if we walked in and found Sara working at her desk?"

"Fine by me." Jason hoped it was true.

Michael raced up the steps to the second floor with Jason stepping behind. "Looks like the perfect place for a private detective's office," he said.

"Sara says a bookie works here."

Bell-shaped light fixtures ran along a high-ceilinged hallway just wide enough for two people walking abreast. They crept down the corridor to Sara's office.

A voice came from within.

Jason raised a hand to knock, but Michael grabbed his arm, pointing to the open transom above the door. "Listen," he hissed. "It's Dad."

"For the third time, I'm telling you Sara will *not* be returning. She's sick and out of town. And you don't need to know where. From now on you get your orders from me. Do as I say, or I'll fire you on the spot."

It *was* Pop.

A trio of small voices humbly agreed.

"Now, I have a few rule changes. First, there'll be no more personalized letters. You'll type one basic 'thank you for writing' letter and send it along with the South Wind Ministries leaflet. Take down the names and addresses of donors, and the amount they gave. If a letter comes with no donation, you throw it out and don't respond. I'm not wasting postage on people who fail to contribute. At the close of each day, I'll gather the money and donor lists."

Jason cupped his hand to Michael's ear. "So this is why Pop left early."

"One more thing," McGurk's voice continued, "I'm looking for a home-run fan letter for my debut program. A letter that will captivate the listeners. It could be a hard-luck story or a request for help. If it involves a government program, so much the better. I'll gather that mail as well. Now I've already spent enough time with you people. I need to get to work."

Jason gasped, pointing behind them. "Quick, beat it downstairs!"

They scurried back to the vacant lobby. Jason scanned the area. *No where to hide.* He led the way down the first-floor hallway. "We need a place where Pop won't find us."

A washroom near the rear of the building provided a safe hideaway. They waited, listening for signs of their father, ready to take cover inside. Three minutes later, footsteps clomped down the stairs, a glass pane rattled, and the door closed. The familiar chattering of the Model A filled the air, fading into the distance. Jason breathed a sigh of relief.

They headed upstairs and found the Mailroom door ajar. The well-lit room contained a central worktable piled with letters, surrounded by four desks. Three women stood by the table huddled in frenzied conversation. As if on cue, all three turned, falling silent.

"We're sorry to bother you. I'm Jason, and this is my brother, Michael." He pointed to the open transom. "We heard part of what Pop said. Sara's our sister. She's missing. We're hoping you could help us find her."

The small but well-rounded woman with reddish hair stepped forward. "I'm Gladys. Sara and I've known each other since high school. She talks about you fellas a lot." She motioned to a grandmotherly woman fanning herself with a handful of letters. "This is Marilyn. And this is Sylvia." A tall black woman in a simple homemade dress nodded, keeping her eyes downward.

Michael whipped off his cap. "Glad to meet you,

ladies."

Jason took a breath. "Two days ago, Sara and Dad had a doozy of a row. He sent her packing. Sara slept here Saturday night and promised to call home the next day. But we haven't heard from her since."

The three women glanced at each other. "Sara would have told us if she was going somewhere," Gladys said. "The last thing she said to us was that we would hit the letters hard on Monday." Gladys glanced sideway at the other ladies. "Sara said she was in a family way. Is that why the pastor said she was sick? Did *he* send her away?"

Jason narrowed his eyes. *You don't know the half of it.* "A polite way of saying it. Dad practically gave her the bum's rush out the door. Sara needed a place to sleep, so I drove her here Saturday night."

Michael snapped his fingers. "Was anything missing or out of place when you ladies arrived this morning? Did Sara leave a note?"

Sylvia gave a bird-like nod. "I shows Miz Sara a letter I got that day." The black girl's hands appeared rough and calloused. Not the hands of an office worker. "The letter's gone. She's always lookin' for a letter to show her Pa."

Marilyn put down her letter-fan. "We had a talk that day, the four of us. One thing we said was Pastor McGurk didn't seem to know how his show affected the listeners. After today, I'm positive he doesn't care."

Gladys blew out a breath. "We pushed Sara pretty hard. If she talked to him about what we said, it could've sparked an argument." She lowered her head. "I'm truly sorry. None of us expected that to happen."

Jason rubbed his temple. The pieces weren't

adding up. "Sis's trouble with Pop still doesn't explain why she disappeared. Michael, you're the detective. What have we missed?"

Michael shrugged. "Let's go over again what we got. Other than your talk, was the day any different than usual?"

Gladys gestured to the big table. "We came in at the usual time and answered letters until the first mail delivery at ten. We sort letters into different stacks. The volume of letters was enormous that day because of the newspaper article about KSKN joining Alliance. We were still sorting when Sara arrived."

"What time was this?" Michael asked.

Gladys considered. "About eleven."

"Did she say where she'd been?"

Marilyn ambled to her desk, sat, and grabbed more letters to fan herself. "Sara came from the Mercantile on Emporia where she gave Larry Bigger the news. Sara often talked about the places they went to when Larry came calling."

Michael snapped his fingers. "I remember that guy. He ate dinner with us last Christmas. Fancy dresser."

"Sara told us he was the father," Gladys added. "She said their conversation didn't go well."

Jason widened his eyes. "You talk about stuff like that?"

Gladys smiled. "It passes the time."

Michael rubbed his chin. "I wonder if Sara talked to Larry on Sunday."

"I guess we'll ask the man himself." *We'd better get some answers.* Jason held his hand out to Gladys. "Thank you. All of you've been a big help."

"We hope you find her," Marilyn said. "Things

have taken a turn for the worse."

"I just hope she's okay," said Gladys.

"Miz Sara's a good person," said Sylvia. "Bring her back to us."

Jason nodded. "We'll do that."

Back on the street, Jason looked northward. "It's a good day for a walk. We can head up Broadway, cut over to Emporia, and be at the Mercantile in forty minutes. Then we'll have a talk with Mr. Larry Bigger."

Michael sniffed the air. "Maybe we should check someplace a lot closer." He pointed across the street. "I smell bacon. It's making me hungry."

Jason rolled his eyes. "You're always hungry."

Michael wasn't listening. He'd already crossed the avenue, making for the Farmland Café. Jason followed, watching for traffic.

"Come on, slowpoke." Michael held the screen door for him. The door banged shut as they entered the diner.

The joint buzzed with activity. A hand-scrawled chalkboard read:

Breakfast Served All Day

Waitresses in blue dresses and red aprons with white polka dots breezed up and down narrow aisles, bordered by booths and tables packed with locals. Behind the counter, a baldheaded cook hunched over a cast iron stove, cracking eggs into a sizzling skillet. The air sizzled with an intoxicating blend of bacon, fried onions, and coffee.

"Let's get a seat," Michael called. "We may be here a while."

Jason followed his brother, wary of the bustling servers zipping past them. Michael stopped at a booth in the back and the two sat. Jason leaned forward to keep from yelling. "What do you mean, we'll be here a while?"

"Nobody will have time to talk until the rush dies down." He picked a menu from a holder, glanced at it, and passed it to Jason.

He wasn't hungry but studied the sandwich choices. "What are you having?"

"I'm thinking about the barbecued beef sandwich, fries, pop, and a slice of peach pie."

"You pig! That's sixty cents worth of food."

"More like a dollar with tip. Especially if the waitress can give us a lead."

Incredulous, Jason tossed down the menu. "I'm getting the ten cent ham sandwich."

Michael shrugged. "It's not what you order. It's how well you tip that matters."

"Is this how your magazine P.I.'s do it?"

"Smirk if you must. P.I.'s may be broke, but they get leads by being good to their waitresses."

"What kinds of leads are we looking for?"

Michael thought for a moment. "We need to know if Sara came here yesterday. Did she leave alone or with someone? Maybe she took a cab? When did she leave? And did she tell anyone where she was going?"

"This could be a wild goose chase."

"Possibly. But I think she came here—to get away from that empty office."

Michael had a point.

Minutes later, the waitress took their order. Despite the crowd, the food arrived quickly, and Jason nibbled on his sandwich while Michael tore into his food. Fifteen minutes later, the server left a ticket. Jason drank ice water as the diner's noon rush thinned out. By one o'clock, the front counter was empty except for one lone patron nursing his coffee. The cook took a broom and swept the aisles. Finally, their waitress returned. "I'm going off duty. Anything else I can get you, boys?"

"We're leaving." Michael held up a dollar. "But we have a favor to ask. Our sister may have been here yesterday morning. Is there anyone who would've worked that shift?"

The waitress stared at the bill. "Sundays are slow. The person you want would be Carrie. She would have been the only one waiting tables."

"When does she come on duty again?" Michael asked.

"She's scheduled for Wednesday."

Michael pressed his lips together. "Is there any way we can talk to her before then?" He placed the dollar on the table, sliding it forward a few inches.

The waitress snatched the bill and tucked it in her apron. "The boss doesn't like us giving out our numbers. But I'll tell her that you want to talk. She's scheduled for six to three Wednesday. Better come early. The boss cuts our hours if business is slow."

"Thank you," Jason said. He rose to leave. They needed to find a new path forward to find Sara.

"Hold it." The server retrieved their ticket and slapped it in Jason's hand. "Pay up front." She sashayed away, and disappeared into a door marked:

Employees Only

Chapter Twelve

Sara threw the scrubbing brush back in the cleaning bucket. The room reeked of cleaning solution, but all was clean. She examined her chapped fingers. Too much bleach. Did she pack her skin ointment? An examination revealed lipstick and makeup. Her stationery kit spilled from its crumpled box onto the bed. She gathered the flimsy pastel sheets of writing paper and scented envelopes. No stamps. Was writing letters permissible here? She'd have to ask Mrs. Eisner.

The matron's footsteps drew near. Seconds later she appeared in the doorway, surveying the room. "Ah, I see you have some writing material. There's a drawer in the dining room where you can keep it. Are you ready for our tour?"

"I'm ready."

"Follow me. We'll start in the common room."

Mrs. Eisner led Sara to the front of the house. On the left, an oak staircase descended to a landing by the front entry. On the right, the hallway opened into a large living area. She swept her arm in a wide gesture. "This is the common room."

The thirty by sixty foot space contained a jumble of mismatched furniture along the walls: worn armchairs, sagging sofas, and a loveseat sitting on bricks. Three wicker baskets stacked with newspapers and magazines sat between the chairs. In the room's center was a mishmash of rockers, card tables, and folding chairs. An abandoned game of checkers covered one folding table—red was winning. Four tall windows spanned the western wall with three across the front. Amid the clutter, the arm-flapping Mr. Wunch dozed in a rocker, his toothless mouth gaping.

A warped sign hung between two of the windows with large archaic-style letters running across the top: NOTICE.

"I want to show you a bit of history."

Sara followed the matron as she traversed the big room. Gloria pointed to the old sign. "These were the original house rules for the residents. Back then, the county called them inmates."

NOTICE
Rules for Inmates:
All persons shall be clean, respectful, courteous, sober, and act in a civil manner.

All persons shall faithfully and diligently perform all tasks given to them by the Keeper or Matron.

Any person guilty of drunkenness, disobedience, immorality, laziness, disorderly conduct, theft, wasteful behavior, or absence without permission from the Keeper may be punished, expelled, or placed in solitary confinement.

"The first matron of this house posted those rules in 1893. They are still a good set of rules to go by."

Sara pursed her lips. "The rules seem a bit vague."

"The meaning is clear enough. Get along or get out."

Dusty magazines and board games—were they the only choices for diversion? "This room needs something. A piano. Or maybe a radio."

Mrs. Eisner laughed. "Child, we have more pressing needs than noisemakers. Indoor plumbing comes to mind."

Sara rubbed her dry hands. "I couldn't agree more."

The matron left the front room with Sara trying to keep pace. She bustled to the dining area, stopping before a tall bureau. The homemade cabinet held at least twelve small drawers. Taped to the front of each compartment was a hand-lettered name:

Arnesdorff, Chapman, Emerson

The last drawer on the bottom right read:

Wunch

"Many of the residents like to keep personal items nearby. That's what these drawers are for. You can keep your stationery here."

"Then I can send out letters?"

"We allow residents to send letters. One stamp a week on Tuesdays, plus some paper and envelopes and any mail received is placed in your drawer."

"May I be included in receiving stamps?"

The matron nodded. "Our address is Joshua County Farm, RFD 2, Joshua, Kansas. The mailbox is at the road intersection east of the house." She tapped a drawer. "What is your surname, young lady? I'll place it on one of the unused drawers. You plan to stay here?"

Sara swallowed. "It's McGuire. And I wish to stay."

The matron took pad and pencil from her apron, jotting down the name. "Very good." She turned to the pantry. "Now, I want to introduce you to our cook."

They passed through a well-stocked pantry set behind chicken wire on lath framing. Hasps and padlocks joined the makeshift doors. The pantry was nothing more than racks separating the dining room from the kitchen. Wooden shelves held sacks of flour, cornmeal, sugar, and beans. Hand-lettered labels covered canning jars containing fruit, vegetables, pork, and chicken. It was heartening to know there were plenty of staple ingredients.

The kitchen was a narrow space with a six-burner kerosene stove on the back wall, a sink and hand pump on the opposite side, and a large worktable with an overhead pan rack in the middle.

"Stay here while I look for Mr. Wheatley."

Mrs. Eisner disappeared through a passageway around the stove, leaving Sara alone. Now was her chance to examine the kitchen.

Someone left a stove burner unattended. The stockpot over the fire had boiled nearly dry. Frowning, Sara flicked the knob off.

To the left, a door opened to the back porch. To the right, past the stove, a taut rope held a shelved box suspended in a chute. The rope could raise the box upstairs or lower it to the floor below. Past the box was the open doorway to the main corridor that led to the front.

Sara examined the stove. How well did the cook clean? The stove *looked* scrubbed. Sara brushed her fingers over the black surface; they came away oily. She opened the oven door, glancing inside—baked-on food covered the bottom. She lifted a pan off the overhead hanging rack. Grease coated the outside and a ring of burnt on food rimmed the inside. Disgusting. How could she take over these kitchen duties? Her side stabbed her with every move. Lifting and stooping were out of the question. Still, in time, she *could* do the job.

The matron's quickened footsteps returned. "Mr. Wheatley is washing pots. I'll introduce you to him."

Sara pointed to the wall compartment. "What is that?"

"It's a dumbwaiter. We use it to move food and water to the infirmary. Now come along."

Sara trailed Mrs. Eisner through the passageway into a steamy washroom with galvanized laundry tubs propped on railroad ties.

Wheatley sat on a folding chair, rinsing an iron skillet. He was a big man with tousled black hair that merged with a bushy, unkempt coal-black beard. A small white cap seemed lost amid the shrubbery. With a metallic clatter, he dropped the skillet onto an unstable pile of rinsed pots and pans. Without looking up, he reached into the oily water for another pan.

"Mr. Wheatley, this is Miss McGuire. She will be with us for a time. Mr. Wheatley used to cook for the Rock Island Railroad."

Sara did not hold out her hand. Clenching her teeth, she made a half-feigned curtsey. "I've tasted your food, sir. It could stand improvement."

Wheatley scratched his beard, looking at Mrs. Eisner. "What?"

Sara placed her hands on her hips. This man had no business cooking. "What do you have planned for dinner? It's bound to be better than the slop you served for breakfast."

Wheatley's brows furrowed. "I usually make soup."

"You have a fully stocked pantry. You should use it." Sara tried not to look at the dishwater. The smell of grease made her stomach queasy.

"I'm supposed to stretch supplies."

"You must be joking. Use your stock while it's still good. Or do we have to wait for the food to turn bad before we eat it?"

Wheatley stared at her without expression.

Mrs. Eisner gripped Sara's arm above the elbow. "Thank you for your time. We'll leave you to your duties. Come along Miss McGuire." Sara found herself pulled along as the matron hurried out of the kitchen.

I'm in trouble. A talking-to for sure. A cold chill shot down her spine. What if she had gone too far? Mrs. Eisner couldn't turn her out. There was nowhere else to go.

In the dining room, she pointed to a chair at the end of a table. Sara sat, head bowed, as the matron pulled a chair beside her. She gazed at Sara with narrowed eyes. "You're quite the pepper pot, Miss McGuire."

Sara sighed. "I know, I shouldn't have said those things—"

She waved her off. "We'll talk about that presently. First, I'd like to tell you about how this farm got started. The county built this house in 1888. It originally housed twelve inmates and has changed little, except for the removal of the bell from the steeple in front. There are three aboveground levels with the men in the basement. We are on the main floor, and the infirmary occupies the third story. The unfinished attic is largely empty. In times past, the county expected inmates to work for their bed and board and make the farm self-sufficient.

"Since the Great War, the population has grown older due, no doubt, to improvements in medicine.

Now, we rely on the county for our existence. A new truck and tractor has helped with the labor shortage. But this came with a price; the house is lagging behind in repairs."

"The county can't chip in a little?"

The matron shook her head. "That's not my biggest concern. Recently, we lost our chaplain due to illness a month ago. I'm looking for a leader who can take his place. Are you a Believer, Miss McGuire?"

Sara crossed her arms. "It isn't that I don't believe. I do, but I fail to see the good it does. People who claim to have God's ear tend to be judgmental."

She let out a breath. "Pity."

Sara pushed herself from the table. "Mrs. Eisner, I have no interest in saving souls, but I think I can do a better job cooking than the person you have now."

The matron leaned back. "I see. A bold suggestion. It's good to lead with our strengths, but we must also accept with grace the limitations of others. In either case, showing respect is important in both word and action."

Sara's eyes darkened. "I understand the need to be patient with others. I was taught to be respectful. But your cook puts no effort into preparing a meal or cleaning the dishes. The man cannot do his job."

The older woman's eyes flashed. "I suspect you've lived an easy life and haven't felt the hardships others have endured. Millions in this country have lost their jobs and homes. Many families live huddled in tent cities—dangerous conditions for both women and children. For many, the choice is eating garbage or starving. Here, we have food and shelter. Order and security. For that, we must remain civil. You were wrong to disrespect Mr. Wheatley."

Sara jumped to her feet, gritting her teeth against the stabbing pain. "Your cook left a dry pot burning on the kitchen stove!" She pressed an arm against her ribs. "I've cooked since I was a child. If you want a lift in spirits around here, I can provide it by preparing a meal people will enjoy. I know how to stretch a dollar, but I'm not about to serve slop."

The matron raised her head. "Sit down, child." Her quiet voice belied the pinpricks of fire in her eyes. "If you raise your voice again, you'll be looking for a new place to sleep."

Cold fear shot down her back. *I shouldn't have pushed so hard.* She was the outsider. It was silly—no, stupid—to fight a losing battle. *Accept the rules, Sara.* She sank to the chair. "I'm sorry. I lost my temper. It won't happen again."

A faint smile crossed her lips. "I understand you more than you think, child. Cooking is your passion. Dazzle others by serving a Sunday dinner every day of the week. You want to be appreciated."

Sara clenched her fists beneath the tabletop but kept her voice steady. "All I want is to serve a good meal. I'm not interested in gratitude."

"It's understandable, even reasonable. But we have to deal with hard truths. This is not a Harvey House looking for new customers. Let's suppose you serve a good table, and word spreads to every panhandler around. Beggars would overwhelm us. I can't allow that to happen. Mr. Wheatley will continue to prepare the meals."

Sara bowed her head in defeat. She had no more arguments. "I just wanted to make a contribution."

The matron stood up. "You can. I have another labor in mind for you, a bigger one." The matron stepped into the long hallway, walking a bit slower this time to the front of the house. She stopped at the landing by the front door. "I'm about to give you a challenge that will test your fortitude as well as your generosity. It will sharpen your strengths and lay bare your weakness. You will feel wonder, elation, and grief." She inclined her head. "It's all up there."

Sara tilted her head, perplexed. "What am I doing?"

"The infirmary. Your job is simple: feed and comfort ten unique human beings."

Sara surveyed the long flight of stairs. "I don't see how I can get up there. I can't lift those people. My ribs still hurt."

The matron laughed. "Child, you were ready to take on cooking for nineteen residents. Now you're afraid of a few steps? Perhaps I've overestimated your tenacity."

"I can do it."

Her voice became gentler. "Pick who you need to help. Mrs. Robson and Miss Underwood are both capable and experienced workers. Rest now. You'll need your strength tomorrow." She left, rushing down the hallway.

Sara tried the stairs, trudging up a third of the way before clutching her side. She crept back down, one step at a time. The first challenge would be reaching the floor above.

No, that wasn't right.

The first challenge was asking for help.

Chapter Thirteen

At two o'clock that afternoon, Sara paced about the main floor attacking clutter wherever she found it. What started out after dinner as a way to look busy turned into a mission. But her thoughts were not on her work. What happened to the Poor Commissioner? He was supposed to be here at ten o'clock this morning. His absence only added to the intrigue. Now, it was more than mere curiosity. She wanted to talk to this man. Why was he so late?

Sara entered the common room for the third time, glancing out the front windows. Still nothing. Mrs. Eisner said he was a committed young man. What was he like? Would he be a fat little bookkeeper with thick glasses, or tall and brawny? Would he give her the time of day? Or snub her for being uppity?

Stacks of dust-covered newspapers overflowed the wicker baskets. Sara retrieved a frayed pillowcase she found earlier. Stooping aggravated the stinging pain. She winced, slowing her movements. *Think about something else besides the pain.*

It was hard to imagine this place as a home. The structure felt more like an institution. Residents had to conform to overbearing rules. Yet everyone accepted them. Mrs. Eisner called it a community. That was certainly true, but there was more. *We all look after Patrick,* Beatrice had said on her slate. Despite their limitations, residents drew together in support. They depended on each other. For this, they shared a mutual bond. A kinship. They didn't whine. They didn't blame others. They didn't even act poor.

The pillowcase, now crammed with trash, pulled at her aching side. She set it behind a chair. Even when Mr. Krause arrived, did she have anything original to say? Poor farms had been around for three generations, segregating the undesirable from the rest of society, but they weren't prisons. Residents stayed here voluntarily. Few wished to leave. As Mrs. Eisner said, they had nowhere else to go.

A station wagon approached. A Woody with the Joshua County seal on its side pulled into the west side drive. Sara rushed to the dining room and watched it park by the back porch. A figure stepped out, his black homburg pulled down against a stiff wind, hiding his face. He wore a tweed jacket and a loose tie. Medium build, not quite six feet tall.

Sara brushed back her unraveling locks. A couple more days and her curls would disappear altogether. Grabbing the bag of newspapers, she set off to meet the Commissioner.

As Sara came in the kitchen, Mrs. Eisner entered with the administrator in tow. Sara dropped the bag and followed them. The matron ushered the young man into an office on the northeast corner of the building. The door closed with a click.

Sara stamped her foot in frustration. Mrs. Eisner had taken control. She could easily occupy the official's time until his departure. How could she possibly see him now? Sara froze as a delicious idea took form. She would wait her turn while the commissioner and matron talked by going to the one place where she could talk to Mr. Krause—alone.

First, the trash. Sara hauled the pillowcase out the back door and found a burn barrel near a smelly privy. She dumped the newspapers into the container and stuffed the pillowcase in her apron. She would tear it into rags later. Now, she would wait for the Commissioner.

The Woody sat near a stand of cedars, and she slid into the front seat. Minutes of waiting irritated her side. She had to stretch out. Sara moved to the back, lying down across the bench seat. Much better. Now, what could she suggest? Allow the residents a monthly trip into town? Purchase a piano or radio? How about a newspaper subscription? Sara yawned. It was easy to relax, though a bit cool. An old blanket lay at her feet. She pulled the cover, tucking it around her neck. The last thing she remembered was the wind stirring through branches. Soon she was fast asleep.

****

Sara awoke with a start. The car was moving! She threw the blanket aside and sat upright. A man with thinning brown hair drove the station wagon in the middle of the road. She shook her head. What was she doing here? Then it came back. She wanted to visit with Commissioner Krause. Now she had the chance—he was in the seat before her. A bit awkward, but that couldn't be helped. *I hope he has a sense of humor.*

She tapped his shoulder. "Hey, could you turn your car around? I'll be in Dutch with Mrs. Eisner when she finds out I'm missing."

"*Hah!*" He jumped, yanking the steering wheel, sending the car skittering across the gravel road.

"*Be careful!*" Sara yelled, arms clutching both his shoulders.

Mr. Krause pumped the brakes and gained control, bringing the vehicle back to the center of the road. He glanced behind him. "You gave me a start. Who are you?"

I wasn't a question, but a demand.

"My name is Sara McGuire. I just arrived—"

"What are you doing in my car?" His tone was more of a demand then a question.

"It's an accident. I wanted to talk to you—as soon as you came out. But I fell asleep, and—this is embarrassing."

"Are you a resident?" Again the forced tone. *What kind of person does he think I am?*

"Yes. The Eisners took me in yesterday. You probably think I'm crazy."

"I didn't say that."

"You didn't have to. I heard it in your voice. I haven't lost my marbles…just had them rattled a bit."

"Well, you've rattled mine. Are you in some kind of trouble?"

"I hurt every time I breath, and…I'm expecting. Trouble enough."

Was he smiling?

"Well, trouble is the menu for the day. I'm Acting Commission Krause. Just call me Wendell. So you the one…the pepper pot."

Sara drew back. *Did Mrs. Eisner talk about her?* "I don't know what you're talking about." It was too late to play innocent, but it was the only card she had.

"All the same, you've made an impression on the matron. She had a few things to say. But they weren't all bad."

"Like what?" Sara wasn't sure she liked where this conversation was goinng.

"Let's see. She mentioned impetious. Called you unruly. A wisenheimer. And obstinate. I think she was complementing you—in a left field sort of way."

"I think I rubbed her the wrong way. They have a lousy cook right now, and I could have done a better job."

"Mrs. Eisner doesn't like her authhority challenged."

"Oh, I got that. For a minute, I thought she would kick me out. Mrs. Eisner was kind to let me stay."

"I'm stopping here, so you can sit in front." He slowed the car, pulled into the parking lot of a filling station, and stopped. "Now, it will be easier to talk while I take you back."

As Sara eased her way through the door. He moved his hat and some papers closer to him. "Thank you, Mr. Krause," she said. "I know this is awkward."

"This is the highlight of my day. Believe me. Mr. Krause has quit for the afternoon, so you can call me Wendell." He turned the vehicle in a thght circle and headed back to the tenement house, again staying in the center of the road.

"Shouldn't you be in your own lane?"

A quiet smile played at the ends of his lips. "I should. But more tramps on country roads are getting struck by farm vehicles. I'm just playing it safe." Wendell rubbed the back of his neck. He had a worn out look that went beyond the rumpled suit and wrinkled tie. The man might been had been up the night before. Of course, his work wouldn't be easy. Probably had a rough day. She had a few of those.

He glanced at her, raising an eyebrow. "So why did you risk your stay by hiding in the back of my car?"

"I wanted to meet you, but couldn't think of a way to do it. Waiting in you car seemed like the best plan. I must have fallen asleep."

"Should I call you Miss McGuire?" A glint sparked in his eyes. "Or Goldilocks."

"I'd rather you call me Sara."

"Fair enough." The twinkle disappeared. He turned his attention back to the road.

He seemed so serious. A little teasing might lift his spirits. "It's nice to know you don't think I'm crazy."

"No more than anyone else. So, what's on your mind?"

He was smiling more, having a little fun with her. A little less somber. That was better.

"I was wondering what you did on a daily basis. Do people really call you Commissioner of the Poor?"

He smirked. "Well, *nobody* calls me Commissioner of the Poor. It's merely a title. On paper I see to it that services are carried out. Mostly, it means fixing things that go wrong. From missed relief checks to finding a doctor for a poor family. And sometimes it's hunting for some poor old woman's lost dog. At least those programs hadn't been challenged yet."

That seemed an odd thing to say. "How did you get to be commissioner?" If he had something on his mind, he could always tell her—if he wished.

"There's a story. My father ran for the office last fall and won. But he died last January, before he started office. When I came into town to settle his affairs, the county asked me to fill in for him. I inherited the job.

And the thing is…" He bit his lip, swallowing. "Everyday, I keep asking myself what would my dad do. Today, I have no answer." He shook his head, staring at the road as morose as ever.

"What happened?" An uneasiness settled on her, like out-of-tune strings playing off-stage.

"The beginning of he end." He glanced down at the papers beneath his hat. "It's all in there. Everything's done but the doing."

Wendell seemed resigned. Defeated. She nudged the pages. "May I look?"

He flicked the air. "Why not? It'll be public soon enough."

Sara gathered the papers.

Schedule And Procedure
for Public Sale of County Property 0043
Miller Township
Commissioner Wendel P. Krause
8 April, 1935

Most of the twelve remaining pages contained maps and blurry memeographs of old public documents. She gazed at Wendell. "What does it mean?"

"Joshua County is selling the poor farm."

"What?" Sara pressed a hand to her temple to calm the spinning whirlwind within. "They're taking away our home?"

" 'They' is me. The other commissioner outvoted me two to one. But it's my job to prepare the property for auction in August. As soon as I finished typing the report, I brought it to Mrs. Eisner for review. That was hard, but I had to talk to somebody."

"What did she say?" It was hard to catch her

breath. What will happen to this house? To Bea and Patrick? To her? And what would happen to her baby?

"She was furious, of course, and demanded to know the reasoning. 'What posessed these fools to make such a cold decision?' she asked."

"I'm with her." Sara shoved the report back under the homburg. "Why?"

"It boils down to money." He gave a rueful laugh. "Joshua County Farm sits on one-hundred sixty acres of good farmland. Why not sell it? Turn a drain on the county budget into taxable private property? No one would notice an out-of-the-way instituation closing."

"It's more then that. It's home. *Our* home—a place worth fighting for." The words rang like a rally cry. Like those stories of underpaid dressmakers her grandmother told her about—who unionized because no one else would come to their defense. "We must find a way."

He shook his head. "I like the idea, Miss McGuire. But I'm tired. After I drop you off, I'm going home, throw together a sandwich, and write my resignation letter. The battle is already over."

"Would your father aprove?"

She wasn't sure if he heard her words above the wind buffeting the car. He sat hunched over the wheel, ever watchful. A few seconds later, he slowed as he passed a man wearing a shapeless cap and shabby jacket.

"No." Wendell drew out the word. "He'd probably want me to stick it out. Dad left home when I was eleven. Most of what I remember are rosy memories: a can-do man who would take on anything. That's part of why I came out here. Not just to settle his estate but to find out if the man I imagined was the real deal."

"Was he?"

He grinned with sad eyes. "Turned out he was."

"I'm jealous," she said. "You should be proud of him. Does that mean you'll stay?"

He turned, giving her a sideways glance. "You assume I'll carry on?"

"You're his son. His fight is your fight."

Wendell stayed silent for several seconds, then turned to her. "You're different from any poor resident in this county. Yesterday afternoon Mrs. Eisner takes you in—and in twentyfour hours you're taking a stand for the other residents. Most women living in poverty are overcome by the sheer enormity of the problem— they're indifferent, worn down. But you're aware and involved. Why are you so interested in what's happening?"

"I want to stay here. Going anywhere else could mean giving up my baby. All in all, Joshua County Farm is the safest place for me."

Wendell sighed. "Mrs. Eisner certainly needs the help."

Sara sat straighter. "She's given me the job of working in the infirmary."

Wendell chuckled. "Either the matron has the upmost confidence in you, or..."

"She thinks I'm a pain? I don't mean to be. Mrs. Eisner is letting me pick my help. The job should be straightfoward. Except for lifting patients, I see no problems."

"The job entails doing three rounds a day. You're dealing with people. Some of the invalids can be difficult."

"I think I can manage the old folks."

The station wagon topped a small hill, going by a small cemetery. The tenant house with its pointed spire, loomed ahead. "So, do you have some thoughts about saving the county farm? I could use the help."

Sara gasped. "*Me?* I have no ideas." In coaxing Wendell to carry on, she had lapse into her role as mailroom supervisor, employing a little trick she discovered to spur on a faltering worker. But this was more serious then tackling a mountain of mail. Lives were involved. And now Wendell was asking for her aid. What did she have to offer? Was this even her fight? It was so much easier to move away and leave the problem of saving the farm to someone else. Why not jump ship then go down with it?

She could never do that.

Wendell frowned, as he pulled into the back door driveway next to an ice truck. "I can't go this alone, and there's no one else to turn to—not even Mrs. Eisner. She's got enough to deal with. It *has* to be you."

He was right. She did encourage him. She couldn't back out now.

She inclined her head. "I'll do everything I can."

"Great! We should plan. Meet together to decide what to do. How about this Thursday? There's a restaurant in Joshua. We can have supper there. Put our heads together and brainstorm. "

"It's hard to refuse when you put it that way."

"Good. I'll call…um, meet you here at four o'clock Thursday and have you back well before lights out."

Sara looked down at her lap. "I don't have anything to wear in public. Only feed store dresses. What would people think?"

137

Wendell waved the thought away. "Most women wear sackcloth around town. You'll fit right in."

"If you say so. Thursday, then." Sara opened the car door.

"Stay there." Wendell jumped out and hurried to help her out of the car. "I'll come in with you. Can't have you in hot water with the matron. That would interfere with our meeting."

Wendell escorted her into the house. Mrs. Eisner was in the kitchen moving food around a new chunk of ice. "Didn't even know you were gone," she said and turned back to work.

"I hope I can come up with something," she told Wendell before he left.

"We're in this together. We've got to."

A few minutes later she was back in her room, pacing despite the twinges of pain from her side. It didn't seem possible for two people to stop the machinery of government once it started on a project. Failure, however, to stop the closing meant for her—for all of them—an uncertain future.

Especially for the baby.

Chapter Fourteen

Jason glanced at the abandoned buildings along Broadway as he and Michael walked north from the restaurant. Two men in patched flannel shirts lounged on the steps of a boarded up furniture store. Signs of hard times were as glaring as a movie marquee. The only thing separating the destitute and them was a paycheck—and hope. Hope for a brighter future. Or a prayer that the hard times didn't turn worse.

Bigger's Mercantile lay ahead. There, they'd meet Larry and find out what happened to Sara. Mom would be relieved. At the end of the block, a vendor with bright red hair and short skirt sold apples from a wagon to a suited gentleman. As they approached, the buyer shook his head and hurried away. A nickel for an apple the sign said. For a dime, he could get a whole bagful at a store.

With a break in traffic at the corner, Jason hurried across the street. On the other side, he stopped. Where was that brother of his? Lagging behind, no doubt. Jason dashed back across the intersection to find him gazing at the comely apple seller.

She wore a feathery boa and a thin dress. The girl's smile was an invitation. She held the fruit up to her small bosom, the sheer fabric detailing her charms. She couldn't have been more than fifteen. "Would you like to buy my apples?" she cooed.

Michael was transfixed.

Jason grabbed the back of his brother's collar, marching him across traffic. "Come on, Romeo."

Michael squirmed like a fish on a hook. "Leggo! You'll rip my shirt!"

Jason released him on the next block but continued at a brisk pace.

Michael hurried to keep up. "Can you believe that? I could practically see through her blouse!

Jason gritted his teeth, but he couldn't blame his brother. He hadn't seen much of the world. "Apples weren't the only things she was selling."

"Slow down! What are you talking about?"

"She's an apple tart—a floozy. Now, let's get to that store."

Michael pulled his newsboy cap tighter as he rushed to keep pace with Jason. "You're taking this search way too seriously."

Jason whirled around. "You bet it's serious. We're not playing at Sam Spade. Sara may be in trouble. Remember that."

Michael stared at the sidewalk. "I know you're worried, but Sis is probably giving Pop the silent treatment."

Jason glared at his brother. Michael still thought this was a game.

Twenty-five minutes later, Jason led the way into Bigger's Mercantile. The first floor acted as a showcase for new products. Larry wasn't anywhere in sight. They may have to check all the floors. Or *he* would. It looked like Michael was distracted again.

This time, it was a radio the size of an icebox.

The impressive looking Zenith set in the center of

smaller table models. The huge radio had a black dial some eight inches across, centered above a decorative wooden grill. Four ridged columns looking like art deco skyscrapers were at each corner of the massive cabinet. Michael ran his fingers over the smooth finish. "This is a swell looking radio."

Jason's eyes drifted to the stairs. "We haven't got time—"

"May I help you, boys?" A well-dressed man with graying hair approached. He took out a handkerchief, buffing the spot where Michael touched the wood. The floorwalker gestured to the radio. "Gorgeous, isn't it? It's the Zenith Stratosphere, their best model. The cabinet is handcrafted walnut. The speaker clarity beats anything else on the market. Very natural sound."

"How much is it?" Michael asked.

"Seven hundred fifty dollars. It's not just a radio. It's finely made furniture and an engineering marvel."

Michael backed away. "I bet it sounds great, but I was just looking."

The salesman nodded. "I understand. Perhaps you'd be interested in something more affordable?"

Time was a-wasting. Jason cleared his throat. "We're looking for Larry Bigger."

The seller frowned. "He's my son. You can find him on the second floor setting up a display of fabrics."

"Thank you, sir." Jason caught Michael's eye. "Come on."

Near the stairs, Larry stood at a table surrounded by rolls of brightly colored cloth. A wide bandage covered his right cheek. Jason remained behind a rack of clothing patterns as Michael examined the merchandise. Larry kept changing the order of the fabrics. First, he'd alternate solid colors with patterns. Then, he'd group similar colors together. Jason stepped in plain view. "Are you Larry Bigger?"

The clerk took his time before looking up. Sara brought him home last Christmas. Blond hair, skinny, big ears, loud suit.

"Do you remember us, Mr. Bigger?"

"No, is there something I can do for you?"

Michael nudged a roll of cloth, letting it unroll across the table.

Larry glared at him. "Please, leave the merchandise alone."

Jason nodded. "You can help. But we're not interested in material. We're looking for our sister. Have you seen her?"

Larry wrinkled his nose. "I see customers all day. What does she look like?"

"Quit the act. She was here Saturday morning, telling you she was having a baby. Your baby. Where is she?"

Michael tapped the roll again, sending the spool to the edge of the table.

Larry's eyes shifted between the two. He snapped his fingers. "I know you guys. Sara's brothers. I remember now. I had dinner with your family. Okay. You're right. She came Saturday. Very upset. We had a few words. Then she left. Said she didn't want to see me again. I haven't talked to her since."

Jason glanced at Michael. His younger brother shrugged, unrolling a second spool of fabric. Jason turned back to Larry. "We don't care what happened between you two. Did she talk about going someplace?"

Larry tapped his chin with a forefinger. "No. She said her father was upset with her. I was busy and didn't have time to listen. That got her angry, and she left. That's all I know." His voice dripped with insincerity. "Listen, I'm on the clock, guys. Got work to do."

Michael unfurled a third bolt of cloth. Three spools teetered on the edge of the table. He gazed at Larry, touching his cheek. "What happened to your face?"

Larry mirrored the gesture. "I cut it shaving."

Jason's hands balled into fists. He'd heard enough. "You slipped up, Larry. You saw her Sunday. Dad didn't blow up until Saturday night."

Larry scowled. "I told you, boys. I'm busy. Now, scram."

"We'll do that. And you'll be busy as well."

Michael flicked his wrist, sending all three spools flying off the table.

Larry uttered a curse.

The boys rushed for the doors. Once outside, Michael doubled over in laughter. Jason allowed himself a small grin. The last thing he saw before hitting the stairs was Larry Bigger chasing three spools of fabric fanning across the show floor.

Chapter Fifteen

Sara leaned back in the rocker by her bed, savoring the time alone before supper. Tomorrow would begin the infirmary assignment; a grueling, painful challenge compared to today's activities. By July fifteenth, the county planned to close the tenant house. After the house closed she had no choice but go to her aunt and uncle in Hutchinson—and the all-too- real possibility of giving up her child. Unless something can be done.

But for now, she needed to do her assigned duties. Coping with the bedridden up those long steps would be tough. Who should she ask for help?

The supper bell rang.

Sara stood and shuffled to the dining room. Bea and Patrick were already sitting down to a bowl of soup. Dutch sat with the two older men at the other end of the table.

"We saved a bowl for you," Patrick announced. "I thought of it."

Sara smiled slightly, eyeing the container of stew. "Thank you, Patrick. You're very thoughtful."

Sara tasted the food. A bit thin, but at least it was still hot. She ate in silence for a few minutes and then turned to Bea. "The matron has given me a work assignment. It wasn't what I expected."

Bea retrieved her slate.

NOT COOKING?

Sara shook her head. "Something more involved. I'll be working with the people upstairs. Do you have a job you're supposed to do?"

I SEW. REPAIR CLOTHES.

"Mrs. Eisner said you made my dress. Thank you. I'd like to find a belt or cloth to go around the waist. So it looks more like a dress instead of a nightgown."

LIKE A SASH?

Sara nodded. "Or a long scarf."

GIVE ME A DAY.

"Thanks. That would be wonderful." Sara took a breath. "I was also wondering if you could help me with the people upstairs. I suppose you'd call them patients. Two people working together will make the job a lot easier."

WHAT WOULD I DO?

Sara thought for a moment. "Help me serve meals, change bedding, do sponge baths, move people to rockers or potty chairs if necessary. Anything you can imagine making old people more comfortable, that's what we'll do."

I CAN HELP. IS TWO ENOUGH?

"Probably not." Sara pursed her lips. "I can't lift anything without hurting. We could use a strong back."

Bea pointed to Patrick.

"Patrick?" Sara peered at the youth who was tipping the bowl to his lips. The job would require lifting patients, transferring them from bed to chair and back again. He seemed strong. But could he take instruction? Would he be gentle?

Bea tapped her slate.

ASK HIM.

Why not. Sara touched the boy's arm. "Patrick, I

need help with a job. Can you lift a person?"

Patrick's eyes lit with excitement. "I bet I can lift you!" He sprang from his chair, circled the table, and stood behind Sara. Two pudgy hands gripped the seat of her chair and raised her off the ground.

Sara grabbed the table. "Hey wait! I believe you. Set me down, now!" Sara held her breath while Patrick plopped her chair to the floor.

"I'm sorry, Miss Sara. Are you mad at me?" The youth collapsed back to his seat.

"No, of course not. I know you're strong. Would you like to help me work upstairs? You'll be lifting old people from their beds. Work starts tomorrow."

Patrick's face brightened. "Yip-pee!" He leaped to his feet and ran around the dining room. "I can work because I'm strong." The other diners watched as he shouted and careened around the tables. On his third lap, his foot caught on the back wheel of Mrs. Chapman's wheelchair. He crashed headlong, sliding across the rough pine floor, but he rose again and completed one more circuit before dropping in his chair, his mouth in a wide smile. "Hey, Miss Sara?" He rubbed a scrape on his forehead.

"Yes, Patrick?"

"I can help because I'm strong."

Sara gave a polite smile. "You are."

"Hey, Miss Sara?"

"Yes, Patrick?"

"What am I supposed to do?"

Bea tapped Sara's shoulder.

THIS WILL BE FUN.

Chapter Sixteen

Jason sat at the edge of his bed writing on a Big Chief tablet. "We need to decide what our next step should be to find Sara. I've already started a list of what we know, but I need your help to finish it."

Michael flipped the detective story pulp upside down on his bed. "What have you got so far?"

"That Sara told the mailroom ladies she was having a baby. She got the news from the doctor's office, went to the mercantile, talked to Larry Bigger, and headed to work. All during Saturday morning." He stared at the page. "What do we know about their meeting?"

"Sara told him of her situation. Larry said they broke up and denied knowing anything about a baby."

Jason jotted down the main points. "Keep going."

"The ladies at the office never mentioned a breakup, but they didn't think Larry took the news of the baby well."

"So, why would Larry say they broke up and deny knowing about the baby?"

Michael shrugged. "He's hiding something."

Jason rubbed his chin. "What's he covering up?"

"That would answer the mystery." Michael turned the magazine over, flipping pages.

"Hey. I thought you were going to help me with this list."

"I can think better when I'm doing something

else."

Jason moved to Michael's bed, looking over his shoulder as his brother stopped to look at an illustration. *What could he be looking for?*

Michael turned to the title page of "Cross Country Car Chase" showing a tilted angle drawing of a sedan leaping over a hill in pursuit of another vehicle. His younger brother glanced at Jason. "We could turn Larry's lies against him and see how he reacts."

Jason sighed. "I'd like to pin some evidence on that mug."

Michael turned more pages, stopping at a sketch of a man in topcoat standing in the path of an oncoming car.

Jason snapped his fingers. "We can talk to the waitress at the diner this Wednesday. Or search Larry's house during the day. What do you think?"

"Sam Spade would never get caught searching a room, but I don't think we'd be as lucky." He found a two-page drawing of a locomotive smashing into a car.

"There's one thing that bothers me," Jason said. "Remember what Larry said about Pop?"

Michael was on the last page of the short story. The drawing showed a man peering through the smashed window of the sedan.

"Larry said he and Sara broke up Saturday morning. And he said Sara was distraught because Pop was upset with her. But that didn't happen until Saturday night. That means the two of them met Sunday. But if Larry denies it, what do we have left?"

Michael kept staring at the illustration of the wrecked car. *What's gotten into him?* "Hey, Sherlock!" Jason thumped his brother on the back. "Get your head out of that mag and help me come up with a plan."

Michael scowled. "I'm thinking."

"Well write me a letter when you come up with an idea."

"And you shall have it." Michael tapped the picture. "This is what we will do."

Jason stared at the picture. "We're looking inside cars?"

"Not just any car. Larry's car. All we have to do is find it."

Chapter Seventeen

After supper, Sara knocked on the matron's open office door. "Mrs. Eisner? At your convenience, I'd like to go over the infirmary duties."

She was writing entries in an oversized ledger that took up most of the space on her makeshift desk. A finger went up as she continued writing. *One minute.*

The office was well furnished with a Royal typewriter, a rotary telephone, and trays filled with neatly stacked papers. Group photographs of residents hung on the back wall. In the corner set a varnished bookshelf containing several ledgers. The fabric covers of a couple hung in tatters. Sara wrinkled her nose. The room smelled of old paper.

Mrs. Eisner set her pencil aside and slipped a red ribbon between the pages of the book, then motioned to one of the two cushioned chairs in front of the table. Sara sank, delighting in the comfort. "Is that an accounting book, Mrs. Eisner?"

She rested a hand on the massive volume. "Some of it is. I've filled this ledger with narratives as well as transactions. There's information about purchases and those passing through these doors going back six years. I think of it as a journal."

"I can't imagine much changing from one week to the next."

"Oh, but you're wrong, child. Your arrival has

created a quiet stir among the residents. Have you noticed the gentlemen stealing glances at you? Or the reactions of some of the women, especially Mrs. Chapman?"

"The lady in the wheelchair? I don't think she likes me."

"Irene wants to be noticed by the men but likes to be pampered like an infirmed patient. It's an exercise in frustration." The matron sighed. "Even small changes get noticed. Mr. Emerson complained to me this afternoon that someone took his newspapers from the common room."

Sara pursed her lips. "Dust covered those papers. No one has touched them in days. I threw them out."

Her lips twitched, holding back a smile. "My husband will find a use for them. Paper makes a good insulator. I assured Mr. Emerson the culprit would not disturb his reading material again. Consider yourself told."

"Thank you," said Sara.

"I'm glad you did it. Now, you wished to discuss the infirmary?"

"I wanted to understand my duties so I'd be better prepared for tomorrow."

"Of course." Gloria closed the big book. "There are ten invalids upstairs. Nearly all of them are sixty or more. Up to now, Mrs. Robson and Miss Underwood— an amazingly strong woman—have cared for the infirmary. They know the patients and the duties of the job. I'm assuming they will assist you tomorrow."

Sara crossed her arms. "I've asked Bea and Patrick to help me."

Mrs. Eisner tilted her head like a raptor sensing

food. "They are children, Miss McGuire. Infirmary work is not for the immature. You would be wise to go with experienced help."

Sara bit her lip to keep from gritting her teeth. "You told me to pick my help. I've done that. Both have agreed to assist me. Patrick, in particular, seems thrilled to lend a hand."

The matron shook her head. "You'll be serving meals three times a day, and that's the easy part. Neither Bea nor Patrick can handle a real job. Instead of ten patients, you'll have twelve. I advise you to change your mind."

Sara leaned back in her chair. "I've already decided. You're welcome to reassign the work to someone else, but I think the three of us will do a good job."

Mrs. Eisner rested her elbows on the table, bridging her fingers together. "You're a stubborn one. That's not always a good trait." She reached for a sheet of paper. "We'll try your little experiment, but I'll be keeping tabs on your work."

"Thank you for giving us a chance."

She waved a dismissive hand. "We should go over procedures since none of you have any caretaking experience. At the foot of each bed is a clipboard. Acquaint yourself with those notes. Get in the habit of writing your own observations. Some residents, like the woman with leukemia, take medication. The bottles are on the shelf above the bed. Note the time and the number of pills given on the chart. When James and I go into town on Saturday, we'll stop by the drugstore and refill prescriptions as necessary. Are you with me so far?"

Sara nodded. "Write down comments. Keep track of pills and the time."

She produced a small wind-up clock from a cigar box. "This will help you stay on schedule. Don't dawdle. These patients will talk your ear off if you let them."

"I understand."

"Now, let's move on to a less savory topic. Each time you enter a patient's room, take care of toilet matters first. Transfer them to the potty chair, even when they protest about going. Two patients wear diapers because they can't hold their bladders. I'll show you how to fold a diaper before you leave. Make sure all patients have clean hands before mealtime. Good hygiene means less sickness. Despite your best precautions, though, accidents will happen."

"Accidents?"

"A patient may pee the bed. Or worse. In the case of Mr. Evans, it may not always be an accident."

Sara cringed. What had she gotten herself into? Cleaning up messes? Could she do this? What about Bea and Patrick? This job would demand every bit of fortitude the three of them could muster.

The matron studied her. "Now do you see why Mrs. Robson and Miss Underwood would be more helpful?"

Sara sat up straighter, ignoring the flare in her side. "We'll do quite well on our own."

"As you wish." She glanced at the sheet again. "I should tell you about several of the patients. Mr. Byers is in Room One at the top of the stairs. There are dust masks and rubber gloves hanging outside the door. Wear these at all times when you enter the room and keep the door shut. He has consumption."

Sara gasped. "Tuberculosis? In this house?"

"The man is dying and has nowhere else to go. The disease spreads by air, hence, the dust masks. Always wash the masks and gloves with bleach water upon leaving his room. Clean your hands and face with soap in a separate basin, and each of you dry with a separate towel. Don't use those basins or towels again. The idea is to isolate any germs you might encounter. Minister to him last and take no short cuts. This will protect you from exposure. He will probably die within a week."

"How horrible." An icy chill skittered down her spine. Entering a room with a man wracked by the dreaded lung disease was like playing poker with death.

"Would my child be in danger?"

"Protect yourself and your child will be safe."

"I'll wash as you say."

"Good. In Room Ten at the other end of the hall is a leukemia patient. Maxine Hiebert is cordial, warm-hearted, and dying as well. Her bones are brittle, and her blood does not clot. Maxine takes morphine in pill form. It's easier to administer that way. Don't let her handle her own medicine. She'll take extra pills if she gets a chance. I give her the early morning dose, but you will be responsible for the other three. She is in constant pain, but during your morning rounds, she'll be feeling the morphine. Don't let that fool you. She is a delicate patient with no immunity to disease. Be gentle with her. I doubt if she'll see the month of May."

"I'll be careful."

"Then there is Mr. Cyrus Evans in Room Two." Gloria's eyes narrowed. "A thoroughly repulsive individual."

Sara gave a rueful smile. "Sounds interesting."

"He's an ornery, hateful old man with dementia. Lived in Joshua his whole life, beat his wife and daughter and spent his money on hooch. For one who's lost his memory, he still has an evil sense of humor, so be wary."

"Sounds like a handful."

Gloria huffed. "That's putting it mildly."

"What happens when a resident passes away? Does family ever come to reclaim the body?"

"These patients have no family." She pointed out the eastern window. "Look behind you. The county cemetery is about a quarter mile away. There are over a hundred bodies there. Half of the buried came from here."

Sara turned. In the distance was a grove of willows. "The cemetery is under those trees?"

"Yes. It's rather pleasant for a gravesite. Lots of wildflowers and mockingbirds."

As soon as she felt better, she'd have to investigate. "What else do I need to know, Mrs. Eisner?"

"Use the dumbwaiter in the kitchen to transport food and supplies. Like the rest of us, the infirmed want someone to talk to. Be friendly, give them comfort, but move on and complete your duties. Sadly, much of their time is spent alone."

"I'll do my best."

Twenty minutes later, Sara returned to her room. Tomorrow wasn't just a job assignment. It was a trial for Bea and Patrick. And for her.

Chapter Eighteen

Tuesday, April 9, 1935

Sara stared at the congealing gravy covering the bread on her pie plate. She disliked the food, but she needed to eat. Skipping meals for an expectant mother was out of the question. She swallowed a few tentative mouthfuls, expecting another bout of morning sickness. Nothing happened. No cramping. No wave of nausea. Nothing to stand in the way of eating or her new assignment.

Across the table, Patrick clenched his spoon to chase the last bit of bread on his plate. Sara tapped his arm. "Are you ready to help upstairs?"

The youth wiped his chin on the sleeve of his shirt. "I forgot what we're doing."

Bea scribbled on her slate.

TELL PATRICK ONLY WHAT HE NEEDS TO KNOW

"Good point." Sara turned to the youth. "For now, let's meet here after morning chores. Then we'll go upstairs together."

The three left the dining table to tend to their rooms.

As Sara freshened her sleeping area, nagging doubts about her decision crept into her thoughts. Should she have gone with the more experienced women, Mrs. Robson and Miss Underwood? Would they have resented taking orders from a younger, less experienced woman? It didn't matter. This was *her* crew. They would do things *their* way and learn from their own mistakes. The feeble-minded boy, the mute girl, and the unwed mother-to-be would become a team. They could be as good as anyone.

Sara cleaned her room, testing her physical limits. She could bend a tad bit more today. If she planned her movements ahead of time, she could manage the twinges of pain.

It was time to get to work.

****

Just after eighty-thirty, Bea sat with the two others in their usual spots in the dining room. Miss Sara talked about the resident behind the forbidden door at the top of the stairs. So, he was dying from a deadly sickness. She'd seen the dust masks hanging by the door and heard the wretched coughing. From within the shadows of her mind, Sally stirred. *Oh ho! We're about to go in the room and see for ourselves!*

Bea clasped her hands. This was her chance to show she could work. She hoped Sally wouldn't interfere. Sally could ruin everything.

Miss Sara glanced at her notes. "Tuberculosis is also catching. Germs spread through the air because of Mr. Byers coughing attacks. That's why we wear the dust masks and the long gloves—to protect ourselves. We're leaving his room last so we can wash thoroughly afterward."

I have to see this. I can't let you have all the fun, little Bea.

HOW WILL HE DIE?

Bea wrote the words, but Sally wanted to know.

157

Miss Sara peered at Beatrice. "Mr. Byers could simply give out. People still call it consumption because victims waste away. All we can do is keep him comfortable."

Bea slid the slate back in her apron. Sally's urging was satisfied—for the moment.

Five minutes later, Beatrice bounded upstairs, Patrick stumbling behind her. Miss Sara came last, taking each step with care, probably due to her injuries.

Sally scoffed. *No. She thinks she's a princess.*

Bea shook her head. She had to make a good impression.

Humph. A good impression for Lady Sara. Bea imagined Sally turning up her nose.

Two carts sat at the far end of the hall near the dumbwaiter. Mr. Wheatley had already brought up several items in the small elevator. Beatrice retrieved six ceramic pitchers filled with water and a stack of steel basins. The bottom shelf held a huge enamel pot will hold what Miss Sara called "slop" and—Bea squirmed at the thought—the "business" from the potty chairs. She moved the loaded trolley aside as the dumbwaiter dropped back to the kitchen. Miss Sara and Patrick maneuvered the cart next to the shaft. As they waited, Miss Sara and Patrick talked about a musical. Patrick loved movies.

Now was a good time to peek in the mysterious room. Bea crept down the corridor, leaving her cart behind. What lurked behind the "*Keep Out*" sign? It was their last room, but the wait was too long. She—Sally—had to know the secret *now*. She could steal a glance inside and hurry back before Miss Sara knew she was gone.

Bea hesitated outside the closed door. Entering was dangerous.

Sally scoffed. *What could be so terrible? Open it.*

A turn of the knob, and the door squeaked open.

Bea gaped at the sight.

Even Sally was speechless.

The reek was an odorous stew of blood, urine, feces, and vomit. Mr. Byers lay snared in his bed, his head pinned beneath the iron rail. He must have jostled loose the heavy upper bar, and it slammed down like a guillotine. Blood and vomit ran down the side of the mattress, dripping onto the floorboards.

Get closer. Lift his head. Sally was exuberant. *Let's see his eyes.*

Bea shuffled into the room like a marionette, reaching to pull Mr. Byers up by his hair, her eyes unblinking.

"Stop!" An unseen hand grabbed her from behind, jerking her from the room. A well-placed foot kicked the door shut.

Sally shrank away with an exasperated shriek, leaving Bea to face Miss Sara alone.

"What's gotten into you?" Sara hissed, yanking Bea to a cart. The older woman poured water and a generous amount of bleach into a basin, then grabbed Bea's wrists and dunked her hands in the solution. "Never mind. I know, you can't write." She snatched a rag and dipped it in the bleach water. "Close your eyes!" her voice snapped, wiping Bea's face none too gently with the pungent rag. "Now dry off." She thrust a clean towel at her. "That was supposed to be our last room. Why did you go in there?"

Beatrice sighed and drew out her slate.

I WAS CURIOUS

Miss Sara pursed her lips. "Now you know—a dead man." She shook her head and turned to Patrick. "Call down the dumbwaiter to Wheatley. Tell him we need Mrs. Eisner." She turned back to Bea. "That was a reckless thing to do. You've got to follow directions. Otherwise, I'll have to find someone else."

Bea widened her eyes. She raced to put down the words.

I'LL ~~TALK TO~~ DO BETTER

She couldn't allow Sally to endanger her job again.

Miss Sara stared at her. "You promise to follow orders?"

PROMISE

She took a deep breath. "I don't want to break up the team before we even get started. You push the cart. Let's get the rest of the supplies. We're already behind schedule. Mrs. Eisner will take care of Mr. Byers."

Bea steered the trolley back down the hall. She got a second chance. Miss Sara was more than a boss—she was a friend.

Perhaps, a better friend than Sally.

Chapter Nineteen

With both carts fully loaded, Sara, Beatrice and Patrick stood outside of Room Ten. Sara looked at her notes. The occupant was Maxine Hiebert. "This is a delicate woman with cancer of the blood," she said to her companions. "We must treat her gently."

A door closed down the hall. "Sara!" Mrs. Eisner removed dust masks and gloves from their hooks on the door. "Mr. Byers has passed. We'll have to sanitize his room after the mortician has retrieved his body." She waved and headed downstairs.

Bea held up her slate.

THANK YOU FOR NOT TELLING ON ME

Sara gave her a serious look. "This can't happen again."

Bea nodded, eyes lowered.

Sara knocked on Mrs. Heibert's door, and the three entered.

The room was gray with plaster walls and one tall window. It held a hospital bed, rolling table that could extend over the bed, nightstand, raised potty chair, white-painted rocker, and a straightback chair in the corner. A white-haired lady with dull hazel eyes and skin as withered as old parchment sat with the bed cranked to a sitting position, an open Bible propped on pillows before her. Gloria had been here earlier giving the resident her pain medicine.

She crept into the room and curtsied. "Good morning, Mrs. Hiebert. My name is Sara." She gestured behind her. "This is Beatrice and the young man at the door is—"

"Maxie!" Patrick charged at the frail woman, his arms outstretched.

Mrs. Hiebert glanced up as Patrick smothered her in a tight hug.

Sara rushed to separate the two. Patrick was squeezing much too tight. But Maxine clung to him as well, a quiet smile spread on otherwise drawn features.

Sara grabbed Patrick's shoulder. "Be gentle! You're crushing her!"

With surprising tenderness, he lowered her onto a mound of pillows. The gray woman lay on her back, eyes closed, thin chest rising and falling. At last, she said in a voice heavy with emotion, "Thank you for bringing Patrick to me. I'm so blessed." Tears rolled down sunken cheeks.

Patrick turned to Sara. "Maxie is my friend. My *best* friend."

Sara stepped back. "You know each other?"

Maxine wiped away flowing tears. "Patrick and I met four years ago. I sold tickets for the movie theater in Salina at the time. Patrick was our best customer."

Sara grabbed an arm of the rocker. "Amazing."

Maxine gazed at Patrick. "How did you find me?"

Patrick shrugged, unkempt hair falling across his forehead.

Sara stepped forward to place Patrick's chubby hands around Maxine's thin fingers. "I have good news. Patrick lives downstairs. The three of us started work today serving meals to the residents on this floor. So, you'll be seeing a lot of him."

Maxine's eyes lowered. "Except for a little water, I don't eat much these days. Not much of an appetite, but I'd love for Patrick—all of you—to visit. Being alone is worse than the pain."

"We'll be coming often," Sara said. "But we should get working."

Patrick grabbed the basin, emptied it in the big enamel pot and refilled from the pitcher. "Can I stay with Maxie when we're finished?"

"We still have eight more rooms to go. Afterward—with Mrs. Hiebert's permission—you can visit with your friend."

He groaned, his lower lip stuck out.

Maxine brushed his arm. "Young man, you have a job to do. Other people are depending on you."

"I know," Patrick said. "They need me 'cause I'm *strong*."

Sara hid her smile. This was becoming a litany for the man-child.

Fifteen minutes later, the three were finished. Maxine's room smelled of pine oil and bleach. As Patrick and Beatrice rolled out their carts, Maxine motioned for Sara to remain behind. "I need your help. You must talk to Patrick for me. Tell him I'm dying. He needs to know, but I can't bear to tell him. Will you do this for me, dear?"

Sara paled. "I'm not sure I can do that, Mrs. Hiebert."

Maxine's hand gripped hers with surprising strength. "Please. You have a way with him. He listens to you."

Sara swallowed. Maxine's eyes bored into her

heart. "I'll find a way to tell him, Mrs. Hiebert."

She placed Sara's hand against her cheek. "Thank you. I don't feel alone anymore. God has sent me a guardian angel. And you are His hand and feet. Bless you for bringing him to me."

"I don't..." How could she explain her doubts to this devout woman? Mrs. Hiebert suffered constant pain, yet she seemed armored with unshakeable faith. It was unfathomable why a caring God would put a poor old woman through such torment. She stood firm, like a rock. It was a rare privilege to meet such a genuine person. "Thank you, Mrs. Hiebert."

Sara turned away before Maxine saw the tears.

Chapter Twenty

Larry Bigger worked the third floor Tuesday morning, sorting a delivery of hand tools and nails. He'd spent the morning carting merchandise up from the dock. The Old Man had lectured him the day before about customers shopping. "People will buy an item they might need while looking for something else," he said. So, Larry found some work gloves to display along with the tools. Fat chance his father will notice.

Donning a work apron, he cut the drawstring from a bag of nails with a pocketknife and dumped the contents into a large wooden bin. The nails fell with a jangling thump. Four bags to go.

Running footsteps on the concrete floor raced toward him. A kid with a newsboy cap stared at him for a moment, then pointed back the way he came. "Hey, Mister! Your car is leaking gas, and some fella is standing next to it smoking a butt. You'd better take a look. Imagine a car like that catching fire!" The kid turned tail, sprinting down the steps.

Larry pocketed his knife. With visions of his precious Chevy in flames, he hustled out the front door and ran down the street to the parked Roadster. No fire or smell of fumes. A walk around the vehicle showed no sign of trouble. Taking off his panama, Larry peeked under the rear bumper. Everything seemed in order.

He examined his baby one more time, scratching

his head. With a pat on the hood, he headed back to the store, passing a man reading a newspaper. *The stupid kid ought to be throttled.* Larry mounted the stairs and reentered the store.

****

Jason smiled to himself. *That was easy.* He refolded the newspaper. A block away, Michael paid the newsboy a quarter, returning a few minutes later. "Did you see the car?"

Jason nodded. "It's the spiffy Chevrolet at the end of the block."

They sauntered past an alley, hands in pockets. Michael whistled. "Very snazzy." Ahead sat a Roadster with a silver paint job.

Jason walked around the front appraising the flashy car. The windshield had several fine cracks on the passenger-side corner. All came together to form a lopsided Y. "Michael, look at this." His brother peered into the driver's window. "Something cracked the windshield."

A car door clicked shut.

Michael sat looking about inside the clean looking Roadster.

Did anybody notice them? If so, they'd have to leave in a hurry. But the few passersby paid them no heed. Michael didn't seem like he was finding anything. *Hurry it up.* They couldn't stay here much longer.

Jason tapped on the driver's window.

Michael cranked open the glass. "Can't you see I'm busy?"

"Found anything?"

"Nothing yet. The car's clean. No trash. It smells like soap in here."

"We need to get out of here."

"Give me a chance…" His brother scrambled to the passenger side, peering at the upholstery by the window—even sniffing at it. Then he bent over, gazing at the seats, especially on the driver's side. Finally she sat up, a dazed look on his face. He emerged from the car, a bit pale, but his jaw set. He looked back inside.

What gives? He acts like he seen a ghost. "Any luck?" Jason asked.

Michael nodded. "We have to find her." His voice was low and intense.

Jason arched an eyebrow. "Do I detect a change in attitude?"

"You could say that."

"Tell me about it on the bus."

"I'm walking home. I have to think—to believe."

Jason faced him, putting both arms on Michael's shoulders. "Believe in what?"

Michael's worried eyes met his. "There's blood in the car. Sara's blood."

"You think she's hurt?"

Michael swallowed. "Hurt…I just hope she's alive."

Chapter Twenty-One

Sara, Bea, and Patrick came to the last room. Sara read the name from her sheet, "Cyrus Eugene Evans." His room sat across the hall from Mr. Byers. Gloria called him a wife and child beater. He had lost his family. Now he was alone with dementia stealing the last thing he had left. His memories. Who could be more alone than that?

After knocking, the three entered. Sara saw the old man feigning sleep, watching them through cracked lids. She gave him her warmest smile. Both eyes scrunched shut.

"Good morning, Mr. Evans. I know you're awake. We've brought you some breakfast. But first, Patrick will help you to the wooden throne." Sara gestured to the potty chair.

Cyrus scowled, opening his eyes.

Beatrice retrieved the used basin, dumping its contents in the big enamel pot. Patrick stood by to help Cyrus out of bed. Sara placed a new pitcher of water on the nightstand, then faced Mr. Evans with her hands on her hips. "Time to get up, Mr. Evans. As soon as you're finished with your business, we'll serve you a nice bowl of milk toast."

"Don't touch nothin'." His raucous voice screeched like an angry blue jay.

Sara stepped back. "What would you like us to

do?"

He poked his head forward and thrust a quivering finger at her. "Get out. I know who you are. You said you hated me. You never wanted to see me again. Now, you come back."

Beatrice took a quiet step toward the door. Sara stared at the fuming old man with the cantankerous moods. "We're here to help you."

Hiking himself to a sitting position, Evans pulled the rolling table close to form a barrier. "Don't pretend you don't know who I am. Have you come for me? Is that why you're here?"

"You have me mistaken, Mr. Evans. I've just been given this job yesterday."

"Stop it!" he screeched. "Quit calling me Mr. Evans. You know who I am!"

Beatrice had one hand on the doorknob and shrugged when Sara glanced at her.

"Tell me. Who are you?" asked Sara.

Evans snorted in disgust. "Oh, I get it. Pretending not to know me. You've grown uppity, just like your mother. And you act as if I don't exist, yet here you are. I'm your blood, you ungrateful runt. Christ in a bucket," he growled. "*Look* at me!" He shoved the rolling table, sending it rattling across the floor.

Sara gazed at him. "Who?"

"I'm your father."

Chapter Twenty-Two

Wednesday, April 10, 1935

"We shouldn't wait any longer," Jason McGurk said, his eyes steely under pinched brows. "Let's lure Larry to a secluded spot and beat the truth out of him."

During yesterday's trip home, Michael filled him in on the faint signs of blood on the seat and upholstery. Sara had received a beating, and somehow Larry got bloodied as well. So much for his story about cutting himself shaving. From the scent of soap in the too-clean Roadster, Larry did his best to hide what had happened. But what *did* happen? That was their task: to find out.

Michael set his glass of milk on the breakfast table. "Name the last time you've been in a fight. Grade school? For all we know Larry may be a boxer. Stick to the plan: trace Sara's footsteps and see where they lead us. I'm sure they lead to Larry, but knowing how gives us an edge. We need to go back to the café and find out if Sis was there."

Katherine cracked the last two eggs into a hot skilled and stirred the mixture. "Michael's right. You can't go off half-cocked, looking for a fight."

Michael couldn't quite hide his smug grin. "The waitress may give us a lead."

Jason imagined Larry flat on his back with a broken nose. "I still think he would cave in with a little persuasion."

"Then again, he could play dumb," Michael said. "The clues in the Roadster mean nothing unless we can get him to talk. And to do that, we need to know when and where they met on Sunday."

Jason held a hand up in submission. "We'll play it your way. But if we come up empty-handed, I'm going after him."

A door down the hallway opened and closed. Sam entered the kitchen, all smiles. "Boys, I've got an errand for you this morning." He sat down at the table. Katherine set a plate of scrambled eggs and potato cakes before him.

Jason glanced at his father. "What are we doing, Pop?"

Sam explained between mouthfuls. "Go to Ziegler's car lot. It's at Douglas and Grove. I've struck a deal with the owner and will settle with him later today. You and Michael are to arrive by nine o'clock. He'll show you the vehicle I bought, a Mercedes cabriolet. Beautiful car, quite a step up from that assembly-line Model A. You're to drive it straight home and give it a good washing. I can't get the car myself because I'm in meetings all day."

"Sounds great," Jason muttered.

"Swell!" Michael clapped his hands.

Jason balled his hands into fists. Talking about a new car with his sister missing seemed callous. "Sara still hasn't called home, Pop. I'm worried about her. She might be in trouble."

His father's voice was a low rumble. "Sara has brought shame upon this family. She must face the consequences."

"She's my sister." Jason bit his lip. "You can be upset with her, but no matter what she did, she's still your daughter."

Sam McGurk sipped some coffee. "The subject is closed. I've given you an errand to do. Get my automobile. Or you can leave as well. It might do you some good to get a taste of the world. You decide."

"I'll get your car," Jason said. "After that, I want nothing to do with it."

Sam McGurk studied Jason over the rim of his cup. "You've grown a backbone these last few days, son. And you look a helluva lot like your mother when you get your dander up." His voice was conversational, but his eyes held a cold light. "You've forced the topic far enough. Now drop it."

Jason slumped in his seat. To continue would be dangerous.

Five minutes later, Sam left for work. Jason slipped on his sister's apron and washed the breakfast dishes while Michael dried.

Katherine wiped her hands on a towel. "Before you leave, there's a picture I think you should have." She left the kitchen for a minute, coming back with a crinkly, square envelope. She handed Jason a towel. "Dry your hands. Here's a photograph you can show to the waitress."

Jason slid out a snapshot of Sara smiling into the camera. "This was taken eighteen months ago when your father first gave Sara the job of supervising the Mailroom. There was even a write-up in the paper about the new office. This picture went with that article."

"Let me see." Michael gazed at the photograph.

"She looks really happy."

Jason studied the picture. "That job suited her well." He placed the snapshot in his wallet. "This will help." He turned to Michael. "We'd better catch our bus. If we hurry, we can talk to the waitress and still get to the car lot by nine."

Chapter Twenty-Three

Maxine Hiebert laid her Bible on the nightstand as Sara, Patrick, and Bea entered her room. Sara opened the windows to let in fresh air. Patrick brought in a small bowl of gelatin, and Bea switched out containers from the nightstand. Concerned that Maxine's book might get wet, Sara moved the Bible to the chair in the corner. It lay open to a family history page. Maxine had filled out names and dates sometime in the past. The flowing script centered at the top of the page read

"Deaths"

Below was an entry:

"Pearson L. Hiebert
Birth Place: Sacramento, California
Birth Date: September 14, 1884
Death: April 10, 1929
Age: 45
Burial: Monument Hill Cemetery, Denver, Colorado"

Oh, my. Maxine's husband died six years ago today.

Sara returned to the bed to wash Maxine's hands. A minute later, she arranged a bowl of gelatin and drinking cup on the table. Patrick rolled it in front of the delicate woman. Bea cranked the bed to a sitting position. Maxine could choose not to eat if she wished, but how could she survive much longer without food? It was prudent not to force the issue.

Maxine nudged the gelatin away. "Thank you, but I'm not hungry. You could give me three of those orange pills, though. Two barely dims the pain."

Sara removed the pills from a shelf over the headboard. "I'd like to, but I need to check with Mrs. Eisner. The doctor has you down for two pills, four times a day. I need permission to change that." She gave the sick woman a tiny paper cup containing the small, round tablets. Maxine tipped her head back, took the pills, then sipped some water through a straw.

Sara replaced the bottle. "Can we can get you anything?"

"Bring Patrick closer." Mrs. Hiebert held out a thin arm. "I want to hold his hand before he goes."

Patrick shuffled forward while Sara returned the Bible. "I saw the entry about your husband."

Maxine bowed her head. "I've been musing about Pearce all morning, reflecting on our life together. We were married nearly twenty-four wonderful years."

"How did you meet?" Sara asked.

"We met at a dance hall in Austin. I was singing on stage with two other girls. We were part of a vaudeville show that traveled the South. It was November 1904. Vaudeville season was over until March, so we found work at a honky-tonk. One Saturday night, this bear of a man in red flannel and dungarees entered with his crew of boomers."

"Boomers?" Sara asked.

"Telegraph linemen. A dangerous job, and the men could be boisterous when looking for fun. Soon, this man came stomping on stage and asked me to dance. I said no, but the other girls pushed me off, and I landed in his arms. I danced the rest of that night, and I don't remember touching the floor. The two of us became inseparable. I learned to take the joshing from his crew and trade good-natured insults with the best of them." Maxine beamed. For a moment, Sara glimpsed the lively, youthful woman within the withered husk. "Seven months later, we were married."

"I imagine your husband's work kept him away from home."

"No. I traveled the country with his crew while they planted poles and strung wire for the railroad. Later, they moved to building long-lines for Ma Bell. Peace was a careful foreman. I never worried about him getting hurt. Not until Colorado Power hired his crew." The aged singer closed her eyes.

Sara sensed a turn in the story. "Maybe we should let you rest."

"No, please." Maxine held out her free hand, seeking Sara's. "It feels good to talk about the old days."

"You were in vaudeville?"

"For several years before I met Pearce. Two other girls and I developed a singing act with trained birds. We called ourselves The Canary Sisters. Onstage, we wore huge flowerpot hats. Each had a live canary perched on top. The audience gave us song requests, and we'd take turns singing the lyrics. The canaries would hop onto the hat of the person singing, except my canary always returned to my hat. It never failed to get titters from the crowd. The girls would fake irritation, and the anger would build until we'd staged a big argument late in the act. In the end, we made up and sang our finale."

"It sounds fun. I've seen acts in theaters between movies, but I've never seen a full vaudeville show."

Maxine sighed. "Times have changed. Movies have taken over. But if you follow radio, you can still catch the best of vaudeville on some of the variety shows. Ed Wynn, Gracie Allen, and Frank Morgan all got their start on the little stage."

"That was a good story."

"It was an exciting time." Maxine turned to gaze at Sara. "But I want to tell you about Pearce. What happened to him."

"I don't want to stir up bad memories for you, Mrs. Hiebert."

Maxine laid her palm on the Bible. "I cherish every memory of Pearce. Even his passing. When I die, no one but you will know his story."

Sara gave a solemn nod. "I would be honored to keep alive his memory."

Maxine sipped water from her cup. "Pearce and I wanted children, but it never happened. We lived like nomads, going wherever the next job beckoned. He and his crew were a can-do outfit, picking their own jobs and loyal only to themselves. Colorado Power sought them out for a big, dangerous job: rebuilding the electrical transmission lines from the Colorado River to Denver. I begged him to stick with the long-lines. But this was a challenge Pearce couldn't walk away from."

Sara sucked in a breath. "I know so little about electricity, let alone how it gets moved around."

Maxine gave an impish smile. "We know so little about our world, don't we? Pearce and his crew needed to replace fifteen hundred miles of high voltage wire as well as sections of the towers over three mountain passes. Pearce was attaching wire to an insulator when the wooden strut he stood on broke." Maxine covered her eyes with shaking fingers.

Sara leaned over, touching the older woman's brow. "I'm very sorry, Mrs. Hiebert."

Maxine took a breath before continuing. "After the funeral, there was some trouble with the settlement. Pearce's crew threatened to strike unless the power company compensated me. I did get a handsome sum, but I'd have returned it all and more to have my husband back."

"It must have been hard moving on."

Maxine nodded. "My plan was to move to Texas and look up old friends. I got as far as Salina taking a job selling tickets at the new movie theater there. It wasn't long before I met Patrick. He came to the show twice a week, plus the Saturday matinee. We often sat together, and I'd explain some of the scenes he didn't understand. We watched movies together for close to three years. Didn't we Patrick?"

"Lots of movies." Patrick stroked Maxine's arm.

"Last summer, I felt sick much of the time. The doctor and said I had leukemia. With all the days I missed at work, my boss let me go. Treatments and tests drained my savings. Five months later, I became destitute. Saline County closed their poor farm in 1932, so they sent me here. Now I see why. God has reunited Patrick and me. It's a wonder to see His sovereign plan at work."

Sara gazed at this marvelous woman. How could she remain so steadfast in her faith? Sara placed the open Bible on her lap. "Pearce must have been a good man."

"He was the best." Maxine closed her eyes. "I can't wait to see him again."

Chapter Twenty-Four

The breakfast rush was in full swing as Jason and Michael entered the Farmland Café. Jason scanned the eatery to find a booth. *The place is packed.* He settled for a cramped table for two in the middle of the hubbub. He and Michael took their seats and flipped their coffee cups over as the waitress approached. She filled the cups, set down water glasses, and produced menus tucked under her arm. There were deepening lines around the eyes and mouth and lipstick that could stop traffic. Probably Mom's age. The name stitched on her collar read CARRIE. Jason smiled. They hadn't even ordered yet, and they'd already found their source.

Carrie retrieved a pad from her apron and a small stub of a pencil from behind her ear. "You boys know what you want? We've got a breakfast special with eggs, toast, bacon, and coffee for forty-nine cents. Or you can order off the menu."

Michael returned the menu. "I'll have the special with an extra side of scrambled eggs."

She turned to Jason. "And what about you, champ?"

"I'll take an order of toast." He took a breath, hanging onto the menu. "I was wondering. Did you work here last Sunday?"

Carrie's eyes sharpened. "Who's asking?"

"We're looking for our sister." Jason fished Sara's

photograph from his wallet. "She may have been here at that morning."

The waitress peered at the snapshot. "Nice hair." She pointed with her pencil to the front of the diner. "The lady sat at the counter. Two seats from the register."

Michael jerked to attention. "Was she here with anyone?"

Several men in overalls sat at a table nearby. Carrie snatched the menu from Jason. "The lady was alone. Listen, I've got customers." She bustled off, pad in hand.

Michael leaned his head over the table. "I think we hit the jackpot."

Jason pursed his lips. "Let's hear what else she has to say first."

"I pictured her being younger. Isn't Carrie supposed to be a name for a younger girl?"

"Not what you expected?" Jason suppressed a grin. "Remember Carrie Nation? I'm not sure she was ever young."

Michael thumped the table. "I've seen those pictures, an old maid with a hatchet in one hand, a Bible in the other, and a face that would turn a buzzard to stone. She could walk into a saloon and clear the place out by smiling."

"You mean with nothing but a smile?"

Michael pointed a finger at Jason, biting his lip. "Now don't get carried away."

Jason laughed, nodding. "You got me there. That was a good one."

Leaning back in his seat, Michael smirked. "You broke first, so you get to pay."

"I paid last time. Next trip we're going dutch. You eat like a horse."

"Maybe so, but you're the one whinnying."

"And you listen to too much radio."

Ten minutes later, Carrie brought their orders. "Your sister called a cab. I remember that because I told her cabs were slow on Sunday mornings."

Jason nodded. "How did she seem to you?"

"She seemed...in a hurry. Anxious for the taxi to arrive."

"What time was that?" Michael asked.

"You boys act like G-men. A little after nine, maybe."

Michael leaned forward. "Did she mention where she was going?"

She put a hand on her hip. "No, but I can tell you what she ordered."

Jason's mouth quivered. "He thinks he's Sam Spade."

"Well, I've lost a no-good husband. Maybe you can find him." She shooed away the comment. "My customers need tending to. I hope you find your sister." She bustled to another table.

Jason sipped his coffee. Sara took a cab—going where? They needed to pin down her destination. Making the connection was vital. The cab company could provide the answer. He put down his cup. "Finish up, Michael. We need to get Pop's car and then plan our next move."

Chapter Twenty-Five

Sara, Patrick, and Beatrice rolled their carts into Cyrus Evans' room. "Good morning, sir. We have oatmeal this morning." Sara sniffed the air, frowning. All the upstairs rooms had a tainted outhouse stink until they changed out the "white owl." This odor was much stronger. Sara checked under the relief chair. The oval pot was clean.

The old man had messed his nest. He hadn't done that yesterday. Why today?

"Mr. Evans? We need to clean you up and change your sheets before we can serve breakfast."

Cyrus stirred under his covers. One eye and some wispy white hair poked out from between clenched fingers holding his blankets. "Stop calling me that. I'm your father. Do I have to get out of this bed and take a switch to you?"

Sara peered at him, frowning. He had been emphatic about being her father for the last two days. Always angry and belligerent, yet he cowered beneath his blanket like a small child. "If you like, we can come back at lunch and leave you in your messy bed. I'll give your breakfast to the pigs."

Evans stuck out his head, scowling. "You do that and I'll take what's down here and smear it over the walls. You and your little monkeys'll be cleaning this room all day."

Sara stepped back, mouth agape.

Evans hooted, slapping the bed. "You should see the look on your face."

Bea held a basin of water while Patrick stood at the food cart. Sara turned to her helpers. "Both of you leave the room. I'll call you back in a few minutes. Mr. Evans and I will be having a little talk."

They left, and Sara closed the door.

"You have no audience now, Mr. Evans. It's just us." She opened a window for some fresh air. "There has to be a reason for soiling your bed. What is it?"

Cyrus was no longer scowling. He opened his mouth, but no words came. He stared at her; lowering his eyelids. The old man laid down, as if going back to sleep.

Sara stepped to his side, reaching for his arm.

Cyrus snapped awake, focusing on her like an old vulture sensing movement. "You called me a mean drunk and wished you never married me. You said both you and the brat were moving east. I couldn't hurt either of you again. It would have been easy to stop you—but why bother? I got along fine without the harping and the whimpering."

Sara rubbed her temple. Who was she supposed to be now? Five minutes ago, she was his daughter. Was she now his separated wife? "Mr. Evans, I'm a resident of this house, same as you. We're not related."

The old man snorted. "Don't lie to me. Is the runt here too? I can't believe you came back. There's only one reason for it. To get even. Well, two can play at that game." Evans closed his eyes.

Was he feigning sleep? Sara stepped back. Cyrus spoke again, this time his voice was calm and deliberate. "You look so much like her."

Sara stepped closer, bending over him. "Like who, Mr. Evans?"

"Your mother. Same hair. Same uppity nature. So you'd better mind your tongue."

"Relax, Mr. Evans. Your wife isn't here. We'll get you cleaned up so you can eat." Sara crept to the bedroom door and opened it. "I think he's calmer. Let's give him a sponge bath, change his bedding and his nightshirt. His meal will be cold, but that can't be helped."

Bea raised an eyebrow, pointing at the still figure.

Sara blew out a breath. "He's a befuddled old man, still looking for ways to get even with a woman he hasn't seen in decades. And he thinks his daughter is out for vengeance. Don't take anything he says to heart. His mind is dwindling away."

Twenty minutes later, Cyrus sat in his rocker with clean bedclothes. Sara and Bea drew fresh sheets over his bed. The old codger shrugged off Patrick's help and shuffled on his own back to bed. Bea cranked up the bed while Sara rolled the table in front of Cyrus. He shoveled oatmeal into his mouth. Some of it dribbled down his chin. Sara turned away, feeling her stomach churn, and she busied herself with the patient chart.

After breakfast, Evans snuggled in his clean bed and closed his eyes.

Patrick and Beatrice filed out. Sara was about to close the door when the old man pulled himself to a sitting position, shaking a finger. "You people need a bath. You all stink!"

Chapter Twenty-Six

Jason and Michael stood in Ziegler's car lot gazing at the shiny Mercedes. Jason had to admit, it was a splendid looking car. So this was the contraption that was more important than Sara, at least in Pop's eyes. *Probably runs like a dream.* The German-built automobile was a glossy red four-door cabriolet with a slender grill and two large headlamps mounted on a shiny steel bar. When Jason started the engine, it purred like a kitten.

Mr. Ziegler stroked the fender. "It's a Mercedes-Benz W18. The W stands for 'Works.' This marvelous machine has a six-cylinder, 2867 cc side-valve engine, producing 59 horsepower at 3200 rpm. It has a four-speed transmission—"

"How do I put the roof down?" asked Jason.

The dealer showed him the mechanism that folded the roof into the trunk. "I've been instructed to tell you boys to drive this vehicle directly home."

Jason studied the car's dashboard. His fingers itched to feel the steering wheel. "We will, Mr. Ziegler."

"Be sure to tell your father that he is probably the only driver in Kansas who owns a Model 290."

"We'll let him know he made a good choice." Jason put the car in Drive and circled the car lot, heading for Douglas Avenue. The luxurious car accelerated smoothly in traffic. Steering responded with just a touch of the wheel. How fast could this chariot go? He ached to know.

Michael turned a knob at the center of the polished wood-grained dashboard. "This car has a radio. Can you beat that?"

Jason touch the gas, savoring the response of the engines. "There's probably no room for a cubbyhole."

Michael shook his head. "Don't see one. Are we headed home?"

Jason shrugged. "You got a better idea?"

"I just turned on the radio. It'll take a minute for the tubes to warm. Let's circle Riverside Park and hear how it sounds."

Jason turned the car north. As they drove through curving streets lined with budding shade trees, the radio came to life. Michael tuned into a jazz station. They toured past a playground, a zoo, and a pagoda. People stopped what they were doing to gaze at the car as Michael waved back. On the radio, Mildred Bailey sang the newest thing called *swing*. Jason tooted the horn. He had to admit, driving the sleek machine was fun.

Driving on a spring day in the park and listening to catchy music—the mood was intoxicating. Families waved to them, and Jason honked and waved back. This was a blast! They circled the park two for times before Jason steered the car to Parker Street. He turned into the drive still blasting the horn. His mother came out the back door wiping her hands on a towel.

Jason stopped the engine, and Michael jumped out. "Mom! What do you think?" He ran up to her, pointing over his shoulder. "Isn't she a beauty?"

Jason joined them, studying his mother.

She frowned at the vehicle. "It all depends on your idea of beauty."

"It must have cost a pretty penny," Michael said.

"I wouldn't care if it was free," Katherine said. "The price is still too high." She turned back to the house. "You boys come in. I'll make you something to drink."

Jason gestured to the vehicle. "Pop wants us to wash the car. We'll be in soon."

"Cleaning it all day won't make a bit of difference. It would still be dirty." The screen door slammed behind her as she entered the house.

Michael glanced sideways at Jason. "What's wrong with the car?"

The excitement of driving the beast ebbed like a receding wave. "Pop bought an expensive car within a week of kicking Sara out. Mom's right. The Mercedes is tainted." Jason sighed. "Come on. Help me get the top up. Let's get this over with."

Chapter Twenty-Seven

Sara drank from a dipper hanging off the hand pump in the big kitchen sink. Mrs. Robson washed pie tins from the infirmary. It was nearly three o'clock, two hours before supper. Peering out the back door window, she could see James Eisner, the overseer, leaving a tall, castle-like structure, some distance from the house. "I'm going outside to get some air."

She slipped on a jacket hanging from a peg and exited the house. The sleeves went to her fingers. Still, it felt warm against the chill air. She stepped off the porch and closed the distance between her and Mr. Eisner. "Hello, I'm Sara McGuire. Thank you for helping me last Sunday."

Eisner wore faded overalls, a brown shirt of heavy cotton, and a dusty wide-brimmed hat. He stopped when Sara approached. "You were in bad shape that day, young lady. Glad I could help."

"I'm feeling much better now. This is the first time I've stepped out back. Could you show me around the farm, if you're not too busy?"

The wind came up, and James grabbed his hat. "Not much to see. Are you up for a walk?

"If you don't mind going a little slow."

"I'm in no hurry. We've got all the basics—a good barn, a coop and a pigpen, an old smokehouse, a fair-sized garden, and lots of pasture. Where would you like

189

to start?"

Sara gestured behind him. "I was curious about that stone tower."

"The smokehouse? We can peek at it."

They ambled toward the circular limestone building. Thin trails of smoke danced about a tall pipe jutting from the top. A gust of wind kicked up dirt and debris. The stiff breeze made walking over the uneven ground an effort. She jammed her hands in her pockets. "Is it always this windy?"

Eisner grunted. "It can gust a lot harder than this sometimes, but it's the flying dirt that's the real problem."

"Wichita has had dust storms, but not like the ones I've heard about southwest."

"It's the drought. Four years and no end in sight. Dust storms aren't common here, but blowing dust is."

"What causes them—the dust storms, I mean?"

Mr. Eisner bent over, picking up a handful of dirt, letting it fall through his fingers. "A lifetime ago, this land was all wind and prairie grass, then farming came with the settlers. Growers plowed up the grass to make room for crops. With a reliable tractor, a farmer could plow more ground in a day than a horse-drawn plow could in a week. Farms got bigger, and that meant more plowed ground. When the rains stopped, the high winds still blew, and the dirt took to the sky."

"Have you ever been in a dust storm? A bad one?"

"Once. Gloria and I were visiting family in Garden City. My brother runs a maintainer for Finney County clearing the roads of windblown dirt. I was riding with him when a ridge of gray clouds swept over the horizon. Tom shut down the machine, and we ran for cover. We found a shack with a cast iron triangle hanging out front. The duster was on top of us. We banged on the door, but no one answered. So I grabbed the rod to ring the triangle. A bolt of electricity knocked me clean off the porch. Tom told me later there's a static charge in the dry air that worsens when a duster approaches. Touching metal will jolt a person, stop a car from running, or even kill plants. We ended up breaking into that shack because no one was home."

The smokehouse was just ahead. Attached to the back of the tower was a cast iron box, hot to the touch. The smell of smoked pork lingered. "We're curing a hog we slaughtered last fall." Mr. Eisner produced a key, unfastened a padlock, and opened the door. "Don't step inside. The floor is slick with grease."

Sara looked in. A fat carcass hung from a hook chained to a rafter. Her mouth watered as she drew in the aroma of smoked meat. "When will it be ready?" Memories of Easter Sunday ham made her long for home.

"Soon. The longer the better when it comes to curing."

Sara stepped back as the overseer locked the building.

"I'll show you the barn," he said. "Dutch is there. The youngsters from the house are by the pigpen. Our sow is about to have piglets."

The barn was red, trimmed in white. They stopped outside the open double doors. "Excuse me. I need to check on my hog. Dutch is inside. He can show you around." Mr. Eisner sauntered down the side of the barn, disappearing around the corner.

Sara peered inside the darkened interior. A

shadowy figure shuffled about. She crept closer, letting her eyes get used to the gloom. Dutch was cleaning out an animal stall using a wide pitchfork with over a dozen tongs. A heavy, pungent smell hung in the air. The tramp waved to her but kept working. Behind him was a pile of straw and manure. A large animal stirred in the next stall. What was it? She tiptoed around Dutch's work and peeked around the corner.

Before her was the massive rump of a Holstein blithely munching hay. The cow swung its ponderous head, peering at her from one side. A wet, organic flapping came from the cow's backside, and a rich, malodorous cloud enveloped her. Sara jumped back, gasping. Stabbing pain from bruised ribs was one thing, but cow farts were an altogether new kind of unpleasantness.

The ripe, earthy smell of dung was even stronger. She glanced down. A wave of dizziness hit her. *Oh, no. I'm in it!* She stood in a mound of cow poop, her shoes heavy with the stuff. Tears rolled down her cheeks. How was she going to explain this to Mrs. Eisner?

Dutch leaned his manure fork against the cow pen, moseyed over, and held out a hand. "Take a big step toward me."

Sara lunged, nearly falling into his arms. Clods of manure clung to her shoes.

Dutch led her to a bale of straw near the big doors. "You've just met Cloris. I think she likes you."

"I can't say the feeling is mutual." Sara slumped down on the bale staring at her ruined shoes.

"She's a gentle beast, unlike the sow." Dutch knelt to take off her shoes. "I'll clean these for you. Be back in a few minutes." Dutch ambled out the barn door, passing James on his way in.

The overseer pointed to the back of the barn. "Dutch, check on the youngsters when you get a chance. I told them to stay clear of the hog pen. That sow will bite off a finger if given half a chance." Eisner turned to Sara. "Would you like to join them and see some pigs being born?"

Sara shook her head. "Dutch took my shoes to clean. I didn't watch where I stepped."

Mr. Eisner glanced at her bare feet. "I'll stay until he returns. You can sit with the youngsters later, if you wish."

Sara smiled. "That's kind of you." James Eisner seemed more personable than Gloria. An unusual pair. What had brought them together? "Did you grow up around here?"

The overseer leaned back, blowing out a breath. "I grew up outside Abilene. Got my first paying job in the train yards, prodding cattle off the trains, getting them watered, and loading them back on the train for Kansas City."

"Is Abilene where you met Mrs. Eisner?"

James Eisner rubbed the side of his head. "You could call it that."

"What happened?"

"One of the other cowpokes dared me a day's pay to hogtie a steer. I took that bet. Never steer-rassled before, but I was game to try. Just about had his legs lashed together when that sack of beef sent me to the new hospital with a cracked skull. The first thing I saw when I came to was this pretty little nurse cleaning me with a sponge." His eyes brightened. "Well…let's say I opened my mouth once too often, and she had me walking the halls morning and evening saying bed was the last place I needed to be. I was back working in a week. If I ever got hurt again, I wanted her by my side, so I wrote a letter asking for her hand."

Sara's mouth fell open. "You wrote her a marriage proposal?"

"I couldn't bring myself to say that stuff."

She bit a lip before asking. "She must have accepted."

Mr. Eisner stared at the barn's high ceiling. "She had conditions. I had to moderate my language, stay out of the saloons, go to church, and bring flowers on her birthday, but five months later, we were man and wife. Been married now for close to thirty years."

Sara stifled a grin as she imagined a young Gloria taming a brassy youth who fancied himself a cowboy. "Is Mrs. Eisner from Abilene as well?"

"She moved to there with her mother as a child. Her father, I understand, died years ago."

Dutch ambled in and knelt before Sara, slipping clean shoes onto her feet. "Good as new, Miss Sara. I won't even charge you." He gave her a wink.

James Eisner stood and arched his back. "We need to get back to that sow. Care to watch, Miss McGuire?"

"I should get back to the house. Thank you, Mr. Eisner for showing me around. And thank you Dutch for cleaning my shoes."

"My pleasure." Eisner nodded and stepped to the barn door.

Dutch helped Sara to her feet. "I'll have to introduce you to Cloris proper next time."

"Dutch!" Eisner called from the door. "Time's wasting."

The two left.

Sara stood alone in the murky gloom. *What am I doing here?* Farm work was beyond her. She left the barn, making her way back to the house.

She felt so out of place here, but she had nowhere else to go. If only she could go home again, but that meant that, somehow, she had to bridge the rift between her and Daddy. He saw her as a shameful daughter. But he was a neglectful father. Could there be a way to mend their differences? Both would have to change, to make amends. But at what cost?

What was the price of atonement?

Chapter Twenty-Eight

Thursday, April 11, 1935

Sara awoke Thursday morning long before the din of Mrs. Eisner's bell. Today's sackcloth dress was pale yellow with white daisies. Sara slipped into the garment and cinched it with the strip of red cloth Bea provided. It would have to do for this evening's supper with Commissioner Krause—Wendell.

What would she say to him about saving the county farm? The last three days had been a whirlwind of activity with staying on top of the infirmary duties. With breakfast rounds over, she had maybe two hours rest before serving dinner. Another two hours to relax and then supper chores would commence. A grueling schedule. It was hard to think about the next day, let alone two months from now.

But she had to. Her home was about to close, and Wendell asked for her help to keep it open. What could she offer besides encouragement. She was only one resident soon to give up her sanctuary with the others. She had no choice but to stay with relatives and give up her child in seven months.

It wasn't just her. There were Bea and Patrick— and the patients upstairs. All they wanted were a few extra minutes of companionship each day. Who would take care of them when the tenant house closed?

She needed a idea.

The trip into town this evening, gave her an opportunity to write mother and tell her she was safe. No return address, though. A return letter would jeopardize her identity as Sara McGuire. In the time she had left, nothing must interfere with staying here.

Sara lit her lantern, walked to the dining room, and retrieved her stamp and box of stationery. She took the items back to her room and closed the door.

She selected a thin sheet of scented paper, wrote a few lines to her family, stuffed the letter in an envelope of pink roses, and sealed it. Sara was about to affix the stamp when a thought struck her.

What if she could never go home again?

Home meant so many things: family dinners, listening to the radio, and warm baths. *Here* felt like home. Again, the question loomed.

How could she save her home?

Stopping the county's plan to sell the land seemed impossible. But what if someone could buy the tenant house and the land it rested on from the county? A buyer who would let the residents stay. A radio personality could use that sale as a way to increase his fame.

Daddy acted on listener mail when it suited his purpose. She could post a letter to him or—better yet—to Gladys. That would get it noticed. The note would have to grab his interest—and spur him to action.

Sara pulled out another sheet of paper. She couldn't use her name, of course. It would have to be Beatrice. She'd tell her friend later about the letter. Not that it mattered. Hundreds of letters arrived every day at the Mailroom. The chances of Daddy noticing her message were next to zero. Still, it was worth a try.

Word by word, she constructed each paragraph. The breakfast bell rang as she signed Beatrice's name, addressed the envelope, and attached the stamp.

Chapter Twenty-Nine

Jason picked up the kitchen phone after breakfast. Getting Sara's taxi destination would be a simple matter of calling the dispatcher. He picked up the telephone receiver. "Michael, could you look up the number to the cab company?"

Michael retrieved the directory from the cupboard and plunked it on the kitchen table. "Found it." He read the telephone number.

"What are you doing, Jason?" his mother asked. She placed coffee mugs in the cupboard and hung the iron skillet by the stove.

"We know that Sis took a cab. I'm hoping the taxi service will tell us where they took her." Jason dialed.

A chirpy female voice answered. "City Cab."

"I need to get some information about a ride taken last Sunday morning. My sister took a taxi—"

"Let me connect you with my supervisor."

"Yes, I'll—"

Click!

Before he could get the words out, he was talking to dead air.

"What's going on?" Michael asked.

Jason stared at the phone. "I'm not sure. The lady said she would connect me to her supervisor. But it sounded like she hung up."

Katherine sighed. "The telephone company says

direct dialing is more convenient, but I always liked the help of telephone operators. They made sure you were connected to the right party."

Jason raised a hand. "I think someone's on the line."

A harsh, too-loud male voice came from the receiver. "This is Peters. Help you?" The words sounded more like *"'Ep ya?"*

"Hello? My name is Jason McGurk, and I'm trying to locate my missing sister. She took a cab last Sunday downtown. I need to know where the taxi took her."

His mother sat with Michael at the table, giving him an earful. Michael was leaning back in his chair, not liking what she was telling him.

"Give me the information." Peters seemed unhappy but resigned.

"The cab picked her up at the Farmland Café on South Broadway between nine and ten a.m."

"Destination?" the voice asked.

Jason gripped the phone harder. Wasn't this guy paying attention? "Sir, I don't know where the cab went. If I knew that, I wouldn't be calling."

Across the room, Michael gave him a sideways glance.

"You won't get anywhere talking like that."

With an effort, Jason forced himself to remain calm. "Sorry. My sister has been missing for four days. We're at our wit's end. All I want is an address."

"That information is with the dispatcher."

"Then can you transfer me back to her?"

His mother was still giving Michael the third degree, but he was watching Jason.

"Won't do you any good. Our policy is not to give

out information unless the person asking is the law. Are you a cop?"

Jason thumped the back door with a fist. "Why didn't you tell me this in the first place? Can I at least find out who drove last Sunday?"

"'Fraid not. Unless you got a badge."

Jason sighed. "I got nothing."

"We make it a point to answer all police queries. If you're that concerned, you'd be calling the law."

"Yessir." Jason dropped the phone on the hook.

"What happened?" Michael asked.

"I got the runaround. They'll give out information to the law, but no one else." Jason rubbed his eyes. "I was hoping to get that address."

Katherine turned to Jason. "You boys have gone as far as you can. Step aside. Let the police take over."

Jason stared at the back door. Defeat pressed on him like a physical weight. Unless Michael had some bright idea, their search for Sara was over.

Chapter Thirty

The gut-wrenching odor of stale vomit hung in the air as Sara and her crew entered Maxine Hiebert's room. The diminutive woman lay huddled on her side, eyes scrunched shut, the meager contents of her stomach splattered on her pillow. Sara rushed to her side. Tears trickled down the older woman's sunken cheeks; her bloodless lips were pulled back in a grimace.

"Maxie!" Patrick charged forward and grabbed her hand. "What's wrong with her?"

"Mrs. Heibert needs her medicine." Sara reached for the pills on the shelf above the bed.

No bottle.

A cold icicle pierced her stomach. Sara scanned the bed. "Bea, help me find her pill bottle! Patrick, you too!" Panic edged her voice.

Sara patted the bed covers. Nothing. Scouring the floor produced eight pills and a cotton ball. She opened the door to the nightstand. Inside was a large ball of newspaper-wrapped paste smelling of garlic, earth, and rotten leaves.

Beatrice discovered the bottle stopper under the rocker.

"I found it!" Patrick yelled, pulling the empty bottle from beneath Maxine's pillow. Frowning, he handed the container to Sara and turned back to hold

Maxine's hand. Sara checked the chart. The bottle had twenty-four pills left. Sixteen were unaccounted for. She glanced from the chart to Maxine. "Patrick, get Mrs. Eisner. We need help."

Patrick shook his head. "I'm not going."

Sara stepped forward, gripping his arm. "There's no time to argue. Get moving."

Patrick planted his feet, turning away.

A tap on her shoulder. Sara whirled around.

Beatrice held out her slate. I'LL GO. Without waiting for an answer, she scurried from the room.

Sara glanced at Patrick. What was she thinking? Of course, the youth wouldn't leave her side. Sara let out a breath and bent to examine the dying woman.

Maxine's eyes were now open, the irises large but unfocused. Breaths came in short, quick, gasps. Her face lay on a wet splatter of bright orange. Sara moved the soiled part of the pillow away from her nose and mouth. Patrick stroked her arm while wind rattled loose windowpanes.

"Maxine, we're getting the matron."

No response.

The hallway echoed with measured footsteps. The matron strolled in with Beatrice behind her. She glanced at Maxine, then stepped to the nightstand and removed the wrapped wad of paste.

Sara held out the empty bottle. "Maxine somehow managed to get her medicine and—"

"I gathered what happened, child. She's lucky to be alive." Gloria pointed to the spot of orange on the pillow. "She became nauseous—morphine will do that—and regurgitated most of the pills." The matron unwrapped the newspaper. "Help me with this, Sara.

Patrick, you'll have to leave the room." Mrs. Eisner tore off a hunk of the earthy smelling stuff, working it with her hands.

Patrick sniffed the gunk, wrinkling his nose. "I'm not leaving."

"We're about to rub ointment on Mrs. Hiebert. You'll have to step out when we do this."

Sara put a hand on the youth's shoulders. "I'll walk you to the hall. Bea will keep you company."

The matron shook her head. "Beatrice stays. We'll need her help."

Patrick crossed his arms, sulking, but Sara managed to get him out of the room.

"Lock the door."

Sara turned the latch. She eyed the gray paste. "What is that stuff?"

"Oh, this and that. It's a theriac, a salve of sorts. Time's wasting. Soften up the ointment with your hands. You'll be surprised how pliable it gets. Rub it on Mrs. Hiebert's skin. She'll thrash a bit when the theriac begins its work, she'll feel better afterward."

"Shouldn't we call the doctor?"

"Later. Dr. Zwiefel would give her a shot of morphine or even heroin. The theriac will soothe her without making her nauseous. I've been a nurse for thirty years, Miss McGuire. I've learned to appreciate folk medicine."

Sara removed Maxine's gown, and the three rubbed the homemade liniment on chest, arms, and legs. Body heat made the ointment easy to apply. After they finished, Gloria drew covers over Maxine's thin frame. "Now comes the hard part."

"Hard part?" Sara asked.

"You'll see. Go to the foot of the bed. Beatrice, stand on the opposite side and grab her shoulders."

A few minutes passed. Maxine stirred, rocking her head from side to side. A low moan escaped her lips. "Hot…" She kicked the covers, flaying her arms. Sara took a step back, wide-eyed, mouth agape. The scene was nightmarish. Was Maxine having a fit? Was she possessed? Sara stood frozen, heart quickening, ready to bolt for the door.

"Sara! Hold her feet down!" Gloria snapped, gripping one arm and shoulder. "Beatrice, hold her down."

Sara stepped in to grasp her legs. Maxine let out a piercing cry as spasms wracked her body. Patrick pounded on the door. The dying woman's strength was uncanny. Sara lost her grip. One foot broke loose, kicking her in the head. The blow sent her reeling. With her eyes teary and blurred, she felt her way back to the bed and hung on. The moans and the convulsions went on for long minutes. Was this really helping Mrs. Hiebert? They could be killing her.

Slowly, the shuddering diminished, whether from the salve or sheer fatigue, Sara wasn't sure. At last, she lay still. Sara retrieved her water cup and held a straw to her lips.

Maxine sipped some water then shook her head. She turned a haggard face to Sara, but her voice was strong. "I want to see Patrick."

With a nod from Mrs. Eisner, Bea unlocked the door, and Patrick rushed in. The three women filed out of the room.

The matron peered at the couple from the doorway. "I'll call Dr. Zwiefel and see about increasing her dosage. Injections would be more suitable for her. If you wish, I can teach you how to give an injection."

"Anything to help Mrs. Hiebert."

"I understand Mr. Krause is calling on you today."

Heat rose up her cheeks. "Yes, Mrs. Eisner. We're having supper in town. I should be back well before lights out."

"Land sake, child, I'm not your mother." She waved the subject away. "I'll call the Commissioner. With any luck, he can bring the morphine and syringes from Dr. Zwiefel's office. We need to keep Mrs. Heibert comfortable in the time she has left." She sighed. "How she hangs on is beyond me."

"She may have found something to live for."

Mrs. Eisner tilted her head. "So I see. It won't end well for Patrick. Keep him busy. The three of you are taking a long time on your rounds. But I understand these patients need the attention. If this home should survive, care for the infirmed will be our main function."

Sara lowered her head. "Mr. Krause told me about his meeting last Monday."

She shot a glance at Bea. "Unspoken prayers, Miss McGuire. And enjoy your supper. I'll do the evenings rounds." She turned and walked to the stairs, but stopped and faced Sara. "Your style of care is breaking new ground. Just don't let it break you." The matron turned away and headed for the stairs once more.

Sara gazed down the hall long after the persnickety woman disappeared. Did Mrs. Eisner praise or criticize her?

Bea wrote.

HOW ARE WE DOING?

"You and Patrick are doing great." Sara squeezed her shoulder.

Beatrice hugged her, smiling.

Fifteen minutes later, the infirmary crew rolled their carts to the next room. Patrick stepped in front of the door, squinting at Sara, arms crossed, blocking her way. "I don't like you." His voice held an edge Sara had never heard before.

She squatted before the disgruntled young man. "I'm sorry about how we locked you out. We needed to help Maxie because she took too many pills."

Patrick shook his head. "She's getting sicker. You're supposed to make her better."

Sara's jaw dropped. She'd promised Maxine she'd tell Patrick of her condition. She needed to honor that agreement. Sara reached for his arm, but Patrick yanked it away. So be it. It was hard to meet his eyes. "I cannot make Maxine better. Neither can Miss Gloria. Nobody can."

"But what's wrong with Maxie? Is it a secret?"

Sara swallowed. "Maxie has a disease. Her blood has turned to poison. There's no medicine to fix it. All we can do is ease the pain as it gets worse."

Patrick squinted, bobbing his head. Sara waited. If this man-child was slow, he was also methodical. "Will Maxie die?"

Sara nodded. "Soon." The word felt like a death sentence.

For a long moment, the youth gazed at her over crossed arms. He never moved. Did he understand what she said? Did her news send him into shock?

Patrick touched Sara's arm. "You told me like a grown-up. I like that. But Maxie will always be my girlfriend. So you can't be." With that, he turned and led the way to the next room.

Chapter Thirty-One

The last patient for each round was always Mr. Evans. Sara blew out a breath. The last but certainly not the least. She opened the door, allowing Patrick and Beatrice to enter before her. The air reeked with the foul stench coming from his bed. Sara put a hand over her nose. "Not again." The old man was a bit easier to manage later in the day, though he never cared to be sociable. The mornings, however, brought out the worst in him.

He huddled in his bed. "Leave me be."

"Afraid not, Mr. Evans. After we clean you up, you'll be wearing a diaper from now on."

"The hell I will." His voice was a growl.

"Two other patients wear one, and they're not complaining, so you're in good company. Bath first, then breakfast." Sara glanced at Beatrice. "Get his wash basin ready. Patrick, add new water to the pitcher."

"No one touches me!" Evans pushed himself to a sitting position. "Get out and take those freaks with you."

Patrick retrieved the pitcher, but Beatrice stopped, eyes cast downward. Evans glanced her way. There was a glint in his eye and a lopsided smirk. The ornery coot never smiled. What was he up to?

Sara slipped an arm around Bea's shoulders. "Don't listen to him. He's trying to get under your skin.

Prepare his bath water. Go on."

Evans jerked his head around. "Why are you coddling those oddballs? They belong in a sideshow. Are they your trained pets? Have you taught them to dance for their supper?"

Sara leveled blazing eyes at the spiteful old codger. "You can snipe at me, but leave my friends alone. Any more mean remarks and I'll leave you here stinking until dinner."

"Don't worry, mother hen," Evans chortled. "I don't care about your monkeys. I tried to teach you when you did wrong growing up. And I'm telling you now. Don't try to get even with me. You think you got me in your pocket, but you'll learn different."

Bea returned with a water-filled basin and set it on the nightstand.

"Thank you, Bea. Now get the sponge and some soap."

Evans eyed the nightstand.

"We'll be done before you know it, Mr. Evans."

Patrick re-entered, placing the pitcher beside the basin.

Without warning, Evans shoved up against the headboard, twisted his body, and kicked out. His right foot connected with the nightstand, tipping it sideways. For a long moment, the top-heavy cabinet hung suspended on two legs, and then toppled over as if in slow motion.

Crash!

Water splashed against the wall. The ceramic pitcher shattered, and the metal basin rolled in a tight circle, spinning to the floor.

Evans thumped his fist on the bed, hooting with

delight.

Sara's hands clenched into a tight fist. Enough was enough. She stepped close and grabbed Evans by the nightshirt, slamming him against the wall. Bewilderment replaced his satisfied leer. She leaned in, her face inches from his. "Good work, Mr. Evans." Her voice was quiet, conversational, and altogether menacing. "You've given us plenty to do." She motioned to the hand restraints hooked to the bed. "Have you noticed these manacles by your head and the straps near your feet? Twitch one muscle. Make one more remark, and I'll bind your hands and legs. You are the last person we'll be tending to until dinnertime. If I remember, I'll look for the key. But don't get your hopes up."

Evans' jaw fell slack. Sara grabbed his right hand, pushing his wrist inside the restraint.

"Do you understand, Mr. Evans?"

"No! No. Please don't." Evans' voice shook with fear. "I won't do nothing else."

"That's not good enough. I want to hear a promise." Sara began closing the manacle on his left hand.

"I promise! I promise. Stop! I beg of you." Evans' voice rose to a trembling wail.

She gripped his hand a moment longer, glaring at him from six inches away. Then she released her hold.

Evans collapsed, gasping as he held his left wrist.

"Thank you. We'll have you smelling better in no time."

Evans remained silent while Sara, Beatrice, and Patrick bathed him and attended to his room. He ate a breakfast of cornmeal mush and stretched out on clean

sheets, wearing a fresh nightshirt.
    And a diaper.

Chapter Thirty-Two

One of the chores Jason helped with since Sara left was the laundry and ironing. That Thursday afternoon, both he and his mother stood over the kitchen table. As his mom sprinkled water over the clothing from a pop bottle, he rolled each item and placed it in a cloth-covered basket.

Since the fiasco with the cab company, searching for their sister had stopped. He had no idea on how to proceed, and his detective brother had nothing as well, not even with the help of his hack-written pulps. Mom wanted them to present what they had to the police. "Let them take care of it," she said. "You boys have gone as far as you can."

His brother wanted to wait until three o'clock before calling the cops. If he couldn't come up with a plan by then it was finished. Jason glanced at the wall clock. Two forty-five. Michael better think of something soon.

"I'm running out of room to work, Jason," his mother said. "Quit woolgathering and roll those shirts. Or else, you'll be doing the ironing."

"I was just thinking about what we could have done to find Sis."

"You and Michael should contact the police. You boys have been putting it off for way too long."

"We'll do it today, I promise."

Footsteps thumped down the living room stairs. A few seconds later Michael burst into the kitchen. "Ten minutes left and I got an idea!"

Katherine McGurk never missed a beat while shaking water from the Nehi bottle. "Michael, you can set up the ironing board in the sewing room and gather some hangers. You need to help your brother."

"In just a second, Mom. I have an idea how to find Sara." Michael stepped to the cupboard drawer, retrieved the telephone book. "We didn't speak to the right people at the cab company."

Jason glanced at him. "Oh yeah? And who would that be?"

Katherine frowned. "I thought we agreed you boys would let the police take over."

Michael picked up the receiver. "We will, Mom—if this doesn't work. We can have another cab driver get her destination for us. It'd be perfectly safe." He dialed the number. "Hello, I'd like a cab at 2234 Parker Street. Thank you." He hung up the receiver.

Jason rolled a towel and placed it in the basket. "What's your idea?"

Michael waved a five-dollar bill. "A big tip for a little information."

"So you're bribing the driver?"

Michael shrugged. "Call it an investment. Care to ride along?"

Jason shook his head. "I need to finish with the laundry."

Katherine set down the bottle. "The clothes can wait. I'm coming along."

Michael frowned. "Mom, we'll tell you what happened when we get back."

She set her jaw in a firm line. "If you boys won't listen to me, then I'm getting involved."

Michael pursed his lips. "The cab driver might chicken out if there's too many people. Right, Jason?"

Not necessarily. Jason exhaled. "A mother's concern could make a difference. It's your show. You can do the talking."

Michael grabbed his cap. "I'm waiting on the front porch. The dispatcher said ten minutes." He dashed from the kitchen to the front of the house. The screen door slammed a few seconds later.

Katherine retrieved her sprinkling bottle. "Let's get these clothes finished before the taxi gets here."

"Sure, Mom." Jason rolled more clothes. *Will Michael's bribe scheme work?*

"Offering money—that sounds…shady. We should be watchful," Katherine said.

Jason glanced at his mother. Her words echoed his own thoughts. "Michael can be naïve. I'll do that. Best to err on the side of caution. At worst, we'd only be out the cost of the cab ride."

Fifteen minutes later, Jason and Katherine finished the pre-ironing, Michael called from the front porch. "Cab's here!" She reached in the closet and donned a pleated green jacket and a Robin Hood style hat tilted at a slight angle. Jason escorted his mother to the cab. Michael ran ahead to the car.

The cabbie jumped out and opened the back door. That was a good sign. He was a young man with loose-fitting pants patched at the knees. He tipped his newsboy cap as Katherine and Jason entered the vehicle. Michael sat behind the driver.

The cabbie slipped behind the wheel. "Where to?"

"Drive around the neighborhood." Michael said. "We're hoping you can get us some information. There's a nice tip if you can help us. As soon as we strike a deal, we'll return home."

The taxi driver pulled away from the curb, heading east. "What's the story, Mack?"

Jason pursed his lip at the cabbie's flippant attitude. Michael produced his fiver. "We want the names of the drivers who worked last Sunday morning. Keep the Lincoln if you take the job. You get another five when you come up with the names. There's also a bonus, if you're interested."

The cabbie rubbed his chin. "An easy ten bucks. What's the bonus?"

Michael got out a ten. "We'll double the fee if you can get us an address."

The cabbie whistled. "Tell me about the address."

"It's a cab destination. A driver picked up a fare at the Farmland Café downtown, around nine-thirty, last Sunday morning. The passenger was a twenty-three-year old woman. Short brown hair with big curls. We want to know where the cab took her."

The cabbie chuckled. "That's it? Twenty bucks for a ride destination?"

Katherine bent forward. "What is your name, young man?"

"Harlan."

She touched his shoulder. "Harlan, it's very important that we get this address. The young woman is my daughter. She's missing."

Enough with the fiddling. "Will you do it?" Jason asked.

Harlan nodded. "I'll ask around."

"Thank you," Katherine said. "This means a lot to me."

"When I get the address, what should I do?"

Michael sat up straight. "Come by the house and honk your horn. Day or night."

"You got it." Harlan turned south on Waco Street.

They needed a time limit. Jason focused on the driver. "How soon can you get us the address?"

"A day… Two days tops." He shrugged. "It's just a matter of finding who worked that shift. That's not a busy time."

"That'll be swell." Michael grinned.

The cabbie turned the vehicle east on Central Avenue. He held up a hand. "Seems like you're shelling out a lot of lettuce. Aren't you worried I could give you a bogus address?"

An internal alarm sounded. Jason leaned forward, hands clenched, but his mother touched his arm. "Would you do that?" she asked.

"No, ma'am." The driver hunched a shoulder. "I'm saying it upfront to get it out in the open. The wrong person could try and shade you folks."

Jason thumped the inside of the car door. "Michael, don't listen to this guy. Drop the deal right now."

Michael cleared his throat. "You said you'd let me do the talking."

"Not if you're throwing your money away on a shyster." Jason regretted the words even as he said them.

Harlan pulled the cab to the curb and stopped. The driver stuck a thumb out the window. "No one calls me a shyster and rides in my cab. Take a hike."

Jason paled. "Are you serious?"

"As a heart attack."

Katherine put a hand on the cabbie's shoulder. "I trust you. And you will have to trust the boys to come through on their end. My older son spoke in haste. Let him apologize."

Harlan shot Jason a frosty glare, but spoke to Katherine. "Okay, but put a muzzle on him."

Katherine smiled. "Thank you, young man. You should hear the boys at home. It's a wonder the house is still on its foundation. Apologize Jason."

Sometimes a strategic retreat was in order. "I'm sorry for talking out of line."

"That's better." The cabbie pulled back into traffic.

Michael settled in his seat. "We have a pretty good idea where the cab took our sister. Your information will confirm our hunch."

"And if it doesn't?"

"We'll deal with it," said Michael.

Harlan turned the cab north to Parker Street. "I hope I get the answer you want."

No one spoke for the rest of the trip.

A few minutes later, the taxi stopped in front of the McGurk home. Jason walked with his mother back to the house. While she went inside, he stayed on the porch. His brother made the transaction, but it seemed to take longer than necessary.

Finally, his brother loped to the front door while the taxi drove away.

"How'd it go?" Jason asked.

"Pretty well, except he doesn't like you. He thinks you're pushy."

Jason smirked. "What about the deal? Will he provide everything we want by Saturday?"

"He said he would, but I had to promise him the full twenty bucks. I did tear the ten dollar bill and gave him half as an incentive to get us the address. It's my guess we'll hear from him tomorrow."

"Hope so." Jason sighed. "It's been five days." *Way too long.* He missed his sister. She knew more about everyday stuff than anyone else her age. It must be all that letter reading she did every day. Of course, he ribbed her about being a smarty-brain. It was a brother's job, after all. And she gave it right back. It was also a brother's duty to protect his sister. *You certainly botched that one.* Jason cringed at the sound of Pop's voice rattling in his head.

So he had to find her. And if Larry Bigger bruised one curl on her head, then they would have a reckoning.

"We should have our answers as early as tomorrow," Michael said.

"Not quit." Jason stared off into the night. "There won't be any answers until we find her."

Chapter Thirty-Three

Sara sat at the dining table staring out the window hoping the Commissioner wouldn't be late. She glanced at the wind-up clock propped on the table—3:48. Two minutes since the last time she checked. Nearly time for Mr. Krause to arrive for their supper in Joshua.

Was this a date? It had been a long time since a gentleman called on her. Larry was an escape from her father, but certainly no gentleman. Mr. Krause, on the other hand, was a curiosity. He was courteous and open. Straight-laced, but endearing. And impulsive? He did ask her to supper at the last possible minute. She could have said no. Yet, here she sat, squirming in her seat, about to dive into unknown waters. She hadn't been this fidgety about a date since high school. That was silly. The evening would be conversation over a meal. Nothing more.

A dark blue Pontiac, a boxy vehicle of vertical and horizontal lines, pulled into the gravel drive, stopping at the back door. The Commissioner got out, holding a wooden box.

Sara dashed to the matron's office. "Mr. Krause is here. He has a package."

Mrs. Eisner rose from her chair and stepped to the doorway. "It's morphine from Dr. Zwiefel's office. I left word for the Commissioner to bring the supplies with him. We need to start Mrs. Hiebert on her injections as soon as possible."

Approaching footsteps came from the kitchen.

Commissioner Krause appeared around the corner. He tipped his hat with his free hand. "Hello Mrs. Eisner, Miss McGuire. Your cook let me in." He shifted the shoebox size container, holding it flat. "Here are the medical supplies you asked for." The Commissioner produced a key. "The doctor wanted you to inspect the contents before I returned to town."

She unlocked and opened the box.

Strapped to the lid in cloth-lined compartments were four vials capped with rubber stoppers. The bottom half of the box contained two glass cylinders with a large opening at one end and a small aperture at the other. Strapped in place were plungers, small rubber stoppers, and a jar containing needles. The matron shut the case, looking satisfied. "This will do."

"I'll let the doctor know." Wendell Krause turned to Sara. "Are you ready?"

"All set." She pulled the fan letter from her apron pocket. "Could we mail this in town?"

Wendell scratched behind his ear. "Sure. Do you plan on wearing your apron as well?"

She peered down at the stained gingham. "I'll be back in a minute."

Mrs. Eisner bit her lip, her eyes twinkling. "I'll take your apron, child. It'll be hanging by your nightstand when you return."

"Thank you."

They left out the back door. Mr. Krause stepped to the passenger side door and opened it. "*Steigen sie ein, Fräulein.*"

Sara suppressed a smile remembering her high

school German. "*Vielen dank, Herr Krause.*"

They drove to Joshua, stopping at the post office first. Sara ran inside to mail the letter. "When will this be delivered?" she asked the clerk.

"Evening mail hasn't gone out yet. So I'd say tomorrow quite likely." The postal worker dropped the letter in a mailbag. Elated, Sara ambled back to the car.

Wendell parked in front of an eatery that looked like a farmhouse with a wide front porch and a large window made up of many smaller panes. A white sign with red lettering hung over the front porch awning.

The Covered Dish

A group of old-timers sat on the porch, most dozing in rockers. Wendell led Sara inside. A cowbell jangled as the screen door slammed shut behind them.

Sara took in a breath. Pleasing aromas of fried chicken and peach pie filled the air. The interior walls were knotty pine. Handmade quilts with little price tags hung from the woodwork. A stack of newspapers, *The Joshua Sentinel,* set by the cash register. The banner headline read, "Commissioners Announce Closure of County Farm."

"Let's find a seat." Wendell ushered her away from the newspapers. "This place is owned by a Mennonite couple. The food is farm cooking. Nothing fancy." They sat at a table near the back wall.

Wendell picked up a sheet of parchment paper and handed it to Sara. "Here's the menu. I've tried everything here. It's all good."

Sara peered at the list. "Savory chicken pie sounds wonderful."

"Good choice. I'm for a bierock and a bowl of soup." He pronounced it as "beer-rock."

Sara tilted her head. "I've never had that before."

"It's peppered hamburger and cooked cabbage wrapped in a half-moon pastry. You can also get it with sausage. Simple, yet tasty."

"We should share. By the way, thanks for letting me mail my letter."

"Glad to help. Many residents write to distant relatives asking to stay with them. Very few get lucky."

"I wrote to a friend asking for a favor."

"Good luck. I hope your friend comes through."

Sara bowed her head. "I saw the headline by the register. The sale of the farm is public news now. Has there been any letters from residents in the county about the closing?

"That newspaper is only a day old. No one around here does anything in a hurry. But I'm hoping for some kind of reaction."

Sara nodded. "Mrs. Eisner said if the farm manages to survive, it would serve the old and infirmed."

Wendell sat back in his seat. "She talked to you about it?"

Sara smiled. "No. That's when I told her I knew. In so many words she told me to stay mum."

Wendell blew out a breath. "I'd say the time for silence is over."

Their waitress arrived with water glasses and took their orders. After she left, Sara leaned forward. "Is there any chance that the other two commissioners will change their minds?

Wendell pursed his lips. "Not likely. Unless they get an overwhelming negative response, they will pronounce the voters as being in favor of the closure. The commissioners see themselves as practical men

223

saving the county money—with no personal ill will."

Sara slammed her fist on the tabletop. Utensils jumped. Water glasses trembled. Customers nearby glanced her way. "It *is* personal!" Her voice erupted with white-hot indignation. "We *live* there! The residents care for each other. There's understanding and respect—we're a family. You—they—are destroying our home!"

Wendell grabbed her hands. "You're attracting attention. Anger won't help."

Sara drew a ragged breath. "I been so busy with the infirmary I've barely had time to think about what to do about it. My only idea was finding someone who would buy the tenant house and allow us to stay."

"Little chance of that happening. But I like your arguments. Perhaps making this a public issue by writing to the newspaper will stir some interest in saving the farm."

Sara's eyes brightened. "Do you think that will work?"

Wendell took a sip of water. "With hundreds of families fending for themselves because of the Depression, I can't see how the dislocation of nineteen people will matter. A long shot, though, is better than nothing at all."

"I suppose you're right." Sara met his eyes. She wanted to tell this sincere man about her letter to Daddy's radio program. How there was an outside chance he might help. But that meant telling him about her family. She couldn't risk that. Not yet. Better to deflect the conversation away from herself altogether. "You seem like an unlikely champion for the poor. What was your family like?"

Wendell let out a long breath. "It started with law school at the University of Chicago. My parents had divorced when I was very young. Granddad Pinkston ran a huge garment factory and died a rich man. Mom inherited the business. Me becoming a lawyer was Mom's idea. Once I passed the bar, my job would be to act as legal counsel for Pinkston Garments, Chicago's third-largest coat maker. My job would be to keep bad publicity to a minimum, negotiate with unions, and cater to local ward bosses. 'Work hard,' Mom told me, 'and you'll be set for life.' "

"So, what happened?"

"Last January, she called. Dad died of a heart attack somewhere in Kansas. Mom wanted me to settle Dad's affairs. So I came out here. It felt good to quit law school. I had no wish to be a mouthpiece for a big company. Mom's control over me ended the day Dad died."

"I'm sorry for your loss. What did your father do?"

"He worked with his hands. Building. Repairing. While I was here, I learned he ran for County Commissioner and won. But he died before he took office. The commissioners asked me to serve out his term. The Commissioner of the Poor has been full of surprises."

"Mrs. Eisner says you're doing a wonderful job."

Wendell fiddled with the cloth napkin, unrolling and rolling it back up again. "That's nice to hear. I knew my dad was a handyman, but I never knew he had this Will Rogers ability to hit it off with people. Mom, on the other hand, liked the good life: theater, shopping, and making life miserable for the help."

"Your parents sound so different from each other.

How did they meet?"

"My father wired Granddad's big house for electricity. The story goes that my mother married him because he wasn't cowed by her demands."

"So father and son left the Big City and moved west."

Wendell rubbed his neck. "Let's just say Mother is not the easiest person to live with."

"Do you plan on going back to law school?"

Wendell chuckled, his hands spread apart, encompassing his surroundings. "What? And leave small-town politics?"

The server brought their orders, refilled their water glasses and left.

Sara's slice of chicken pie looked marvelous. The thick wedge covered half her plate, its golden crust filled with thick chunks of white meat, potatoes, carrots and peas in a creamy sauce. Sara dug in, relishing the blend of tastes and textures. The colors, the aroma, even the *feel,* demanded that she savor each flavorful bite. The creamy sauce was the key, light and buttery with an array of spices. It was a privilege to be here to enjoy such a feast. She hadn't tasted anything like this since her retreat from home. Too bad the others had to eat Wheatley's watery potato soup, but they were used to it. She wasn't. She deserved a good meal.

Sara stopped eating, setting down her fork. What was she thinking? Here she was, stuffing her face while Bea and Patrick ate the same bland fare. A hollowness yawned within her, but not from hunger. How could she betray her friends? How could she be so selfish?

It was shameful.

"This is a mistake. I shouldn't be here."

Wendell looked up, "Something wrong?"

"I can't eat this."

"Is the chicken bad?" Wendell studied her from across the table.

Sara shook her head. "It's wonderful. But...I shouldn't have it." She gulped water to rid her mouth of the taste. "I need to step out."

Wendell looked aghast. "Are you sick?"

"No. I have to go." Sara rose to her feet. No explanation could excuse her actions. No use trying. "This is all my fault." She turned and dashed for the door.

She didn't remember getting into the Pontiac—just the headlong flight from the restaurant, bursting through the screen door, and the scolding jangle of the cowbell on the way out. Inside the car, she drew her knees to her chin and wrapped arms around them. She didn't know where she wanted to go. Or what to do. But eating at a place where her friends could never go seemed like hypocrisy. Was she any better than her father? It was so easy to be disdainful of him, yet for a few brief moments sitting at the restaurant seemed like just another day of dinning out. Nothing special.

Yet, for Bea and Patrick—even Dutch, it would be an experience out of reach. In two months the closest they'd be to a restaurant would be to hunch in alley, going through garbage and fishing for scraps. The thought made her stomach turn.

The car door open and Wendell dropped behind the wheel. He watched her, brows raised. "Are you feeling better?"

"A little." It came out more as moan.

"What happened back there?"

227

She stared ahead over her knees, speaking in a far-away voice. "I was eating... Marveling at the taste... Knowing that the people I live with never had such a feast. And I didn't care. Everything soured after that."

"You were enjoying yourself and feeling guilty because of that?"

"I suppose I was. How did you know?"

"Sometimes a farmer gives me eggs or milk to pass on to a poor family. Needy parents often accept the food for their children—never for themselves." He reached for her hand and squeezed it. "You're not alone in how you feel."

"That may be true. But I still want to go home."

Wendell started the car and headed for the city limits. "I just now realized how much I dominated the conversation at supper."

"That's because I asked all the questions." The queasiness made grinning an effort.

"And I fell for it. The more I talked about myself, the fewer questions I'd be asking you."

That brought a smile to her lips. "I hoped you wouldn't notice."

"Next time, it will be your story."

"I gave my history to Mrs. Eisner." She turned to look out the passenger window.

They drove in silence. After the car topped a small rise, the silhouette of the tenant house came into view, blocking the setting sun. Just ahead was the poor farm cemetery. She was almost home.

Wendell slowed the car and parked by the cemetery gate.

Sara sat up straighter, an image of Larry swinging at her splashed across her thoughts. "What are we doing here." She already had her fingers on the door handle, ready to make a run for it. Not likely she'd get far.

"Before we call it a night, I wanted to show you the cemetery." He gestured to a gleaming picket fence. "This is the quietest spot in the county, and it's a six-minute walk from where you live."

"A cemetery?" Sara peered at the rows of wooden crosses. Wendell came around and helped her out of the car. Here and there were spots of color on the ground. Mid-April and wildflowers were already blooming. She heard how cemeteries could be fertile ground for an assortment of plants. It was certainly true for this little gravesite.

The burial ground was rectangle-shaped with eight markers set side-by-side going back some twelve rows. A simple wooden cross topped each grave with the first initial and last name in black paint on the crossbar. Most of the markers showed little sign of weathering. Six bare-limbed willows stood just east of the cemetery. The largest tree bent like a stooped-shouldered sentry, its limbs bowing over the resting place as if protecting it. A rabbit munching on bits of grass watched from a pile of railroad ties behind the gravesite. Wendell and Sara passed through the picketed gate.

A stiffening breeze blew from the west. Sara hugged herself as a shiver coursed down her spine. It may be a tranquil place, but she wouldn't want to be alone here.

"Are you chilly?"

"It's gotten cooler." Sara rubbed her upper arms. "Is Mr. Byers buried here?"

Wendell pointed. "On the back row." He took off his suit jacket and draped it over her shoulders.

"Welcome to the Joshua County Cemetery."

She trembled, pulling the jacket tighter. "Mrs. Eisner told me about this place."

"She avoids the cemetery. I come here to repair some of the markers or patch the fence. It helps me to unwind. So few visitors come here. But if anyone should visit, they'll see this is a good resting place."

"You are the caretaker?"

Wendell shrugged. "I've always thought that an odd title. I'm more of a steward." The sun hovered over the horizon. Shadows from the grave markers created lines that stretched to the willows. Sara turned in a full circle, clasping the jacket. "It's lonely out here."

"Anything but lonely. Over ninety souls lie here." He gestured to the eastern end of the graveyard. "Not everyone in this cemetery is from the county farm. There are two tramps who died while passing through town. And then, there's the Boy."

He showed her to a single marker set against the picket fence. The black paint was faded but still readable:

NEGRO BOY

"I don't know why. Every time I come here I spend time in front of this grave imagining where he came from."

"Who was he?"

"Nobody knows. He may have died on one the orphan trains that passed through here. Another story says he was riding atop a sand car and fell in. No documents exist showing when he was buried. I've considered moving the body so his grave is aligned with the others. Then common sense prevailed. Someday, I'll fix his marker, but I'm reluctant about disturbing his resting place."

Sara removed a tree branch from the cross. "That poor child. To die without a name."

Wendell nodded. "An unknown orphan—and yet, my thoughts are drawn to him every time I come here."

A gust of wind whistled through the bare trees like mournful spirits who had lost their way.

Wendell took her arm, and they hurried back to the car. Sara expected him to start the vehicle. Instead, he turned to her. "I have to ask you something. In my job, I ask many personal questions of people who apply for relief. I don't do it to pry, but to justify the need. Clients lie to me daily—to protect themselves, their family—their pride. So I listen to what the person is saying—and *not* saying. The hidden truth. And here's my question. What is your unspeakable truth?"

Sara turned toward the graveyard in the fading light, twisting her fingers.

Wendell gripped her hands.

She turned to him, her voice edged with insolence. "You want a list? I fear for the future of my child. With the house closing, I'll have to move on, but where will I go? Will I be able to keep my child? I can't go home. Daddy called me a disgrace. We don't get along—but we'll have to find some kind of peace, or I'll never see my family again."

Wendell blinked. "Tell me about your child. What would you like to happen?"

Sara pursed her lips. "I want to keep my baby— watch her grow. I can live with the shame of being an unwed mother, but I will not allow others to shame my child. I'm told that giving up the baby is the only way to give her a future. I fear that may be true."

Wendell gripped her hands tighter, but she pulled her fingers free. "Other women have been in your situation and raised children. Don't sacrifice your child before she's even born."

"You sound like one of those writers telling people to think like a winner."

"I don't want you to give up. What's your father like?"

Sara cast her eyes downward. "Daddy is so ambitious. He has his eyes on fame and notoriety. His need for celebrity blinds him to all else—including his own family. That's partly why I'm here. He saw me as a threat to his career."

"What happened?"

Sara pulled the jacket tighter. "We had an argument. I'm barred from my own home."

"How can you solve this problem? For that matter, how can you change your father?"

Sara stared at him. "I don't know."

"You're feeling guilty about situations and events you cannot control. You don't have to leave immediately. Stay at the house for as long as you can. "

"I want to talk to Daddy again. He could be a thousand miles away, yet he's never far from my thoughts. I have to end the rift between us."

"Don't worry about that. You're a mother-to-be. Your goal is to stay healthy. Try not to let your father haunt you." Wendell drew her close, wrapping his arm around her shoulders.

"He called me a threat!" Faint light caught her glistening eyes. "Me! Larry said the same thing the very next day before dumping me." She pointed ahead with a trembling hand. "Lying in the cold, hurting and alone…I wanted it to be over."

"You survived. You're stronger. How do you feel now?"

Her eyes were like reflecting pools, brimming with tears. "Now? I've found a purpose here and a sense of…belonging." It was hard to talk, to force each word past the lump in her throat. "I've never felt that way before. Each day, the ties keep getting stronger. This place has been a sanctuary. And now…I can't stay here. I can't go home. I have to show Daddy…to prove…I'm worthy." Sara leaned into his shoulder, weeping.

Wendell bent forward tipping her face upward; his lips touched hers in a tentative question. She responded with a crushing answer. He circled her back with his hands and she pulled him close. She closed her eyes, drinking in his presence.

Time and place faded. The moment hung suspended. They melted together in a universe all their own. There was no past. Only a never-ending now and a yearning desire for a fairytale future. Both had a simple wish for the world to leave them in peace. And both knew with certainty it would never happen.

They kissed, not as lovers, but as two desperate souls finding a reprieve from loneliness, fearful of asking for more, but reluctant to break their tender bond. They broached no questions. They made no promises. Only prayers. Fervent hope. Solace. They held each other in a tiny piece of forever. A land of tender beauty. A world of roses.

Sometime later, Wendell returned Sara to the house.

"Goodbye," she murmured, opened the door, and darted up the steps. From the back door, she waved to him as he backed the car out to the road. Sara didn't go in until the engine's chattering receded into the stillness of night.

Chapter Thirty-Four

Friday, April 12, 1935

Beatrice awoke in a cold sweat in the middle of the night. Through the curtained window, speckled moonlight spread across the floor of her room.

She had dreamed of the bookkeeping office again.

For the last six months, it was the same unsettling vision. Some nights it was a shadowy jumble of impressions, but this time she felt the broom handle and tasted the bitter ink. Tonight wasn't so much a dream as a reenactment.

Bea stared at the pattern of moonlight on the floor. It was just like that evening when the light went out, and the office turned to spotty points of light and shifting shadows.

It was so easy to remember...

Move that dust. Sweep with care.

Push too fast will fill the air.

Making up rhymes made the work more enjoyable. Otherwise, cleaning Mr. Bergkamp's office was boring. Beatrice swept dust into a pan and dumped it in a nearby bin. She tugged on the back door to take out the refuse, but the knob wouldn't turn. Why would the bookkeeper lock the back door? She was supposed to empty the office trash every night. Beatrice shrugged and returned to work.

Gather rubbish. Empty trash.

Make it quick. Make it fast.

There were three trashcans: two were nearly empty and a third under the roll-up desk spilled over with papers. After she set the trash by the back door, she could go home to help Miss Beth with her niece's gown.

Prepare the dress. Work with haste.

Wedding's coming! The lady waits.

At eighteen, Beatrice Mullens had to leave the Kansas City orphanage, but she needed to learn the skills to survive in the outside world. The social worker found a sponsor, a couple who would take her in and teach her the things a young woman needed to know. On the day she left the orphanage, the social worker drove her to Union Station and gave her a one-way ticket to Joshua, Kansas. When she arrived in the small town, Frank and Elizabeth Bergkamp met her at the depot. A nice couple. Mr. Bergkamp was a bookkeeper. Miss Beth was a dressmaker. Bea's inability to speak didn't bother them. She soon learned to cook, clean, and sew. Miss Beth even let Bea pick the fabrics for her own dresses.

Mr. Bergkamp promised a small allowance if Beatrice would clean his downtown office. Stirring up dust, he told her, bothered his breathing. Four weeks after her arrival, Sally hadn't stirred from within her mind. Life with the Bergkamps was working out.

The cool October evening seeped into the office as Bea gathered the refuse together. She crawled under the roll-up desk to retrieve stray wads of crumpled paper that had fallen out of the waste can. Behind her, the front door squeaked opened and rattled shut. Bea scrambled out from under the desk. Before she regained her feet, the lights went out.

Someone else was in the office.

Dappled light filtered in from streetlamps and surrounding businesses. Beatrice concentrated on the shadow standing between her and the front door. Heavy, labored breathing approached. Headlamps from a passing car fell on the figure as he passed an opened window. It was Mr. Bergkamp, his arms outstretched and a strained smile played across his reddened face.

Beatrice sensed the familiar stirring of Sally as she emerged from the depths of her mind. Sally adopted a singsong tone. *Uh-ohhh. We've got com-pa-nee.*

Bergkamp crept closer. "Don't be afraid. I'm not going to hurt you. I just want to be friends. Good friends. A good friend who deserves some affection."

Bea retreated a step, bumping against the roll-up desk. Her fingers found a desk lamp and turned on the light.

Light caught Bergkamp's shifting eyes. Beatrice had seen those eyes before. In the orphanage, a night watchman found one of the prettier girls to his liking. His eyes shifted as well.

What was she going to do?

Sally pulsed with excitement. *I do believe he wants to play.* Beatrice could almost feel her friend rubbing her hands.

There was no way out except through the front door. Sitting on the desk behind her was an open ledger, its pages filled with tiny numbers. Beside the ledger sat a small dark bottle.

Bergkamp stepped closer, his eyes hungry, and his grin contorting into a grimace.

Bea picked up the bottle. The label said WATERMAN'S BLACK INK.

Sally loomed from within. *Don't throw it—pop it open!*

Bea flipped off the stopper.

Let him come closer. Art class is about to begin.

Bergkamp didn't notice what Bea held. He was an arm's length away, his hands about to encircle her.

Let's finger-paint.

Bea upended the ink bottle over a page of figures. It was like pouring corn syrup over pancakes. Bergkamp screamed like a little boy, stepping backward. Bea grinned as she rubbed her hands over the page, making little stars and spirals with her black fingers.

Time for lipstick!

Bea swiped a finger across her mouth. The ink tasted horribly bitter. She spat; a stream of black goo landed on Bergkamp's shirt.

The little man looked at his chest as if he was bleeding. His eyes became giant saucers. For a moment, he stared at Bea as if assessing her. Then with a roar, he rushed at her.

Give him what he wants.

With blackened hands and lips, Bea hugged the man, kissing him on the lips, face, and neck.

Bergkamp tore her arms loose, staggering back. "Get away from me!" He turned around, making funny little noises in his throat, and ran smack into the door. After fumbled with the lock, he dashed out, bending to his knees on the front porch. There, he heaved up his supper, gulped a lungful of air, and bent forward again, his body shaking. Finally, he disappeared from the open doorway, still wheezing.

Sally shrieked with delight.

Bea grinned. She sat in the swivel chair by the desk, toying with the spilled ink. Someone would be along soon. By then Sally would disappear from conscious thought. She—Beatrice—would be left alone to answer questions. Sally was that kind of a friend...

The dappled square of moonlight on the floor held no more magic. Bea turned over, facing the wall. So ended her time with Miss Beth. Frank Bergkamp accused her of destroying property. The Joshua County Court agreed and sent her to the county asylum for observation.

It wasn't so bad. Living here wasn't scary like staying at the orphanage. She had new friends: Miss Gloria, Patrick, and now Sara. She seemed like a princess who had lost her palace, pretty as a porcelain doll and just as fragile. Regal, yet friendly. It was easy to imagine her wearing jeweled bracelets and a long, flowing gown. And she was her princess-attendant. Bea smiled in the darkness. Working with Miss Sara was pleasant. There was only one problem.

Sally despised her new friend.

Since the death of Mr. Byers, Sally remained quiet. *Too* quiet. Was her friend jealous of Miss Sara? Bea hoped not.

There was no telling what Sally would do.

Chapter Thirty-Five

"No, no, no. You're holding the syringe all wrong." Gloria Eisner took the glass tube from Sara and held it with the tip pointing upward. "When injecting, you hold the needle like you're throwing a dart."

Sara stood at Mrs. Eisners's desk, which held a bottle of rubbing alcohol, some cotton balls, a bowl of water, a potato, and the open box of syringes. A folded newspaper sat on a corner of the desk. It was a copy of the same paper she saw at the restaurant yesterday.

Breakfast was over and the residents were doing morning cleanup. Infirmary rounds would begin soon. The matron had been patient up to now, drilling Sara on giving shots. The potato used in the exercise leaked water from at least four punctures. Soon, Sara would inject a dangerous solution into a dying woman.

The matron handed the syringe to Sara, taking care to point the needle away. "Now, give the injection. Recite the steps as I've instructed."

Sara wetted a cotton ball with rubbing alcohol. "First I sanitize the area. Then I take the syringe and push the plunger forward to eliminate air bubbles inside. That way the patient gets nothing but medicine." A small bit of water sprayed from the end of the needle.

"What's next?"

Sara inserted the inch-long needle into the potato. "Next, I pull back on the plunger slightly to see if I hit a blood vessel." Sara drove the plunger forward, shooting more water in the potato and removed the needle. "After the shot, I massage the muscle to spread out the drug." Sara replaced the glass cylinder in its place and closed the lid.

Mrs. Eisner nodded. "You did excellent."

Sara beamed, Mrs. Eisner did not give compliments often.

"Training is over. You're ready."

Sara nodded. "Thank you." The steps in giving a shot were easy—yet scary. But what filled her thoughts was yesterday. What was she to make of the evening with Commissioner Wendell Krause?

She'd always thought cemeteries were frightening, but the small pauper graveyard dotted with spring flowers felt tranquil. Like the Commissioner, she found the mystery of the Negro boy's grave enchanting. Who was he? Where did he come from? What happened to him? Feeling pity for the child—and herself—brought about a rising emotion impossible to control. Confessing her fears to Mr. Krause—Wendell—felt like a release. She offered no resistance to his touch and responded to his kiss with surprising passion. What must he think of her? Should she explain her feelings and actions? Avoid seeing him alone again? Or should she wait to see what happened next?

Wendell was kind and thoughtful. But the timing was all wrong. She didn't need romance. Not now.

Mrs. Eisner moved the box aside. "I'll prepare two syringes. Mrs. Hiebert will require morphine every four hours. With that many injections, a third person should assist. I'll train Mrs. Robson and set up a schedule. The three of us will each administer two shots per day."

"That would be a big help."

The matron dropped the waterlogged potato in a nearby trashcan. "I want to be there when you administer your first injection. It will remind me of those days when I watched over new nurses." A faint smile played across her lips. It dwindled when she glanced at the folded newspaper.

"I don't know if I'd make a good nurse."

"You have gifts, child. Natural abilities." She unfurled the paper. Beneath the headline of the announced closure, a smaller line read: "Commissioners Disagree Over Closure Decision." The story recounted the heated discussion between the three commissioners. Residents would be vacated by July 15th, and the property would be sold in forty-acre parcels by August 5th. "Have you mentioned this to any of the other residents?"

"I thought that should come from you."

She folded the paper. A wry grin lingered for a moment. "I almost wish you had. It'd be easy to blame the messenger. I'll tell the group at dinnertime."

"Is there anything we can do?"

"I'm not sure if doing anything is a wise idea. I don't like the attention we will draw from this article. Dozens of people will come to inspect the farm. Or to gawk. I hope we can remain a safe place before…" She sighed. Behind her stern mask, Sara glimpsed the weary in her eyes and the set of her mouth. Mrs. Eisner met her gaze. "You best get ready for your rounds. Never mind me. I'm feeling my age today, and prone to worry. Shut the door on your way out."

As Sara left, she saw the matron bowing her head, hands clasped before her.

Chapter Thirty-Six

Sara steeled herself before leading Bea and Patrick into Mr. Evans' room. He was often at his conniving worst in the morning. *Let's hope he'll limit his anger to me.* She knocked twice and entered, feigning a smile. As her helpers went about their chores the old man watched them without comment. "Good morning, Mr. Evans," said Sara. "We'll change your drawers and have you eating breakfast in a few minutes."

She turned the long rod, bringing him upright. Still he said nothing, though he had a sour expression, the old codger hadn't launched into his usual belittling assaults. "Is there something wrong, Mr. Evans?" Sara stepped forward, leaning over him.

"Nothing wrong," he muttered, cringing. "Go about your business and leave me be."

He hadn't move at all. "There is something amiss," she said. "What is it?"

He licked dry lips. "I don't like being called Mr. Evans. Not coming from you."

She stepped back, crossing her arms. "What should I call you?"

Evans scowled. "Call me Daddy, It's my privilege."

She studied him. "Oh, that's right. I forgot. After we freshen the room, would you like to sit by the window…Daddy? Then we'll get breakfast ready."

He sighed. "A window seat would be fine."

Patrick helped him to a rocker. Curious why he remained so reserved, Sara stood by him as he stared outside. *Perhaps I was too harsh with him yesterday.* She didn't mean to scare him—at least unduly. But a manageable Cyrus Evans seemed too good to be true.

From his window, Sara glimpsed a deer grazing among the cedars. Bits of red, yellow, and white dotted the scraggly grass. The color reminded her of the wildflowers in the cemetery.

Mr. Evans seemed interested as well. He leaned forward with effort in the rocker, muttering to himself. "Weeds... Nothing but weed wrapped with paper and bows." He leaned back, the chair swaying as he rubbed his eyes.

"Paper and bows, Mr. Evans?" she asked.

"What?" He peered at her as if coming out of a stupor.

"You mentioned weeds with bows. Do you mean the wildflowers?"

"Flowers?" Mr. Evans' eyes drifted back to the window. For a few seconds, his gaze intensified as he peered outside. "Dandelions and lilacs strung all over the kitchen. Then, they'd be rolled and tied inside a paper holder with bit of ribbon." Sara wasn't sure if he was talking to her or to himself. A moment later he fell back in the rocker, closing his eyelids. His face melted into a deepening frown.

Old memories must be slipping past the veil of his dementia. Was there any way she could help him?

"Are you thinking about May Day baskets?"

Mr. Evans jolted awake. "That's what they're called. Do kids still do such nonsense?"

Sara stifled a smile. "Afraid so."

"Waste of time." He glowered. "And a mess to clean."

"Did you get a May Day basket, Mr. Evans?"

He stirred in the chair, shifting his back and shoulders, as if he could not find a comfortable position. "Don't remember."

Bea set a bowl of oatmeal on the rolling table by the rocker.

"Would you like to eat breakfast in front of the window?"

The old man bobbed his head.

Sara moved the straight-backed chair next to the rocker. "Patrick will help you move to this chair. We can lower the table so you eat while watching out the table."

"I can take care of myself," he grumbled. Mr. Evans leaned forward to stand, but the rocker continued to sway with him in it.

Patrick lifted him to his feet. Sara steadied him. He hobbled to the other chair while Beatrice rolled the table in front of him.

Usually Mr. Evans had a good appetite, but today he continued to watch out the window, leaving his food untouched. Other than the bits of color, there was nothing else interesting outside. The deer wandered away, its tail disappearing behind the cedars.

"You did that." His voice seemed to come from far away. "You used to bundle those weeds in paper holders and run from house to house."

Mr. Evans was having a rare moment of soul-searching. Perhaps she could help him in his search for old memories. "I made them in the kitchen?"

"Back door must have been banging all day with you running in and out." It was hard to tell if he was disgusted or amused. His remarks bordered on the sarcastic. Still, there was a hint of re-discovery in his words. "I threw out all the dead plants, the ribbons, and the rolled papers with the names of neighbors. 'Til I saw mine."

"So you did get a May Day basket," she said. "From me."

For a moment, Mr. Evans raised his head, his eyes alive. Then his chin sagged to his chest.

"To Daddy." His voice was barely audible.

"What did you do?"

Evans furrowed his brow. "What needed to be done."

That sounded ominous. But if Mr. Evans did remember, he needed to get the words out. Even if they hurt.

"What had to be done?"

She wasn't sure if he heard her. Sara motioned for Patrick and Beat to take the carts out of the room. He roused in his chair, fully alert. "What *did* I do?" He seemed to ask himself. "I came home from the foundry early. Not much work that day. Kitchen table and floor were covered in grass and picked flowers. Then you came running in, squealing with excitement about who you delivered your flowers to. All I wanted was a little quiet." He paused. "After you were in bed I found mine."

"How old was I when I made your basket?"

"You were..." Mr. Evans fiddled with his nightshirt. "Eight or nine. So small."

"You was my father. I loved you."

"I don't know what you're blathering about." Mr. Evans grabbed a spoon and shoved food into his mouth.

Ten minutes later, Patrick helped him to bed. Cyrus drew sheets to his neck, Sara tucked him in. Before she left, she had one more all-important question. "What name did you give your little girl?"

The old man gazed at her, his head wavering. "I dunno."

She held his hand. "I'll help you."

Cyrus gazed at her.

"I'm Sara."

"Sara." Evans repeated the name. "I'm glad you're home."

Chapter Thirty-Seven

Gladys Pickering watched Pastor McGurk stuff the day's donations into his satchel. "Any interesting letters today?" He zipped the bag closed.

For the last five days, it was the same routine. Pastor arrived at four o'clock, looked over the list of donor names, counted the cash—paying little attention to the checks—and asked about notable letters. Gladys had shown him more than a dozen messages, but none suited him. He kept insisting on a "home run" for his network debut.

Today, she might have just the one.

The letter came in the two o'clock delivery. Sylvia discovered it and handed the envelope to Gladys. Above the address, the writer penned *Attention: Gladys Pickering*. Who would write her a personal letter? Gladys tore it open. The note, however, was for Pastor. That was odd. Why put it to her attention? The penmanship seemed familiar. Insistent thoughts nagged at her to check out a hunch, but she'd have to wait until later.

"We got this note two hours ago." Gladys offered him the pages, keeping the envelope hidden. "You might find it interesting."

He sniffed the paper, raising his eyebrows. "It smells like flowers." Shaking his head, he unfolded the sheets, reading the letter aloud.

"Dear Pastor McGurk,

"I am a resident of Joshua County Farm. Before the misfortune that brought me here, I used to listen to your program. Just hearing your voice gave me comfort and hope. Other residents here have heard you as well. Since we do not have a visiting pastor, your voice and message would be most welcome.

"We work hard earning our keep here. One of my chores is caring for the old and the infirmed. The job requires me to lift and move the patients. It is tiring work, but worthwhile. The people I watch over are happy and comfortable. Since we do not have indoor plumbing, we are constantly hauling in new water by hand and taking out the old. My back aches from all the lifting and carrying. Running water would ease my burden and add to the comfort of our older folks.

"Your Sunday program made me feel like part of something bigger. Your words explained the world in an understandable and reassuring way. Your solutions would set the nation to a prosperous future. I long to hear them again.

"I wanted to ask for a radio, but events which we cannot control imperil our world.

"Leaders in our community have deemed it necessary to abandon us. They wish to sell our home and land in a public auction as a way to cut expenses for the county. We will be turned out with nowhere to go. I don't fear for myself, but what will become of the infirmary patients? Where will they go?

"In a few weeks, our home will dissolve. As time grows short, I pray for a miracle: a way for us to keep our home.

"Pastor Sam, can you save us?

Sincerely Yours,
Beatrice Mullens"

McGurk turned to Gladys. "Excellent. Very perceptive of you to bring this to my attention." He paced the office floor, pocketed the note, then whirled around. "This letter has a story that will draw listeners in. It will turn my debut into an event." He scrutinized the top of the page. "Joshua County Farm. What kind of place is that?"

Gladys shrugged. "A poor farm. They harbor the needy."

"Exactly. A group of indigent workers living in isolation. What do you suppose they wish for? What would they want the most?"

Gladys turned her palms up. "Shelter?"

McGurk scowled, "Shelter..." He brushed the idea away. "Open your eyes. They're alone and want to be a part of the outside world. They need a place to gather, and a radio would suit that purpose. I suppose they'll need one with a battery."

Gladys pursed her lips. "Aren't you forgetting? Their shelter is about to close."

McGurk wrinkled his nose. "I'm not about to take on the expense of saving a poor farm." He continued pacing, eyes furrowed, one hand covering his mouth. "I need to know more about this place. All of you will need to make calls. Where is it? What are the people like there? Who runs it, and how can I contact them? I want this by eight tomorrow."

Gladys gasped, "It's after four now. How do you expect us to get that information by morning?" She spread her hands. "Do you see a telephone in here?"

McGurk grunted and reached into his satchel,

drawing out some bills. He counted out five dollars and handed the money to Gladys. "The Allis Hotel has a row of phone booths in the lobby. Make your calls from there. Tomorrow is my last day of meetings with the Alliance representative. The brass from the radio station will be there too, so I need to have my facts straight when I'm convincing them to do the impossible."

"What do you mean?" It was impossible to follow this man's thinking.

McGurk glared at her. "Haven't you been listening to anything I've said? The premiere will be live from Joshua County Farm. I'll present a nice radio to this Beatrice during the program. Think of the publicity it would generate."

Gladys bit her lip for a moment. "You're going there?" Apprehension washed over her.

McGurk smirked. "No doubt the engineer will balk. But a remote broadcast could work. With more information, I'll be able to sell the idea to the Tabors. William and Meredith Tabor own the station. Bill likes a challenge. But it's his wife, the Snow Queen, who will be the tough sell. If she agrees, then it's simply a matter of engineering."

Oh, no. He mustn't go there. Not if her guess was true. "The poor farm won't have electricity. Broadcasting requires power."

"Engineer Gorham touts himself as a problem solver. He'll figure out the solution."

Gladys' mind churned, looking for another obstacle. "The Alliance broadcast is only a month away. There won't be enough time to prepare for such a broadcast at a location you know nothing about. Doesn't this sound a bit risky?" Showing Pastor this letter was a mistake. Who would have guessed he would want to go to a poor farm?

McGurk sighed. "Possibly. But the pay-off will be a historic broadcast. You do your job. Mine is to sell the idea. The rest will take care of itself." Pastor grabbed his hat and satchel. "You have phone calls to make. Good day, ladies." He strode to the office door, opened it, and stamped out.

Gladys waited a minute before creeping to the door. No sign of the pastor in the hallway. Satisfied, she hustled to Sara's desk. The handwritten draft of a letter lay in the top tray. Gladys took a page to her desk, produced the envelope, and laid it on top of Sara's note. For a long moment, she studied the handwriting between the two.

They matched.

She motioned to Sylvia and Marilyn. "You need to see this."

Marilyn stood up. "What is it?"

Sylvia raised a hand to her lips. "Something wrong?"

"Just the opposite. I know where Sara is."

Sylvia and Marilyn rushed to join her.

Gladys pointed to the envelope "My first clue was how the envelope was addressed. Nobody writes *Attention* on a fan letter. But the handwriting was the real giveaway. See how Sara prints a capital A in Alliance? She makes a diagonal line from the bottom to make the crossbar. It matches the A in Attention. The B in Broadcasting is curved at the top just like the B in Broadway on the envelope. There's no doubt in my mind. Sara is staying at Joshua County Farm."

Sylvia's jaw dropped. "What should we do?"

Marilyn frowned. "We should get her. Drive up there now and bring her back."

Gladys rubbed her chin. "It's tempting. Joshua is about sixty miles from here. My husband could take us there. Still...the best thing might be to write her back. Find out what she wants us to do."

Sylvia clasped her hands together. "Sara's brothers came here askin' about her. Shouldn't we tell 'em?"

Gladys pressed her lips together, thinking. "Good point. If she wants her family to know where she is, she could have written to them directly. Or gave us instructions what to do. Nowhere is there a plea for help. She may want us to do nothing."

Marilyn tapped the corner of the envelope. "The return address says Beatrice Mullens. We should write back to that person."

"You're right. Sara may be using a false name."

"We should tell Miz Sara how we miss her," Sylvia said. "Find out how she doin'." The ebony-skinned woman steepled her fingers before her lips. "Iffin' you think so, Miz Gladys."

Gladys smiled. "You're part of this, Sylvia. Those are good suggestions."

"That letter..." Marilyn's voice held a serious tone. "The pastor must never learn it came from Sara."

Gladys lowered her eyes. "That's why we're warning Sara. Pastor Sam has stars in his eyes, and he's about to come calling."

Marilyn shook her head. "I still think we should bring her back. We can stop any trouble before it happens."

Sylvia's eyes became liquid. "But what if Miz Sara sets her mind to stay? Surely, we can do something to help."

Gladys set her jaw. "There is. We'll be there when they meet."

Chapter Thirty-Eight

Jason McGurk lay on his bed rubbing his eyes. Michael was already asleep. It was nearly midnight and the cabbie had not shown yet. Through the open window, a far-off train whistle pieced the night. A nighttime mockingbird trilled in a nearby tree.

Harlan was late. The taxi driver made it sound so easy to find Sara's destination. He seemed sincere enough, but there was things he said that made him less than trustworthy. Surely, he wouldn't take the money and run. No, he wanted the cash—all of it—so he wasn't likely to disappear.

Jason picked up one of Michael's pulp magazines. The cover story was King of the Sky and showed a giant airship engulfed in flames with red biplanes circling about. One plane streaked downward trailing black smoke. He flipped to the story and read from where he left off.

"Jackson King, Commander of the Aero Knights, scoured the skies as his zeppelin, The Monarch, burned like a bonfire in the heavens. The only thing keeping the hydrogen from exploding was the insulating layer of lightweight beruvium coating the buoyant vessel. The armor could sustain bullets, but could it protect against heat? It had to. They blew one of Red Murdoch's flyers out of the sky. The aircraft fell in a spiral, trailing flames and smoke. That left four planes, each loaded

with lethal machine-guns. King needed a miracle or his crew would perish in a fiery explosion."

Somewhere outside a car honked.

Michael rolled over, muttering in his sleep.

Jason leaped to his feet, crossed to the window, and peered out. A taxi sat in front of the house. Harlan came through! Jason waved his arms, hoping the driver would notice. Headlights blinked. He stepped to his brother's bed and shook him awake. "Get up. Cabbie's here."

Michael blinked, rubbing his nose. "What time is it?"

"Midnight. Get your cash and follow me." Jason darted out of the room and descended the stairs with as little noise as possible. He flashed out the front door with Michael catching up as he neared the taxi.

Harlan rolled down his window. "Step into my office, boys. We need to talk."

Jason and Michael glanced at each other, then climbed into the backseat.

The cabbie turned to face them, lighting a cigarette. "I talked to two of the three drivers who drove last Sunday morning. Not many fares so they knocked off early. That leaves the third guy, and he's out of town. Funeral, I suppose. He'll be back Sunday. I can't get an address for you until then."

"So why are you here?" Jason asked. "We got a deal. No address, no money."

Michael tapped Jason's arm. "Let him finish."

The tip of the cigarette glowed in the dark. Harlan exhaled, filling the cab with smoke. "Yeah, we got a deal. The third driver is scheduled for a double shift starting noon on Sunday. I can catch him then and have your address to you by twelve-thirty."

Jason waved smoke from his face. "We can take it from here by calling for a cab Sunday and asking for the cabbie who just returned. We don't need you anymore."

The driver sucked in another drag. "No can do. I've spent a lot of time on this. You give me the other half of that Hamilton tonight and that other five and I'll get you the address on Sunday. Otherwise, I drive off, and spread the word that you guys don't pay your fares."

Jason narrowed his eyes. "Are you welching?"

Michael handed the driver some money. "Here's the other half of the ten and the five. We've honored our half of the bargain."

Jason gritted his teeth. Michael just gave away any control they had in their agreement.

"Thanks," Harlan said. "See you Sunday."

"We'll see," said Jason.

"Easy, boy scout." the driver said. "I remember your ma the day we made the deal. I saw how she looked when she talked about her daughter. I'm not going to stiff you."

Michael sighed. "It's been a tough week. We're not sure if our sister is even alive."

Harlan whistled. "Maybe you should call the cops."

"It's an option. In the meantime, you'll still get us that address?" Michael asked.

"Will do."

"Thanks." Michael got out. "You coming?"

"I'll be along," Jason said. "See you at the house."

After his brother left, Jason turned to the cab driver. "I know you can renege at any time, but I believe you." Jason thrust out a hand. "Care to shake?"

The cabbie seemed to hesitate, but shook his hand. "You're not the trusting sort, are you?"

Jason inhale the stale air. "I suppose not."

"I'll prove you wrong."

"Do that. My brother will make sure I eat plenty of crow."

Harlan chuckled. "That I'd like to see."

"Sunday then." Jason left the cab and joined his brother on the front porch.

Michael yawned as he approached. "Now don't you be yelling at me. I had to give him the money to show good faith."

"Don't worry," Jason said. "We kissed and made up."

Michael burst into laughter.

Jason turned away to hide his smile. Too bad they weren't at the café. He'd have won that round.

Chapter Thirty-Nine

Saturday, April 13, 1935

Jeremy Gorham rose to his feet, both hands on the conference room table. "Pastor McGurk's idea of a remote broadcast is impractical." He hated these daily meetings. With KSKN's debut with Alliance in four weeks, he ought to be testing the control board they received last week. Sure, the equipment might be new, but the vacuum tubes that made up the insides could have been damaged during transit. Troubleshooting took time, and time was growing short. Crazy endeavors as the last minute wasn't what they needed. "Our station would have to pay for building a telephone line to a location where a single show will air. Moreover, we don't even know if a remote is feasible from there. Our resources for such a grandstanding experiment are limited."

There were four others in KSKN's smoke-filled conference room. William Tabor, the owner of the station, continued puffing on his long cigar and wiping non-existent ash from his gray suit. Pastor Sam McGurk leaned back in his leather chair scowling, as if he cared less what the hired help said—except he, too, was a hired worker. Charles Lam, the dapper representative from Alliance Broadcasting Systems, gazed at a photograph on the far wall. *None of them matter.* Jeremy retook his seat. Only one opinion counted—The Snow Queen's.

Meredith Tabor swept back her feathery white hair with long elegant fingers, peering at him with cool blue eyes. Those cobalt peepers could freeze mercury. She reigned as the radio station's bookkeeper, chief producer, scriptwriter, and wife to the owner. It was rumored she often dined with Olive Beech, bookkeeper and financial guardian of Beech Aircraft. "And what do you suggest we do instead, Mr. Gorham?" Her voice was quiet, but firm. Joan Crawford could learn from such a voice.

Jeremy shrugged off an icy chill. "Broadcast from here in Wichita, the way we've always done. Since Alliance requested a choir to perform on Pastor's program, we've constructed a new studio—one large enough to hold a dozen singers. Let's use what we have."

Tabor blew another puff from his cigar. "Sam, go over again what you wish to do, but leave out the sales pitch."

McGurk glanced at his notes. "I wish to create a singular radio event, a network premiere from a unique remote location about sixty miles from here. The centerpiece of the program would be to present a radio to a deserving group of people."

Tabor waved his hand with the cigar. Acrid smoke permeated the air. "Yes, yes, I get that. But what is this place—did you say a poor farm?"

"Joshua County Farm is an institution where the indigent pay for their keep by working in the fields. According to the county clerk, they have a telephone."

Meredith jotted some notes. "Tell us, Pastor, how

did you come up with such an extraordinary idea?"

"I received a fan letter from a person living on the premises."

"Do you have the letter with you?"

"Yes, ma'am."

"Hand it over, please."

McGurk gave the folded note to Jeremy, who passed it to the Snow Queen.

Tabor laid his cigar on a mahogany ashtray. "Jeremy, what would it take to get a remote up and running by May twelfth?"

Jeremy considered. "First, we run network quality telephone wire from this station to the broadcast site. That location would become the end link to Alliance's radio network. Second, we'd need to set up a broadcast station, complete with mixing board and amplifiers. Third, to haul all this heavy, bulky equipment up there, we'd require a large truck, one big enough to hold a generator or batteries since there's probably no electricity. Generators are noisy. Batteries are quiet, but I would have to convert DC battery power to AC current." *Insane.*

Tabor lifted an eyebrow. "Is that possible?"

He wanted to say no. "It's dicey but workable. Dry cells, like car batteries, would work best. We should have an engineer and director at both ends to coordinate the broadcast. A backdoor communication line is a must in case problems arise. When the broadcast is over, the remote crew packs up and goes home. How long a show are we talking about?"

McGurk shrugged. "A half hour, same as a regular show."

Jeremy shook his head. "The station would lose

money."

McGurk leaned in, scowling. "Surely, alternatives can be found. Perhaps we can use the existing telephone line. Or broadcast using a shortwave transmitter."

Gorham sighed. *Everyone's an expert.* "Both would work after a fashion. What it comes down to is sound quality. The tinny voices of a choir singing over a telephone line sounds terrible—not acceptable for a commercial broadcast. If you were trying to communicate with Admiral Byrd over the South Pole, shortwave would make sense. These signals travel thousands of miles because the waves bounce between the ground and upper atmosphere. They become less reliable as the sender and receiver come closer together. Reception becomes spotty. One area may sound clear, but another location can get distortion. At sixty miles, you're asking for a perfect bank shot from earth to atmosphere and back down to the ground again. The most reliable signal will always be through high-quality telephone wire."

The Alliance representative cleared his throat. "You know, there is another way to get a perfect signal without spending a dime for telephone line."

Tabor picked up his cigar. "How is that, Carl?"

"The same way some of our other stations broadcast baseball games. As your engineer suggests, it's cumbersome to take the studio to the ballpark. But some stations re-create the ballpark from within the radio studio."

"Impossible," McGurk scoffed.

"It works like any radio drama. A telegraph operator climbs a pole and sends in the play-by-play to the station. A writer composes a script based on the game's progress. About four innings into the game, while the scripter is still hammering out the action, a couple of announcers and a soundman will simulate the game, following the script. The listeners hear a realistic sounding ballgame complete with commentary, mitts slapping, the bats, crowd noise, and umpire calls."

Jeremy clapped his hands. "That's it! Pastor can do his presentation at the county farm, but we bring everyone involved to Wichita and re-enact the program in the studio on the day of the premiere."

McGurk shot to his feet. "I won't allow my radio event to be cheapened by studio tricks. My broadcast will be done live at the poor farm. If money is an issue, I'm willing to pay the cost of running the telephone line there. This is my show, and I want it my way."

Tabor turned to his wife. "Do you see a way for this to work?"

Meredith laid her pencil down after totaling a neat row of figures. Her moniker fit her well. The Snow Queen expected results without ever raising her voice. Was she pushy? Always. Intimidating? Like a hawk. But never brutal. Meredith wasted little time on fabricating punishment or inspiration. She demanded excellence and paid well when her staff delivered.

"Gentlemen." Her smooth, clipped voice commanded attention. "Pastor wishes to devote his program to donating a radio to a workhouse that is about to fold. A pointless gift when you think about it. Pastor neglected to mention that the writer and other dwellers will soon have to leave. Keep in mind, this is more than a workhouse for penniless fieldworkers. It's a resting place for the old." Her eyes turned back to McGurk. "Perhaps you should give each inmate a share of the money you were so willing to spend on wire—as a going-away present. It would save us all a lot of bother." Meredith took up her pencil again.

McGurk jumped to his feet, his chair falling over backward. "Those remarks are insulting! The future of that house is not the subject of my broadcast. This is my show. I decide the content. Alliance chose it over two other programs, one of which you produced—"

Meredith's pencil snapped, sending bits of wood skittering across the tabletop. McGurk jumped when a piece of lead struck the wall by his head.

"Be seated, sir." Meredith's tone remained cool. She set the shards of her pencil aside and reached for a new one. "Some enlightenment is in order. You signed a contract with this station. That means you work for us. As long as you continue to make this station money, we will entertain your employment. This fits with your gospel, I believe."

McGurk's red face stared back without expression.

Meredith smiled benignly. "While we are on the subject of ownership, we're modifying the name of your program. The sponsor wants name recognition, so on May twelfth we are renaming the program *Carey Salt Presents Heaven and Earth*."

McGurk's eyes flashed. "Do I have a say in this?"

"Only if you wish to pay for your own sponsorship."

Jeremy bit off a chuckle. The Snow Queen seemed to take pleasure in toying with the preacher.

Pastor shook his head, loosening his tie.

She turned to address the group. "On the face of it, the pastor's notion of a remote at a doomed workhouse is a ridiculous idea, but remotes are the future of radio.

Broadcasting from large hotel ballrooms in New York and music halls in Nashville have become popular. Audiences are demanding more. As broadcasters, we cannot stay hidden in our studios indefinitely, and so we must venture out to become listeners as well. Our opportunity now is to relay the story of the workhouse lodgers along with the larger story of its closing. The real story is how losing their home will affect the lives of the infirmed and those caring for them."

Jeremy cringed. A series of remotes? This project was bigger than what their station could handle. "Are we producing these shows within our studio?"

Meredith nodded. "Rest assured, Mr. Gorham. Further broadcasts will originate from the studio here. I don't imagine the workhouse overseer will want us taking up residence there. Shows about their own community get listeners involved. How does the Depression affect the people here? How will it affect the area? Has the role of these home changed over time? If so, what will the future hold? Learning these answers will lead us to discovering ourselves."

"I'm not interested in the future." McGurk flicked his hand like batting away an irritating fly. "And I'll have no part in this grandiose scheme of glorifying the destitute."

Meredith Tabor turned her chilling gaze upon Samuel McGurk. "Oh, Pastor, you misunderstand." Her smile showed perfect teeth. "It will be your job to sustain the audience from the start. You will show the plight of the dwellers and be a part of the narrative."

"I agreed to the offering a radio. And to pay for the telephone line. You're demanding that I involve myself in their affairs?"

"Of course, the cost of the network line is the least of your duties. Do what you do best. Sell yourself. Fail—and you can retire to your pulpit."

McGurk hunched forward, gasping like he'd just run up three flights of stairs. He mopped his sweaty brow with a handkerchief and gulped down the glass of water before him. With some muttering, he regained some measure of composure. Jeremy slid his untouched glass to the pastor. Was he counting backward?

Meredith turned her gaze to Jeremy. "We'll need to gain permission from the authorities to use this site. You will go to Joshua and see the county official in charge of the workhouse. Get his permission to proceed with the broadcast and inspect the site. Decide if it meets your requirements. And locate a choir if you can. I'm leaving the engineering details up to you as well. Much of this is on your shoulders. I'm expecting miracles, Mr. Gorham." She gave him one of her rare genuine smiles.

"Yes, ma'am." There it was. They were going through with the pastor's crazy scheme. Only now, it was the Snow Queen's crazy scheme. And he was tasked with making it happen.

Meredith turned to McGurk. "Pastor, I want an hour-long script of your premiere. Assume there will be no music. We can always edit down later. Give me your best draft in ten days."

Pastor McGurk lowered his eyes. "Yes, madam."

"Splendid. If everything looks promising, then it's a small matter of hiring a crew of linemen to run the telephone wire. Our premiere is in a month so speed is essential. Mr. Lam, you have your contracts. Let's make history, people. You're all dismissed."

As Jeremy Gorham left the conference room, he wondered if the history they were about to make would be a grand victory. Or a disaster because they overextended themselves.

Chapter Forty

Sunday, April 14, 1935

Jason McGurk scanned the neighborhood from the porch as Michael read from his *Black Mask* pulp. It was twelve twenty-five. The cabbie, if he were coming, should be along soon. It all came down to waiting for an address, the last known place where Sara went. They'd been seeking this answer for a week.

Kids squealed playing tag across the street. In the branches of a neighboring elm, squirrels quarreled over shared territory. To the east, a man in a straw hat mowed his grass. Jason watched as he leaned into the handle, pushing the two big wheels with its whirling blades. Why bother? There'd been little rain. It seemed like a waste of time.

"Cab's coming." Michael pointed to the west. The approaching taxi tooted as it chattered to a halt in front of the house.

Jason followed his younger brother running to the car. He agreed that Michael should do the talking. This was his idea, and the driver trusted him.

Michael peeked into the passenger side window. "Have you got an address for us?"

Harlan handed him a slip of paper. "I was lucky to catch him starting his shift."

"Thanks." Michael waved as the cabbie pulled

away. Jason glanced over his shoulder. He unfolded the paper.

"1217 River Boulevard." Michael refolded the slip. "We can walk there in thirty minutes."

"Forget that." Jason jangled a set of car keys. "We're taking the Model A. Dad's still at the radio station. It's a good time to go."

Michael crooked his thumb to the house. "Shouldn't we tell Mom?"

And tell us to sit by while the cops question Larry? "Would you tell her?"

Michael sighed. "No."

"That's what I thought. Let's go."

A few minutes later, Jason steered the Model A south along the winding street bordering the river. Five years of drought had not been kind to the Little Arkansas. The river used to be nearly sixty feet wide. Now, it was little more than a creek, crisscrossed with sandbars and grass. Houses on the west side of the street faced the forlorn river.

Jason rubbed a well-scratched spot of dry skin on his arm. He'd never started a fight before, but Larry would talk—one way or another. He parked the car two houses north. Larry's residence was not visible because of the curved street.

He killed the engine. "Stay here."

"What're you doing?"

"I'm ending this. If anyone gets in trouble, it'll be me." Jason got out of the car.

Michael jumped from the vehicle, slamming the door. "Nuts. I'm coming too."

Jason held up an arm. "We're done playing detective. Stay put. I mean it." With that, he set off for the house.

The Roadster sat in the driveway. Jason entered through the gate and up to the front door. A radio played inside. Several chairs sat together on the covered porch and a bench swing hung from hooks screwed into the ceiling. Jason rapped hard on the doorframe. Behind him, a board creaked. He turned around.

Michael leaned on the porch rail, crossing his arms. "You know, there's another way to get our bird to sing. You act the part of the angry brother, and I'll be the nice brother. That way, you won't have to go to jail for fighting." He shrugged. "That's assuming you win."

Jason furrowed his brow. *Wise guy.* What kind of pretend game was Michael talking about? "Okay, Sam Spade. How's it work?"

"Just threaten him. I'll take it from there. The two of us will play him like a piano."

The door opened. Larry stood, eyes not quite focused. "You guys again? Get off my porch."

Jason stepped forward, blocking the front door from closing. "Not a chance. There's blood in the front seat of your car. Sara's blood. You tried to clean it off, but it's still there." Jason pointed at Larry's bandage. "Yours too, I'll wager."

Larry touched his cheek. "How... What do you want?"

Michael drew up beside Jason. "We want Sara. Our parents have issued a reward. It should be in this evening's newspaper. As I see it, we can either tell the cops about the blood. Or...you can be the hero. Bring our sister back, and collect the reward."

Jason blinked. What was Michael talking about? Then it dawned. Play him like a piano. And he was the angry brother. Not exactly a stretch. He balled his hand into a fist. "The reward is good only if she's alive. If something happened to her, *you'd* be the one paying."

Larry focused on Michael. "How much?"

Michael spread out the fingers of one hand. "Five grand—cash money. That'll get you a nicer car. A new car beats getting grilled by the cops."

Larry's eyes sharpened, shifting between the boys.

Jason turned to Michael. Time to set the hook deeper. "He doesn't deserve the money. Send him to prison. He won't last long in the Big House."

Michael grabbed Jason's arm. "No. Give him a chance. Larry can help." Jason struggled to keep a straight face. And he thought Jackie Cooper was a ham.

"No cops. I want the money," said Larry.

Jason glanced at Michael, tapping his chest. *My turn.* Michael shrugged. Jason pointed at Larry. "You've got the rest of the day. Bring Sara back home safe and sound. Or else."

"Have the money ready." Larry pushed Jason back and slammed the door.

Jason passed a shaking hand across his forehead. Michael's plan worked. He turned and trudged out of the yard. His knees wobbled, and he head reeled from the adrenaline.

Michael loped ahead, clapping and rubbing his hands. "We got 'im! Did you see the look on his face? He believed every word we said!"

Jason grabbed his brother by the collar. "What got into you? There's no reward. That's crazy! He thinks we'll pay for Sara."

"That's the point!" Michael broke away and danced around Jason as he lumbered back to the car.

"Who cares about the reward? All that matters is Larry bringing Sara back. We can watch the house and see if he makes a move."

As they reached the car, Jason pulled out the keys. "He confessed to taking Sara. We got the goods on him. Maybe we should go to the police." Jason started the engine. "This business of flushing him out seems like—"

"Save it!" Michael pointed. "Look!"

Around the curve, the silver Roadster was just visible backing onto the street. It turned north, coming their way.

"Duck!" Michael yelled. "He'll see us!"

Jason bent, knocking heads with his brother while diving below the dashboard. He rubbed his forehead as the rattle of the Chevy engine passed, dwindling to the north.

Jason sat up, engaged the car, drove to the nearest driveway, and turned around. Their canary was loose. Now, they had no choice but to follow. Where would their songbird fly?

Chapter Forty-One

Sara and her crew went about serving Sunday dinner to Mr. Evans. Like yesterday, he didn't taunt or bicker, but hummed an out-of-tune song. After eating, he allowed Patrick to help him. to the rocker by the window. He settled in with a sigh. Then, he took up the off-kilter song once again. He gestured to the window. "Can you get some fresh air in here?"

What was the name of that tune? She'd heard it before.

Patrick lifted the window, but it kept falling down. "Miss Sara? It won't stay open."

She stepped to the window, pushing the sash to its fullest extent. It slipped a couple of inches, then held.

Cyrus inclined his head. "Thank you." When was the last time he said that?

Sara turned. "Why, you're welcome!"

Mr. Evans gazed out the window, taking deep breaths. "Nothing but blue skies."

Blue Skies. That's what he was humming.

"I remember more about the May baskets you made."

She bent forward. "Tell me."

"You made a little tag that said 'To Daddy.' Only the D faced backward. For years after you left, I thought about that tag."

"Bea and I are going to the cemetery to gather

flowers. Would you like us to bring back a nice bouquet for you?"

Cyrus nodded, closing his eyes. "But it needs the tag."

Sara's voice held her smile. "One flower basket with a badly printed tag, coming up."

HIs chair creaked as he leaned back. "I recall growing up, near a train stop called Watch Horn. Our farm had a quarter horse named Babe. I took her riding each week. One day, a cougar shadowed us. Its screams kept getting closer and closer. The thing sounded like a woman, but its screams would curdle your blood. Babe spooked and bolted for home. I lay flat on her back, my fingers wrapped around her neck. That cougar kept pace with us, screaming the whole time. I knew if I fell, I was done."

"What happened?" She imagined a small boy clinging to terrified horse. A mountain lion urging the horse to rear up.

"Babe got back to the house, practically climbing on the porch. By the time Pa got his shotgun, that cougar left, its screams faded with the wind."

"Thank you for telling me that story."

Mr. Evans shrugged. "Just something I remembered." His smile faded.

"Sara." He cleared his throat. "I've done a few things wrong in my younger days." His voice took on a gravely tone. "Things I'm not proud of. If I'd made a few middling changes, life would have been different. I might have kept my wife. And you."

He's apologizing. Sara bowed her head. "That was a long time ago. You were a different man then."

The old man looked beyond her to the window.

She tried to meet his eyes. But he averted her eyes. "T'ain't no excuse. I know what I did. I'm not proud of it. Seems like once a body goes far enough down a certain road, it's easier to keep on going. Not so easy to turn around. I could've done different. Changed my ways. I didn't. Now, I'm not making sorry. That won't change what happened between your ma and me. All I can do is make good with you."

A small moan escaped her lips. If only her own father could say those words to her. Ask her forgiveness or merely offer a word of love. Daddy had his flaws—pride and vanity. His own self-blindness could well wreck his family as Cyrus destroyed his. But Cyrus atoned, though it was way too late.

But even for Mr. Evans, it was redemption. He had just apologized to the image of his grown daughter.

She held his hand. "If Ma was here. I'm sure she'd forgive you."

"I don't see why. She'd dune right to walk out. It took brass to do that. I could have gone after her. Guess I was too proud. Never really appreciated her 'til I grew old alone."

"You're not alone now. I'm here."

Cyrus smiled.

The three finished with their chores. Sara pulled back the bed covers. "Would you like to lay down?"

Cyrus shook his head. "I'd rather look out and see the sky."

Sara took the blanket off his bed and tucked the edges around him in the rocker. "That should keep you comfortable." She moved the table closer and set his water cup on it. "We'll be back at suppertime with your May basket."

"Remember the tag."

She kissed his forehead. "Of course. I'm glad we can be friends."

"See you."

"Goodbye, Daddy."

Mr. Evans rocked in his chair humming off-notes as he looked out the window.

The three filed out of the room.

Chapter Forty-Two

Larry Bigger drove on Highway 15 north from Wichita, his Panama hat pulled low over a sweaty brow, his head rang like a cracked bell. If only he could sleep at night, but rest eluded him. Instead, an endless parade of questions kept him awake. Would anyone link Sara's disappearance to him? How much trouble was she going to cost him? What if she came back and accused him of kidnapping? Would the police arrest him? He imagined the cops knocking at his door in the dead of night. So he stayed awake. Listening. Waiting. He nodded off often during work. One customer complained to his father about him dozing on the job. That got him a thorough chewing out.

Now, Sara's brothers were nagging him. Threatening him. To get out of this mess, he had to return the broad. Then, he could collect the reward and sleep like the dead. He brushed a shaky hand over his forehead. Sara still had to be at that county asylum.

Dating Sara was pleasant at first. There was that familiar anticipation of another conquest. But then she became friendlier with his father, charming him, and always acting interested in his business. The old fool loved it, of course. The vamp wormed her way in, turning father against son.

"Larry, you need to adopt a better work attitude."
"You should show more respect."

"Learn to develop a nose for business like Sara."

And finally, *"What I'd give to have a daughter like that."*

News of the baby was the final straw. Sara wanted to marry. *Ha!* How convenient was *that*? When he ran across the asylum, an idea shaped itself into a plan for getting her out of the picture. Last Sunday, that plan became an opportunity.

With Sara's return, the prospect of marriage would rear its ugly head again. How could he stop that? A punch to the stomach? Could that abort the baby? Would a car accident work? Larry patted the steering wheel. Sacrificing his Roadster for an uncertain plan didn't seem worth it. He'd have to think of a better idea. And if he could keep the five thousand dollars, so much the better.

****

Jason McGurk found it easy to keep Larry in sight. Few cars were on the flat highway. Little disturbed the expanse of grass and sky except fencing, farmhouses, and a few trees. He and Michael had been driving north for over an hour and Larry Bigger showed no sign of slowing down.

Michael stretched his arms. "Where's he going— Salina? Concordia? Nebraska? He'd better get to where he's heading. I'm hungry. What time is it, anyway?"

Jason pulled out his pocket watch and flipped the cover. "Two-thirty."

Michael took off his newsboy cap and scratched his head. "Whose idea was this to follow him?"

Jason snorted. "I believe it was yours."

"I'm not saying it wasn't. But you're the one driving."

"We've gone too far to turn around. He's bound to stop soon. When he gets to where Sara is, we'll step in and take her back ourselves. Are you with me?"

Michael glanced at Jason, one eyebrow raised. "Are you expecting trouble?"

"I think we need to take control when the time is right."

"Gotcha. Speaking of trouble, what do you suppose *that* is?" Michael pointed to the northwest.

Jason slowed the car to gaze at the strange sight. A gray-black band rose just above the horizon. Even as he watched, it grew taller, topping far distant trees. It wasn't a cloud, more like a curtain, dividing day and night. The mesmerizing band climbed higher, becoming an approaching dark wall. And it would soon be upon them.

The tires were kicking up sand. They were on the shoulder of the road. Ahead, a bridge—more like a road of wooden planks—spanned a dry creek bed. Jason drew in a sharp breath and yanked the steering wheel. The car swerved. Tires caught the edge of the uneven boards, rattling the car. Terror jolted him. *Hang on!* The Model A bounced across the expanse, its front tires popping over a bump and landing on a plank that snapped beneath the weight. With a final jolt they made the other side.

"Holy cats!" Michael stared out his side window, one hand clutching the dashboard, the other grabbing the backseat. "It's a wonder we didn't fall in the creek! Watch where you're going next time."

"What creek?" Jason mopped his brow. Michael was right; they could have sailed off that bridge. "That's some kind of storm. Think we should go back?"

Michael shook his head. "Keep going."

Jason glanced at the ominous sky one last time, then searched the road ahead for the silver Roadster.

The highway was empty.

A cold chill washed over him. He stomped on the gas and shifted into third. Gears ground, but the Model A lurched forward like an old but valiant horse. The pleasant clatter wound to a strident rattle.

"Michael! Do you see his car?"

Michael searched the road. "He's just ahead. I'm sure of it."

"I can't go any faster." Jason's fist pounded the wheel. "I know he's no Houdini. But he's gone!"

Chapter Forty-Three

With afternoon rounds over, Sara and Bea changed into leggings for their flower hunt. Before they headed for the cemetery, however, they stopped by the barn to bid farewell to Dutch. Don Holland was heading to find work in McPherson. A pang of sadness touched her heart. Perhaps even dread. The lovable, self-deprecating tramp provided a layer of stability to the dining room. *Will I even see him again?*

He made his announcement that morning, sitting across from Sara at the breakfast table. Patrick dropped his spoon, staring down at his oatmeal in sullen silence. The tramp placed a hand on his shoulder. "Now don't be sore at ol' Dutch. I have to make a living. Can't do that here. McPherson is only one county over, and I can come back to visit anytime. While I was helping the Eisner's, a fellow in town told me about the jobs there. Oil companies are looking for help. In McPherson, they're saying, 'What Depression?' I have to go. So, what do you say? Still friends?" Dutch stuck out a hand.

Patrick crossed his arms, keeping his head down.

Dutch glanced at Sara and Bea. "How about you, ladies? Would you come out to the barn later? Say goodbye to an old tramp?"

Sara smiled. "Sure, Mr. Holland. We'll stop by this afternoon. Bea and I are going to the cemetery to gather wildflowers." Sara turned to Bea. "You still want to go?"

Bea nodded.

"Great!" Dutch stuck up both thumbs. "Say, there's some old baskets in the barn. They might come in handy."

"Thank you. We could use some baskets."

After breakfast, Sara found some work gloves. She longed for a nice wide-brimmed hat, but she saw nothing suitable. Leaving the back door, Sara and Bea made their way to the barn. Dutch stood inside the double doors talking with James Eisner. A cloth bag with a rope handle sat at his feet.

"We came to wish you luck on your journey, Mr. Holland." Sara curtsied.

"No formalities needed, young lady." With that, Dutch grabbed Sara in a tight bear hug. "And how about a squeeze from my little Spelling Bea?" He bent over, giving Beatrice a tender embrace.

Beatrice retrieved her slate.

I'LL MISS YOU

"That goes double for me. I doubt if I'll find any lovelier dinner companions than you and Miss Sara. You two headed out to pick flowers?"

Bea inclined her head.

"Then I've got a surprise. I fixed these up myself." Dutch gave Sara a theatrical wink. From the shadows, he retrieved two wicker baskets and gave one each to Sara and Bea. The handles and frames were wicker, but Dutch had replaced the bottoms with two layers of stout burlap.

Sara fingered the heavy stitching. "This is wonderful, Mr. Holland. You've gone to a lot of work.

Thank you."

"My pleasure. Now bring back some pretties."

"We'll do that." Sara kissed the surprised tramp on the cheek.

Dutch raised his brows. "I may have to visit often. I could get used to these kinds of goodbyes."

Sara and Bea left the barn, walked down the side-drive to the country road, and turned east. A slight breeze ruffled Sara's hair, but the day promised to be pleasant and mild. They passed the gravel lane that stretched south. Larry assaulted her on that road nearly a week ago. She'd do well to avoid him in the future.

The stroll evoked thoughts of pleasant walks in the park or exploring the neighborhood as a child. Such peace and solitude. There wasn't a cloud in the sky. *Blue Skies smiling on me.* Sara found herself singing the words to Mr. Evans' song. Bea glanced at her with a peculiar scowl on her face. That seemed odd. Must have been an errant thought. No reason to be a sourpuss. They had a few hours to themselves on a glorious spring day. No hard times could touch them out here. It felt so good to leave their cares behind for a little while.

She led the way to the cemetery gate. Along the fence, they found white violets and flowering milkweed. Sara knelt, cutting flowers while Bea placed some mint and parsley in her basket. "We'll leave the milkweed. Butterflies like it, but it sets me to sneezing."

Yellow and cream flowers inside the cemetery fence beckoned. These turned out to be fawn lilies. Star-like blooms tapered to five points on thin stems. Sara placed a few stalks in her container. "These would be good flowers for Mr. Evans' basket."

The hunt continued. Bea found white poppies hidden by a willow, while Sara discovered spurge and daisies. Often, they leapfrogged from one plant to another, examining likely groups of flowers. In spite of the dry spell, early spring wildflowers were abundant. And cemeteries provided a fertile environment for blooms.

Finally, after examining a cluster of wild onions—mostly out of curiosity—she waved to Bea. "Pull me up. My side is throbbing." After Bea helped Sara to her feet, she pointed to the stack of railroad ties at the rear of the cemetery. "Let's rest a bit before heading back home."

They sat under the bare branches of the willow, facing the sun to the south. The railroad ties were uncomfortable, but sitting eased the stitch in Sara's side. Bea leaned back, her shorter legs swinging inches off the ground.

"Thank you for coming out with me. I couldn't have done this without you."

Beatrice produced her slate.

I HAD FUN.

Sara smiled, glancing at her friend. It was tempting to kid her for frowning earlier. Bea was such a mystery. What was her past like? Why couldn't she talk? And why did she go to Mr. Byers' room?

"Something tells me you rarely get to enjoy yourself. What was it like growing up?"

Bea averted her face for a moment before answering.

MAMA HANGED HERSELF WHEN I WAS 5.
I FOUND HER.

Sara gasped. "That's terrible! I'm so sorry."

Bea wiped the slate clean with her apron.

PAPA SAID HER SADNESS WASN'T NATURAL

Her mother committed suicide. Was it due to depression? "Do you remember your mother?"

YES. MAMA TAUGHT ME TO SING

Sara drew in a breath. "You could talk at one time?"

A far-away look came into her eyes. She crammed her words together into one long string of letters.

I COULD TALK, BUT WITH MAMA I SANG. SHE SAID I COULD BE ON STAGE SOMEDAY

"Your mother must have been special."

SHE WAS EVERYTHING

Sara drew her arm around Bea, holding her shoulder. "What happened later, with your father?"

I QUIT TALKING. PAPA BLAMED MAMA'S MALONCHOLEY FOR MY STATE. HE SENT ME TO A CHILDREN'S HOME

"And you've never lived with a family since?"

Bea pursed her lips.

ONCE, IN JOSHUA, AFTER I LEFT THE ORPHANAGE

"What happened there?"

I LEARNED TO SEW. MR. B. HAD WOLF EYES, BUT I SCARED HIM OFF. THAT'S HOW I GOT HERE

Sara wiped her brow. Bea delivered her messages in broad strokes. The gaps in her story were yawning, and the process of verbal questions and labored written answers was tedious. Sara knew facts, but little about her silent friend.

"If you could do anything, what would you like to do? Would you like to talk?"

Bea scrawled the single word in large letters.

SING

Sara tilted her head. "Aren't we talking about same thing?"

Beatrice dashed the words down with her stub of chalk.

TALK IS LIKE THE THORNS ON A ROSE—SINGING IS THE ROSE ITSELF

"But to enjoy the rose, one must endure a few thorns."

Bea cleared her slate and wrote the letters in careful block letters.

I WANT TO SING!

Sara removed her arm from her friend's shoulder. Bea was serious. Surely, this was nothing but a child's fantasy. If she couldn't—or wouldn't—talk, how could she sing? "What's stopping you?"

For a second Beatrice looked blank. Then her mouth twisted into an ugly scowl. Worse than the one earlier. The frosty glare from the slight girl curled the hairs on the back of Sara's neck. It was a cold, appraising examination from the eyes of a malevolent stranger. Sara shivered.

Just as quickly as it came, the shadow passed. Beatrice bowed her head and wiped the slate with deliberate care. She wrote a single word and turned the slate around.

SALLY

Sara scrunched her eyes, trying to fathom the power of this person. Was Sally from the orphanage? An old companion? An enemy? A stray thought thrummed in the back of her mind. But that was too improbable. "Is Sally a friend?"

YOU ARE MY FRIEND. SALLY IS...

The remnant of chalk flipped from Bea's fingers, falling in the grass. Bea jumped to the ground and retrieved the stub. When she stood to face Sara, her face went ashen.

Bea had a flair for the dramatic, but enough was enough. "Who is Sally?" Impatience edged Sara's voice.

Bea pointed beyond Sara's shoulder. She mouthed the words, *Turn around.*

Sara glanced to the northern sky.

An impenetrable black wall took up a quarter of the northwestern horizon, dwarfing distant objects. Faint wisps of smoke curled within the rising curtain.

It looked like the end of the world.

"God help us." Sara heaved herself to her feet, holding her side. She couldn't run, but a steady pace should get them home before the cyclone rolled over them. "We need to get back to the house. Leave your basket."

Sara hustled the best she could and kept a wary eye on the approaching storm. It rose higher and seemed to be coming faster. They needed to hurry.

Each step sent a jolting stab of pain across her ribs. The good news was they were halfway home. She sucked in a breath as another sting pierced her side. The second half didn't promise to be so easy. *Endure it— then rest.*

From the north, hundreds—maybe thousands—of birds approached. They filled the darkening sky, making no calls as they flew. The flapping of countless wings sent shivers down Sara's spine. Geese, songbirds, bats, hawks, and a pair of eagles soared past, trying to escape the coming maelstrom.

Sara pointed ahead. "Run home. I'll be right behind you."

Bea shook her head, motioning back and forth. *We stay together.*

Sara nodded. "Come on. In three minutes, we'll be there."

They were nearing Carriage Road, but the black curtain covered more than half the sky, rising higher by the second. The race would be close.

An ominous calm settled around them. But not silence. There was a tremor, more felt than heard. Like a train coming. Icy fingers stroked Sara's back. A horde of creatures approached, pounding down the center of the road.

A stampede!

She gasped. *It's not fair! We're so close. We could have made it.*

Deer, coyotes, fox and other wildlife fled as Sara and Bea crept along the ditch. Like the birds, they made little noise, but the fear in the air was palpable. One coyote carried a pup in its mouth. Several raccoon kits clutched the back of their mother. No creature paid them any attention. All concentrated on fleeing from the rolling black cloud.

This was no cyclone.

Sara pointed a trembling finger before grabbing Bea's hand. "Run! It's a dust storm!"

They took off. She gritted her teeth against the flaring pain. But the idea—drowning in dirt—made the sting almost laughable. Get to safety. The earth trembled as the granddaddy of all freight trains was coming at full speed, carrying a sky full of dirt. At the base of the black wall was a tumbling wave, like a long cyclone flipped on its side and rolling on the ground. Cold dread replaced the stitch in her side.

What if they didn't make it?

A large deer hurtled toward Beatrice, striking her in the shoulder and knocking her into the ditch. Sara ran to the still figure. *Please, Dear God. Don't let her be hurt.* She bent and assisted the dazed woman to her feet. Bea grimaced with pain as Sara helped her onto the road. Blood ran from her shoulder and down her left arm. Sara stepped back, biting her lip to keep from screaming. Bea needed help, and shelter was less than two hundred feet away.

"Lean on me. We can make it." She hoped it was true.

A distant horn blew, its blast rising in pitch. A farm truck bore down on them, the young driver motioning frantically for them to move aside. Sara and Bea leaped for the ditch as the huge truck roared past. Behind the vehicle swirled a fantail of fine powder, a faint imitation of what was to come.

Sara climbed onto the road on hands and knees, pushed to her feet, and helped Bea up. The air thundered. Darkness drew around them like an enveloping cloak.

Bea took a step and collapsed. Sara heaved her up, wrapping her arm around her waist. "Come on! I'll help you. The driveway is just ahead!" She yelled to be heard.

They set off with Bea leaning on Sara's shoulder, pacing in sequence like runners joined in a three-legged race. With time all but gone, they left the road, entering the curving driveway. The wind shrieked. The steps were just around the curve. But even as they neared the porch, the storm rushed upon them.

A black wave surged around the tenant house and obliterated it from existence. Before Sara could scream, a blast of cold air gave her goose bumps, and dirt pelted her like buckshot.

The darkness swallowed them.

Sara and Beatrice were trapped in the belly of the storm.

Chapter Forty-Four

It is impossible, Jason thought. The roadster *couldn't* have disappeared. *I just took my eyes off the road for a second. And then the bridge appeared.* Larry would lead them to Sara, but they had to find him first.

Michael grabbed his arm. "Look! We're not licked yet. Larry must have turned." Michael jabbed a finger ahead. "That dirt road up ahead. Take it!"

Jason wheeled the Model A around the corner, hitting a bone-jarring pothole, followed by a rock that brought one wheel off the ground. The path ahead promised more dips and bumps.

Michael grabbed onto the dashboard. "Slow down!"

Jason hung onto the wheel with both hands. "Not now. We have to catch up."

The car pitched ahead, bouncing along the rutted lane. Before them, dust still stirred from Larry's car. At least Jason hoped so. Through the haze, Jason glimpsed a flash of silver. They found their runaway bird.

Michael licked his lips, glancing out the rear window. "The storm is closing in. Can we still follow Larry in the dark?"

"We'll have to," Jason said. "Sis has to be close. Why else would Larry turn from the main road?"

"Maybe someone is holding her prisoner?"

"You need to switch to zeppelin stories. They're

more realistic."

"Ha, ha."

"How close is that storm?" Jason asked.

Michael glanced back one more time. "Close. Stay with him. As long as you can."

****

Larry Bigger glanced in his rearview mirror. A Model A trailed behind him. Probably the same one that followed him out of Wichita. It had to be Sara's nosey brothers. He was just minutes away from the asylum. Soon, these ruts would smooth out, and his vehicle would have the advantage of speed. He'd lose those clowns, grab Sara, and take a different route back home. There, he'd make the exchange, Sara for the money.

As the lane flattened, Larry jammed the gas. His head pounded, as much from the jarring road as last night's drinking. Driving was more of a chore than it should have been. But he knew his limits. More important, he knew the capabilities of the car and the conditions of the road ahead. Those boys couldn't keep pace. They were beaten, and they didn't even know it.

The Roadster hit loose gravel, sending his back tires fishtailing. Larry applied just enough brake to maintain control. Then, he pressed hard on the accelerator. Tires bit into packed dirt, and the car surged ahead. Speed and danger. Much better than coffee and whiskey.

He couldn't wait to get to the looney bin, to hear Sara beg and plead for him to take her back home. He was in control. Sara and those idiots behind would soon find that out.

Carriage Road was coming up. Homestretch to the

asylum. Here's where he would lose those guys. He'd whip his car around the corner, just like last time.

Movement registered from the corner of his eye. Cattle had broken through the barbwire fence. A few of the stupid beasts lumbered toward him on the road. How was he going to get through? He had to make his turn. Wait. An opening! A tight fit, but he could make it. Larry swerved the wheel hard, shooting the gap. His right hand touched the metal knob of the gearshift.

Snap!

A tremendous static charge jolted him backward, numbing his right hand. He lost his grip on the steering wheel. The Roadster flew off the road, jumped the ditch and hit the rise on the far side. The impact jerked Larry's head forward, his nose smashing into the steering column. The car shot upward.

For a few brief seconds, the Roadster became a flying machine.

Larry screamed, blood gushing from a broken nose, He leaned into the door writhing in pain. Pain blotted out all thought. Breathing was impossible. He brought up his hand to protect his face, dislodging a lever. The door beneath him flew open. With dim surprise, he sensed a rush of air.

Falling. Why was he falling?

He didn't remember hitting the ground. Gray loomed over him, fading to black. A low groan escaped bloody lips. The pain in his nose was excruciating, but something else was wrong. Searing heat burned at the base of his neck. Below that—nothing. Fancy that. Driving back would be hard with a broken neck. Where *was* his Roadster? He was driving it a minute ago. He wanted to find it, but he couldn't turn his head. All he could do was stare into the darkening heavens.

Black waves rushed toward him. That was worrisome, yet all he felt was a profound lethargy, urging him to rest. Was he about to die? A pity. Too bad. He missed getting his reward. The money would have come in handy. The sound of a tremendous locomotive filled his ears. That's it. He could sleep on the train.

He stared ahead, blinking. Churning darkness rolled toward him. It looked like dust. He tried to swallow, but his throat didn't work. Moving was out of the question. Dirt would cover him. Too bad he couldn't brag about what was to come.

How many people get to see their own burial?

****

Jason somehow closed the gap between the two vehicles. Thank goodness, this road was more drivable. He had to stay with Larry. No telling what would happen when the dust storm overcame them. Ahead, the Roadster pulled away. Larry must be standing on the gas. If he got too far ahead, they might not find Sara.

"It's almost here." Michael turned to the front. "On the road! Cattle!"

Jason slammed on the brakes. Livestock wandered about. But it was the Roadster that held his attention. The Chevy veered off the road and launched skyward like a silver rocket from a catapult. The vehicle smashed into the earth seconds later, rolling end over end. He grabbed Michael's arm. "Larry just crashed!"

The Model A's engine popped and died. The world dimmed to black.

"It's got us," Michael said.

The storm slammed into the vehicle, causing the

car to lurch from side to side. Sand and loose rock pelted doors and windows. Cold wind howled, looking for a way in. Jason touched the lifeless ignition and jerked his hand from the stinging shock. He rubbed feeling back into his fingers, but he couldn't see any damage.

He couldn't see anything at all.

Wind shrieked. Jason sensed the dust creeping in and rolled his window as tight as he could. "Lousy, rotten timing…" Jason shook his head. "I never imagined a dust storm could be this bad."

"I hope the windows hold," Michael said. "I wasn't looking. What happened to Larry?"

"His car shot off the road just before the storm hit."

Michael groaned. "So he's out there in a wrecked car?"

Jason touched the car door, then let go. Larry could be dying. The only person who knew where Sara was, and they couldn't save him. A person could get lost in that blackness. "He's probably dead already. Or will be soon. We need to stay put. Save ourselves."

Michael stirred. "Turn on the headlights. Honk the horn. We need to do something. If you're too afraid, I'll go after him."

"Michael, the car is dead. Nothing works. You'd never find him or make it back." Jason coughed up a wad of dust that turned to mud in his throat. "Breathing's going to be a problem. Find a cloth to cover your mouth." Jason ripped the sleeve of his shirt and tied the torn cloth around his face. "Have you got anything?"

Michael's voice sounded muffled. "I've got my cap over my face."

Jason leaned back in his seat. No one knew where they were. It came down to survival: keeping the windows closed, protecting their lungs, and praying that the windows wouldn't shatter from flying rocks. Grit settled on hair and clothing. The air even tasted dirty.

Jason removed his watch, but it was impossible to tell the time. If he needed to, he could pry off the crystal and read the hands like a blind man. In the meantime, they would have to sit and wait out the storm. At least the car quit rocking as much. Their plan of rescuing Sara had turned into an exercise in self-preservation. All they could do was stay alive and try again another day.

Nobody knew where they were. How many others were in their situation? Was this the end? If God was blowing the world out like a candle, He was doing it in grand style.

The howling wind seemed muffled, and the Model A sat as solid as a rock. That didn't seem right. It should be bucking and shaking like before. The car didn't move even when Jason shifted his weight back and forth. Could he open the door? It was an insane idea, but he had to know.

He pushed, then pounded on the side of the vehicle. It wouldn't budge. He couldn't get out. A strange calm settled over Jason.

"Michael. We're in trouble."

"What is it?" Michael coughed between words.

"We're buried."

Chapter Forty-Five

Sara kept her eyes shut against the flying dirt. The wintry gale assaulted her. She staggered, trying to stay on her feet. With one hand clutching Beatrice and the other shielding her face, Sara crept forward, keeping to the path pictured in her mind. Tears dried on her cheeks. She was in a cold, black void of shrieking wind, pelted by wind-driven dirt. The tenant house should lay just ahead. Don't panic, she thought. Curve left. Find the porch. Climb the steps. Get inside.

Sara grasped Bea's arm, leading her forward. "We're almost there!" A blast of wind from an unexpected quarter sent both women stumbling backward. A branch hit Sara's wrist. For an instant, her grip loosened, and Bea's fingers tore away. Sara reached out to snatch her hand, wrist—anything—but she disappeared.

Gone!

Sara fell to her hands and knees, crawling in a frantic circle, fanning her arms in all directions. *Nothing!* She scurried in a widening arc, sweeping her arms from side to side. How could she have lost her? Breathing was difficult. Grit filled her nose and mouth. She coughed up balls of muddy phlegm only to breathe in more dirt. Whipping cold stole the warmth from her. How could the temperature have spiraled down so quickly?

Sara slapped a yielding form and lunged forward. She found an arm, staggered to her feet, hauling the smaller woman up as well. They embraced—an island of comfort amid the fury raging around them.

Sara cried with relief and raised a fist at the monster storm. "We're not dying here!" The maelstrom whisked her voice away and answered with a mocking boom. The chilly wind filled her mouth with dust.

But there was a problem. Her mental path to the house had whirled away in her scramble to find Bea. Where was the porch? She couldn't see. Wind shrieked in her ears. Dust covered grass and driveway alike. She had no landmarks to go by. The house could be anywhere.

They were lost.

Sara tried to peek under lowered eyelids, hoping to glimpse the house. No luck. The world was darkness and stinging dust. All she could do was listen and pray for a stray sound to guide them in the right direction.

Sara sensed Bea was nearing her limit. Desperate measures would soon force her to pick a direction and hope for the best. And if she was wrong?

Concentrate! The wind wailed around them, but not always in the same direction. Sometimes, the current struck from a different direction, the way it blows around a large structure. And there was a subtle clue within the wind. An occasional *thump* more felt than heard. The big wind bursts also brought a booming sound, like a gunshot. Two separate, distinct sounds: the subtle thump and the boom. Were the sounds connected?

Boom!

There it was again. Not quite like a gunshot. The

sharp report was more like a heavy mass bouncing off a high barrier. *Like a wall*. Where was it? It was hard to pinpoint. Sara tried to form an image that matched the sound. She listened, seeing with her ears. *Come on. One more time*.

A gust of wind, a subtle *thump* and…*Boom!*

Heavy boards slapped against a wall above, almost overhead. A feminine figure had watched her that first day, sitting outside a window. A high window with heavy wooden shutters.

Bea leaned against her side, sliding down. No more time. Sara took her bearings, grabbed Bea's arm, and pointed where she intended to run. They dashed together. Eight. Nine. Ten paces.

She tripped and fell. Wood barked her shins, and she sprawled on steps. Ignoring the pain, Sara pulled Bea to her feet and charged at the door. *Locked*! Both women pounded on the entry until it opened. A surprised Mrs. Chapman stood in front of her wheelchair, gaping at them as they rushed inside.

They were safe at last. So why did she feel so uneasy? As if the storm just claimed a part of her.

Chapter Forty-Six

Sara staggered into the house, reaching for the banister. She bent over the rail, gasping for breath. Gray dirt covered her from head to toe. She sank to the stairs, wiping grit from her face. Even in the shelter of the house, the air was thick with dust. Drawing a careful breath, she scanned the murky common room, trying to fathom the frenzied activity amid the dim light.

Bea sat huddled in a nearby rocker. At the entrance, Mrs. Chapman was on hands and knees, stuffing rags beneath the front door, her wheelchair to one side. But it was the rest of the room that held Sara spellbound.

Kerosene lanterns gave the air a hazy glow. Ghostly forms cast distorted shadows. Mrs. Eisner stood on a chair nailing one corner of a quilt over a window while Miss Underwood hammered in the other end. Mr. Emerson and toothless Mr. Wunch shredded bedding while Mrs. Robson dunked the rags in a bucket and stuffed the wet cloth around the front windows. A battle was being fought; the shrieking elements wanted in and the residents strove to keep the fury out.

Gloria and Miss Underwood stepped away from the window as Patrick slogged into the common room, setting down two buckets of water. The matron pointed to the quilt, and Patrick threw sheets of water on the bedspread with a ladle. Glancing her direction, the matron made her way to Sara, swabbing her face with a rag. "You're alive! We thought you two were lost in the storm. Can you help us fortress the house?"

Sara nodded and pointed to the small form in the chair. "Look after Bea. She has a shoulder wound. Deer struck her."

Mrs. Eisner glanced at Beatrice. "We've had our hands full down here. I can't spare a person to check the infirmary. Will you do that? I'll tend to the girl."

Mr. Evans' open window!

Sara bolted up the darkening stairs, heedless of the ache in her ribs. The infirmary hallway lay in total darkness. Sara thrust an arm before her, feeling her way to his room. Wind howled behind the thick door. Cyrus Evans was in there. *Dear God.* Grabbing the oval knob, she steeled herself, ripped open the door, and tore into the room.

It felt like being outside again. A solid mass of dirt, sand, and cedar needles streamed through the wide-open window. Sara grabbed the sash and slammed it down. She felt for the rocker, finding it and the overturned rolling table. A blanket lay on the floor but no Cyrus. Was he hiding under his covers? She lunged to where the bed should have been. Nothing but gritty, dirty sheets. Maybe he made it to the hallway. No, that was wishful thinking. He was here in this room. With a groan, Sara dropped to the dirt-covered floor, scrambling to find the old man.

Her friend.

She found him lying in a corner, buried under a mound of dust and sand. Sara uncovered his head. Dirt encrusted his eyes, nose, and mouth. Where grit met drool or tears, it hardened. With a cry, she brushed his face clean, pulled his mouth open, and used her fingers to clear his throat. Sara put her ear to his mouth, hoping for a sign of breath. Nothing. Her hand dug under his thin shirt, feeling for a heartbeat. Her fingers quivered so badly it was impossible to tell.

Sobbing, Sara swept a portion of the floor free of the dirt. Gently, she rolled the old man to his stomach, making sure his mouth wasn't blocked. Then she knelt over him and pressed down on his back with the palms of her hands. She remembered a demonstration about life-saving in a high school class six years ago. *I hope I'm doing this right.* She released, waited a moment, and then pressed again.

Out goes the bad air. *I left him with the window wide open.*

In goes the good air. *I left him to the dust storm.*

Press. *I am responsible for this.*

Release. *I killed him.*

Push out the bad air. *Please, God. I'll make a deal.*

Let in the good air. *I'll do anything. Just bring him back.*

Push. *I'm his guardian.*

Release. *And if he's dead?*

Push. *I've failed.*

Precious minutes passed. She needed to check on the others. Save the living. Give up the dead.

But I can't abandon Mr. Evans.

The air was thick with dust. She bent over, overtaken by a spasm of coughing.

Face the truth.

He was gone. She must take care of the others.

Face the music.

It was her fault. She would have to pay.

Sara staggered to her feet, feeling in the darkness for the bed. She grabbed a cover and found her way back to Mr. Evans, drawing the sheet over him. With tears streaming down her face, she ran her hands along the wall, found the door, and stumbled out of the death chamber.

In the hallway, Sara found a wall lamp. She fished in her apron for a match, found one, and struck it. Turning the wick brought the light to full brightness. That was better, though dust was creeping into the passage. What should she do about the patients? No one should be alone. Everyone needed to be safe and together. Drawing a breath, Sara lit more wall lamps and opened the door to the next occupied room.

A few minutes later, she opened Maxine's door. Sara held up a lantern she found on a nightstand. "I'm moving you to the hall with the others, Mrs. Hiebert. You can't stay in here."

"What's happening?" Maxine held her bed sheet over her mouth. Her muffled voice held a raspy edge. "It sounds terrible outside."

"Dust storm. It's easier to breath in the hallway." Sara grabbed a rail and pulled the rolling bed past the door, slamming it behind her. She parked Maxine near a smiling little man.

"I'll be right back."

Maxine seized her arm. "Where's Patrick?"

"Helping downstairs. He's very busy right now."

"I just wanted to know if he's safe. Could you sit me up? It's easier to breathe that way."

Sara cranked the bed to sitting position. "I have to block the doors. Dust is coming in the hallway."

The east side patients weren't in any direct danger,

but a child-like woman poked her head out asking questions. When Sara told her about the dust storm, she crossed her arms. "Well, bring out my rocker. I'm not about to miss on any gathering."

She moved two more beds and another rocker. One man wanted his potty chair carried into the hallway, but Sara refused. "Do your business in your room. Everyone will still be here when you come rejoin us."

As Sara made her way back to the stairs, she grabbed dusty sheets off beds and stuffed them in the door cracks, working her way back to the stairs. She sighed with relief after wedging a pillowcase under Mr. Evans' door. She had sealed off the hallway. No more dust came in, and there were no other weaknesses in their makeshift fortress. The patients were safe. But the temperature was dropping.

She rummaged through the big bureau, pulling out clean sheets and quilts. The patients needed warmth. At least she had enough blankets for everyone.

The stairs creaked. Beatrice ascended the stairs. She looked refreshed; face clean, hair combed and a raised area on her left shoulder indicated a bandage. Sara waved her over. "I'm glad you're here! There's still plenty to do."

Bea studied the crowded corridor. Finally, she looked down and moved her toe over the dirty floor.

MR. EVANS??

Sara leaned her head against the bureau. "He died."

Bea wandered to Cyrus's room, her hand reaching for the doorknob.

Sara lunged for the door, slapping Bea's arm away, her voice a low hiss, "Stay out." Grabbing Beatrice by the hand, she pulled the smaller woman to the dresser and piled her arms with bedding. "We need to replace dirty covers with clean ones." She slammed the drawer with her hip. A flurry of stabbing needles fell on her side like dumped coals. Sara gritted her teeth, marching toward the beds. "Cover the patients and then check the doors. We need to keep the dust out." Sara turned and glared at her.

The silent woman stood with downcast eyes.

Sara hurried back. "You don't have your slate. Where's it at?"

Bea shrugged. A tear rolled down her cheek.

"Is it lost? Worry about it later. You need to get busy."

She shook her head and bent to the floor, writing with her finger.

I'M SORRY MR. EVANS DIED

Sara stared at Mr. Evans' door, wiping silent tears. "I tried to save him. Too late." She turned back to Beatrice. "Come on. We've got work to do."

They changed covers, cleaned faces, and ripped strips of cloth to use as dust filters. Howling wind lashed the window at the end of the hall. Dust rolled across the attic floor, sounding like a serpent slithering overhead, looking for a way inside. The patients hardly noticed. Conversations buzzed throughout the well-lit passage. Neighbor met neighbor—many for the first time.

"What's your name again?"

"Why, I'm right next door. Come visit anytime."

"Cottonwood Falls? I've been there. Do you know…"

"We should do this more often."

Sara found Bea dusting off a fallen pillow. "I'm

sorry for snapping at you. I've been thinking about Mr. Evans. Remember how I left him next to the open window? What if I had done things differently? What if I never opened the window? Or we came back sooner? He'd still be alive."

Bea produced a serving tray and a stub of chalk.

WE SURVIVED

"That's not enough. I should have saved him as well."

WHAT IF WE DIED?

"I wouldn't have let it happen."

WE'D BE LIKE THE FLOWERS COVERED IN DUST

Sara tilted her head. "I don't understand."

MR EVANS WAS A FLOWER

What was Bea trying to say?

BEFORE THE STORM—HE BLOOMED

Bea scurried off to help a tottering woman trying to get into bed. Sara gazed in wonder at the baffling young woman.

Patients were calling for something to drink. Bea scribbled on her tray that she would send up water and then dashed downstairs. Before long, pitchers and cups appeared in the dumbwaiter, and Sara moved among the old folks, filling water cups like a maid at a house party. Outside the north window, darkness turned to gloomy gray. None of the elders noticed. The social event of the year was in full swing. No storm was going to dampen that. Sara moved some of the beds together. Those who wanted to chat could do so without yelling.

Bea returned with supper: bread sprinkled with brown sugar. No one complained.

Chatter continued into the late evening. Sara tried to coax the east side patients into going back to their rooms. All refused, preferring to stay the night in the corridor. No one noticed the wind had ceased. At nine o'clock, Bea helped Sara put out most of the lamps, leaving two flickering at each end of the hall. Most of the patients were settling down to sleep. Only two residents, like balky children, persisted in murmured conversation. After lights out, Bea returned downstairs.

At last, Sara was alone. She pulled the pillowcases from beneath Cyrus's door and entered. Kneeling by his body, Sara took his withered hand. "I guess you know now I'm not your daughter. You insisted, and it was easy to play along. You remembered so much. I saw you for the first time. If only I could have known you a little longer." She squeezed his limp fingers. "Forgive me."

Knock, knock.

Sara jumped.

Mrs. Eisner stood in the open doorway holding a lit candle. Bea stood beside her. "Forgiveness generally works best when the other person is still alive." The matron stepped forward, held out a hand and drew Sara to her feet. "From what Beatrice tells me, Mr. Evans' death was an accident."

"Is that supposed to make me feel better?"

The older woman waved her remark away. "You made a difference, though. Despite his nastiness, you worked with him. In six days, you did more to improve his disposition than anyone else had in months. I saw nothing but a bitter old man losing what few memories he had left. Beatrice says you two snapped at each other those first few days."

"We did."

"Maybe that's what it took. I refused to let him bait

me. As it is, you gave him back his humanity. That's a great accomplishment."

"I failed him."

"Beatrice said it was his choice to keep the window open. Providence took him. No one, least of all you, should feel responsible."

The stark outline of Evans' face flickered in the candlelight. "It doesn't matter. I can't do this anymore."

"Nonsense. Tomorrow is a new day."

Sara licked dry lips. "Tomorrow, I'm leaving."

Chapter Forty-Seven

The wind had quit blowing for some time now, and the world was quiet. Jason took a breath. He nudged Michael, and his brother stirred. They survived the storm. Now it was a matter of getting out of the car and surveying their situation. What did their car look like from the world outside? Just another mound of dirt, a little bigger than the rest? He wiped the dust from his eyes. At least it wasn't completely black outside. No details could be discerned, but a shade of dark gray came through the passenger window.

Light! They could still get out.

"Try your door, Michael," he said. I can't budge my, but you might have better luck."

Michael pulled the handle and shoved. "It won't move." A note of fear edged his voice.

"Then roll down your window. We're getting out."

"Do you think it's safe?"

Jason smiled in the murky darkness. "You got a better idea, Houdini?"

"Suppose not." There was some movement. "Can't tell how deep the dirt is on this side, but I can climb out the window."

Jason breathed a sigh of relief. Being buried alive gave him the willies. "Well, get going. I'll be right behind you."

A few minutes later, Jason circled the Model A,

appraising their task ahead. South of them the world looked black, but to the north and west sky were gloomy, but clear. Along the windward side, of the car, fine granules of dust lay heaped to the windows. Even the hood was covered. But sand only covered half the wheels on the leeward side. Michael, with a torn bit of shirt wrapped around his face, was already scooping dirt by hand away from the rear compartment. Digging tools were in there. Once they got the back end open, they could make better progress. Jason assessed the road from which they came. The storm filled in ruts and holes. That was the good news. The bad news? Road and grassland were a single rippling plain of dust.

"Come on! Help me out!" Michael bent over the rear, throwing dirt with hooked arms. He looked like he'd been mining in a sandbox. Jason went to the front of the car to work. He wasn't about to have his brother throw an armful of dirt in his face.

The top layer of earth was the finest dust he'd ever seen. Just moving it filled the air with minute particles, making it hard to breathe even through his makeshift dust filter. Unless scraped carefully away, the powdery grit sifted through his fingers and rolled back in place like a thick liquid. Swiping with his forearm worked much better.

The brothers labored at opposite ends of the car making slow progress. Around them, the world grew, if not brighter, at least less shadowy. Michael popped the rear door. Jason peeked at his watch. Seven o'clock. "Here's the shovel," Michael called. "And look! Something for you." Michael tossed a hoe in Jason's direction. Pop always carried tools in case the car became stuck on bad roads. Today those tools would be lifesavers.

Jason grabbed the tool. "Thanks. We might get ourselves out if this yet."

Michael scooped dirt from the rear bumper, while Jason cleared the hood and grill. As work progressed, each made their way to the driver's side; Jason scraped around the front tires while Michael shoveled out the back. Their unspoken goal was to meet in the middle. Moving the earth was tedious and grueling. Jason's shoulders already ached. This was thirsty work, and they had no water. It had to wait. Digging out came first.

After an hour, the scarred, dust-blasted side of the Model A came in view. Jason tapped Michael's shoulder and pointed. "The old man will have a conniption when he sees what the storm did to his car. I can hear him already, bellowing about getting it repainted."

Michael drew his cap across his forehead. "Pop's all wind. He'll fume and growl, but a couple of hours later, he'll give us something to do like nothing ever happened. I never listen to him. You shouldn't either."

"It must be nice to have it all figured out."

Michael laughed. "Well, I didn't figure on getting waylaid by a storm and stuck in the country." He turned to look to the road ahead. "That reminds me, shouldn't we try to find Larry? He might still be alive."

Jason pointed to a patch of hazy red above the horizon. "We have maybe two hours of daylight left, and we're nowhere near finished digging out. Do you want to be here after dark?"

"I'd rather be at home with a Nehi."

"I'll buy you a carton of Nehi if we get out of here

before dark."

"You're on."

They dug with renewed effort.

With dusk closing in, Michael cleared the rear wheels. Jason scratched a path for the front tires. "Check the tail pipe. Make sure it's clear. A plugged exhaust would not be good."

"Yes, boss!" Michael called back.

They were free. With tools stowed away, both jumped in the front seat. Now, the decisive moment. A clogged engine meant further delay. Jason hesitated, and then turned the ignition.

For several anxious moments, the Model A coughed and sputtered—then backfired with a resounding *bang!* The old car was cranky but awake.

Jason turned the vehicle around and retraced their route to the main road by dead reckoning. "Let's hope there won't be piles of dirt on the roads. I don't want to dig our way home."

"What time is it?" Dusk was turning into starless night.

Jason retrieved his pocket watch, but couldn't read it. "Too dark. Sometime after eight."

Michael stared out the window. "This whole day has been a wild goose chase."

"Not completely. We know Sara is alive somewhere in Joshua County. That's something."

"And Larry Bigger is probably dead. Who should we tell? What do we say? The police could decide we had a hand in his death."

Jason drove around a mound of dirt. "He killed himself. And we would have died trying to look for him. We lived. That's all that matters."

The drive seemed eerie. The countryside around them was devoid of light. Hours later, they entered Newton. The town seemed abandoned. All of the streetlights were dark and the houses seemed to be without power. No businesses were open. Too bad, they would have gotten something to drink. Only one other car moved about as they passed through the deserted streets.

Some ten hours after they left, the highway turned into Broadway Avenue at the edge of Wichita. They entered a darkened city with only a few sections lit with streetlights. Few vehicles moved about. Parked cars had drifts of dust well above the tires. At a quarter past eleven, Jason pulled into their parents' driveway. The neighborhood was dark, but a light moved near their house. Their mother held a lantern. She set down the lamp and rushed to the car as it came to a halt.

Jason turned off the engine. Michael pulled himself out of the car and trudged to meet her, falling into her arms when they met. Jason eased himself onto wobbly legs. Arms and back ached with each movement. When he reached the two of them, his legs nearly collapsed. The three embraced, Katherine weeping on Jason's shoulder.

"We were so worried about you!" She thumped Jason on the shoulder. "Thank God, you're both okay!" Tears streamed down her cheeks. "Telephone lines are down, and the power is out. All we could do was pray that you'd be safe."

"We're fine, Mom." Michael put on a brave face, but his eyes betrayed his weariness. "We had a line on Sara, but the storm caught up with us. We had to wait for the wind to pass before we could dig the car out."

"I'm not happy with you boys. You left without a word where you were going." Katherine paused, then added, "Your father is in the kitchen. He's been drinking. Jason, don't provoke." Katherine wiped her eyes with her apron. "Despite appearances, he worried about you boys."

"More likely he's worried about the car." Jason left his mother and Michael to enter the back door, his thoughts centered around a tall glass of water. Inside the kitchen, he headed for the cupboard. Pop could say anything he wanted. But first, the water.

He sat at the kitchen table with a single flickering candle in the center. A square bottle lay on its side. He remained seated as Jason plodded in. "Take those filthy shoes off," McGurk said in a heavy, carefully enunciated voice. "And I want those car keys."

Jason pulled the keys from his pocket. "I can explain."

"Not interested."

Jason tossed the keys toward the table. Incredibly, his father snatched them in mid-air. He heaved himself to his feet. Without another word, he took the candle, and lurched to his bedroom, one hand leaning against the wall. A moment later, the door slammed shut.

Jason clutched a glass and filled it from the sink, drinking it. He couldn't think of a time when something as simple as water tasted so good. He refilled his glass and gulped it down as well. Only then did he allow weariness to overtake him. He slumped in a chair and rested his head on the table. They came so close.

Now, they had no car.

And no way to find Sara.

Chapter Forty-Eight

Monday, April 15, 1935

Sara awoke from a restless sleep in Mr. Evans' rocker outside the door to his room. The rest of the infirmary residents still lay sleeping in beds scattered throughout the corridor. Morning light peeked around the blanket covering the window by the big bureau. It must be past six o'clock, and Mrs. Eisner had not rung her wake-up bell. There was a serene quiet in the hallway. One that could go on indefinitely. Sara had no such luxury.

Stifling a sneeze, she straightened from the chair, stretching overworked muscles. Her neck and shoulder ached, and it wasn't from sleeping in an odd position. Bright red marks ran across her shins from where she barked them on the outside steps yesterday. Even her knees hurt from kneeling on the hardwood planks and stuffing sheets under the doors. What she'd give for a long soaking bath. Shaking off the fantasy, she padded downstairs to her room.

First thing was to clean herself. She prepared a basin of soapy water, removed her filthy clothing, washed, brushed her hair, and slipped into a clean dress. At least look presentable enough to travel. From here, she'd go to Hutchinson and live with her aunt and uncle. Once the child was born, she would give it up for adoption. Maybe then, the remorseful daughter could return home.

A light knock on the door jerked her away from her thoughts.

"Come in."

Miss Eisner's voice called through the door. "Breakfast in twenty minutes."

"Thank you. I'll be there."

No annoying bell. The storm had even changed Mrs. Eisner's steadfast routine.

Saying goodbye to Patrick and Bea would be hard. They were good friends. Leaving them felt like desertion. Abandoning Mrs. Hiebert in her final days was especially hard. What else could she do? This was her day of reckoning.

Sara left her room and knocked on Bea's door. No answer. Bea liked her coffee. She was probably already at breakfast.

Only three residents sat in the dining room: Patrick, alone at one table, Mrs. Robson and Miss Underwood at the other. Streaks of dirt covered the chairs, walls, and floor.

No Bea. She could be upstairs asleep.

Sara found a sheet of newspaper, draped it over her seat, and sat down, Wheatley rolled his cart to the table and served what looked like porridge, passing a tin to her and Patrick. She scrutinized the mixture.

"Cream of wheat," the big man said as he lumbered to the next table.

Sara picked up a spoon and dug in. A bit gritty—Wheatley could have rinsed out the pot better—but not too bad. This past week certainly taught her the errors of being too fussy with food. Besides, she was hungry.

Patrick sat across from her, eating with his usual gusto. Sara reached out, touching his arm. "Have you seen Bea?"

"No." He barely slowed eating.

She'd have to find her. Sara gripped his arm harder. "There's something you should know. I'm leaving today. You're a true friend. I'm going to miss you."

Patrick squinted, following Sara's hand up to her face. "Can't. You have to take care of Maxie."

"Miss Gloria will help you look after Mrs. Hiebert."

Patrick's slack jaw drew into a tight frown. "Why?"

"I'm leaving. Mr. Evans died. It's my fault. He'd still be alive if I closed his window."

"Oh." Patrick bobbed his head. "I get it. You're sad about Mister Cyrus."

"I grew to like that cranky old man."

"You were friends. But not like me and Maxie."

A faint smile touched Sara's lips. "You're a wise man, Patrick Arnesdorff."

"Funny kind of friends, but not ha-ha funny."

Sara's eyes glistened. "Funny friends. I couldn't agree more."

After breakfast, Sara knocked again on Bea's door. No answer. She turned, heading for the stairs when Mrs. Eisner's voice beckoned. "Miss McGuire, I have your bags in my office. Would you come back here, please?"

Sara bustled up the hall. Mrs. Eisner didn't like to be kept waiting.

She sat at her table with a sheet of paper in her

hands as Sara entered. Her travel bag and purse sat nearby. "Here is an inventory of your belongings. Check to be sure nothing is missing." She handed Sara the slip of paper.

Sara took a seat, looking through her purse. Her Max Factor makeup, wallet, and the money were untouched. The travel bag felt as tightly packed as the day she left home. "It's all here. Thank you for storing my things, Mrs. Eisner."

"You're welcome. Where will you go?"

"To Hutchinson. I have relatives there. After the baby is born, I can give the child to the children's home there. After that, I may try to return home."

"I wish you luck, Miss McGuire."

"Thank you."

She leaned back in her chair. "Some men are coming to take Mr. Evans away. Could you show them to the body?"

"Of course."

"The commissioner will be visiting as well. After our meeting, he can take you to the train depot."

Sara nodded.

Mrs. Eisner rose to her feet. "You'll want to change into your own clothing before the Commissioner arrives."

"I'll do that. And thank you for everything, Mrs. Eisner." Sara stood, picked up her belongings, and stepped to the door. "Have you seen Beatrice today?"

The matron glanced up from her ledger. "I assumed you assigned her duties in the infirmary."

"No. But I'll check up there. I want to say goodbye to her before I leave."

"Make it quick. I don't want you dawdling while

the county men are waiting."

"Yes, Mrs. Eisner."

"Goodbye, Sara. Write to us. You've left your mark here."

"I will." Sara left the office and returned to her room. After the morning cleaning chores, she drew out a purple lilac dress from her travel bag. No way to iron out the wrinkles, but that couldn't be helped. She put on the dress, running her hands over the pliant fabric, enjoying the texture. It felt good to wear her own clothes again.

She left her bags and scaled the stairs to find Bea.

The hallway was still full of sleeping patients, including Mrs. Hiebert. Sara picked her way through the cluttered passage, looking under beds and inside doorways. No Bea. Sara avoided Evans' room but peeked in the rest. No luck. Where was she? She couldn't think of anywhere else to look. Shaking her head, Sara wandered back downstairs to wait.

At nine-forty, Wendell parked the station wagon in front. As the commissioner came through the entrance, he raised his brows. "My, you look nice today. Going somewhere special?"

Sara swallowed, trying to form the words. "I'm leaving."

His mouth fell open. "You can't. Not now. The New Deal is coming to Kansas. Big changes are on the way. I've got a job set up for you."

"Wendell. Stop. I *have* to go. I need a favor, though. Would you take me to the train depot after your meeting?"

Wendell pursed his lips. "Only if you explain to me what happened."

Sara let out an exasperated sigh. Why did she have to explain herself?" A man choked to death from the dust after I left a window open. He died under my care. I can't stay here anymore."

Brakes squeaked outside. A large box truck stopped behind the county vehicle.

"That's unfortunate." Wendell gazed out the front window as two men in uniform stepped to the ground and headed to the rear of the truck. "The Feds started a new program. Thousands, if not millions, will get work. It means you can stay—"

Sara stepped back. "I've decided. Don't make this harder for me than it already is." Doors slammed, and the two men came up the steps. "Please excuse me. I'll talk to you later." She dismissed him and turned to answer the door.

Wendell trudged down the hall.

Two men stood at the entrance. The taller one tipped his cap. "Good morning, ma'am. We're from the County Medical Office." He was a balding, mustached man holding a folded gurney. Behind him, a shorter, heavier man held sheets of cloth. Both wore dirt-stained coveralls and name tags on the front pocket with the county seal beneath. The taller man's tag said *Stewart*. "Could you direct us to the body?"

"Cyrus is upstairs." Sara wrinkled her nose. Why were these men so filthy? She turned to go up the landing. "Follow me."

"Appreciate the help, lady. It's been a trying day— our second pickup," the shorter man said. His nametag read *Toliver*.

Upstairs, Sara opened Evans' door and stayed outside as the workers entered, unfolding the gurney next to the bed. They lifted Cyrus and plopped him onto the wheeled stretcher. How could they treat a body with such disrespect?

Stewart sneezed into a handkerchief. "It's not often we retrieve two bodies a mile apart on the same day. We had to dig him out. Not sure if he died from his car accident or if he suffocated from the storm."

"How awful."

Toliver shrouded Mr. Evans with a white sheet and cinched him tight to the stretcher. Sara followed them down the stairs and outside. It looked like another gusty day.

Stewart opened one of the big back doors and detached the stretcher from the gurney. Toliver jumped inside the truck, and together, they secured Cyrus in place. The smaller man leaped out, ran to the cab, and started the engine.

Stewart strapped the gurney to the back door and reached for the handle when a gust of wind blew a dingy white hat out the rear door. The heavy door flew shut and knocked Stewart to his knees. Groaning, he staggered to his feet clutching his head.

Sara ran to him, holding him steady. "Are you okay?"

He rubbed his forehead, eyes scrunched shut. "Give me a minute. That smarts." He blinked a few times before pointing a shaky finger to a spot on the driveway. "The dead guy's hat is blowing away."

Sara dashed to pick up the topper, a bloodstained panama. She dropped her jaw in horror. Was it possible? Her head reeled. She planted her feet to steady herself. Was Larry the other body in the truck?

With numb fingers, she returned the hat. "What

321

kind of car did this man drive?"

Stewart tossed the hat back inside. "Hard to say. Dirt covered most of it. The sheriff said it had a Sedgwick County license plate. He'll call Wichita to get the owner's name. We couldn't find his billfold, either. For now, we're calling him John Doe."

Sara's mouth was dry. "Can I see him?"

The man stopped rubbing his forehead and gave her a strange look. "He's a horrible sight. The neck is broken, and he's covered in dirt." He tilted his head. "You think you know this guy?"

Did she really want to see Larry this way? "No. I'm thinking of somebody else." She backed up a step. "Take care of Mr. Evans. And put some ice on your head to ease the swelling."

The truck honked. "Quit your lollygagging back there!"

The tall man tipped his cap. "I will. Bye now."

Sara watched the truck head east to Joshua. She stood, turning one way and another. Mounds of dirt collected around the cedar trees like brown snow drifts. The wind methodically erased tire tracks and footprints. No grass anywhere. And to think—it was like this for miles around.

Oh Larry, what were you doing?

Shaking her head, she turned to the house.

Chapter Forty-Nine

Sara stood outside the door of her room with her bag, waiting. Wendell and Mrs. Eisner stepped out if the matron's office and were ambling toward her. She was about to leave this unlikely home, and she still had not found Bea. A twinge of disappointment squeezed at her heart. *Where could she be?*

Wendell nodded, "Mrs. Eisner told me about Cyrus Evans. A terrible accident. It's commendable you tried to resuscitate him. Few would have made the effort."

Sara retreated a step. "I never told anyone about that."

"You didn't have to," the matron said. "I examined Mr. Evans while you were sleeping. He was on his stomach with his mouth and nose cleared, and you swept dirt away from his head. Knee imprints in the dust were visible. You tried to revive him."

Sara gaped. Not much got past this woman. "It didn't work."

"I think you should stay," Wendell said."

"I have to go."

He nodded. "If you wish. Where do you want to go?"

"The train station. I'm going to Hutchinson."

"We best be off, then. There's a southbound to Newton. You can transfer from there." He pointed to her carrier. "I can stow that in the car."

She handed the case to him, and turned to Mrs. Eisner. "Beatrice wasn't upstairs, and she hasn't answered her door. I don't know where she could be."

Mrs. Eisner stepped to the girl's door, rapped once, and opened it. "She not here. I'm sure the child is about. She can be mischievous. Or she may not want to see you go."

Sara bit her lip. "We have to find her."

Mrs. Eisner narrowed her eyes. "I'm not going to spend the rest of the morning looking for Beatrice. Especially if she doesn't want to be found. We have an immense cleaning project ahead of us. She'll show up in due time."

"I could stay long enough to help."

Wendell cleared his throat. "I don't expect to be coming back for another week," Wendell said. "Mrs. Eisner said you wanted to leave today."

Sara nodded. "I only wish I could have said goodbye to Bea."

Mrs. Eisner took her hand. "You can write her. Don't worry about young Beatrice."

"You're right. Goodbye, Mrs. Eisner."

"Goodbye, Sara. You'll be missed."

Wendell led Sara down the front steps to the station wagon. "I have an appointment at the courthouse in an hour, and the roads are in terrible shape. Hopefully, the county maintainer will be along soon. It will make getting to town easier."

"A few detours won't bother me."

The commissioner dropped the tailgate and stowed her carrier inside. "I'm glad to hear that. This will give us a chance to talk. A job opportunity has opened for you."

"Wendell, I don't feel like talking right now."

He slammed the tailgate and escorted her to the passenger door. "You won't have to. Just listen. If I don't convince you to stay by the time we reach town, then you're free to leave with my blessing."

"Nothing is going to change my mind."

Wendell sighed and opened the passenger door.

"*Sar-r-aaa!*"

Her name was a piercing cry that echoed off the cedars. Sara glanced around. Where did it come from? She turned to the house. No one stood on the porch. She drew in a breath. *Please, no*. With terrifying certainty, she peered up.

Bea sat on the ledge outside the attic window as she had a week ago, arms gripping the sill on either side of her.

Rooted in place, Sara gazed upon her troubled friend. Her heart pounded. Around her, she sensed the wind stirring, drawing a mighty breath. There was a moment of stillness, and then the gust blew. A shutter flew inward, catching Beatrice on her hurt shoulder. She cried out, flailing her limbs, grabbing for the battered wood. The shutter bounced away. She missed, teetering on the edge of the sill.

And fell.

One hand shot up, catching the ledge. Beatrice scrambled to find a hold for both arms as she hung over the porch.

Her spell broken, Sara dropped her purse, darted up the steps and threw open the front door. Inside, she grabbed the curled end of the banister, sprinting upstairs. How did Bea get to the attic? Biting her lip, Sara scanned the ceiling.

Over the linen bureau was an opened square hatch and a pile of dust sat atop the big dresser. Two drawers were pulled out, making steps.

"*Sara!*" Another cry. This one more urgent.

With her heart beating in her throat, Sara clambered up the bureau. As she climbed higher, the massive chest of drawers wobbled. She pulled herself over the top and stood upright, grabbing the edge of the hatch opening. Inside the attic, mounds of dust covered the floor. Nearby was an open window.

Crack! Brittle wood snapped just outside. The ledge was breaking!

She clutched the splintery frame that held the hatch in place, then jumped, scrambling for a perch. Her face burrowed through dust as she pulled her legs inside the attic.

"I'm coming!" Wendell pounded up the steps.

Sara stood, gasping for breath. No time to wait. She leaped for the open window.

It was a reckless act. A mistake! The position she found herself in was awkward, if not downright dangerous. Sara gripped Bea's wrist with her right hand; her left clutched the broken wooden ledge. Her left foot, wedged behind the window frame, kept her from falling out while the right leg remained suspended in the air, maintaining a precarious balance. One hand and one foot held her in check. For now.

They were both in trouble.

"Wendell!"

"Coming up." Downstairs, wood splintered and a sharp yell came from Wendell. Moments later, creaking wood gave way to a thunderous crash. The bureau toppled.

"Wendell?"

No answer.

Cold fear pierced her heart, but she had her own hands full. One slip of her foot or hand and both she and Beatrice would fall and tumble off the porch roof. Sara swallowed hard, pushed aside her fear, and met Bea's terrified eyes. "I got you. When I pull you up, grab for the window frame with your free hand." Drawing a breath through clenched teeth, she pulled on Bea's arm, bending her own arm back like an archer drawing a bow. Bea strained but couldn't reach the side of the window. Sara exhaled, easing the smaller woman back down, letting her leg take the weight.

"Let's try again," Sara hissed. "On three." She took another breath to steady her nerves.

"One…Two…*Three*." Arm muscles tensed as Bea came closer to the window. Sara's left foot dug into the sharp corner of the framing. Bea reached out, fingernails scratching the gnarled wood, but she couldn't get a handhold.

Sara's head filled with the roar of pumping blood. Dizzy with fatigue, she eased Beatrice back down. Her limbs ached for release.

Her foot slipped, scraping along the side of the rough wood. Long slivers of dry, brittle wood drove into her flesh. Tears welled in her eyes. A small voice plucked at her thoughts.

Let go.

No. Never.

Save yourself.

She's my friend.

You were going to leave her.

Sara gritted her teeth. No more thinking. Be done

with this.

With every limb aching, Sara took in a ragged breath. "Bea." Her voice was dead calm. "One last time. Count out loud. You can do it."

Bea nodded. "One."

Sweat made her hands slippery. She gripped tighter.

"Two."

She set her jaw; muscles coiled.

"*Three!*" Bea screamed as Sara whipped her arm back. The younger girl rose, clawing for the window. And then she was gone, yanked out of Sara's grasp.

Firm hands grabbed Sara around the waist, pulling her from the ledge. She fell backward, landing inside the attic on top of another body.

A man groaned. Sara looked down. Wendell lay beneath her, glasses dangling off one ear, and an earpiece bent upward like an antenna.

Wendell grimaced. "This is almost pleasant. Except for the board cutting across my back." His arms were still around her.

Sara thumped him on the chest. "You took your sweet time getting up here."

"You're welcome." He groaned, releasing her.

Sara rolled to one side, careful to keep the splinters from driving into her skin and sat next to Bea.

Wendell gritted his teeth and scooted near the open window leaving a trail of blood. The torn fabric of his left pant leg revealed a ragged gash down the middle of the shin.

"What happened?" Sara asked.

"Oh." Wendell glanced at his injury. "I was climbing the bureau. A board scraped my leg when my foot broke through the bottom of a drawer. That's when the dresser fell over. I'm still not sure how I scrambled out of the way."

"How did you get up here?"

"I found a ladder in a storeroom behind a stretcher."

"Thank you."

Wendell nodded. "I think we both need Mrs. Eisner's nursing services."

Sara glanced at her scraped ankle then turned to Beatrice. "What were you doing outside that window?"

Bea reached in her apron.

Sara glared with green fire. "We're long past that. Talk."

Bea crossed her arms. "Sally said you were leaving because of me." Her little-girl voice had a resonant alto timbre. "I feared it was true."

"I thought Sally was a friend from the orphanage? How can…" Sara drew back with understanding. "Sally's not from there. She's a part of you."

Beatrice cast her eyes downward. "Sally wanted to prove she was the better friend. And so I had to watch you leave. When I called your name, Sally left."

Sara rubbed her temple. It was hard to imagine another personality living inside one's head. "This has happened before. You were on the ledge the day we met. Did Sally send you out then?"

Bea shrugged. "I agreed. It was like a dare. But you were hurt. So I had to help. Even then, I knew you were different."

Wendell blew out a breath, "Amen to that."

"Stay out of this," Sara said.

"Can't. I fell."

Sara gave him a lingering stare before turning her attention to Beatrice. "I'm not special."

"But you are! You're alive. You do exciting things. That's what I want to do."

Sara touched her hand. "You will. I promise."

"You can't promise," she whispered. "You won't be here."

She's right. I said I was leaving.

It all came down to this. She could take the sure road, live with her aunt and uncle, and give up her child. Or she could stay and find a new and different path to follow. Start fresh. But could she free herself from the past?

Sara lifted her chin. "I'm staying."

Chapter Fifty

Sara lay on the bed with her foot elevated on two pillows. Mrs. Eisner stood with a pair of tweezers and a sewing pin scrutinizing her scraped ankle. All the larger wood fragments were pulled. Now, it was a messier process of digging into the skin for the smaller pieces. The extraction of these tinier splinters hurt more with the matron pricking her skin with the needle. "Your leg is looking better now." Mrs. Eisner said, snaring an elusive bit of wood.

"*Aww.* Are we close to finishing?"

"Quit complaining. Just a few left." More sharp stings and the matron held the last tiny splinter up like it was a prize. "That's the one I was looking for. Now, some salve and a bandage." The matron rubbed on some ointment. "The wrap should help the salve draw out any splinters I might have missed." She pinned the binding in place.

"Thank you, Mrs. Eisner."

"Think nothing of it, child. I hope both you and Beatrice have had enough adventures."

"I certainly hope so. Is her shoulder okay?"

"Her shoulder is bruised and battered. A simple job of re-bandaging. I'd suggest rest for the two of you, but we have a lot of cleaning to do."

"I don't think I can rest. The entire house needs a good sweeping."

"Do what you can," Mrs. Eisner said. "I have one more patient to examine."

"Mr. Krause was gracious to have you look after us first. Of the three of us, his injury looks the worst."

"Probably so. There now, you're fixed up for now. I'll look at your leg again tomorrow. Now bring a pan of hot water to the dining room. I'll stitch the commissioner's leg there."

"Yes, Mrs. Eisner."

Sara found Wendell sitting in the dining room with his injured leg propped on another chair. He held a wet cloth to his lower knee. "Has the bleeding stopped?"

"Still oozes a little and it throbs like the dickens." Wendell peered at her. "I still can't get my mind around what just happened this morning, and what we should do about it."

Sara drew back. "Why should we do anything?"

"You may be right." He pursed his lips. "Still, the question won't go away."

"Maybe you should be more concerned about your leg. I'll be back in a few minutes with some hot water. Be prepared—it will sting."

"Anything to ease the pain." He squirmed a bit. "Don't go far. There's a decision about Beatrice Mullins I have to make, and your thoughts on the matter will be important."

A judgment about Bea? She went into the kitchen to heat the water. Did the commissioner have the authority to make such decisions?

The matron was with Wendell when she returned. She left the hot water and returned to the kitchen. Rounds still had to be done, and Wheatley was nowhere in sight. She loaded the dumbwaiter with filled pitchers, tin plates, and leftover cream of wheat. Then knocked on Bea's door. "Come out, Bea," she called. "You and I need to get breakfast for the residents upstairs."

Bea opened the door, peeking through a crack in the door. "What about Patrick?"

Thank goodness she is still talking. "No time to find him. I've got the food loaded. Let's get moving."

Upstairs, they pulled up the elevator and loaded their cart. "With everyone in the hallway, breakfast rounds will go faster."

"I'm glad you stayed, but why are we in such a hurry?"

"I've a hunch Mr. Krause doesn't understand how important your work is. You need to tell him how good it feels to work. I can help, but it has to come from you."

"Is he wanting to turn me out?" Beatrice cringed. Water from a pitcher dribbled to the floor.

"Not sure, but we can't let that idea take hold."

"I don't know if I can do that. Isn't it easier to let things happen on their own?"

"Even if that's not what you want?"

Beatrice shrugged. "What can I do?"

"Defend yourself by proving your worth. Working here is a good example. We may have to argue the point today, so be ready."

They worked their way through the scattered beds and chairs. Some of the patients were still groggy from sleep, but most were awake and hungry. Even Mrs. Hiebert seemed more energized by the buzz of voices in the hallway. "I know the storm was dreadful, but I hardly noticed it with so many people around."

"Would you like some breakfast, Mrs. Hiebert?"

The dying woman barely shook her head. "A little water, though. I'm thirsty all the time."

Bea poured some water in a tin cup. Sara slipped a straw between the older woman's lips. "Will I see Patrick today?" she asked.

"Of course, you will," said Sara. "The storm has disrupted our routine, but we'll get that fixed by this evening." It sounded plausible.

Forty minutes later, Sara lowered the bed for a patient. Bea took the cart of dirty tins to the dumbwaiter for cleaning. Catching up on laundry and sweeping dust will demand a big chunk of time in the coming days. With the on-going needs of the residents, it was hard to imagine where to begin the formidable task of cleaning after the storm. Behind her, the steps creaked.

Gloria Eisner stood at the top of the banister. "You and Beatrice are to come to my office immediately. Before the commissioner returns to town, he wants to sort out what happened this morning."

"if this is about Bea, can it wait? We have a lot to do here."

Mrs. Eisner narrowed her eyes. "He's cancelled his morning meetings." She bowed her head for a moment. "I'm not sure if this meeting is proper, but his is the commissioner for relief programs in this county. We must defer to his judgment."

We'll see about that.

The conference started at eleven that morning. James Eisner leaned back against the rear wall in his chair. Mrs. Eisner wrote some notes in her giant ledger while Sara and Beatrice sat in nearby chairs.

Wendell stood facing the group. "We must understand the reasons behind this morning's events.

Why did the resident Beatrice Mullins exposed herself to danger on a high ledge? Was she a danger to herself? A county farm is no place for possibly suicidal behavior. The question before us is to decide whether the resident remains here until closure, or should we move her to a hospital that can treat her condition?"

James plopped his chair down on all four legs. "I can nail the shutters closed and push the bureau upright again, then put a hasp and padlock on the ceiling hatch. That should be enough to keep her or anyone from climbing into the attic."

"Can we get it done today?" Wendell asked.

"I'll need to pick up the hardware when I run into town for new seed. Hopefully, the county won't mind footing the bill. The duster wiped out all our work this spring. We will have to replant. Another concern is the amount of dust that's collected in the attic. We should sweep it out. I've heard of ceilings collapsing under the weight of too much dirt."

Wendell frowned. "Do what needs to be done with the attic. But new seed is out of the question. We're selling this land in four months. Sorry Jim, the new owners will have to replant."

James stood up. "I can't let the land go fallow. Something needs to hold the ground together. That's why the damn dust is blowing in the first place."

"I don't think the other commissioners will accept that."

James hooked a thumb, pointing backward over his shoulder like a man hitchhiking. "Fallow land is worthless. You'll get more for your auction with crops growing."

Wendell rubbed the back of his neck. "I suppose

you're right. Tell the clerk at Claasen's the county will be good for the bill. I'll remind the other commissioners they wanted the farm in salable condition. It won't make them happy, but it'll keep them quiet."

"I better get going." Eisner stepped to the door. "It'd be a shame to drive into town and find supplies out of stock. By the way, if it makes any difference, I think the kid should stay. She's never been any trouble. I can think of a few questionable things I did when I was eighteen." He tugged down his hat brim and left.

Wendell shut the door and regarded Beatrice. "My next questions are personal ones. Can you tell us why you were in the attic today?"

Sara rose to her feet. "I can explain."

Wendell held up a palm. "I'd rather hear it from Miss Mullens."

Bea looked around. "Sally told me to. She's my friend. Or was. She's been with me a long time."

Wendell stood before her. "When did you first notice Sally?"

"It's hard to remember. Sometime after Papa put me in the children's home. Sally told me never talk to others. Friends couldn't be trusted, but she would protect me."

"Did you speak before Sally came to you?"

Beatrice closed her eyes for a moment before answering. "When I was little, I sang and played with Mama. When I found her hanged, I turned silent. Papa said Mama was melancholy, and I'd be the same way. The children's home could help me, he said. When I arrived there, the other girls whispered that I was touched and stayed away from me. Sally told me I didn't need them."

"How old were you then?"

"Six."

Wendell paced several steps. "Why did Sally send you to the attic today? Did it have anything to do with Sara leaving?"

"Sally wanted to show she was the better friend by having me watch Sara leave."

He bent forward. "Why was that important?"

Beatrice swallowed. "She didn't like Sara. It was okay when we worked together, but we couldn't be friends. Sally thought Sara acted the princess to hide her failings. 'Just you wait,' she told me. 'Her majesty is bound to slip up. And when she does, she'd fall apart.' When Mr. Evans died, Sara wanted to leave. Sally called Sara a weakling."

Sara bit her lip but remained silent.

"Did Sally want you to jump?"

"Not today."

"But in the past?"

Bea stared at the floor. "It's hard to explain. Sally is—was—tough. And she could be bossy. She liked to goad me into doing scary things. Sometimes she came to my rescue. Today she didn't. I felt helpless. My slate was lost, and my friend was about to leave forever. I had to stop her."

"You called out."

"I broke Sally's rule. Never talk."

"And by calling out Sara's name, you chose her over Sally."

Bea stared at the floor. Sara grasped the smaller woman's hand.

Wendell bent over, hands on knees, before Beatrice. "Is Sally still with you? Is she listening to our conversation?"

Sara jumped to her feet. "That's enough! Bea has gone through a terrible ordeal. Let her rest."

Wendell straightened. "Stay out of this. We need to know if this house is the right place for her. Beatrice may be better off in a state hospital or even an asylum back east."

Sara stepped forward. "Her place is here. She has friends, and she helps in the infirmary. Check your records. If those doctors in Baltimore knew so much, why did they send her to an orphanage in Kansas City? They have nothing to offer her. We do."

Wendell raised his brows. "That's patient information you're not privileged to know."

Mrs. Eisner cleared her throat. "That was my fault. I didn't see the harm in telling Sara about Beatrice. I wanted the two to be friends."

Sara placed her hand on hips. "It's not important how I know. Why should you assume that doctors, who've never met Bea, know more than we do? Come to that, what gives you the right to decide?"

"I have to bring these questions up. We need to look at our options."

The urge to stomp her foot was overwhelming. She leaned forward keeping her words low. "I wonder if you even have the authority to send Bea away. The simple truth is this: Bea is better off here, than among strangers. Doing that would be heartless."

Wendell stepped back, bumping the door. "You've made your point. Now, sit. One more remark and you're dismissed from this room."

Sara glared at him as she sank to her chair.

Mrs. Eisner laced her fingers together. "I believe

the Commissioner has a point. Let's suppose Beatrice stays. What if she hurts herself in the future? Would you be able to live with that, Sara?"

"But she *wouldn't* hurt herself!" Sara's hands balled into fists. "She didn't jump. When the shutter struck her, she hung to the ledge for dear life."

"Enough. I still need an answer." Wendell crossed his arms, caught himself and shoved his hands in his pockets. "Beatrice, is Sally still with you?"

Sara drew in a breath through clenched teeth.

"She's gone."

"Where did she go?"

"I don't know."

Wendell blinked. "Will she come back?"

Bea shook her head. "I don't think so. It feels quiet."

"Incredible." Wendell squeezed his eyes shut, rubbing his forehead. "Mrs. Eisner, do you have any suggestions?"

"I think we should accept what Beatrice says. Call it a miracle and leave it alone. To be on the safe side, she should room with another resident. If this phantom should return, we will have to reconsider the state hospital."

Sara touched Bea's arm. "She can room with me."

"I'd say this problem is solving itself." A hint of a smile slipped across the matron's lips. "Mr. Wheatley should have dinner just about ready. After that, we have a lot of cleaning to do."

Wendell dismissed the meeting.

Sara stood in the hallway with Beatrice. "We should get back upstairs. Anyplace is better than staying down here." Footsteps came from behind. The voice of the last person she wanted to hear from spoke in her ear.

"Come with me. We can get your bag from the station wagon. Now that you're staying, this will work out swell."

"I can get my own bag." Despite not wanting to be near him, she found herself walking to the entrance. She stared at him sideways. "We have nothing to talk about. You went too far in pushing out Beatrice."

Wendell frowned. "Those questions deserved answers. I consider it part of my job to made an ironclad decision. An extraordinary event occurred this morning, and someone may ask how later how we handled it. Both Mrs. Eisner and I will write a summary of what happened. Believe it or not, I was on your side the whole time."

Sara shook her head. "You were ready to send me out of the room so you could grill Bea even more."

"That was a warning for you to calm down. You were pushing your point pretty hard in there."

"I did it to protect her. I don't like people threatening my friends."

Wendell sighed. "Your stubbornness is losing its charm. Can we talk about this later? I have great news. It's about that special job I mentioned: it might even be a career."

They reached the entrance and walked down the steps to the back of the station wagon. Instead of taking the bag, Wendell grasped her hands. "I recommended your name to the program head for this area. The job is screening clients for a federal project called the Works Progress Administration. Roosevelt will pay people to work. Your job would be to interview eligible workers and pick the ones who most need a job. You'd get your own desk and a secretary. The position is practically yours, and there's a good chance for advancement. Please tell me you're interested."

Sara pulled her hands away, seized her bag, and picked her purse off the ground. "I've just committed myself to helping a friend, and now you want me sitting behind a desk and passing judgment on one poor person over another?"

Wendell passed a hand across his forehead. "You're missing the point. There'll be guidelines, sure. But you'll be in a position to shape those guidelines. The program will help thousands—millions—of families to make ends meet. It might just get this country moving again."

Sara's expression hardened into a pensive frown. She took a step toward the house. "I have to go."

"Why are you turning it down?"

Listen to me. Was it really possible he didn't understand? "My job is here." She turned, going up the steps.

"Can I call on you later this week? A movie on Friday? I promise no sales pitches."

"I don't think so." Sara reached the door and made a half-turn. "Goodbye, Wendell."

He rasped out a breath. "I don't get it. What happened? To us?"

She turned to face him. "It's not you. Not all of it. You cannot imagine what the last week has been like. I need time to sort out my priorities." She turned away, opened the door, and disappeared.

Part III: Convergence

"It is to the telephone, not to radio, that we owe the development of the equipment whereby speech and music are made available for broadcasting. More than this, it is the telephone wire, not radio, which carries programs the length and breadth of the country. John Smith, in San Francisco, listens on a Sunday afternoon to the New York Philharmonic Orchestra playing in Carnegie Hall. For 3200 miles, the telephone wire carries the program so faithfully that scarcely an overtone is lost; for perhaps fifteen miles, it travels by radio to enter John Smith's house. And then he wonders at the marvels of radio!"

~R. T. Barnet, "Network Broadcast Historical Summary," Bell Telephone Quarterly, April 1934

"There's no better cure for the fear of taking after one's father, than not to know who he is."

~Andre Gide, The Counterfeiters (1925)

"Acceptance of what has happened is the first step to overcoming the consequences of misfortune."

~William James

Chapter Fifty-One

Tuesday, April 16, 1935

Jason studied a roadmap of Kansas on the kitchen table while Michael read a letter from the Radio Club of America, inviting him to join their association. Katherine set iced tea and baloney sandwiches before them.

For the last two days, the boys had helped the neighborhood clean up after Sunday's big dust storm. Since early Monday, the entire city had jumped into action. Neighborhoods organized to clear the streets and yards full of drifted dirt. In every home, women swept floors, beat rugs, and scrubbed houses. Men carted wheelbarrows full of drifted dirt to waiting pickups, which hauled it to locations east of town. Sparse patches of grass still grew on the south side of buildings. Dirt covered everywhere else.

The radio called the storm "Black Sunday." A newspaper man from Oklahoma even coined a name for the South Plains. He called it the "Dust Bowl."

Jason drank his second glass of tea as he studied the map. "I found the road we took when we lost sight of Larry. Based on that, I'd say Sara should be...here." He drew an oval covering the eastern half of Joshua County, including the county seat. He pushed the map over to Michael. "What I don't understand is why he didn't continue north and take the highway east into Joshua. Driving would have been much smoother."

"Maybe Larry took the first turn-off to see if we were following him."

"It's possible." Jason pinched his chin. "But I'm guessing he was driving to a specific place." He tapped the map with his pencil. "We should talk to his parents. They may know where this place is."

Michael was incredulous. "Are you serious? You saw Larry wreck his car. You said yourself he could be dead. If his parents find out we were there, they could blame us for causing his accident."

Katherine rinsed and wiped a stack of plates clean. "If I were Larry's parents, I would want to know what really happened."

Jason rose from the table. "That's it then. I'm going."

"Hey! Wait up!" Michael grabbed his cap, hustling to follow his brother out the front door.

Banned by their father from using the car, Jason and Michael had no choice but walk along Parker Street to the house on River Boulevard. There was little traffic on the streets as they kicked dirt with each step. The sun was a burnished red in the sky, a sign that the atmosphere still held a large amount of dust. Jason rubbed a patch on his arm. The dry air could drive a person crazy with scratching.

When they came to the street bordering the Little Arkansas, they turned south. Incredibly, the big storm hadn't buried the river. The water still ran in sluggish, muddy rivulets. Around a small bend in the street, they came to the two-story home where they had confronted Larry just two days earlier. There was no Roadster, but several cars sat in the driveway and along the front of the house. Jason led the way through the wooden gate and onto the front porch. He knocked on the door.

A young man, about Michael's age, wearing church clothes and slicked-back hair answered the door. "Can I help you?" he asked.

Jason stepped back. "We'd like to speak with Mr. Bigger. Is he home?"

"Uncle Jerry is busy. Are you relatives or friends of the family?"

"We know Larry." Jason glanced inside the front door. Large arrangements of flowers filled the living room. A group of well-dressed people stood in small circles talking in hushed tones.

"Everyone here is family. What are your names? I can tell my uncle who you are."

As Jason and Michael introduced themselves, an older man in a dark gray suit came to the door. It was the floor man from the mercantile. "I'll take care of this, Gordon. Get yourself something to eat." Mr. Bigger stepped onto the front porch, closing the door behind him. "I know you, boys. You were at the store last week. Sara's brothers, I believe."

"Yes, sir. I'm Jason. This is Michael."

"We always enjoyed Sara's company when she came home with Larry, and I know she meant a lot to our son."

Jason and Michael exchanged glances. "Mr. Bigger, I have to ask. Where is Larry?"

Gerald Bigger took a step sideways as if the world had just shifted beneath him. "You mean you don't know?" The store manager wiped his brows. "Of course, you wouldn't. The sheriff from Joshua County called yesterday and broke the news. My son died in a car accident. We have no other details. Could you boys bring Sara by later? I'd like to give her the news myself."

Michael met Jason's eye, mouthing the words *Play dumb.* Jason wet his lips. This wasn't going to be easy. "We can't, Mr. Bigger. Our sister is missing."

"Dear Lord." Bigger sank down on one of the porch chairs, one hand covering his forehead.

Jason sat down beside him. "We've been searching for her over a week now. A few clues have turned up." Michael shook his head no, but Jason waved him off. "Some of it is disturbing. We think she's somewhere in Joshua County close to where Larry had his accident."

Michael slapped his forehead.

Gerald Bigger lifted his head. "I didn't tell you where Larry died. You couldn't have known that...unless..." The storekeeper focused on Jason. "I think you'd better tell me everything you know. And spare no details."

Jason, with reluctant assistance from Michael, went over the events of the last ten days avoiding details about Larry's behavior. Mr. Bigger bowed his head when Jason told about Larry's vehicle during the last moments before the dust storm hit. After the boys finished, he removed a handkerchief from his pocket and wiped his eyes. "That answers a lot of questions: Larry arriving home late that Sunday night, the gash on his cheek, and his pre-occupied state. We—my wife and I—thought the demands of the job were too much for him. I may have mentioned Sara's name as a way to urge him to work harder, but I can't imagine him holding a grudge against your sister."

"Do you have any idea where he might have taken her?" Jason asked.

Bigger shook his head. "I knew he drove his car for hours at a time. But he never told us where he went. Larry was always secretive about his life outside of work."

Michael tapped his chin. "Larry may not have talked to you, but he must have had other friends."

Mr. Bigger looked down at his clenched hands. "I wish he did. Larry was pretty much a loner."

"We're sorry about not being able to save Larry," Jason said. "After the storm hit, the world turned pitch black. Even if we found the Roadster, getting back to our car would have been impossible. Our headlights wouldn't come on. Nothing worked until the storm passed."

The store manager glanced from Michael to Jason. "There is something I don't understand. Don't take this the wrong way, but I need to know. Why did you two live and Larry die?"

"I guess we were lucky." Jason clasped his hands together. The question seemed unfair, but Larry's father was trying to understand. "I stopped the car because cattle wandered onto the road. Larry somehow shot his way through. When I tried to restart, nothing worked. The air tingled with electricity. Larry may have had the same trouble with getting shocked. And he was moving fast."

Gerald nodded. "Larry always did like the thrill of speed."

The nephew Gordon stuck his head out the front door. "Uncle Jerry, the funeral home wants to talk to you."

"I'll be there in a minute."

Gordon ducked back inside. Bigger turned to the boys. "I wish I could help you find Sara. Right now, Lois and I need to grieve for our son. It's possible Sara may come back on her own. She's a resourceful woman."

"Yes, sir." Jason averted his eyes to hide his disappointment.

"I'd better answer my call." Bigger rose to his feet.

Jason and Michael got up as well. Jason balled his hands. The storekeeper turned to reenter the house. Mr. Bigger had a car and could help them continue the search in Joshua. What could he say that would cut through this man's grief and get his attention? His chance was slipping away.

"Sir." Jason's voice was urgent. "There's one more thing you should know."

Bigger didn't bother to turn. "I have to go."

"Sara is having Larry's child. You're about to become a grandfather."

Chapter Fifty-Two

Sara and Bea were in Mrs. Hiebert's room after dinner rounds, giving it a thorough cleaning. Maxine, as well as the rest of the west side residents, were rooming with residents on the east side. Now, Sara and Bea could sweep, scrub, and mop each of the empty bedrooms without disturbing anyone. Downstairs, Patrick and the other men were washing sheets and blankets while the women residents cleaned the main floor. Three women from the Mennonite Church also volunteered to help. The trio brought laundry baskets, extra clothespins, cleaning supplies, and food for an evening feast.

Bea wandered to the open window, tilting her head. "They're beautiful." She stood mesmerized by the small group of women singing outside.

Sara joined her. "They harmonize well together."

Between the house and a row of cedar trees, three women with baskets hung blankets on the clothesline while taking off sheets and pillowcases. They wore full-length aprons and bandanas over their hair. A stout woman wearing a red-striped apron, led the other two in a chorus of "Praise Him! Praise Him!" Stooping to pick up the baskets, they strolled back to the house, never breaking a note.

"I wish I could sing like that," Bea said.

Sara grinned. The gift of speech had awakened a

curiosity within the young woman. "You could ask to join their choir."

"Oh, no!" Bea backed away from the window. "I could never do that. I don't even know the words to the songs."

"You can always learn." The small choir stirred Sara's memories of growing up. Choir practice was an essential part of church life for a pastor's daughter. Fifteen years old and she stood out as the youngest member of the adult choir. All the other members praised her for her beautiful gift of singing to the Lord. That was partly true, but she really sang to Daddy. If only he noticed her, or mentioned how proud he was of her. But he never did.

Perhaps because he sought to be noticed as well.

"Sara...Sara!" Bea shook her arm.

"What?"

"I called your name three times. What are you thinking about?" Beatrice peered at her with concern.

"Home, mostly." Sara passed a hand over her eyes. "It's not important."

"Yes, it is. Tell me." Beatrice gripped her arm. "I want to hear it."

Sara bit her lip. "The music reminded me of when I was younger, being in a church choir and feeling all grown up. Bittersweet memories, I suppose. It was a long time ago. You should ask those ladies about joining their group."

"We both can ask. Wouldn't it be grand to sing together?"

Sara slowly shook her head. "I can't. Those times were enjoyable, but I don't care to sing anymore. I wanted to please my father, but he had his own calling to think about. His pursuit of a new career led to a dispute between me and the rest of the choir. Since then, I've never gone back to church because of what those hypocrites said about Daddy."

"What does your father do?"

Sara picked up the broom, sweeping dirt from a corner. "He's a pastor with his own local radio show. In three weeks, his program will broadcast over much of the country."

"Is there some trouble between you and your father?"

"You can say that. When Daddy learned I was with child, he demanded I leave his house. I've defended him and worked for him, but now I'm not sure if I'll ever see my family again."

Bea placed her hands in her apron pocket. "Still, at least you had a home. How many brothers do you have?"

Sara stopped sweeping and leaned on her broom. "I have two. Jason is twenty, and Michael will be nineteen in July." Sara tilted her head. "Why do you ask?"

"I found a letter in my drawer this morning. It has my name on it, but I think it belongs to you." Bea withdrew an envelope.

Sara grabbed the letter from Bea's outstretched hand. Inside was a sheet of paper in Gladys's distinctive combination of print and cursive penmanship.

The note was short, friendly—and devastating.

"Dear Beatrice,

We got your note and hope you are well. I recognized your handwriting. You didn't ask for a reply, but we feel you need to know that your letter created quite a stir. Pastor plans to use it for his debut program on the Alliance network. The radio station is seeking permission to broadcast from Joshua County farm. There, Pastor will interview "Beatrice" during the program.

Also, your brothers came to the Mailroom asking questions. So far, we've remained quiet. Please write and tell us what to do. Keeping this kind of secret is driving all of us batty.

Take care of yourself. Write soon.

Gladys, Sylvia, and Marilyn

P.S. If there are any supplies you need, please let us know. We can make up a parcel and send it up there.

P.P.S. Using a poor farm as a hideaway is a clever idea. Well done!"

Sara's hands trembled as she refolded the letter. "I can't believe it. He sends me away from home. And now, he's coming here."

"What does it mean?"

Sara bit her lip for a moment. "Another storm is coming."

Chapter Fifty-Three

Jeremy Gorham parked his four-year-old Plymouth in front of the Joshua County Courthouse, a three-story limestone structure that sat on one corner of a town square. The other three structures in the quadrangle were the police station, city hall and post office. He grabbed his clipboard and entered the main doors. A directory in the lobby guided the engineer to the third floor. Mrs. Tabor said he was expected. Gorham climbed the wide circular stairs to the top floor where he found a small office marked W. KRAUSE, Commissioner. Inside the open doorway, a medium built man in a wrinkled brown suit and loosened tie punching keys on a large adding machine. Jeremy knocked.

Krause glanced up and waved him to a wooden chair and continued tallying figures from a pile of receipts. Krause made quick work of pecking keys and pulling the ratcheted crank, tearing off a long ribbon of paper and writing the total in a thick ledger. "Sorry for the wait," he said, getting to his feet. "It was easier to finish adding figures now, rather than come back to it later." He stretched a hand. "I'm Wendell Krause. How can I help you?"

"Jeremy Gorham from KSKM Radio. I'm here to ask about the workhouse."

"A Mrs. William Tabor called earlier today and

asked if I was interested in keeping the workhouse going. Before I could answer, she said an engineer would arrive this afternoon to give me details and examine the location firsthand to see if a radio broadcast from there is possible. Then, she hung up—too quick for me to ask questions. I take it you're the engineer."

Jeremy nodded, smiling. "That's our Meredith. I work with her. She's a hard person to say no to."

"We'll see. What exactly do you wish to do?"

"Our station carries a Sunday morning program called *Heaven and Earth*. It's a commentary on politics and society. Very popular with the listeners and generates lots of fan mail. The show's host received a letter from an occupant at the county workhouse. She mentioned the farm was slated for closure by the county. Pastor McGurk would like to interview the writer during his broadcast on May twelth. This is also the show's national debut on the Alliance network. Would you allow me to visit the property to see if broadcasting from there is feasible?"

"And if it is?"

"Then, with your permission, we'd proceed with airing the show. Our station doesn't want to intrude on the people who live there any more than necessary. After the initial remote, any further reporting on the future of the workhouse will originate from our radio studio in Wichita."

Krause rubbed the back of his neck. "This is amazing. I would never expect a radio station to be interested in a county farm."

Jeremy nodded encouragement. "This is a big deal. Think how this story would affect listeners. It's a world people usually don't contemplate."

The Commissioner bowed his head, nudging the receipts scattered on his desk. "I am."

"So, is that a yes? I can drive to the farm today. We'd need an open space with solid flooring. Some of the equipment is bulky and heavy. If the space is adequate, we complete the broadcast and go home. Pastor gets his show, and your tenants will get an experience they'll be talking about for days."

Krause sighed. His voice took on a cheerless tone. "I'm afraid I can't accept your offer, Mr. Gorham. The closure process has already started, and I'm in charge. We're dismissing the residents in July. After that, the county will auction off the land. You've made a trip for nothing."

Jeremy leaned forward. Time to put his salesman's hat on. "We're aware of the workhouse closing. That is precisely why I'm here. Together, we can make a case for keeping the building and population intact."

"I don't see how. It's now become a county mandate."

"Is this what you want to see happen?"

"Of course not, but my colleagues believe adding more taxable land and eliminating a relief program will get them re-elected."

That sounded like a defeatist answer. Jeremy needed a commitment. He wasn't about to leave without getting it. "You're a commissioner as well. Are you going to stand by and do nothing?"

Krause rose to his feet. "I am carrying out my duties the best I know how, but I'm fighting a defensive battle here. There's other programs to protect as well. People think I dole out taxpayer money and food to

Wes Brummer

freeloaders. That's not true. Most of my recipients are women, children, and the aged. They need relief to survive. The poor farm, however, is a unique example of how a group of dependent people can band together to live a life of quiet dignity. I would not care to put a price tag on that. Somehow, we have."

Gorham smiled. "It's good to see a politician who stands for stands for basic values."

"Well, it's not helping me. I've been looking for any way possible to keep the county farm open. I haven't found it yet."

"Maybe I'm your answer."

Wendell retook his seat. "Listen, good intentions aren't enough. Times are changing. We live in the twilight of what you call the work farm. Other county farms have closed in recent years. You're from Wichita. You should know Sedgwick County sold the land out from under its poor farm five years ago. Saline County closed theirs after a group of residents rebelled against conditions. We are not unique. County farms are dying. Someday, they will cease altogether."

"So you're declining our request?"

"There's no point, sir."

"I see. That's unfortunate." Gorham stood. He couldn't get past this county official. It was a long drive back to Wichita—with Meredith Tabor standing at the end of the line.

Wendell rose as well. "Sorry this was a fruitless trip for you."

"Thank you for your time, Commissioner," Jeremy said. "I'll inform my boss. She'll be disappointed to hear the bad news."

They shook hands. Gorham turned to leave but

stopped in the open doorway. Time for his final pitch. "You're wrong about one thing, Commissioner. Joshua County Farm *is* unique because we can give the dwellers a voice. Our station is providing you an opportunity to speak to the world. Stir emotions. If the program is successful, then listeners will be reaching out to you through fan mail by Tuesday."

Krause was gathering his receipts together. He peered at Gorham, tilting his head. "How many listeners are we talking about?" he asked.

Jeremy considered. "Alliance anticipates at least twenty million listeners will tune in at some point during premiere week."

"I can't fathom a number that big. You mentioned fan mail. Do people really write about your shows?"

"It's how we understand our customers. Some programs like Pastor McGurk's have a loyal following who write frequently."

"That's hard to believe."

Jeremy looked down. "Listeners like dramatic stories full of dialogue. Not a dry narrative. Stirring emotions will lead to an outpouring of letters that will soon die unless we keep the story alive. Our station can start the conversation, but we need your help." Jeremy held his breath.

Krause looked to the ceiling. "Still sounds like a long shot." He rubbed the back of his neck. "I can't imagine a story about a Midwest poor farm getting the attention of a radio listener in New York. Do you follow baseball, Mr. Gorham?"

Gorham chuckled. "Sure. Who doesn't?"

"Well, I feel like the left fielder running to catch a bouncing line drive. Anything I do may be too little too late."

"Well, you can't give up the ball."

Krause drew in a breath. "Good point. Okay. Do what you need to do, Mr. Gorham. Let's see how this game plays out."

****

Ten minutes later, the engineer drove to the work farm. Brown ridges of dirt bordered the country lane. Road crews were certainly busy these days. His car topped a small hill. He drove past a cemetery buried in dirt. The big house weathered the storm well, but the land around it looked stripped and bare.

Gorham parked in front, retrieved his clipboard, and climbed the porch steps. As he stepped to the door, flying dirt and billowing dust shot through the entrance. Jeremy leaped back coughing. A stout woman with a straw broom glowered at him before turning back inside.

He peeked in the doorway. Two other ladies were cleaning the muddy walls of a large front room with rags and buckets of murky water. The menace with the broom lurked in the back, sweeping around the fireplace. Forlorn, mismatched furniture lined the walls of the day room. Rockers, wooden chairs, and small tables for games dotted the center of the dank space. An old wheelchair with a missing footboard sat in a corner.

On the plus side, the floor was solid. They could move the furniture and whatnot aside, and the women were making progress on their cleanup project. This room would serve well as a place for the broadcast.

Jeremy knocked on the open doorway. "Hello?"

"Who are you?" one asked.

"Sorry to intrude. I'm looking for the person in

charge."

The glowering woman leaned her broom against the unlit fireplace and pointed to the rear of the house.

"Could you show me the way, please? I'd be grateful."

She waddled across the room, and plopped in the dilapidated wheelchair. "Push me."

Jeremy rolled her through a large dining room and pantry, stopping in a long, narrow kitchen. Water splashed farther back. The woman pointed to a passageway. "The matron is in the laundry room." She rose to her feet and pushed her wheelchair out of the kitchen. Shaking his head, Jeremy stepped around the corner to the source of the ruckus.

Three men, soaked from head to foot, were washing clothes. A large, bearded man fed laundry into a handwringer. A grandfatherly old man heaved the crank. Bed sheets rolled from the wringer into a basket. The third man, a hooked-nosed old codger with a chin that nearly met his nose, stood in a galvanized tub full of water. He wielded a laundry stomper, pounding away at the wash like he was digging a post hole. Water flew everywhere. Jeremy shielded the clipboard, but drops still hit the paper.

"Welcome to the circus!" A woman's voice broke through the racket. A howl of pain erupted. The big man whirled about, yelling and clutching his fingers. "Just a second." The small matron led the bearded man from the room. Three minutes later, she returned alone. "Let's step into my office."

"Is that man okay?" Jeremy asked.

"Mr. Wheatley will be fine. I wrapped his fingers with a rag and some ice chips. The swelling should go down in a day or two." She led Jeremy to a small corner workspace. "Take a seat. I'm Mrs. Eisner, matron of this house. How can I help you?"

"My name is Jeremy Gorham and I'm an engineer with station KSKN in Wichita. I talked to Commissioner Krause. He's agreed to allow us the use of your front room for a remote broadcast on May 12th."

The matron tilted her head. "Did the Commissioner mention that the county plans to close our doors?"

"We discussed that. Both of us believe there is a chance that listener reaction could extend your operation."

The steely-eyed woman waved him off. "That's so much falderal."

"I assure you, Mrs. Eisner, this is a serious matter. Pastor Sam McGurk, the host of *Heaven and Earth*, plans to do a story about your home and the people who live here. It's all part of a special live broadcast airing across the nation on the Alliance network."

"We make do on our own, Mr. Gorham. Your charity is not needed."

"This is not charity. It's business. Our station will gain new listeners, and reaction from the show could delay the closure."

"How cozy." The matron frowned. "Why did you choose us for—what did you call it—a remote?"

She wasn't convinced. Were country people always this bullheaded? "Actually, that came about from a fan letter sent to the pastor. The note was a plea for help. The powers that be at KSKN saw this as an opportunity to tell a dramatic true story. One that loyal listeners will talk about. Which reminds me, is there a choir or singing group, perhaps affiliated with a church, near here? We need music for the program."

"You're in luck, Mr. Gorham. Step outside the back door and you'll hear a group from the local church helping us with the laundry. I'm no judge of music, but they have a pleasant harmony."

"I'll do that. So have I made my case, Mrs. Eisner?"

"You should have been a salesman instead of an engineer, Mr. Gorham."

Jeremy grinned. "In radio, you wear many hats."

"I can imagine. Tell me, who wrote this letter?"

"Well…" Jeremy looked at his meeting notes. "I understand the writer lives here. Her name is Beatrice Mullens. To be frank, Mrs. Eisner, we want to create as much drama as possible for this program. That includes an interview with her and the pastor. Can she articulate well?"

Gloria scrunched her lips. "Beatrice is not the person I'd have guessed to write such a letter. Someone else comes to mind. But to answer your question, Beatrice can put a sentence together."

"Great. I want to get your telephone number so my director can keep in touch with you. We will install a new phone line in the front room in two weeks or so. On May twelfth, we will be bringing in some equipment in order to make the broadcast."

"I can't believe Commissioner Krause agreed to this escapade."

"This endeavor might well save the farm."

"Wishful thinking." Gloria took a towel out of her apron and wiped her hands. "It's against my better judgment, but I'll go along with this silliness. The house rules are posted in the common room. I expect you to follow them like everyone else. And you better put the room back together the way you found it when you're finished."

"Yes, ma'am. Should I be discussing this with the overseer?"

"With James? He'll be finding things to do in the barn while this is going on. You'll be dealing with me, young man."

"It will be a pleasure, Mrs. Eisner." Jeremy suppressed a sigh. Another hurdle jumped. "Just imagine. Your workhouse will be the subject of conversation for millions of people. Our program could be on any radio between here and New York City."

"Young people spend too much time listening to the radio. They should be reading a book or working with their hands."

"They do, Mrs. Eisner. In just eight years, radio has gone from a hobby to a major part of our lives. Today, we can send a human voice or a Beethoven symphony across the country or across the ocean. Who knows what we can come up with in the next eight years?"

"Hopefully," said the matron, "A better way to clean the house."

"Someone will have to work on that," said Jeremy. "Now, let's hear this choir."

Chapter Fifty-Four

Sara sat at her usual spot in the dining room that evening. She had gone into the kitchen to offer her help, but the church ladies shooed her back to the tables. Now, she waited with the others in anticipation of the evening's feast. The tables were covered with red-checkered tablecloths. Pie plates set besides evenly spaced tinware placed on carefully folded cloth napkins before each person. The mouth-watering aroma of seasoned meat and vegetables whiffed from the kitchen. Across from her, Patrick rubbed his hands. "It's supposed to be a secret, but I know what we're having." He leaned forward, cupping his mouth as if to whisper, but his voice was too loud. "It's spaghetti casserole!"

Mrs. Chapman shushed him, but the old coot, Mr. Wunch, cackled and thumped the back of Wheatley who sat beside him. The cook must have hurt himself today. Three of his fingers were bandaged together.

Sara glanced about the room. The cupboards and walls were shiny white instead of dull gray. Mrs. Robson, Miss Underwood, and Mrs. Chapman did a fine job cleaning. All the sweeping, mopping, and scrubbing had paid off. The house never looked so clean. Too bad Dutch wasn't here to see this.

Two ladies in aprons and long dresses filed out of the kitchen each carrying a large bowl of meaty casserole. Both went to the head of each table. The third volunteer brought out a cart containing two bowls of green beans and a deep dish of apple crisp. She tapped the dish with a wooden spoon. The room quieted.

"We've all worked hard today cleaning. I know you've built up big appetites. What better way to celebrate than by sharing our bounty. Mr. Eisner, would you say the blessing, please?"

James stood, clasped his hands, and bowed his head. "Dear Heavenly Father, thank You for the fine food and the generous service of these wonderful neighbors. I pray that each of us find ways to serve others by giving of ourselves as our sisters have done today. We cannot thrive on our own, but only through Your Grace. You touch our lives, and we practice our faith by touching the lives of others. This is the source of our true bounty. Through serving others, we serve ourselves. In this way, we bring home the harvest of Your Glory. And for that we give You thanks. And we thank these generous ladies for their kind help today. Amen."

Bowls of food passed down the table to lifted hands waiting eagerly to fill their plates. The spaghetti sauce was thick with plenty of hamburger meat. The green beans held bits of bacon and onion. Sara watched several residents stare at their untouched food. Probably thinking the same thoughts she had at the restaurant nearly a week ago. Well, that wasn't going to happen tonight. She picked up a fork and ate.

One of the volunteers, a full-bodied woman with calloused hands, soft brown eyes, and a wide smile, drew a chair next to Patrick, who was well on his way to being the first person to clean his plate. Beatrice kept her head averted. After looking around, the visitor turned her attention to Sara. "Mrs. Eisner told me how the three of you care each day for the aged souls upstairs. Tonight, you can take your rest. My friends and I will serve the elderly folks."

"Thank you for the help. I'm Sara. Next to you is Patrick. And this is Beatrice."

Bea nodded.

"We were in the infirmary and heard your singing outside," Sara said. "You sound good together." She nudged Beatrice with her knee.

"The songs were pretty." Bea cupped a hand over her mouth as if she said too much.

"We were being playful with the Lord's music, but it makes the labor so much more enjoyable." She smiled, her brown eyes beaming, "I'm Priscilla Rohlman. Friends call me Cilly."

"Music is always welcome here." Sara nudged Bea again.

Swallowing, Beatrice leaned forward. "I want to sing… To learn, I mean."

Priscilla glanced at Sara as if asking for confirmation. Sara nodded.

"Do you, now? I'll introduce you to the others later. We're always looking for new voices to add to the choir."

"I'd like that," Bea said.

Sara finished her meal, saying no more. She helped planted the seed. Now, to see if it would grow.

After supper, Priscilla came around the table and embraced Sara. "I'm so glad to meet you. Go relax. You deserve some time to yourself. After we serve the elders, we'll do the dishes, and then make a joyful noise upstairs. You're welcome to join us."

"Later, perhaps. I'd like to write a letter first."

"Splendid." Priscilla turned to the younger woman. "You come along with me, Miss Beatrice. I'll introduce you to the other ladies."

They left. Sara stood alone in the kitchen.

The church ladies would get home late tonight, and she couldn't walk away from a kitchen full of dirty dishes. Sara tied on an apron and set to work filling the two metal dish pans in the big sink with hot water from a teapot mixed with cool well water. Then, she grated some flakes from a bar of borax soap. Rounding up someone to dry would make the job easier, but it felt good to be alone. In a few minutes, she had a pile of dishes in the rinse tub, Sara found a towel and put away the tinware and utensils.

Nearly all the residents were in the common room doing jigsaw puzzles, playing checkers, cards or waiting for the singing to begin upstairs. The Eisners were gone—possibly helping upstairs as well. *That's what I should be doing.* Sara backed away from the group, satisfied with the relative solitude of the dining room. It wasn't that she was uncomfortable with the others. Working simply made it easier to avoid saying something that would expose her identity.

Still, she needed something to do. Sara opened the bureau drawer with her name on it, taking a stamped envelope and a sheet of paper. Sitting at the dining room table, she wrote:

"Dear Ladies,

Thank you for telling me what's happening. I can't believe my sanctuary is about to be invaded. It's my fault, of course. I never thought my letter would lead to this.

I'm staying here. This is my home, and this is where I stand. The fact that a broadcast will take place here means Daddy will need to stay focused on the program, so I don't think anything will likely happen.

One thing for sure. Daddy's arrival will force my true identity to come out. Friends I've made could see me as a fake. Even if they don't, I will still have to leave. I could avoid any trouble by leaving early, yet, I feel I must meet him face to face and attempt to mend our differences.

Don't tell my family I'm here. Let me handle this my way.

I love you all,
Sara

This would be her last message. Sara addressed the envelope, stuffed the letter inside, and sealed her decision.

As she walked past the landing, choral voices rang from upstairs. Sara walked out the door and down the steps. Sunset was giving way to twilight. The mailbox for the county farm sat with two others at the intersection of Miller and Carriage Road. Sara set off to mail her letter.

The short walk was comforting. Despite the promise of relaxation, the free evening felt like a rebuke. Working in the infirmary gave her purpose. But this evening she felt aimless. What if the choir asked Bea to sing with them? She couldn't do that. Was she and Beatrice drifting apart?

Sara reached the mailbox, slipped her message inside, and raised the flag. In the fading light, she returned to the house.

The common room was deserted, except for Mr.

Emerson and Mr. Wunch huddled over a game of checkers. Hands clapped in applause upstairs. Sara hovered by the staircase, one hand on the banister. A new hymn began. Was Bea with them?

She climbed to the infirmary.

This end of the passage was dark, but at the far end, wall lamps burned bright on either side of a makeshift stage. Beds and chairs filled the hallway. All eyes faced the churchwomen as they stood in a row, singing a rousing call-and-response standard, "Get Away Jordan." In the center, beside Priscilla, Bea stood holding a sheet of paper. She wore a radiant smile as her rich, contralto voice blended with the other singers. A few of the residents clapped to the beat while others swayed to the music. Bea's eyes beamed as the audience broke into more applause.

The group began another gospel favorite, "Just Over in Glory Land." Peppy songs must be the order of the day. Bea faltered on the lyrics, but came out strong on the chorus, her foot tapping to the music. Here she was, with newfound friends, singing to people she knew. Sara had never seen her so happy.

Lingering on the edge of darkness, Sara watched several more minutes. No one knew she was there. She turned away and descended the stairs, one long step at a time. Halfway down, a wave of despondency overcame her, and she sat on a step, leaning her head against the banister.

Beatrice was a wounded creature when Sara first met her, haunted by a darker half that no one knew existed. Yet, in the last two days, the mute caterpillar had turned into a joyful butterfly taking wing with new friends. She found her calling. Maybe even a way out of this place. Bea achieved it on her own. Could she survive outside these walls? She was such a dependent creature.

Or maybe not.

Bea could leave, and she'd be the one left alone.

It would be easy to sabotage Bea's good fortune. Tell the church ladies of Bea's dark past. *Be careful, ladies. Your little butterfly could turn into a wasp.*

Sara gasped, her fingers covering her lips. These were treacherous notions. Not even her father would do such a thing. Could the coming meeting with her father be affecting her judgment? She must consider the consequences of her actions. Her reunion involved the lives of her friends. Confronting Daddy may be the wrong thing to do. Wasn't he supposed to help save this home? So why was she feeling so much dread?

One thing mattered most. She lived here. This was her house. Her father was the visitor. And she wouldn't tolerate threats from a visitor.

Even if her home was already doomed.

Behind her, the choir sang "A Shelter in The Time of Storm."

Chapter Fifty-Five

Saturday, April 20, 1935

Sara couldn't put her finger on what it was, but something was going on with Beatrice. Her friend said little during afternoon rounds. After storing their supplies, she and Beatrice relaxed downstairs. Bea fidgeted in her chair and watched out the front windows.

Sara turned to her companion. "Is something wrong?"

Bea leaned back in her rocker. "I'm going to choir practice with Cilly. She invited me to church on Easter Sunday. That's tomorrow."

Sara blinked. "I'd forgotten all about Easter. We've been so busy with the patients. Will you be singing?"

"I don't think so. But I do want to listen to the music."

"Easter hymns can be beautiful."

"Cilly told me that singing is not an amusement, but a prayer to the Lord."

"We may sing for any number of reasons. But the ear doesn't know the difference. You told me when you were small you sang for the sheer pleasure."

Bea bowed her head. "I still do, but I can't tell Cilly. She'd be disappointed in me. It *is* fun. But in church it's serious fun."

Sara nodded with one eyebrow arched. "Church choirs are people with all-too-human emotions who can kill the enjoyment. I envy your innocence."

"These ladies aren't like that."

Sara remained silent.

At four o'clock, Priscilla and her husband arrived in a mule-drawn carriage. Bea bolted for the front door with Sara lagging behind. Priscilla waved to her. "We'll have Beatrice back to you folks by eight. The church is having a potluck supper after practice, so she'll be eating with us."

Mr. Rohlman helped Beatrice to her seat. "Does Mrs. Eisner know Bea will be out?"

"I told her a few days ago. Tomorrow, we will be singing three special hymns for Easter service. We're all very excited about the new music." Beatrice waved goodbye as the mules set off.

Sara and Patrick worked evening rounds alone. Without a third person, it did take longer. "Did Bea tell you she was going to music practice?" Sara asked Patrick as they were finishing their last room.

He nodded.

"I wonder why she didn't mention it to me."

Patrick stared at her, blinking.

Sara flashed a false grin. "It's okay. I'll ask her about it when she returns."

By seven-thirty, Sara sank exhausted into one of the couches in the front room, a four-month-old *Saturday Evening Post* lay crumpled in her lap. Daddy had a subscription to the magazine. She read the short stories and poetry but nothing else. Today, she found an article by Garet Garrett, a free-market thinker who blamed the Depression on government debt. Garrett argued that the New Deal was disguised Socialism. Quit government spending, he suggested and let the downturn play itself out. This sounded like one of Daddy's talks. He probably read this same article.

A few minutes later, Beatrice bounded in. "Mrs. Eisner!" The small woman tore through the entryway, dashing down the hallway. Sara peeked out the front window. The carriage still sat outside. What was going on?

Sara opened the front door. Priscilla waved her over. Sara descended the steps.

"The choir has asked Beatrice if she would like to sing during Easter service. She's gone to ask Mrs. Eisner if we can pick her up early."

"I see." Sara took a step back. "It's getting dark. Will you be able to make it home safely?"

"We live just a couple of miles away. Once old Sulky knows we're heading home, he'll pick up the pace. We'll be there in no time."

Bea flew out of the house, jumped into the carriage, and hugged Priscilla. "She said I could leave whenever I needed to."

"That's wonderful, sweetheart. We'll be by about seven. Service starts at eight. Don't worry about clothes. I can scrape something together for you."

"Thank you, Miss Cilly. You've been very kind," Bea said.

"Nonsense. God had a hand in making this happen. He wants your voice to be shared. Now, we best be going."

"I can't wait for Easter." Bea's eyes twinkled in the dimming light.

Mr. Rohlman flicked his wrists and the mule jerked

the wagon to life. Sara and Bea watched the Rohlmans turned south.

"Why didn't you tell me about going to Easter service?" Sara asked.

"I…didn't think you wanted me to go." Bea continued to watch the vanishing wagon.

"I'm not interested in church, but you're welcome to go. I'm very proud. You're getting your wish to sing."

"You could come with me."

"No." Sara shifted her feet. "I can't go back to that."

"Whatever happened to you, it doesn't mean it will happen again."

Sara looked down. "I can't dismiss the past."

"But Sara—"

"Don't ask me again." Sara rushed up the steps, hurried in, and slammed the door.

Chapter Fifty-Six

Monday, April 22, 1935

Sara massaged Mrs. Hiebert's hip after her six a.m. injection of morphine, working the medicine into the muscle. Maxine moaned as Sara rolled the bed-ridden woman onto her back and drew the covers. She was thinner now—and weaker, having eaten little in the past week. Last evening her Bible slipped from her hands at least twice. Yet, despite the medication, she stayed alert during their room visits.

Sara laid a hand on her forehead. "You're looking a bit pale. Can I get you anything?"

Morning rounds would begin soon enough with the clatter of changing pitchers, pots, and basins, followed by the rush to clean and move on to the next room. It was nice to have a little quiet time with Maxine. In all the bustle, it was easy to forget that Mrs. Hiebert was a person and not a patient.

The older woman swallowed. "Could you raise my bed? My mouth is dry, and I could use some water."

Sara cranked the bed to a sitting position and rolled the bedside table in place. She filled Maxine's tin cup, found a straw, and held it to her lips.

She took a couple of sips. Sara wiped water from her chin.

"Thank you, young lady. I wish for all this to be

over. I so wish to be with Pearce again. Will you pray with me?"

Sara pursed her lips. She didn't have the heart to voice her thoughts on the injustice of a supposedly kind God inflicting needless pain on a dying woman—a devout follower, no less. There was plenty of evil in the world to draw His wrath. Much easier to remain silent and go through the charade of praying.

Maxine tilted her head as if sensing her hesitation. "You're not a Believer, are you?"

Sara lowered her head. "I want to believe. But it's hard…"

With an effort, Maxine grasped Sara's hand. "It's not always easy, especially if you're going through a personal trial. But you must know this; God has sovereignty over your life, whether you believe in Him or not." She focused on Sara with intensity. "Even if you've lost your way."

Sara blinked. "What do you mean?"

"You were a Believer once, but your faith has fallen. Yet, you still serve Him."

Sara's eyes widened. "How did you know? About losing my faith?"

"You lack the conviction of a true atheist. For them, Jesus is a subject to avoid, or they reject Him with pride. For you—it's an apology."

"You're a perceptive woman, Mrs. Hiebert."

"If perceptive means having lots of time to think of the obvious, then I suppose so. Still, you believed once, growing up. You fell away, or perhaps an event shattered your faith."

Sara glanced about, looking for a task to do. "I shouldn't burden you with my problems. It would be selfish of me."

Maxine's gentle laughter was like soft bells. "Oh Sara, hearing your story takes my mind off myself. What was your childhood like?"

Sara closed her eyes. "I don't know where to start. I don't like talking about myself."

"Start with your parents."

"I've always gotten along with Mom. Not so well with Daddy. He sees me as a nuisance. As a child, I tried different ways to please him. Few things worked. I loved drawing pictures. When I showed him my art, he would tell me to pick up my crayons. When I was seven, Daddy bought some tools. I took them out of the car, and the teeth of a saw touched the door paint. He yelled at me about how I scratched his car, and now he'd have to re-paint it. When I was a little older, Mom taught me how to cook. I wanted to do all the cooking one day a week. He didn't like anything I made. The biggest shock of my life was when Daddy asked me to manage the fan mail for his radio show."

"Is your father an actor?"

"Daddy calls himself a radio pastor. But he doesn't bring up much scripture. He's more of a social commentator." Sara brushed the air with her hand. "It doesn't set well with me."

Maxine nodded. "My pain is temporary. Yours will never end unless you take action. Open your heart. Ask God for comfort. And there is another task you must take. The hardest task you'll ever do. You've built yourself a cross to carry, and you must learn to cast it off. It will take forgiveness."

Sara shook her head. "There's nothing to forgive. Every time I'm around Daddy, I'm that little girl who can't do anything right. There's still a lump in my throat every time he scolds me."

"I'm not talking about forgiving your father."

She puckered her brow. "What do you mean?"

Maxine made a small gesture. "You must forgive yourself."

Chapter Fifty-Seven

Saturday, April 27, 1935

After her Saturday afternoon choir practice, Beatrice entered the tenant house. *Where is Sara?* Her friend's dark mood was aggravating. Ever since Sara learned of her father's upcoming visit, she hadn't been the same cheery person. These days, Sara showed little interest in conversation before meals, sitting on the porch, or even taking walks. And she wanted no part of choir practice or attending church. Sara used to stroll about like a princess who just discovered the countryside. Now she seemed like a whipped child.

The coming reunion with her father must be bothering her. Tonight, she would do what she meant to do before Easter. Wake her from her doldrums.

Bea loved telling her new friends how she and Sara worked together and how Sara saved her life. Cilly wanted to know Sara better. "Invite her to church," she urged Bea. "Keep asking until she says yes."

Tonight she would do more than just ask, and she wasn't taking no for an answer. Miss Sara was normally a generous person, but lately, even the bedridden folks upstairs have noticed her sour nature. Today, she would challenge her friend.

I hope she'll still be my friend tomorrow.

Bea found Sara with Patrick in Mrs. Hiebert's

room. Patrick leaned forward in Maxine's rocker, stroking her hand while Sara sat in a corner chair, a handkerchief in her hands. Mrs. Hiebert was asleep.

Beatrice stepped inside the door. "Should I get Miss Gloria?"

Sara leaned back in her chair. "No. Maxine is failing. Patrick won't leave, so I'm keeping him company."

Bea touched Patrick's arm for a moment and then turned to Sara. "I wish to speak to you."

"Go ahead."

"Not here." Bea was firm. "Let's go down the hall."

Sara sighed but stood and followed the smaller woman out of the room.

Bea led the way, entering the room once occupied by Mr. Evans.

Sara looked sideways at Beatrice. "This room gives me the heebie-jeebies. I'm surprised it doesn't make you uneasy as well."

"I'm learning to face my fears. Maybe you should too."

Sara crossed her arms. "What's *that* supposed to mean?"

Bea stepped between Sara and the door in case she tried to bolt. "I want you to come with me to worship tomorrow. I've been telling everyone about the work we do together—even about the black storm. Everyone wants to meet you. They say I'm so lucky to have you for a friend."

Sara backed up a step and tried to duck around the smaller woman, but Bea rushed to the door, blocking her way. Sara blew an exasperated breath. "How long do you intend to keep me here?"

"Until you become honest with me. What's wrong with attending service?"

Sara placed hands on hips, her voice edged with anger, she said, "You want a reason? I'll give you several. Church is full of phony people pretending to be pious and noble, but they're a bunch of two-faced judges. I was once in a choir singing my heart out. The choirmaster told us we were singing to God." Sara hesitated, biting her lip. "That may have been true for the others, but I was singing to Daddy, hoping he would notice. Instead, he left the church to start a new career, leaving my mother and I to face their judgment."

"It must have been hard."

Sara closed her eyes. "Daddy left so abruptly, I took the rebukes in silence. Perhaps I even agreed with them. Daddy's behavior *was* insincere. How could I say anything? That was five years ago. I've never been able to forgive them, and I can never go back to church again. Never."

"These feelings—your irritation—it's misplaced. You're really angry at your father."

Sara reeled backward, her palm stuck out, as if fending off a blow. "No. It was the choir. They were all pretenders—"

"*Stop it!*" Bea stepped forward, heat rising up her neck. Blood pulsed in her temple. She thrust an accusing finger at Sara. "*You're* the pretender."

Behind glaring eyes, Bea's thoughts whirled. What was happening to her? The clenched teeth... The shallow breaths... A feeling like surging water bouncing off rocks... A roaring cyclone. And she was in the center, buffeted by swirling unrestrained feelings.

Each one fierce and demanding.

Anger. That was it. She was *furious* at Sara. All these years Sally had harbored these emotions. Kept them to herself—blocking them. Bea only knew the depths. Now, for the first time she sensed the heights of body and mind acting in tight orchestration.

It was...*exhilarating!*

Sara blinked. "What did you call me?"

Beatrice took a breath to calm herself. She wanted so much to share her wonderful discovery: feelings, emotions, and the instant leap from thought to action. But not now. "You heard me." Bea glared, savoring the heat. "Your make-believe story about being wronged is a mere excuse."

Sara gaped. "That's not what I meant."

"Poor Sara," Bea said, chastising her in a Sally-like voice. "You can be such a damsel. You suffer the words of others. Your job and your home were taken away. You've lost more than any of us will ever gain. I've only lived a single month in a real home. Never worked or gone on a date. Yet, you've done all these things."

"But you're accusing me—"

"Let me finish. Yet, here you are with a different name and a story to go with it. Hiding with the invisible people. So, tell me. Who is the pretender?"

Sara shook her head. "You're twisting my words."

"None of us have anywhere to go. None of us can change from a pauper to a princess. No one but you."

Sara slumped to the floor, her hands covering her face. "Is that how you see me? A fake?"

Beatrice sat beside her, steadying her breath. *Whew. Anger is exhausting.* "Of course not. But you hide behind your father's words and the work upstairs.

It's easy to act the hurt daughter or the busy boss. But it's not so easy to trust. To take off the disguise and let others see who you are."

Sara tilted her head, her eyes full of wonder. "I've never heard you talk like this before. How did you put this together?"

Beatrice reached into her apron. She missed her slate. It was so easy to jot down some words and make a few gestures. "I'm no different. For years, I never uttered a word. Wishing for a normal life was always a constant thought. But it was so easy to hide behind Sally. You led me out of the darkness, Sara."

"You did it yourself."

Bea touched her arm. "Since you came here, I felt like you were better than the rest of us. But today I realized how hiding behind a mask is so easy. That has to end."

Sara gripped her hand. "I'm so sorry for the way I acted. How can I make it up to you?"

"You can come to Sunday service with me."

"You're relentless." Sara shook her head in surrender. "How can I refuse? I'll go, but don't expect me to sing."

They embraced. Bea hid a sly grin. "I wouldn't dream of it."

Chapter Fifty-Eight

Wednesday, May 8, 1935

There may be better ways to travel, Jason thought, stretching his legs, but riding in Mr. Bigger's roomy La Salle made for a smoother ride then the jittery Model A. He sat in the passenger seat while Michael dozed in the back. The car was long and stylish, with a tall radiator in front and small portholes running along the side of the hood. An elegant, yet sensible car. On this trip to Joshua they stuck to the main road. Not that bumpy, rutted lane they used to follow Larry. Maybe today they'd have better luck finding Sara.

It was more than three weeks since Larry's death. Twenty-four days since they followed him on the day of the biggest dust storm since, well, ever. Now they were beginning the search again, thanks to Mr. Bigger lending his time to the effort. And his car. They could ask around—find out if anyone seen her. And if they were lucky—bring her back home.

"Boys, I need gas and I can hardly see out of this filthy windshield. I'm pulling in, here."

Bigger pulled into a Sinclair station. The attendant, a young man with a blonde brush cut and stained overalls, hopped out of the small cubbyhole of a building and loped to the car. "Fill 'er up, sir?"

Bigger leaned out the open car window. "Do that.

And check the oil and tires."

"Glad to, sir." The eager employee jumped to fill the gas tank.

He turned to Jason. "Where would you like to start?"

Jason glanced down the street, toward the center of town. "I'd like to talk to a few people. See if anyone spotted Sis."

Michael stirred in the backseat. "We could put some of the leaflets in the restaurants and on telephone poles, especially downtown."

"Sounds reasonable. How many flyers do you have, Jason?"

Jason glanced down at the thick envelope on the front seat. "About forty."

"I'll stop at the county courthouse and talk to the sheriff. You boys distribute the flyers and see what you can dig up. I'll meet you at the newspaper office."

"We appreciate your help, Mr. Bigger," Jason said.

"It's the least I can do. Larry's death has been tough. He was our only son. And to find out he has a child... I imagine your parents are horrified, but we—Lois and I—are excited. It means a part of Larry still lives."

"I'm sorry for the way I told you about Sara." Jason sighed. "We came at a bad time. But I wanted to get your attention."

"You did that, son. After you left, I relayed the news to Lois, and she called your mother to see if it was true. That's something women have over men. They're not afraid to talk about sensitive matters. I should do the same with your father."

The gas attendant opened the hood of the car.

Jason shook his head. "You better wait until after Sunday. Dad's got a big show planned that morning. It's all very hush-hush."

"I'll call on him later this week, then." Bigger slapped Jason's knee. "Liven up. Today, we might get lucky and find your sister."

"Fine by me." A brief smile passed Jason's lips.

Michel gestured to a large Nehi sign mounted on the side of the filling station. "Is it okay to drink pop in your car?"

Bigger glanced at the advertisement.

Drink Genuine Nehi in All Popular Flavors!

Along with the bottle was a pair of women's curvy knees beneath a bouncy skirt. "Sure. We all can do with a soda pop."

The attendant closed the hood, wiped down the windshield, and came to the driver's side with a ticket pad. "She took a lot of gas. It'll be $2.45. Anything else I can get you?"

"How about three bottles of Nehi? What'll you have, Michael?"

"I'll take chocolate."

"Jason, get me two of those flyers. What would you like?"

"Peach for me." Jason handed Bigger printed leaflets with Sara's picture.

"And I'll have a Grape Nehi. If you can tack up these posters, you can keep the change." He handed the attendant three dollars bills and two leaflets.

The attendant glanced at Sara's photograph and whistled. Jason frowned. Wolfish behavior was acceptable—but not when it was directed at Sis. "There's a reward for finding this girl?" he asked.

"Fifty dollars," Gerald said. "Call the sheriff if you see her."

"Yes, sir. Be right back with the pops. And I'll take care of these posters."

"Thank you, son. One more thing. Can you give us directions to the newspaper office?"

About ten minutes, the green La Salle drove along Joshua's single main street.

"The Sentinel building should be ahead and on the left," said Bigger.

Jason nodded. "I see the sign. Pull over where you can. Michael and I can tack flyers to the poles. Then we'll talk to the newspaper people."

"I smell food." Michael pointed at an eatery on the corner called The Covered Dish.

"My brother was born hungry," Jason said. "We'll see you in a little while, Mr. Bigger."

"See you later, boys." Bigger set the car in gear and drove away.

Jason took half the flyers from the envelope and handed them to Michael along with a box of tacks. "Let's get these posted."

"I'll go across the street and work my way around the block and meet you at the newspaper office."

"You're just interested in that restaurant."

"I'm only going to peek in and leave a flyer."

"Sure," said Jason.

His brother crossed the blacktop street with leaflets in hand. Jason set to work tacking the "Our Sister Is Missing" posters on utility poles, giving some to shopkeepers and pedestrians, and stuffed a few in the door handles of cars. Twenty minutes later he tacked a flyer in front of a feed store. With one sheet remaining, he headed to the newspaper office. And sat on the front steps of the news building to wait for his brother.

He didn't have to wait long.

"Hey, I got a lead!" Michael yelled, running across the street. "A waitress remembered seeing her," he said, catching his breath. "Sometime before the big dust storm."

"That's great." Jason clapped him on the back. "That is a break. Did she have any details?"

"Not much else. She ate supper with a young man, but he didn't look like Larry."

"If one person saw her, others should have too. Come on, let's get our poster in the paper." The two rushed inside the Sentinel office.

Jason expected to find a secretary, but the only person in the office was a rotund man at a typewriter, wearing a white shirt and suspenders.

Jason and Michael stood before him, but the man kept typing. Finally, Jason cleared his throat. "Hello?" The desk a plaque read "*Editor.*"

The man nodded, hit the carriage and continued hitting the keys. Three paragraphs later, he yanked the sheet from the machine, snatched a pair of reading glasses, and peered at the words. "What are you doing in my office," he said, still scrutinizing his work.

Jason placed his remaining poster on the editor's desk. "We'd like this in your paper."

"A missing sister," he mused. "This has the makings for a good story. I can get it in the next edition. Too late to for this week. Paper goes on sale noon tomorrow. Too bad you didn't come in this morning— might've been able to squeeze it in the classifieds.

"A whole week?" Michael shook his head. "That's

too long a wait."

"Hold it." Jason held up a hand. "You said this could be an important story. Couldn't you replace this for a minor story. We'll still pay for it like it's an ad."

"I said it could make for a *good* story. It would take a fair amount of work to make changes at this stage. Tell me the back story."

"What's that?" Michael scrunched his forehead, looking at his brother.

"He wants to know what happened up to now," Jason said.

With frequent corrections from Michael, Jason went over Sara's disappearance. "So you see. We've been worried that Sis might be hurt. But today, my brother says someone might have seen her."

The editor rubbed his chin. "You convinced me. It's a hot story. Ernestine Graber's nuisance dog can wait another week. It will take a pot of coffee and a few hours' work, but I'll change things around. Might even put it on the front page. It gives me an excuse to move the dust storms to page two for one week."

"Thanks, sir." Jason held out his hand.

"Glad to help, son," he said. "The name's Mel White. No relation to that hotshot newspaper man from Emporia."

Jason and Michael met Bigger as he emerged from his car. "The editor will run our poster," Michael said. "Sara's story will be in Friday's paper. She might even be on the front page."

"Good job, boys. Is there anything else we need to do here?"

"No, sir," Jason said. "Our job is done."

"Fine," said Bigger. "One more stop, and we'll be

home by supper."

A few minutes later the La Salle drove west on Miller Road. Jason leaned back in his seat. It was disappointing not to have found Sis. The news from the waitress, though, was encouraging. Between the leaflets and the newspaper, something was bound to happen.

"Where are we going, Mr. Bigger?" Michael asked. "This isn't the way we came."

Bigger rolled up his window to keep dirt from blowing in. "We're going to where the storm overtook you boys."

Jason raised an eyebrow. They were stopping at the place where Larry died. He'd better stay close by Mr. Bigger, in case he needed help. They passed a small cemetary, then slowed at an intersection.

Michael pointed to a large formidable-looking structure ahead. "What's *that*?"

"A poor farm." Bigger turned south. "The sheriff said if I drove past it, I went too far. In my day, we called them county asylums."

"It looks creepy." Michael turned to stare out the back window at the tall building with the wide porch and short steeple. "It must be full of ghosts."

Jason rolled his eyes. "I didn't know Sam Spade was afraid of spooks."

"No spooks," Bigger said. "The people who live there are real enough."

Near the next intersection, he stopped the car at the side of the road. The storekeeper got out with Jason and Michael followed. Bigger took off his suit jacket and tie, and handed them to Michael. He stepped to the rear compartment, removed a bundle of cut flowers, stakes wrapped in twine, and a hammer. The three crossed a shallow ditch to a barbed-wire fence. The pasture beyond held little grass and no cattle.

"Stay here," Bigger said. He tossed the items over the fence.

"You'll need help with those things," Jason said.

"Suit yourself," Bigger said.

Jason helped him climb through the wire. In the pasture, he retrieved the flowers and other things and followed the merchant into the field. Michael stayed behind. Dirt still covered much of the area, but patches of prairie grass had begun to reclaim the pasture. A small, disturbed spot showed where a tractor pulled out the Roadster. Bits of broken glass littered the area. This was Bigger's destination.

He wants to make a memorial.

Jason knelt, tied a length of twine around a stake and hammered it into the ground. He positioned the flowers under the twine, tied the other stake, and drove it into the earth. The arrangement held the flowers secure. He rose and nodded to the store owner. Both men bowed their heads. The older man began speaking. It wasn't a prayer. More like a one-sided conversation.

"My son, I worked hard to teach you a trade. More than that, I wanted you to be a man. One who would gladly take on new responsibilities. I failed in that. I may have put too much pressure on you. Or too many expectations. In any case, I know you hated your work. That's why I introduced you to the McGurk girl."

Jason swallowed. Larry did hold a grudge.

"I was hoping she'd bring out the best in you. I know now, you despised me and the principles I hold dear. But I can't understand what you had against that young woman. Was it more than anger? Were you jealous? I remember that night you came home drunk. It's now so clear. You knew you were going to be a father, and you kept it a secret. If you had told us—trusted us, you'd still be alive."

He stooped forward, knees bent. Fearing that the older man was about to collapse, Jason put an arm around his waist, but Bigger thrust it away. He stiffened his back and called across the empty pasture, "Where is she, son? Where is Sara? I want to know. I demand it!"

To the north, a lone train whistle blew. Bigger looked down at the flowers one last time, then turned and trudged back to the fence.

Jason helped him through. Michael had his jacket ready, making eye-contact. *Is he okay?*

He waved a palm. *Tell you later.*

The store owner glanced back to the empty pasture, then kicked a small rock on the roadside. "What a desolate place this is. Get in the car, boys. We're going home."

Chapter Fifty-Nine

Friday, May 10, 1935

Sara led the way into Mrs. Hiebert's room but stopped just inside the doorway. Maxine's breath crackled like a straw sucking up air and thick liquid. There was a pause, and then the wet crackles began again.

Sara knew that horrid sound. The day Grandpa McGurk died those slow, burbling rasps sent her fleeing from the room as a child. Her parents and relatives remained seated around Grandpa's bed. Now, it was her turn to sit with the dying.

Patrick rushed to Maxine's side, calling her name and reaching for her hand. Inching her way to the bed, Sara bent over the small form. Maxine's frail body lay unmoving; her mouth gaped open.

Patrick patted her wrist. "Why doesn't she wake up? She's breathing funny."

Sara stepped to his side, resting her hand over his. "She's leaving us. Hold her hand. That's all you can do. Hold tight."

"I wanted to be more than just friends." Patrick leaned forward and squinted, trying to study Maxine's slackened features. "She's snoring loud."

Sara bit her lip, forcing the words out. "Her body is saying goodbye."

"Is her soul leaving?"

"Yes. Keep holding her hand. You're doing what any husband would do for his wife."

"I am?" Patrick's eyes were bright as he grasped her limp fingers.

Bea stood outside the open door, her hands covering her ears. Sara gasped. Was she merely fearful or would this event trigger Sally's return? Sara rushed out of the room, pulling Bea aside. "Are you all right?"

Bea stood trembling, staring through the doorway. "I can't go in there. It sounds like death."

Sara hugged her, sighing with relief. "You don't have to. Find Mrs. Eisner. Tell her Mrs. Hiebert is passing."

Long minutes went by as Sara and Patrick stood their vigils. A squeaky cart rolled in the passageway. Sara peeked out the door to see Mrs. Eisner and Bea completing morning rounds.

The rasps were much shallower now. Each interval between breaths grew longer by the minute. Sara found herself holding her own breath during those moments of silence.

Twenty minutes later, Gloria entered the room. "I helped Bea with serving the rest of the meals. She told me she couldn't bear to see Mrs. Hiebert. So I sent her downstairs. How are you and Mr. Arnesdorff holding up?"

Sara shrugged. "I'm okay. I worry about Patrick. I don't think it's really hit him yet."

Gloria glanced at the sixteen-year-old grasping the hand of his dying friend. His eyes were expectant as if searching for movement.

Anytime now.

Sara's thoughts returned to that day a few weeks ago when Maxine and Patrick reunited. What a joyous event that was. What a pleasure to see two devoted friends happy these few weeks together. They made an odd, yet endearing couple. Sara's eyes brimmed with tears. Each one was so protective of the other. For both, it was an end to loneliness, however brief.

The dreadful rattling paused. Silence hung heavy in the room. Patrick still held Maxie's hand, while Gloria placed her fingers on Maxine's neck.

"She's gone."

The matron stood with her head bowed for a moment, then leaned over to whisper in Sara's ear. "Stay with Patrick. I'm concerned that when the county picks up Mrs. Hiebert, the reality will hit home. We could see some temperament. Talk to him, Sara. Prepare him for Maxine's departure." Mrs. Eisner left the room, closing the door.

While Mrs. Eisner spoke, Sara glanced at Patrick to see if he was paying attention to them. He continued to stroke Maxine's hand. After the matron left, she sat beside the youth, placing his hands in hers. "Maxie's gone to a better place. She's not hurting anymore."

"She's still my best friend."

"And you did what a best friend would do. You said goodbye." Sara gave him a tender embrace.

Clumsy, unsure arms wrapped around her as he leaned his head against her. Sara held him, lightly stroking his back.

"What will happen to my friend?"

"Some men will come today and take her to a safe place. In a few days, she'll be placed in the cemetery not far away. You'll be able to visit her anytime you want."

"I didn't want her to die."

He understands. A feeling of quiet elation came over her. "Nobody did. But she was sick. You protected her and gave her comfort. Dutch was right when he called you a shining knight."

Patrick broke their embrace and stood facing Maxine. "I want to stay here 'til they come."

They continued their vigil for the next two hours. When the county men arrived, Patrick stepped aside while they placed Maxine on a gurney and took her downstairs. He stayed in her room while Sara followed the men downstairs and watched from the porch as they loaded Maxine's body into the truck. Mrs. Eisner stepped outside and stood beside her. Both watched as the truck drove away.

"I was wrong to worry about Patrick," she said. "He seems as meek as a kitten. What did you say to him?"

Sara shook her head. "I tried to console him by comparing him to a knight. I'm not sure he understood. I probably made no sense to him at all."

Chapter Sixty

Article from the front-page of *The Wichitan*,
Saturday Evening edition, May 11, 1935
KSKN Debuts on Alliance Network Tomorrow
*Wichita radio station KSKN will officially premiere
on the Alliance Broadcasting Systems at 10 a.m.
Sunday. "The Alliance will carry our locally produced
program, Carey Salt Presents Heaven and Earth," says
William L. Tabor, KSKN Director. "It's a commentary
program about society and politics, hosted by Pastor
Sam McGurk."*

*Tabor said tomorrow's hour-long program will be
special, originating from a location outside of Wichita.
"It's a remote broadcast, something we hope to do
more of in the future." Mr. Tabor would not divulge
where this setting would be. When pressed, he said the
site is unique. No other station has broadcasted from
such a setting. "Tune in tomorrow morning at ten to
find out where it is," he said.*

*The show's commentator, Pastor Samuel McGurk,
has avoided much of the controversy that follows
Father Charles Coughlin. "Pastor's program will offer
an uplifting message about communities large and
small," the station owner said. "It will open your
ears."*

Wendell Krause finished a day of paperwork and
strolled to the Covered Dish Café for a bit of supper on

his way home. Today's special was baked chicken and noodles. Eating while listening to a variety show on the radio made a passable evening.

He ordered his meal to-go, and the waitress hurried back to the kitchen. The restaurant was busy this evening. They always were on Saturdays. He stepped aside from the growing line behind him to wait for his order.

Farmers huddled in groups, catching up on gossip. At a separate table, several women, probably their wives, chattered away. A well-dressed young couple sat together on the same side of the table. He really needed to get out more. Meet new people outside of work. But he really wanted to win back Sara. He still caught glimpses of her during his visits with Mrs. Eisner. She was starting to show now. Motherhood looked good on her. Did that change his feelings about her? Wendell shook his head. Of course not. At least she would be around until the residents had to leave in July. A little time remained to call on her again.

On the countertop before him a few copies of Joshua's ten-cent weekly paper still remained. The top fold of the front-page story was about the continuing effects of the big dust storm over three weeks ago. He picked up the paper.

The headline below the fold riveted his attention:

Missing Woman May be in Joshua County

A picture showed Sara McGuire in big curls, smiling into the camera. He clutched the paper as he read the article.

Her name was Sara McGurk, and her two brothers had been searching for her since April seventh. The article contained her description: height five feet six inches, weight 115 pounds, and she liked to wear long, patterned dresses. The boys were offering a fifty-dollar reward for information on her whereabouts. If anyone had any information, they were to call the Joshua County Sheriff's office or MO-55545 in Wichita.

"Here you go, Mr. Krause. That will be ninety-eight cents."

Wendell paid for the meal and the paper and left the eatery. Home was four blocks away.

Her brothers somehow traced her to Joshua. She came here injured but stayed after her ribs healed. Why didn't she return home? And why did the name McGurk seem so familiar?

His thoughts turned to the evening in the cemetery. She talked about her ambitious father and how he saw her as a threat. They had harsh words that resulted in her retreat from home.

The radio show! Wendell snapped his finger. Pastor Sam McGurk was the radio preacher coming to the tenant house tomorrow. Was it a coincidence that he had the same last name? Could he be her father? Wendell rubbed the back of his neck. Too many questions. No way to connect the dots. He could jump in his car, go out to the county farm, and demand answers from Sara.

Or he could use the phone.

Wendell unfolded the paper and read through the article again, memorizing the telephone number. The dry goods store had a pay phone. He felt in his pocket for change. He had enough. With quickened steps, he hurried to make a long-distance call.

In the store he dropped a nickel in the coin slot and dialed O.

"Number please."

"MO five, five, five, four, five."

"Just a moment please," the operator said. "That will be thirty-five cents for the first three minutes."

Wendell dug in his pocket and found the right change.

"Thank you. Just a moment. I'll connect you."

The line droned several times before a woman's voice answered. "Hello?"

"Go ahead, please," the operator said and disconnected.

"Hello, my name is Wendell Krause. Whom am I speaking to?"

"I'm Mrs. Samuel McGurk."

McGurk. That was name of the preacher visiting tomorrow. Was he Sara's father?

"Is anyone there?"

"Sorry. I was gathering my thoughts. Do you have a daughter named Sara?"

A gasp. "Yes, I do."

"Are your sons looking for her?"

"They are." Then, her voice became more urgent. "What is this about?"

Wendell reeled. He thrust out an arm against the side of the phone booth to steady himself. Connections were falling into place. "Bear with me, Mrs. McGurk. One last question. Is Sara with child?"

A long pause. "What is this about, Mr. Krause?"

"I'm holding a Joshua County newspaper with Sara's picture on it. It says she is missing. But she is staying at the county farm a few miles outside of town. Doing quite well, all things considered. She misses her family."

There were muffled voices. Mrs. McGurk must be relaying the news to the people around her. In a minute she came back on the line. "I'm so glad she's safe. Thank you, Mr. Krause."

"You're welcome. Things will be hectic at the tenant house tomorrow. Pastor McGurk is arriving tomorrow for a special radio show. There may be some tension between father and daughter. I could bring her home tonight, but it would be late. Otherwise, I suggest she leave with someone other than her father tomorrow—"

"Please deposit twenty-five cents to keep this connection."

Wendell found his last quarter and jammed it in the coin slot.

"Go ahead please," the operator said.

"No," Mrs. McGurk said. "Sara can't come home tonight. I'll find a way to come up there and get her tomorrow."

"I'd better give you directions to the poor farm before we get disconnected."

"No need. My oldest son told me he knows where it is."

"The broadcast starts at ten. I suggest you come before that time. The house will be in an uproar. You can retrieve Sara and leave without anyone noticing."

"Thank you for the advice, Mr. Krause. We'll try to do that."

"Sara has been a great service at the tenant house, but she goes by a different name there. Her true identity is bound to come out tomorrow. A quiet exit will be best for all concerned."

"My sons and I will be there as early as we can."

"I hope we'll have a chance to meet, Mrs. McGurk. Sara has been a joy to be around."

"That's very nice of you to say so, Mr. Krause. Bless you."

"Just doing my job. Glad to give you the good news. Good night." Wendell eased the receiver back on its cradle. He no longer had two months to renew a relationship with Sara. By ten tomorrow she would be a memory.

Chapter Sixty-One

Sunday, May 12, 1935

I shouldn't have sat so close to the front. Sara covered her ears after the tractor's third backfire, and the exhaust fumes made her dizzy. She and Beatrice sat in front of a long wooden hay wagon driven by an old farmer. Behind them, the three women calling themselves The Joymakers chattered like schoolgirls about the upcoming broadcast. Can you imagine? People would hear their voices from here to New York. Nearly fourteen hundred miles! Wasn't that a miracle?

The hitch joining tractor to hay wagon screeched as they turned into the tenant house driveway. In front of the building sat a box truck with the KSKN logo and a trailer attached in back. The wagon bumped to a stop, and the three choir women jumped to the ground. Stacked on the hay wagon were a dozen wooden folding chairs from the church. The women formed a line and relayed the chairs to the door. Before long, both the chairs and singers were inside the house.

The farmer set a stool on the ground and helped Sara and Beatrice step down. Sara turned to him. "Thank you, Levi, for your help."

"Welcome." Levi took off his battered Stetson and scratched his balding scalp. "If it's all the same, ma'am, I think I'll go help in the barn." With that, he ambled off, rounding the corner of the house.

Sara stepped forward to examine the radio station truck with Beatrice close behind. The logo was a black circle with KSKN flashing over a stand microphone in electrified blue. Lightning underlined the letters, implying speed. Bea drew beside her. "Is that the radio station you wrote to?"

"Yes, it is." Icy hands squeezed her stomach. Was Daddy inside? Did he know she was here? This was her home, at least for now, and she would protect it. Sara and Bea walked around the truck to the porch. Mrs. Eisner stood at the top of the steps, hands on hips.

"I want both of you in my office. Now."

The matron led the way, bustling up the hallway to her office. Sara followed, glimpsing the activity in the common room. One workman—Jeremy Gorham—was attaching cables from a row of car batteries to a square metal box with rows of dials and switches. The choir ladies were examining large capsule-shaped microphones mounted on tall floor stands. Another man stood on a ladder covering windows and walls with heavy blankets. Sara hurried to keep up with Bea as they trailed the matron.

Once inside, the matron closed the door, gesturing to chairs in front of her desk. "I was never for this in the first place. Strangers have taken over my house thanks to a showman who brings a circus wrapped in a box." She narrowed her eyes. "Someone, it seems, sent a letter to this preacher asking him to save us."

Sara leaned forward. "I wrote the letter, Mrs. Eisner."

The older woman tilted her head. "I figured as much. Why you did puzzled me until James and I bought supplies in town yesterday." She tossed a printed sheet onto the table. Large headline letters read "Our Sister Is Missing" over a picture that Mom took more than a year ago. "Can you explain this, Miss McGuire? Or should I say Miss McGurk?"

Sara closed her eyes. "It's a long story."

"I'm sure." She turned to Beatrice. "The choir is practicing. Go join your friends. Sara and I have matters to discuss."

Bea glanced from Sara to Mrs. Eisner. "Sara only wanted to help."

"I understand, young lady. Go on. She'll be out in a few minutes."

"Everything will be okay." Sara smiled, but she clenched her hands.

Beatrice drifted to the door and opened it, but seemed reluctant to leave. "I love you, Sara." She scurried out, leaving the door open.

The matron rose to her feet and closed the door. "Priscilla Rohlman talked to me yesterday. She would like Beatrice to live with her family. This is an opportunity for her. She deserves a life in a real home." The matron sat looking down for a moment. Then she lifted her eyes to Sara. "James found the poster on a pole in front of the dry goods store."

Sara retrieved the sheet and read the text. Jason and Michael had mounted their own search. Somehow, they tracked her to Joshua. A wave of homesickness hit her like a physical blow. She gripped the paper, ready to tear it apart. Instead, she pushed it away.

"Commissioner Krause will be here for the broadcast. He can make arrangements for you to return home." Her voice took on a gentler tone. "I understand your deception. But why are you not with your family? Having a child out of wedlock is shocking, but families are protective of their own."

Sara glanced at the closed door. "My father considered me a disgrace. I complicated his plans for fame. For that reason, I had to leave home."

She arched her brows. "The preacher coming today is your father?"

Sara nodded.

"When I saw your poster, I wondered about the name. Did you mean to draw your father up here?"

Sara stood up. "Of course, not! You know I intended to leave here when Mr. Evans died. I only stayed for Beatrice." Sara put her hand on the edge of the desk, anything to keep from waving her arms. "I wrote that letter because I wanted to do something for the residents. Before I came here, my job was answering Daddy's fan mail. I knew the kinds of stories he liked to use for his program. So I wrote the type of letter he couldn't resist. But I never thought he would come here."

"I'd say you succeeded all too well."

Sara sat down. "When Daddy wants to give money to a listener, he sends a letter to the lucky person, telling them to expect a wired check. Then he would drum up his good deed on his show. KSKN was never involved in these transactions. At least, not until now."

"Your father's employer shows more ambition. They ran a special telephone line to the house. Mr. Gorham said the program will be aired on a national network."

"Daddy wants to make a splash. It's his big debut."

"There is something you should know. Your father

wants to talk to the author of the letter. This brings up a problem. I cannot have this man talking to Beatrice. She is too fragile. That person will have to be you."

Sara drew back, shaking her head. "I can't. My father has a temper. We had a terrible argument the night I left home. Can't somebody else do it?"

The matron smiled. "No. You have to do the interview. There shouldn't be any trouble. Your father will want this program to succeed. He'll have a big audience, and will want no trouble. That would leave matters pretty much in your hands."

"I'd rather be upstairs minding the patients."

"Stop running, Sara." She leaned forward. Steely eyes bore into her. "You've never been shy about sharing your opinions with me so don't start now. You started this process. Now you have to finish it."

"Daddy will be courteous while the microphone is on, but he can be irritable as well. He won't hold back."

"Should you?"

"Maybe I should forgive. Isn't that what we're supposed to do? Let go and move on?"

"Forgiveness is admirable. But too much forgiveness without action will leave you empty. You have a backbone. Use it."

"Now may not be the right time. The radio program should come first."

The matron shot her a level gaze. "Child, the program means nothing. Talk honestly with your father. You may never get another chance like this again."

No one, not even her mother, ever talked to her like this. Sara studied the matron, trying to fathom what experience she went through to gleam such ideas. "Who are you?" she whispered.

"The question should be, who was I? Before I married James, I was Gloria Evans. Cyrus Evans was my father."

"No!"

"Yes. So follow my advice. Talk to your father as an adult. Not as his child. Otherwise, this day will haunt you for the rest of your life."

"Did you and Mr. Evans ever come to an understanding?"

Mrs. Eisner bowed her head. At that moment, Sara knew the weight the matron bore, seeing her father's dementia worsen before her eyes. "We never had a chance to talk. Mother and I fled Joshua when I was very young and settled in Abilene."

Sara tilted her head "So you never expected to see Mr. Evans—your father—ever again?"

She nodded. "Whenever people asked about my father, my mother always said he died of diphtheria. I saw no reason to change that story. When James and I came here to oversee the farm, I wanted to look Father up and settle accounts between us. But I never did. Too easy to put off, I suppose. Then, a year ago, the sheriff found him wandering along the tracks. By then, he was a cranky old man who didn't know his own name. Turned out he had a stroke. Dementia had already settled in. With no money, he came under my care. I waited too long. Don't let this happen to you."

Sara drew in a breath. She had to do something. But what?

A knock brought the conversation to a halt. The door opened a crack. "Gather your people, Mrs. Eisner." Jeremy's voice was urgent. "Pastor McGurk just arrived. We'll be on the air in thirty minutes."

Chapter Sixty-Two

Sara dashed to the infirmary after Jeremy's announcement. It was easy to slide into the role of attendant. Why not wait and go downstairs until she needed to? Mrs. Eisner was right, though. She got her father up here; it was her obligation to see it through—in due time. Now she was seeing patients. *Her* patients.

She went from room to room visiting, fluffing pillows, and adjusting beds. She would miss them all, but the ones she'd miss the most were already gone. Maxine and Mr. Evans. Living at opposite ends of the hall, they seemed as different as night and day. Yet, part of the same coin. They were the anchors that kept her stable. And helped her grow. For that, she would always be grateful.

She stood at the dumbwaiter, about to return downstairs, when she noticed Maxine's door open. Patrick had closed it hours after the county men took Maxine away. Was someone in there? Sara peeked inside.

Patrick lay asleep in Maxine's rocker by the stripped bed. He must have slept there all night. It was tempting to let him slumber, but he needed to be downstairs.

Sara knelt beside the rocker, patting his hand. "Wake up. The people from the radio station are here setting up for their program. Beatrice will be singing.

410

We can watch the show together."

He blinked open bleary eyes. "Maxie?"

"No. It's Sara."

"I want Maxie back."

She nodded. "I do too."

"She's still my friend."

Sara brushed his unruly hair to one side. "You took good care of her."

"I carried her and put her in this chair." He pounded the arm of the rocker. "Every day!"

"You gave her a lot of love, Patrick."

He reached out to touch the mattress.

"Come on," Sara said. "Downstairs there is a machine you should see. It has dials and switches and wires. Big as a movie projector."

Patrick shook his head, gripping the rocker. "I can't leave. What if Maxie comes back?"

Sara extended a hand to lift his chin. "She can't. Remember all those times you waited for Maxie in the movie theater when she had to stay in her booth and sell tickets?"

"I didn't mind."

"I bet she won't mind if you come downstairs with me. This machine works with sound the same way a movie projector works with pictures."

"Only if you say so." Patrick pushed down on the armrest and rose to his feet, and they left the room.

****

Wendell Krause parked his Pontiac beside an impressive looking Mercedes. A large man in a black suit and flat, wide-brimmed hat pounded on the back door. Wendell jumped from his car and hurried up the steps. "Can I help you, sir?"

The red-faced stranger held a sheaf of papers. "I'm expected, and nobody is answering the door. Time's wasting, and preparations are needed."

"I'm with the county. The name's Krause." Wendell stuck out a hand.

"Pastor Samuel McGurk. I'm the commentator for *Heaven and Earth.*" The big man had an abrupt handshake.

Wendell opened the door and showed McGurk to the common room. The pastor weaved between an assortment of chairs set in rows to confer with the engineer. Gorham sat on a wooden stool in the center of the room listening through a headset. A wire from the earphones led to a large box of dials and switches. McGurk tapped Gorham on the shoulder. They talked a minute and Gorham produced some papers—probably a script—handing it to McGurk. The pastor shook his head, waving his own pages. He stepped over a row of car batteries separating the chairs from a makeshift stage. There, he lengthened an already long microphone stand, tilted the oblonged-shaped microphone, and began reading. Gorham made adjustments on his machine. At the other end of the stage, the singers moved chairs, examined the hanging blankets, and talked among themselves.

Abruptly, the pastor stopped reading and shot a glance at the engineer. "Director, kindly inform the women to be silent while I'm completing my sound check."

Jeremy gave McGurk a sidelong glance. Then, he clapped his hands twice. "Ladies, stay quiet while I finish with Pastor's microphone test. Then, it'll be your turn."

Three minutes later, Gorham made the okay sign with his fingers and waved the singers to their microphones. "Hurry, ladies. Twenty minutes until show time."

Two ladies sang at each microphone. The engineer concentrated on two dials to fine-tune the sound. Wendell didn't envy Gorham. He was the ringmaster of this tightly wound production. Keeping Pastor McGurk and the singers focused on their tasks would be a job in itself. Several of the residents were already drifting in and finding seats. Sara was not among them. She must be upstairs.

From the beginning, Sara was like a breath of fresh air. Maybe an unpredictable gale at times and opinionated. Still, he wanted to be her husband and the father of her child. In a couple of hours, she would walk out these doors, never to return. No, that wasn't true. Once her mother appeared, she was free to leave anytime.

Brakes squeaked outside. Wendell peeked beneath a blanket blocking the window. A Model T parked behind his Pontiac. Several women jumped to the ground and hustled to the kitchen entry. The driver, a lanky man in straw hat and coveralls, lagged behind. Wendell stepped to the back door and opened it. "Are you folks here for the broadcast?"

"We're here to see Beatrice Mullens." The short auburn-haired woman seemed to be the leader of the group. "I'm Gladys Pickering. These are my friends, Sylvia and Marilyn. Hiding behind them is my husband, Eddie."

"I'm Commissioner Krause. Come in." He led them to the front of the house. "Are you old friends of

413

Beatrice?"

"Yes. How did you know?" Gladys smiled. "Beatrice and I went to high school together."

"Lucky guess." Wendell pointed to a set of chairs. "Have a seat. You friend is busy at the moment. Did you and Beatrice talk to each other much?"

"In high school we chattered all the time."

Wendell pointed to the stage. "We have some singers with us today. Recognize any of them?"

Gladys peered up front. "No. Should I?"

"No reason." Wendell glanced at the staircase, tiring of the game. No more time. "She's upstairs. I'll get her down here before the broadcast begins."

Marilyn tilted her head. "I hear someone knocking on the back door."

Wendell stood up. "That should be Mrs. McGurk. Mrs. Pickering, could you let her in? I'll be back with your friend."

As the group left for the back door, Wendell rushed to the stairs. He slipped out his pocket watch. Ten minutes left.

****

Sara stood at the top of the stairs. Patrick tromped down the steps, passing Wendell coming her way. Parting shots or a moment of truth? She owed him an explanation before she left this place.

Wendell climbed to the top of the stairs, blocking her path. "Good morning, Sara McGurk."

"Good morning, Mr. Krause." *He knows my name.* Everyone probably knew by now. "I should be getting downstairs. There's somebody I need to see."

"Sit down." Wendell pointed to the top steps. "If it's your father, he can wait."

She sat, moving over as Wendell settled beside her.

He held her hand. "You are the last thought I have at night, and the first person I think about in the morning. If I don't say this now, I won't get another chance." He stared at her though narrowed eyes, though he didn't seem angry. But there was an intensity about him.

Sara lowered her eyes. "I'm listening."

He drew in a breath. "I love you. I want you to marry me."

A small quiver skittered down her back. Of all the times for this to happen. She had demanded a proposal from Larry, and he rejected her. Now, *she* had to answer.

Wendell squeezed her hand. "I've known this for a while now. Since the day we went out for supper. You were hiding your thoughts earlier that evening, but you trusted me enough to share your secrets. I knew then I wanted us to have a life together. To be parents. I know people will be counting down the months to when the baby will be born. Let them. I've got a small nest egg saved up. After my term as commissioner is over, we can go anywhere you want. Start over."

"Long ago, I demanded this very thing," she said in a broken whisper. "It seemed so simple. I could carry on with my job and still visit my family. That evening, Daddy called me a disgrace and threw me out of my own home. Now, I have to go back."

"Things will change for the better."

"You don't understand. Since I came here, no one has judged me. No one has called me shameful. I was just Sara. I did my job, and people appreciated my work. A poor farm would be shunned by respectable people, yet it became my refuge. If I could, I'd stay. But now I have to be what I was.

Wendell pulled her in close. "That's not important anymore. Say you'll marry me."

Sara leaned her head on his shoulder and wet her lips to speak.

Voices filtered up from downstairs. An argument. "I don't have *time* for this!" an angry, familiar voice roared nearby downstairs. "It's five minutes before airtime, and I need *somebody* with me at that microphone. If *she* won't do it, then who *will*?"

Sara jumped to her feet. Didn't he understand anger wasn't good for his blood pressure? She hustled down the stairs.

Her father stood in front of the singers' microphones, pointing an accusing finger at a frightened Beatrice. She huddled next to Mrs. Rohlman who extended an arm, keeping her father from coming any closer. Jeremy sat at his controls with hands cupped over his headset. A group of voices—familiar voices— approached the big room. Those things didn't matter. Bea was in trouble.

Sara rounded the landing and advanced on Bea's attacker.

"Stay away from her! You're frightening the child." Mrs. Rohlman planted herself between Beatrice and her father.

"I need to interview her." He threw his arms wide in mock supplication. "She only has to say a few lines. Why did she write the infernal letter if she didn't want to talk to me? What's wrong with her?"

Priscilla crossed her thick arms, eyeing him with distaste. "You are a man of God. Be more respectable."

"If I can't get a response from her, then I need someone else. This is radio. All I need is a grateful voice."

Sara tapped her father on the shoulder. He whirled around. "You can talk to me," she said. "I'll be your stooge."

The crowd of voices entered the common area. Michael's voice yelled from across the room, "There's Sis. By the front door!"

"Sara!" Chairs scooted as family and friends rushed to greet her.

Mouth agape, her father stared at her. "You! What in God's name—"

The rest was lost. Mother, Jason, Michael, Mr. Bigger, Gladys, Sylvia, and Marilyn converged on Sara. Her head reeled as she grabbed onto Jason—the first person to reach her. Jason held her as she wept on her mother's shoulder. The people she most cherished were all here. In a few minutes, she would have to face her father on stage, but she would always remember this blissful moment.

****

Jeremy removed his headset, remembering the stream of last minute instructions from Mrs. Tabor. And now she wanted to speak to the pastor. The time was 9:56, four minutes before airtime, and the place was a madhouse. He found the pastor scrutinizing the group surrounding Sara. "Follow me, sir. Meredith Tabor is on the backline. She'd like a word with you."

McGurk placed the headset over his ears, picked up the hand microphone, and spoke into the dimpled surface, "This is Pastor McGurk."

The Snow Queen's faint tinny voice was

discernable, even without the headset. "Mr. Gorham tells me you are getting distracted. Is there a problem?"

"No. I took care of it."

"Stick to your script. Mr. Gorham is acting director up there. Refer any problems to him. Now, take your place and give us a great performance."

"Yes, madam." McGurk handed the headset to Gorham. "My daughter will act as Beatrice." He motioned to Sara, still surrounded by friends and family.

"Stand by, Mrs. Tabor." Jeremy sat the hand microphone down on its thick base, grabbed a script, and hurried to Sara.

"I understand you'll be on stage with Pastor." Jeremy handed her the papers. "Follow the cues marked BEATRICE. Good to see you again. By the way, I like the feed sack dress. You look like you live here. Now get on stage." Jeremy turned to the crowd gathered in front. "Choir! Take your places. Everyone else be seated. Quiet please, we're on the air in two minutes."

Chapter Sixty-Three

Jeremy Gorham sat at his console with one ear pressed to the headset. He positioned himself so that the singers, Pastor, and Sara could see his signals when to speak. A small speaker rigged to the "front line" played the choral music lead-in to the show.

"Ten...nine...eight..." Meredith's clipped voice came over the backline as the soothing baritone of the announcer introduced the program.

"From subjects as far-reaching as Genesis to tomorrow's headlines, the *Carey Salt Company Presents...Heaven and Earth!*" The final words sounded like echoing thunder. An "*On the Air*" light hanging over the stage blinked to life. The engineer flipped a switch marked *MiC 1* and shot a finger at McGurk. This was his cue to speak.

"I am Pastor McGurk. Friends, today is our debut broadcast with Alliance Broadcasting Systems. It is my honor to be talking to you from Joshua County Farm in the heart of rural Kansas. Some would call this institution a poor farm. That is untrue. Though, it is a community of impoverished souls, it is also a group rich in spirit. They labor for their own food. Make their own clothing. And care for fellow residents too old or sick to work. It is a demanding existence. Yet, for many, the county farm is their first real home."

McGurk bent forward projecting a soft Irish

brogue, "Today, we celebrate the eighteen residents of this large house that looks older than its fifty years. The structure is without electricity or running water, yet, a group of dedicated workers minister to eight invalids every day. In a few minutes, we'll talk to one of those care providers. Her story will amaze you. But first, we have music from a local choir called The Joymakers. Ladies, it's all yours."

On cue, Priscilla led the choir as they sang "Count Your Blessings."

****

Sara flipped through the script, searching for her lines. They weren't much. What few words she spoke were meek and humbling. She remembered Dutch's words the day she met him. A deserving poor person was a docile one. Go along with the script? She had a choice to make.

"What are you doing in this dump?" her father's whisper hissed with venom.

She glanced up from the script. "I live here."

"That's impossible. We're in the middle of nowhere. I've kept this location a secret. Your mother doesn't even know. Why is she sitting out there? What's going on?"

"You're making your show. I'm taking Beatrice's place. There's nothing else."

"That's not enough. I want to know how you got here."

"Larry Bigger brought me."

"Ridiculous." His voice was a low growl. "He's dead. Your mother must have found out and told you."

Sara smiled. They were drawing attention from Patrick and Jason. Jeremy glanced in their direction and drew a finger across his lips. *Zip it.* "Mother told me a few minutes ago she got a call from an official last night saying I was here." She drew in a breath. "She's taking me home."

McGurk leaned forward. He, too, smiled for the audience, but his tone was poisonous. "You have no home. Not under my roof. I'm still waiting to hear how you got here."

Sara sighed. "I called on Larry the day after you threw me out, and he suggested we go for a drive. Along the way, we argued, and he left me in front of this house. Looking back, it seems clear he had the trip planned from the beginning."

"That means you've been here five weeks. Plenty of time to think of a plan to sabotage my debut." His voice became more livid with each word. "You must have written the fan letter that brought me here. This is a trap. Look at me when I'm talking to you!" His voice ended in barely suppressed rage.

More heads turned their way. Jeremy put an index finger to his lips. *Quiet.* He flipped a switch, picked up the handheld microphone, and spoke into it.

Sara gestured in Jeremy's direction. "Keep your voice down. I did write the letter. But I never thought—"

"I knew it!" he said.

Jeremy glanced over again, this time giving her father a sharp look.

The choir reached the final refrain of their hymn.

McGurk turned away from the engineer and yanked out a pair of reading spectacles from his suit pocket. "We're not finished. My intro talk is coming up, so stay quiet. I've got more to say to you later."

As the last note of the hymn faded, Jeremy cued the singers to silence, flipped several switches, and gave McGurk his cue to speak.

Sara followed her script as her father began his first talk. "When I was a young boy, one of my favorite authors was Horatio Alger…"

****

Jeremy bent to listen to Mrs. Tabor's voice coming through his headset. She was not happy. "I discernible heard McGurk's voice twice during the interlude. The second time his words were distinct. What's gotten into him?"

The engineer kept his voice as low as possible. "I admit the start was awkward. For one thing, Pastor is not interviewing Beatrice. He has a daughter, and she's sharing the microphone with him. They were arguing during the opening hymn."

"What about?"

"I don't know. He was fine until he saw her just before airtime. Sara—that's the daughter—is wearing a feed sack dress and worn slippers. She looks the part of someone living here. I'd say he wasn't expecting her, but she seemed ready for him."

Meredith sighed. "It's too late to separate them. Their dialogue is right after the commercial. How is the situation looking now?"

"Seems normal. Pastor's reading his spiel. Daughter's following along. No fireworks."

"That is fortunate. Caution our friend about his outbursts. And let's get the daughter off the stage as soon as she plays her part."

"Would you like to talk to him?" Dealing with Pastor McGurk was like dealing with a pompous idiot.

"No. You are the director. Handle him as you see fit."

"What if he won't control his temper?"

Meredith's voice was sharp, "Please refrain from that course of thought, Mr. Gorham. That is uncharted territory where I prefer not to tread."

Pastor's talk ended ten minutes later. A commercial promoting the benefits of Carey Salt played over the speaker. Jeremy shut down the on-the-air light and all microphones. He approached Pastor and Sara on stage. "Having a bad day, Pastor?"

"I'm having a fine day, engineer. This is my national debut."

"Then I suggest you cut out the shouting. Your job, and probably mine as well, are at stake. So let's play our parts like professionals." Jeremy turned to return to his console.

"Are you the Snow Queen's messenger boy?"

Jeremy whirled around. "No. I'm the director." He grabbed the microphone stand. "Keep your mouth shut during the hymns. Or I'll pull the plug on you. Now get ready. Your dialogue with Beatrice—I mean Sara—is coming up." He hustled back to his console and donned his headset.

****

Sara found her spot on the script. She was about to play her role in this charade. Jeremy sat with his fingers outstretched. Three. Two. One.

"Hello, friends. This is Pastor McGurk speaking to you from Joshua County Farm. I'm standing here with Beatrice Mullens, the author of a most inspirational fan letter. Before she introduces herself, I wish to read the letter that moved me to journey here and meet her in person."

Her father read the letter from his script. Except it wasn't her letter. His version made her letter sound like a simple request for a radio and running water. No mention of the closing. Any attention generated by this program would be meaningless. In three months, the county would sell the farm and furnishings. Sara scrutinized the upcoming exchange between "Beatrice" and her father.

Pastor: (encouraging tone) *"Step up to the microphone young lady. Don't be shy. Everyone, give her a big hand.* (applause)

Beatrice: (meekly) *My name is Beatrice. I care for the elderly here.*

Pastor: *Tell the people how long you work during an average day.*

Beatrice: *Usually from early morning to well past supper.*

Pastor: *Those are long hours. How do you relax?*

Beatrice: *Often I sleep in my chair while soaking my feet. I think about the time before I came here when I listened to your Sunday mornings talks.*

Pastor: *Bless you for your thoughts. But tell us about how you get water up to your patients all day without plumbing.*

Beatrice: (hopelessly): *We carry it by the bucketful up the stairs every day. Enough to drink and to bathe. We have so many sick and bedridden here. It's impossible to provide enough clean water for all their needs. That's why I wrote to you. I could think of nowhere else to turn.*

And what of her? At best, home was a way station. She would have to leave again. Odd. An unknown future didn't seem so terrifying anymore. She could deal with it when the time came.

That left the radio broadcast. Time to end the make-believe. Not with sabotage, but with the truth.

Her father flipped a page, finishing her letter.

"We live frugally and spend what little free time we have in solitude. I wish for the day we have running water and a radio, but as long as these hard times continue, I don't think either is possible. Pastor Sam, can you help us?"

Her father held out a hand. "This ends an impassioned letter from a unique resident. Now, I'd like to introduce you to the author of this letter. Step up to the microphone. Don't be shy. Everyone, give her a big hand." McGurk clapped while Jeremy motioned for the audience to applaud as well.

Sara glanced at her script, then tossed the pages in the air, letting the papers flutter to the floor. Her father's head jerked around in surprise. She stepped to the microphone. "I'm your daughter. And we don't want your gifts."

Chapter Sixty-Four

Oh, no. Jeremy Gorham spoke into his headset. "The daughter is winging it. Her script is scattered all over the stage." His hand hovered over MIC 1. Improvising on live radio often ended badly. "I'm ready to switch off. We can always say the lines went down."

Mrs. Tabor's steady voice came over the backline, "Keep broadcasting."

"Are you serious? Sara has a look about her. Calm, but—I don't know—determined. She could say anything. I can't predict how the pastor will react. Terminate the broadcast."

"No." The Snow Queen's voice was firm. "Let's see where this little drama takes us. We have three minutes until the choir's medley. If listeners are riveted to the show, they'll stay tuned even during the musical interlude. I can stop the transmission from here if the situation warrants."

"Will comply." This was nuts. Sara could well turn her father's show into a train wreck, and Meredith was letting it happen. Why?

****

Sara held the microphone stand in her hand. She could sense a stirring in the room. Like them, listeners were sitting by their radios hearing every word. *What kinds of letters will they write? How will they remember this day?* "I'm unwed and with child. That's why you sent me away. But why is banishing the daughter from home always the answer? Does it lessen the family's sense of humiliation?"

Pastor leaned back on his heels. "You're Beatrice, remember?" He chuckled into the microphone. "I've been told by the matron that Beatrice thinks she is someone else—"

"Mother is sitting in front of you. Perhaps she can remind you who I am."

He grabbed the microphone stand. "Folks, this is my daughter. She is asking a question as old as time. Of course, the daughter has sinned. She has brought shame upon the family because of that sin. It's also against the rules of society. The family has their reputation to protect, and the daughter must bear responsibility for her disgrace."

"Why is that? I am your daughter. This is the time when I need the security of my family the most."

McGurk crossed his arms. "You had to leave for the good of the family."

"I see. Your reputation outweighs my safety. I'm sorry that I mean so little to you, Daddy."

"Now is not the time to discuss family matters."

"Now is a grand time. You're not the only father with a less than perfect daughter. Families look to you for guidance. Talking about how to keep the family intact makes more sense than raving about the government."

"Don't be twisting my words against me. I don't make up the rules. I follow them. Maybe you should have considered that before you…sinned."

"We're all sinners, Daddy. There's a sin of pride—"

"That's enough." McGurk raised a fist, looking like a boxer ready to pounce. "You've always had a slippery tongue that never kept quiet. I came here to present this deserving place a radio and the means to provide indoor plumbing. Can we at least agree on that?"

"Those things aren't important. You know why."

Her father gaped at her, shaking his head. "You mentioned a need for a radio and plumbing in your guise as Beatrice. But first—"

"The county is closing us down," she said. Seated in the back of the room, Wendell rose to his feet with an upraised fist.

Her father scanned his script. "We'll talk more. But first let's listen to a medley of hymns sung by the Joymakers, starting with 'Every Time I Feel the Spirit.' Ladies?"

Caught off guard, Priscilla, Beatrice, and the other two singers scrambled to their microphones while Jeremy collapsed on his stool, flipping switches. In a few moments, Priscilla led the choir in song.

Sara looked down at the script scattered on the floor. No matter what happened here today, she would leave with her head held high.

****

Jeremy Gorham leaned his head against the control board waiting for his head to quit spinning. The last few minutes were like watching a verbal boxing match, all the while he was torn between cutting off the confrontation and seeing how the drama would end. For now at least, the pressure was off. "That was extraordinary," Mrs. Tabor said on the backline. "Stand by. I need to consult with my husband." For several seconds, muffled voices came over the line.

He had no idea how this was going to end. He was in a remote location with one—no, two—loose cannons at the microphone in what was turning into a radio drama without a script. So far, they were still keeping the show alive, but this was a runaway train. Sooner or later, they were bound to crash.

"You there, Mr. Gorham?"

"Yes, Mrs. Tabor."

"We want to hear what Pastor is saying during the medley. Can you patch the feed from his microphone into the backline?"

"I can switch *MIC 1* to my stand microphone. You won't hear me, but I can still receive through the headset."

"Get cracking."

It took but a few seconds for Jeremy to splice the stage line to the stand microphone cord. He flicked open MIC 1.

****

Sara pursed her lips. Daddy was using Gladys, Marilyn, and Sylvia as bargaining chips again. She kept her voice low, not wanting her voice to be heard over the air. "What kind of deal are you talking about?"

"It's simple. After the hymns, you apologize for your behavior. Say that you're distressed and moody from being with child. I couldn't care less what the reason is. Apologize and I'll let your friends at the mailroom keep their jobs."

"Daddy, you're grasping at straws—you would fire my co-workers just to get back at me? If I wanted to destroy your program, these ladies—my friends— would lose their jobs anyway. Please, no more threats. You've already taken away the things I care most: my family and my work. You have nothing left to bargain with."

"Then what is it you want?" There was an edge of fear in his voice.

"Spend an hour or two each day reading your listener mail. And change the content of your show. Forget the doings of government, and talk about the stories behind the letters. Set up a charity. It's time to give back to your listeners what they have given to you."

"You care about those hayseeds? Most of them can barely spell their own names."

"Those listeners got you where you are today."

"Nonsense. Next thing you'll be telling me is you care about this dump."

"I care about the people here. In two months, everyone has to leave. Most have nowhere to go."

He chuckled. "So another dozen tramps are riding the rails. Why should I care?"

Sara bowed her head. "I will be one of them."

The choir was starting their final refrain of "Time I Feel the Spirit."

****

Jeremy cringed as Mrs. Tabor's voice blared in the middle of his head. He turned down the volume. "I've heard enough. Patch everything as before. We're proceeding with the broadcast. But we're cancelling Pastor's four minute talk before the half-hour station identification. There will be a minute commercial, and director?"

"Yes, Mrs. Tabor?"

"You will need to coax three minutes of music from the choir."

"Is that advisable? Listeners will tune their dials to another station."

"Noted, Mr. Gorham. Proceed."

He sighed, setting the wires to their original positions. His pocket watch showed twenty-six minutes past ten. With a sixty-second commercial running, he hustled to the choir's end of the stage. "Okay, ladies, I need for you to come up with three minutes of music. Whatever you got. Be ready on my cue." He stepped to the other end of the stage. "Pastor, we're cutting your second talk. Stay quiet. The second half-hour will remain unchanged."

McGurk scowled but said nothing.

Jeremy hurried back to his console and retrieved his headset. "All set."

"Good," Meredith said. "I'm betting listeners will stay glued to this broadcast. Thirty seconds."

"Choir ready."

"Thank you. One last thing, keep all three mics open. Twenty seconds to air."

"Is this wise? What if Pastor talks during the hymn?"

"We're aware of that. Fifteen seconds. It won't be the first time an emcee destroys his career because he thought his microphone was dead."

"But nobody's done it on purpose."

"Live in five. Don't be so sure."

Jeremy counted down using hand signals and then motioned for the choir to begin. The four singers huddled around their microphones and sang "It Is Well with My Soul."

All three microphones were on. *MIC 2*, and *3* registered sound. *MIC 1* remained silent.

431

****

Sara stretched her shoulders while standing on stage. Sparring with her father was tiresome. He would not budge from his position. If only this broadcast would end. In two months, her fellow residents would have to leave. What will happen to the house after that? A farmer could make use of the structure. Or it may sit abandoned and left to rot. In fifty years nothing would be left but a limestone hulk: porch rotted away, doors gone, and windows broken. A poor ending indeed.

She smiled at the irony.

"What are you grinning about?" Her father had given up all pretense of smiling. He glowered like an old man who had lost all joy in life.

"I was thinking of the people living here. Everyone will soon have to leave. A public auction will take place a month later. You could use the plumbing money as a charity for the residents when they move on."

"Let the county deal with them. I'm still going through with the presentation. With a little luck, I'll still be able to keep my money. No reason to spend good cash on an empty building."

Sara averted her eyes from the audience. "And you're saying no to the charity?"

"You know the answer to that question. I entertain. If it makes you feel good playing nursemaid, then find yourself a sugar daddy who cares."

Sara gave her father a sideways glance. "Why did you really come here? You could have had the radio delivered. Or wired the money like you've done in the past. Why go to all this trouble?"

"For my debut. That's always been my goal."

Sara flicked a hand, dismissing the notion. "That's

not a goal. That's an excuse. No, there's got to be another reason."

Her father inclined his head. "Well, it did cost me a pretty penny to make this show possible. Call it overhead expenses. In the end, though, my investment should pay off."

Sara blinked. "What do you mean?"

McGurk smiled, leaning close. "With a national broadcast, the donations will pour in. All tax-free cash—day after day, week after week. When the flow slows down, I'll find another worthy cause to hoist up the flagpole, and the donations will fall again like rain. In the end I can be my own sponsor. Buy airtime on any network I like. Endorse the right people for public office—for a moderate fee, of course."

"So you'll con your listeners into sending more money?"

"Before you get ideas about bringing me down, think about your position. You wrote the letter that brought me here. And you are standing on stage with me pretending to be someone else. You're part of the plan. Hell, you *made* the plan. I've couldn't have done it without you."

The boldness of his scheme stunned her. Sara raised her hand to slap him.

McGurk snatched her hand in his large fist as if he anticipated her move. Sara gasped from the wrenching of her arm. He squeezed.

Then the pain began.

****

A harsh grating sound erupted between Jeremy's ears. *Aww!* Gritting his teeth, he yanked off the headset. On the front row, a small thick-necked boy with curly

433

brown, and too-big trousers stood. He shuffled forward, bumping his way through the car batteries in front of him. On stage, Pastor gripped Sara's hand in his larger fist. He should go help her, but Mrs. Tabor was demanding his attention. No one in the audience except the boy rose to advance on the stage. It was as if the on-the-air light held them in check. On stage, the chubby kid gazed up at pastor, then glanced at Sara.

Then, without a word, he lowered his head and charged.

****

Tears flowed down Sara's cheeks. The bones in her hands were being crushed. "Please. Stop."

"Promise you'll remain quiet and far away. Don't come home for a year. Make it two."

"Anything." She groaned.

"I have your word?"

Sara could only nod. Through bleary eyes images were fuzzy. A small figure stood looking at her. Was that Patrick? He put his head down. She'd never seen him move so fast. A streak of brown hair brushed passed her and rammed into her father, tipping over the microphone and knocking her father on his back.

She shook her hand. *Oh, the relief.*

"Get this moron off of me!" Daddy was red-faced, slapping at Patrick who sat on his chest.

Members of the choir shrieked. Chairs fell backward. People rushed the stage. Wendell drew Patrick off her father. Moments later, Mr. Bigger pulled Daddy to his feet and assisted him to a chair. He took a step sideways before sitting and held a palm to his temple.

"Let's see that hand." Mrs. Eisner led her to an

empty seat. With Mother, Jason and Michael huddled around her, the matron felt her fingers and wrist. "I'll fix you an ice towel. Don't think anything is broken." With that, she disappeared.

"Who was that?" Michael asked.

"A friend." Sara wiped moist eyes. She was going to miss her new friends.

The room seemed strangely quiet. Jeremy wasn't at his post by the control board. Instead, he was staring at the ceiling, his headset around his neck.

"Who was that little guy?" Michael asked.

Sara shushed him, her attention riveted on her father. Daddy rose from his chair. Mopping his brow, he tottered over to the engineer. "Why aren't you getting these people back to their seats? We got a program to finish."

"Not anymore, Pastor. Meredith terminated the broadcast."

Daddy brushed a hand across his discolored face. "Why would the Snow Queen terminate the broadcast?"

Jeremy looked away. "Go home, Sam. We'll sort this out tomorrow."

Her father gritted his teeth. "We'll sort this out right now. Is the Queen still on the backline?"

Jeremy nodded, handing the headset to her father.

He donned the device, picked up the hand microphone, and rasped some words into the device. Daddy bowed his head, holding the headset with both hands. He stayed like that for a full minute.

Afterward, he removed the headset, rubbing his left arm. Then, he crumpled to the floor.

Chapter Sixty-Five

Thursday, May 23, 1935

Sara blew out the single candle on her birthday cake as the six others in the McGurk kitchen finished singing.

"Happy birthday, dear Sara. Happy birthday to you."

Twenty-four years old! She never thought she would spend her birthday at home. Not after what happened eleven days ago. She gazed around the kitchen. A folding card table extended the seating space to eight. On her right sat Gerald Bigger, his wife Lois, and Michael. On her left were Gladys Pickering, Jason, and her mother. Daddy will soon sit adjacent to Mother at the foot of the table.

"Did you make a wish?" Michael leaned forward, fork in hand. "You need to tell us what it is."

Katherine passed a long-bladed knife to Jason. "A mother-to-be has only one wish. Sara, will you cut the cake? I need to help your father."

Jason passed the knife to Gladys who handed the utensil to Sara. "How is Pastor, Mrs. McGurk?" Gladys asked.

"Since his stroke, Sam has been able to get around with a walker, though his right side is weak. And he can't use his writing hand. That reminds me. Sara, leave your father's slice on the cake platter. He'll eat later."

"Why, Mom?"

"He doesn't want me to feed him in front of company."

"That's silly."

"We must respect your father's wishes."

Gladys received a slice of cake and passed it on. "How long has Pastor been home, Mrs. McGurk?"

"Riverside Hospital released him two days ago."

"Is he able to talk?" Gerald Bigger waved off his wife's finger to her lips.

"Sam can say two or three words at a time. Sometimes they're jumbled and don't make sense, so don't be surprised if he doesn't answer questions. That makes it hard to know what he remembers."

Sara cut more pieces of cake, passing the dessert plates to Gerald Bigger and Gladys.

Katherine handed Michael his slice. "Don't be alarmed if Sam appears irritated. He doesn't think he's a whole person anymore. We have many changes to get used to."

Gerald picked up his fork. "We'll treat Sam with respect, Katherine."

"Thank you. He's been quiet since coming home. Meek, really. He's never mentioned the broadcast. On the other hand, he's more curious about the rest of us—like a man who just woke up and discovered he has a family." Katherine wiped a glistening tear. "I have to go. He doesn't like being alone for very long." She stood and hustled from the kitchen.

Sara set the knife aside. "This morning Daddy held Mother's hand at breakfast. I've never seen that before."

Michael thumped his fork. "Can we eat now?"

Sara rolled her eyes. "Dig in, Michael."

Lois Bigger glanced down the hallway. "I think your mother is holding up well with the new responsibilities of looking after Sam."

Sara rose to her feet and put the remains of the cake under its glass dome. "Daddy needs lots of help. The boys and I do what we can to ease the burden on Mother. We're talking to each other more. And we're not arguing as much."

Gladys touched Sara's arm. "Has he mentioned anything about the Mailroom?"

"No. Although he could have and we misunderstood."

"There's a reason why I'm asking. An avid group of listeners is waiting for Pastor to return to local radio. Some even think the broadcast was all staged—part of a radio drama."

Sara's jaw dropped. "You're joking! Daddy can't form a full sentence. The few words he can say aren't always sensible."

"You could help us write a letter explaining his condition. Marilyn and Sylvia would love to see you back at work."

"You don't need me. The radio station canceled Daddy's show. Hasn't the mail fallen off?"

"Oh, no. Mail is up. Eight hundred letters a day are pouring in—with no end in sight. I've hired new help, but we're still behind. Come downtown. Even if it's only for a few hours a day. We need you. Donations have gone through the roof."

"Are listeners still giving to Daddy's church?"

Gladys shrugged. "Some. Most folks are sending

money in to pay for Pastor's doctor bills. I've put the money in the bank. Eddie said we're not having that kind of cash sitting in the house."

Sara squeezed her eyes shut. "I can for a few days, but I'm leaving next week to visit my aunt and uncle in Hutchinson for a few months."

Gladys drew back. "Why? Your father's not in a position to force you to leave—"

"Daddy doesn't know I'm with child. The stroke has left him with a hole in his memory. He draws a blank when it comes to recent events. It makes no difference. This is my decision. My choice. I'm going to have the baby in Hutchinson. When I return, I can think about a normal life again."

Gerald and Lois's eyes met. Mrs. Bigger turned to Sara. "What will become of the child?"

Sara heaved a heartfelt sigh. "I'm giving the baby over to a children's home. It was a hard decision to make. Daddy has destroyed himself. Sometimes, I find myself wondering: if I gave up the baby from the beginning, would events have turned out differently? Impossible to say. All I know is this child may be better off with a different mother."

Lois Bigger gasped as her hand sought Gerald's. "Don't say that! And don't give up the baby. I implore you. This is our only chance at having a grandchild. We can't tell you what to do, but we can't bear to see our grandchild disappear. Promise to keep an open mind."

Sara peered at the couple. Since her return from the tenant house, the decision to give up the child seemed clear. Now, Larry's parents were anticipating the baby's arrival the way Larry should have. She must offer some glimmer of hope for these good people, even

if she saw no other recourse. "I'm not due until November. Nothing can happen until then. I promise not to be hasty."

Gerald gave a solemn nod. "Thank you, Sara."

The mercantile owner showed streaks of gray Sara never noticed before. The lines under his eyes were deeper. Mother said he wasn't spending as much time at the store, and some of the lights in the ceiling were out. The loss of Larry must have hit hard.

Lois Bigger pursed her lip. "What I find odd is that KSKN has not said much about Pastor since the station canceled his show. On the other hand, newsies from other stations are having a field day taking shots at him, especially that awful man, Walter Winchell."

Sara sighed. "We've stopped listening to the news. Mother made a point of unplugging the radio the day Daddy came home. She also canceled the newspaper subscription."

"Then you haven't heard the latest." Gerald extended his hand. "It seems the Joshua County Commissioners voted unanimously to cancel the closure of the poor farm. In a left field sort of way, your father may have saved that place."

"I can't believe it." Sara shook her head. All these changes were hard to sort out.

A hallway door opened and a steady *thump-thump-thump* approached the kitchen. With a determined look on his face, Sam McGurk lurched forward with each step of his walker, arriving at the foot of the table. Sara jumped to her feet and rushed to take her father's arm. Katherine pulled her husband's chair in place as he dropped in his seat. Katherine retook her seat and gestured across the table. "Sam, this is Gerald and Lois

Bigger. They own Bigger's Mercantile downtown. And sitting by Jason is Gladys Pickering. She and Sara went to school together."

Sam peered at Gladys as if trying to place her. His head bobbed in recognition. "Schoolgirl." He held a shaky finger and grinned. "Troublemaker."

Gladys leaned back in her seat. "I'm married now with two children. I haven't pulled a school prank in years."

Katherine flashed a bittersweet smile. "Sam remembers you girls growing up together."

Gerald peered at the pastor. "Sam, I have a few questions for you. I know it's hard for you to let us know what you're thinking. So answer with a nod or a shake."

McGurk sat unmoving, one eye bright with expectation.

"Did you know I had a son?"

Sam bobbled his head. *Yes.*

"Did you know he died?"

A moment's hesitation, then a sway of the head. *No.*

Gerald touched Sara's arm. "Look at this young lady. Is she your daughter?"

Yes.

"Did you know my son and your daughter were seeing each other?"

No.

"They were. Now look at your daughter, Sam. Really look. Do you see fullness? A radiance? What could that mean, Sam? What's the only possibility?"

Sara's mouth went dry. Dear God, don't let it happen again.

Katherine gasped. "He doesn't know!"

Gerald leaned forward. "If I were in his shoes, I'd want to know. Don't protect him. The man deserves some dignity."

Katherine thrust out her hand in a signal to stop. "I can't allow this. We've been through too much."

"Gerald's right. Daddy deserves to know." Sara sensed an inner calm she'd never felt before. For the second time, she told her father of the baby.

Gerald clasped his hands together. "I envy you, Sam. My son is dead. He never met my expectations when he was alive, but I'd gladly take him back, faults and all if I could. But you have a second chance. Sara is alive. And we can be grandfathers together. I'll have to take up fishing. And you will, too. Our wives shouldn't be the only ones spoiling our grandchild."

Sam gazed ahead. The right side of his face sagged. His left side showed no expression. Did Daddy understand? Was he upset? She should tell him of her plans to leave. Anything to appease him.

Sam's head slowly dropped to his chest. Sleeping?

"Don't be alarmed," Katherine said. "The doctors warned us that social gatherings would tire him."

"It was the right decision to tell Sam about the child," Gerald said. "Sleeping on it could be a good sign."

Lois said, "We're sorry for disturbing Sam. Sara's child means a lot to us."

Katherine grasped her husband's limp hand. "Sam reacted harshly when he first heard of Sara's baby. I don't want events to repeat themselves."

Knocking came from the front door.

Jason glanced at her. "Who can that be?"

Sara got to her feet. "Probably another newshound. I'll get rid of him." Sara crossed to the living room. A man stood behind the thin curtain covering the front door window. Sara opened the door.

"Hi, Sara." Wendell Krause stood before her, wearing his Homburg and a rumpled suit. He fumbled in a hip pocket and produced a small square box. "This is for you." He opened the lid. Inside was a simple band with a small green stone. "I couldn't afford a diamond ring, but the stone matches your eyes. Will you marry me?"

She took the ring from the box and tried it on. "A little big, but I know a place that can fix it." Sara stepped onto the porch, closing the door behind her.

"Do you like it? The jeweler called it green amber—"

She rushed into his arms, knocking his hat to the porch. Her lips met his with a fiery kiss that raised his eyebrows. "Hold me," she whispered in his ear. "Don't talk. Just hold me. And the answer is yes."

Wendell drew her close.

She rested her head on his shoulders, smiling. Late at night, she had imagined this moment, but never dreamed their reunion would happen. Wendell was the answer to everything.

He sighed. "What do you think about a wedding at the tenant house?"

She tapped his chest. "Don't get ahead of yourself. I have to ask you something first."

"Sure. Anything." He stepped back.

"I've been waiting eleven days. What took you so long?"

"Today's your birthday. Mrs. Eisner said so. I

figured my best chance of finding you would be on your birthday."

"You could have come sooner."

Wendell rubbed his neck. "Since the broadcast, the tenant house—the entire area—has been in an uproar. Newspaper reporters, radio people, even newsreel photographers, have swarmed the county. A constant parade of vehicles passed in front of the tenant house every day. Then, there are the letters. I've been overwhelmed with mail. The other commissioners as well. Much of it demanding we reinstate the county farm. Last week, the commissioners voted to table the closure. For now, at least, the farm is out of danger. But I need your help. The matron has parcels and bags of letters stacked in her office, and she's running out of space."

"Welcome to my world."

"I'm serious. Some of the letters—quite a few really—contain cash. This whole letter business is taking up a lot of her time. She's demanding I do something about it."

"Hire a secretary."

"I intend to." Wendell retrieved his hat, holding it in his hand. "Sara, will you take the job and return with me back to Joshua? Mrs. Eisner told me she'd send Patrick if you said no. I'm offering you a paid position to manage the mail and keep the reporters at bay."

"Will I be staying at the tenant house?"

Wendell nodded. "Unless you'd rather stay in town."

"Will Mrs. Eisner allow me to stay until the baby arrives?"

"Of course she will. And I have an idea about that.

We can talk about it later."

Sara shook her head. "No. You can tell me now."

His gaze wandered to the street. "It's just an idea. Mrs. Eisner still has you on the books as Sara McGuire. You'd continue to stay at the tenant house under that name and have your child there. Gloria is a trained nurse, and Dr. Zwiefel is a phone call away. At some point after the baby is born, Sara McGuire will disappear, leaving the baby behind. After we're married, we adopt the child. You won't have the worry of gossipers counting the months on their fingers and making those knowing nods."

Sara thought it through. "No, I can't hide behind a story like that. When our child ever asks how we came to be married, I'm going to tell her the truth. Maybe it will break the string."

"The string?"

"The past repeating itself."

"People may call you a tramp."

Sara grinned. "Some of my favorite people are tramps."

The front door opened. Jason and Michael stared at the couple. "Mr. Krause? Sara? Is everything okay?" Michael asked.

Sara beamed. "Couldn't be better." She held out her hand, showing the ring. "Everyone is here. Let's go inside and make an announcement."

Michael looked puzzled. "What's going on?"

"You and Jason are going to be uncles after all."

Forty minutes later, Gladys stood by the back door of the McGurk kitchen, pinning on her hat. A Model T sat in the driveway with its motor running. "Write to us, Sara. The girls will want to hear from you."

"I'll do that, Gladys. I'm glad you came."

"It was swell. Did I tell you Eddie is teaching me how to drive? Marilyn, Sylvia, and I may wind up on your doorstep soon. You can show us around on that farm."

"Be sure to bring an old pair of shoes."

Al-ooo-ga!

Gladys patted her cap, a feminine Robin Hood style with a small silk flower. "That's Eddie being impatient. Someday, I'd like to stuff chewing gum in that car horn. Is my hat too tilted?"

Sara stifled a grin as she embraced her friend. "You look fine. Tell Eddie hello. Oh, and tell Marilyn and Sylvia I'll visit the Mailroom in a couple of months. Michael's birthday is in July."

"Will do. Hang on to that man," Gladys whispered. "He's no Doc Savage—more like Johnny Littlejohn—but he's a keeper. Take care." Gladys dashed out the door, wiping her eyes, as the car horn blared again.

Gerald Bigger took his derby off a peg in the kitchen and shook Wendell's hand. "It's good to meet you again, young man. I hope we'll be seeing a lot more of each other in the months to come."

"It would be my pleasure, sir."

Gerald smiled. "No need to be so formal. I miss not having a son. Call me Dad."

Wendell blinked. "Yes, sir...Dad. I'll do that."

"I'm serious. What do you plan on doing after being a commissioner?"

Wendell looked down. "I don't know. Find work—"

"Call me. I want the father of my grandchild to have a steady job. It's important. When Larry died, I nearly gave up, and the store shows signs of my neglect. I even considered selling the store. My wife talked me out of it, though. I suspect she doesn't want me at home feeling sorry for myself. Since then, mail order sales have taken off, and Jason is keeping my delivery trucks running. Where is Jason?"

Katherine washed the last plate and gave it to Lois Bigger to dry. "The boys made their escape upstairs."

Lois stepped over to Sam, still sitting at the table. She gave him a light hug. "You get better, Pastor."

Gerald donned his hat. "Ready, dear?"

"Ready." She moved to join her husband and then stopped. "I almost forgot. Wendell? Did the farm get the plumbing and the radio?"

Wendell glanced at Sam. "WPA will complete the plumbing. The residents still don't have a radio."

Lois smiled. "I think we can remedy that. Walk out to the car with us. We can talk details."

Wendell nodded. "Glad to."

Gerald touched the brim of his derby. "Good night, ladies."

Katherine dried her hands. "I'll walk out with you." She turned to Sara. "Will you stay with your father until I get back?"

Sam McGurk still sat unmoving, seemingly asleep. "Sure, Mom."

"Goodbye, Sara," said Lois.

Katherine, Wendell, and the Biggers left the kitchen, going out the front door to the La Salle parked in front.

Since his stroke, she hadn't been alone with her father. There were hints that he was a changed man because of his memory loss. But his physical handicap could just as easily be masking the same obstinate person inside. It was hard to know. Should she dare talk to him? Sara sat down in her mother's chair. Her father's head bowed down, but his eyes were open. Did he play 'possum?

She patted her father's arm. "Would you like a piece of cake? It's lemon."

His head slowly rose, wobbling. *No*. He raised his left hand and pointed a finger at her abdomen. "When?" His voice was explosive, whether from anger or the effort to speak, Sara didn't know.

"November."

"Marry?" Her father pointed to the front of the house.

Daddy was listening the whole time. Sara looked down, avoiding his sidelong gaze. "Yes."

"When?" That same explosive question.

"Wendell and I haven't set a date yet. Soon."

His eyes narrowed. "Runaway," he said. It sounded like an accusation.

What did *that* mean? A chill went down Sara's back. Her father was getting upset. He was about to split the family again. If only she could keep that from happening.

She touched his arm. "I haven't been the best daughter for you. You and I lived like strangers under the same roof, going our separate ways. Mom held the family together. It must have been tough for her. I've made mistakes and became," she paused, "a disgrace to you and Mom. I'm sorry for that. I can't change the past. But I vow to be a better daughter in the future. I love you, Daddy."

His expression didn't change, but his left arm

twitched. Slowly, he raised it, letting his large hand fall on her wrist. She gasped. Any second now, he would tighten his grip, crushing her. He leaned in close. She felt his breath on her cheek. His frame trembled. Shaking with anger? Had to be.

Four words came with effort—a whole sentence.

"Love…you too…Sara."

A word from the author...

Born and raised in Kingman, Kansas, a small agricultural town not far from Wichita, I grew up with three brothers, two sisters, and many relatives who loved to tell stories of the Depression and life on the farm. I soaked up a lot of background for this story from many family reunions.

I went on to Emporia State University, where I got a degree in Rehabilitation Counseling, and worked as a supervisor in sheltered workshops and as a Rehabilitation Counselor for the State of Kansas. I also worked with cerebral palsy kids at the Capper Foundation in Topeka and spinal cord injured at Rusk Rehabilitation Hospital in Columbia, Missouri.

For the last few years, I've worked with my wife in our snack shop at the Sedgwick County Courthouse.

Dust and Roses is my first novel. I'm currently working on a second historical—about a German soldier in a Kansas POW camp during WWII.